"*In the Shadow of 10,000 Hills* is both an evocative page-turner and an eye-opening meditation on the ways we survive profoundly painful memories and negotiate the complexities of love. I was deeply moved by this story."
— Wally Lamb, *New York Times* bestselling author of
She's Come Undone and *I Know This Much Is True*

"This blazingly original novel is about the illusions of love, the way memory can confound or release you, and the knotted threads that make up family—and forgiveness. Profound, powerful, and oh, so, so moving."
— Caroline Leavitt, *New York Times* bestselling author of
Is This Tomorrow and *Pictures of You*

"Jennifer Haupt has woven an intricate and moving tale of family and culture, of conflict and love, and of the challenges of healing after unthinkable loss. Told with remarkable compassion and grace, *In the Shadow of 10,000 Hills* is a story everyone should read."
— Therese Anne Fowler, *New York Times* bestselling author of
Z: A Novel of Zelda Fitzgerald

"...an exploration of grief, justice, family, and reconciliation ... the focus is on healing rather than revenge and anger. Haupt's debut novel is a good choice for those seeking tales of hope after adversity and it may prove popular with book clubs."
— *Booklist*

"Jennifer Haupt takes readers on a journey that spans from the turmoil of Civil Rights-era Atlanta to an orphanage in Rwanda born of unspeakable tragedy. In this hopeful story that transcends race and cultural differences, Haupt guides both the survivors and readers toward the courage to believe in love again. An important story reminding us that when a crime is unforgivable, only grace will do."
— Susan Henderson, Founder of LitPark blog, author of
The Flicker of Old Dreams

"This astonishing debut novel about an American woman's search for her father in Rwanda knits together intricate, complex stories of love and the destructive forces of society that tear families apart. Haunting and delicately told, Jennifer Haupt enters the heart of Rwanda's darkest hour and shows us where to find the light."
— Jessica Keener, author of *Strangers In Budapest*

"*In the Shadow of 10,000 Hills* by Jennifer Haupt takes readers from Atlanta to New York City to the dark and mysterious hills of Rwanda as three women of different ages, backgrounds, and experiences come together in the most unlikely of places..."
— *Bustle*, 19 Debut Novels Coming Out In 2018
That You Definitely Won't Want To Miss

"*In the Shadow of 10,000 Hills* is a beautifully written novel that tells a compelling story. I was deeply moved by it. Jennifer Haupt is a gifted writer, whose heart is as large as her considerable talents."
— Steve Yarbrough, author of *The Realm of Last Chances*

"I highly recommend *In the Shadow of 10,000 Hills* for a story that moves seamlessly through eras, countries, and heartbreaks without breaking stride. It is beautiful, poignant, and immensely readable."
— Paperback Paris Book Blog

"Haupt was able to produce the true emotion that this novel elicited by building rich and realistic characters that spoke to her readers."
— Drink. Read. Repeat.

"Exploring themes of grief, abandonment, loss, love, healing, the horror of violence, the barbarism of prejudice, and the complications of family, this novel is a glittering gem."
— Dianah Hughley, Bookseller, Powell's City of Books, Portland OR

"Whether you're looking for a fulfilling novel, a transporting reading experience, or a great book club discussion book, choose Jennifer Haupt's debut. *In the Shadow of 10,000 Hills* portrays interweaving journeys in the aftermath of the Rwandan genocide with a sensitivity and universality that make the unbearable bearable."
— Tegan Tigani, Bookseller, Queen Anne Book Company, Seattle, WA

"In her debut novel, Jennifer Haupt explores unforgivable crimes and their lasting impacts on disparate lives, tackling a dark time in history with power and grace."
— Mira T. Lee, Author of *Everything Here is Beautiful*

"While *In the Shadow of 10,000 Hills* remains true to setting, both in place and in time, it is also timely, and reveals how forgiveness is possible even during the trials following the unspeakable acts of a horrific war. Author Jennifer Haupt's experience as a journalist in Rwanda plants the seeds of truth that bloom on every page."
— *Foreword Reviews*

IN THE SHADOW OF 10,000 HILLS

— a novel —

JENNIFER HAUPT

central avenue
publishing

2018

Published by Central Avenue Publishing, an imprint of Central Avenue Marketing Ltd.
www.centralavenuepublishing.com

Published in Canada
Printed in United States of America

1. FICTION/Literary   2. FICTION/Family Life

IN THE SHADOW OF 10,000 HILLS

Trade Paperback: 978-1-77168-133-9
Epub: 978-1-77168-134-6
Mobi: 978-1-77168-135-3

1 3 5 7 9 10 8 6 4 2

Dedicated to everyone searching for *amahoro*.

{ April 14, 1994 — Mubaro, Rwanda }

T HE GIRL WAITS. THERE ARE ONLY THE
silver threads of a spiderweb swooping precariously over
the top left corner of a window frame. There are no rays
of warm light seeping through cracked glass. There is no slight breeze,
no swaying jacaranda branch heavy with purple blossoms her mother
sometimes plucked before church and pinned to the brim of her straw
hat. These simple luxuries disappeared hours, perhaps days, ago.

She is not sure how long she's been curled up in the darkness,
under the frame of a stepladder tented with a blue tarp. Long enough
that there is only the faintest odor of paint, turpentine and a piney
cleanser. Long enough that her empty stomach no longer gurgles, and
the certainty of a machete blade slitting her neck no longer brings up
the sour taste of fear. For as long as she can remember, her family has
lived with the threat of death—maybe today, maybe tomorrow—as
if each day is a gift, easily snatched away. It occurs to her that fear is
what has given the Hutus their power. The boys who sometimes shove

her into the dirt while walking to school, and the men who come to take her father's crops. It is some small comfort that they no longer have power over her.

She presses one eye against a ragged triangle of light, scraped open with a rusty nail. It only distracts her mind for a few seconds at a time but that's enough to suppress the urge to run from this place. There is nowhere to run, nothing to do but wait. Nose pressed to plastic, there is only the shimmering web—no screams, no church bells clanging, no shattering glass, no gunshots that pulse behind her eyes, no ache in her groin, no pieces of prayers.

There is barely enough room, even knees pulled to chest, between the steel rails of the ladder. Still, the girl rocks back and forth, back and forth. She pulls an oversized flannel shirt down over bare knees and hooks it under curled toes. She hums without making a sound, the force of her breath vibrating in her chest, a Kinyarwanda lullaby her mother used to sing every night. Umama sings to her, still, louder than the bass pumping from a boom box, primal and urgent, too loud to be mistaken for music.

She waits, watching the web until the shiny black insect with spindly golden legs floats back into sight. It's a relief to see the spider fortifying her home, spinning away. As long as the spider is in view, there is a small hope that the man who wrapped his shirt around her and told her to wait, to make herself small and quiet and hide somewhere safe in her mind, might also return.

ONE

{ August 15, 2000 — New York City }

RACHEL SHEPHERD BRACES A HAND AGAINST the mattress, and rolls onto her side in slow motion so as not to rock the boat of her bed and awaken her husband. She sips in air and waits out the ripple of achy pain across her lower abdomen, traces a knob of elbow or knee nudging her ribs. *Easy, champ, no kickboxing...* or spin class. There's no standing on her feet mixing drinks, that's for sure, but this is no vacation. Four months of wallowing in bed, not even a walk to Washington Square for a hot pretzel and to watch the acrobatic skateboard punks. She sits up. Another contraction, lower this time. They seem to come in pairs. But that's normal. 'Perfectly normal,' those were the ob-gyn's exact words. Bed rest is merely a precaution. Braxton-Hicks, not real labor. This isn't real.

"Get you something?" Mick mumbles into his pillow. Rachel waits a beat, but he doesn't reach out to her. He doesn't flip on the light.

Doesn't ask again.

"I'm fine, just need to pee." She dips a toe out of bed. Water, lots of water. According to *What to Expect When You're Expecting*, fluids may ease the contractions. But won't that make her have to pee again? Isn't she supposed to stay in bed? The doctor said she could walk around the apartment, but how often? Why didn't she think to ask? She swipes a baby book off the stack on the bedside table and holds it to her chest. Two weeks ago, she sat at her mom's bedside, brainstorming baby names, debating the best diapers (cloth, definitely cloth), comparing cravings, asking for advice on a million little things a mother should know. Who can she ask now?

Across the hall in the almost-nursery, Rachel blinks against walls stark with primer. A dozen shades of yellow paint chips are scattered at her feet like a field of daisies. Against the far wall, within arm's reach of a skeletal, half-assembled crib, is a flea-market-find desk with beveled edges. Her designated study space/future office. She eases into the Herman Miller chair with a wobbly arm, a castoff from Mick's office, and pushes aside a dog-eared catalogue of fall courses at New York University. Mick's right, thirty-three is getting too old to keep bartender's hours, especially with a baby on the way. The beauty of her job, though, is the freedom. That, and the music. When she moved here from Jacksonville fourteen years ago, she couldn't believe someone would actually pay her to listen to up-and-coming bands—new wave and punk, and then grunge—while sliding bottles of beer across the bar.

Now, she shakes martinis at the Blue Note. The classic blues singers are her favorites: Ella, B.B., Etta, Buddy. These legends are from another era, before slam dancing and mosh pits, when music was more sensual than sexed-up. The songs are real stories, told straight from the heart, of love and loss. Sometimes, she finds herself turning away from the stage—restocking the condiment tray or examining the rows of colorful bottles on glass shelves—her face flushed with a vulnerability she doesn't want exposed to customers sitting at the bar. There's a connection, not only with the singer's aching heart but also her own desire. After the song ends she turns back to taking orders for cocktails and making small talk, the desire gone.

The cardboard box wedged under the desk is heavier than she remembers. A nurse's aide packed up her mom's few belongings after she succumbed to a fifteen-year battle with liver cancer. Rachel winces at the scrape and thump of dragging the box out into the room, glances toward the door and then exhales a mixture of disappointment and relief: her dog, Louie, not her husband, pads in from the hallway. The collie mix gives the cardboard box an indifferent sniff. Rachel scratches his ear as she rereads the note that came with it in the mail last week: *Ms. Shepherd, you must have forgotten…* But, no, she hadn't forgotten to pick up these scraps of her mom's life after the funeral.

Nobody leaves. This was their pact. Just the two of them. She was angry that her mom broke it. She rummages through this hodgepodge of her mom's life: a pink silk scarf, a crystal rosebud vase that was a recent Mother's Day present, a plastic bag of glittering rhinestone jewelry, a few photos of the two of them that were taped to the fridge, and a manila envelope that probably holds personal documents. She removes a plastic Macy's bag, plump with the remnants of a half-finished green and blue afghan for the baby's crib. "I'll finish this before she's born," she promises, and then says to her stomach, "Your Gram would have loved teaching you to knit." Merilee would have showed

her granddaughter the right way to apply make-up, spoiled her with
frilly dresses, the kind Rachel refused to wear, spent afternoons sharing her secret recipes for triple-fudge brownies and the crispiest fried
chicken ever. She would have loved recruiting someone else into their
"girls only" club.

There's not much else in the box that's worth saving. Rachel uses
the scarf to wipe a snowy mantle of dust off a silver-framed photo. They look so formal, almost regal: Her father in a tuxedo, brown
curls slicked back off his broad Slavic face. Merilee's shiny dress the
perfect shade of buffed pearl against alabaster skin, waves of auburn
hair swept into an updo, her wedding veil a crown. The newlyweds
gaze at each other like they're the only two people in the room. It's a
little unsettling to see her parents looking as happy as she and Mick
were, exchanging vows under the oak tree in his parents' backyard
at the foot of the Catskills. There were dozens of O'Sheas, members
of their church, and neighbors. A small group of Mick's friends and
their wives, from his Wall Street office and racquetball club, who had
become Rachel's friends too, travelled to the quaint town in Upstate
New York. Her mom walked her down the aisle.

Next, Rachel hooks a finger under the flap of the manila envelope;
it seems to breathe open, exhaling a handful of yellow-edged photos
onto the desk with a crumpled sigh. She vaguely recognizes the pictures
her father shot as a photographer at *The St. Augustine Record*, his dream
job after finishing high school. She lays them out side by side, and slots
them into the photo album of her memory. Some of these images from
the mid-sixties were displayed on the walls of her father's office at the
ad agency where he worked: Martin Luther King, Jr. behind a pulpit;
several burly white policemen standing over a black woman curled up

in a ball on the street; John F. Kennedy on the steps of the Jacksonville City Hall; a young white boy helping an elderly black woman up the front steps of a bus. These photos always struck her as a montage of a different world where her father once lived, where he met a president and took photos of interesting—sometimes dangerous—people. After he left, she imagined him travelling back to this foreign land. Merilee told her the photos were lost; it followed that her father was lost, too. Of course, that's why he never wrote or called. She didn't want to upset her mom, bring on the darkness that sent Merilee to bed with the shades drawn for sometimes days, even before her father left. And so, for years Rachel worried silently: How would her father stay warm? Find stuff to eat? Find his way back to her.

The truth is, she envies the family stories Mick and his three sisters told at their wedding. She envies the way, every year, her husband looks forward to Christmas at his parents' house, with relatives coming from Baltimore and somewhere in Ohio. She envies Mick's easy smile as he strolls through his hometown, waves to neighbors. She never knows quite what to do, where to sit, in the white clapboard house where he still has a bedroom. It was just Rachel and her mom in the tomb-like house in suburban Jacksonville with not enough furniture. *This is still our home*, Merilee maintained stubbornly, sometimes working two secretarial jobs to make mortgage payments.

There's one photo stuck in the envelope, the thin, splintery wooden frame rough against Rachel's fingers as she coaxes it out. She props the timeworn image of a young black woman dressed in a navy suit with a Peter Pan collar on the desk beside the silver-framed happy newlyweds. Rachel studies the woman trapped under dull glass: she stands in a church, her hands braced against a pew, slivers of gold and purple light from a stained glass window falling around her like an exploding meteor. Her expression is heartbreakingly sincere. In the distance is the blurred image of a preacher behind a pulpit. The date in the top corner of the *Life* magazine cover is April 4, 1968, the day Reverend King was assassinated. The bold-faced headline reads: *The End of a Dream.*

Rachel picks up the photo, remembers it in clear view when she used to sit in the leather chair at her father's desk. As a child, she was mesmerized by the young face with grown-up narrowed eyes, her chin jutted forward. The girl in the church window appeared downright fierce, defiant. Hopeful. Rachel came to regard hope as a weakness, a silly wish that couldn't possibly come true. When her parents fought, which was often, her mom called her father a dreamer—said it like a curse. When her father left, she felt guilty, as if she were betraying her mom by daydreaming about where he might be. How he might one day return. Eventually she stopped thinking of him altogether. By the time she moved to New York she stopped hoping for any kind of love to show up, settling instead for affairs with interchangeable men, slightly more hygienic versions of Kurt Cobain. Men who usually insisted on going to her place instead of their own, where Rachel suspected a wife or girlfriend was likely waiting.

One lazy Sunday morning, Mick O'Shea sat next to her on a bench in Battery Park to watch the ferries glide past Lady Liberty. She was impressed that he asked for permission. She said yes, although he wasn't her type: bristly blond hair and a ruddy face, handsome in a J. Crew catalogue sort of way. She was intrigued by this guy—this *man*—her age, but he came off much older, a little stiff and serious. Mick called to ask her out on actual dates, wore Calvin Klein suits and had business cards that read *Junior Financial Planner*. He "court-ed" her for six years, half-joking that his persistence would eventually wear her down. Their courtship was a game and she enjoyed being thought of as a prize. Their wedding day, three years ago, was the hap-piest day of her life.

Rachel chips away at the crumbly wooden frame that holds the *Life* magazine cover, her eyes flitting to the silver-framed wedding photo of her parents. It occurs to her, not for the first time, that be-coming pregnant has been another kind of game during the past three years, a challenge that bonded her and Mick. Finally, she can offer him a real prize. Their baby is what makes them not merely a couple, but a real family.

"Her name is Serena," Rachel confided to her mom during their last visit at the Seaview Nursing Home. "It's a secret, not even Mick knows." It was nice to see a flush rise to Merilee's pale face, cheeks that had held a young girl's blush until recently. Her eyes, blue tinged with violet, like a rare gem, sparkled with the news.

"I won't tell," she promised between labored breaths, tapping a conspirator's finger against coral-pink lips. It was the last secret they shared. She died two days later.

Now, Rachel looks out the pocket window between her desk and the crib. A fog of light emanates from the streetlamp. She cradles her stomach with both hands and makes a wish, aiming it toward where the North Star should be. *Serena.* It's superstitious but she's still afraid to say her daughter's name aloud, afraid to somehow jinx her existence. Still. It's been over a month since the end of the first trimester, when the doctor announced they were officially out of the danger zone. That night, after toasting their future astronaut or rock star with bubbly cider, she and Mick made love on the living room rug for the first time since finding out she was pregnant. She imagined they were being transported back two years, before the pressure of thermometers, calendars, and positioning their bodies for optimum baby-making. Before the miscarriage at ten weeks last year. She bends over, a hand on her lower back, to pluck a paint chip from the floor. Bumblebee Yellow or Golden Wheat. They couldn't decide, went back and forth on what shade to paint the nursery like they had all the time in the world.

One side of the frame snaps in her hand, a sharp edge of glass slicing her palm. Rachel sucks at her wound and stares at the girl in the church window, shattered but still in one piece, on the floor. She picks icy slivers off the photo taped to cardboard, and then examines it more closely. On the back are several crossed-out phone numbers and an address in Atlanta. Why the hell did her father keep track of this woman? Maybe her mom had good reason to suspect he was having an affair. Did he leave them for her?

The laptop computer sputters as if it has been awakened from the deepest sleep when Rachel taps the "on" button. The dial-up connection groans. She drums her fingers on the desktop. What if Henry Shepherd is in Atlanta? Fucking Atlanta, not Timbuktu, only two hours by plane from Jacksonville. Serena stirs; Rachel's hand softens and floats onto her stomach. The other hand reaches for a snow globe from a shelf above her desk containing a tiny snow-capped mountain, above it bright green cursive script: *Merry Christmas from Mt. Kenya.* It's the one and only gift her father has sent to her in the past twenty-six years, the Christmas after he left. The computer screen flickers from black to blue, and she shakes the orb like a Magic 8-Ball. As a girl, before she stopped hoping, she watched these papery flakes and glitter drift to the ground and imagined her father's footprints in the snow. Now, she sees two sets of footprints, one very small.

Alta Vista pops up on the screen and she types the address in Atlanta into the search engine box. The computer springs to life, awhirl with ticking sounds. Rachel leans in closer toward the screen. Maybe the photo her father took, an impression frozen in time, might lead her to him. Bring him back home. A name materializes on the screen along with the address: Lillian Carlson. She hasn't lived at that address since the late sixties. A small flare of hope lights up within Rachel as she scans a short list of website links, one with an email address that's definitely not in Atlanta.

TWO

{ *September 15, 2000 – Mubaro, Rwanda* }

NEARLY THIRTY YEARS, AND IT NEVER gets any easier when a child shows up on the front porch of Lillian Carlson's modest farm in the shadow of the Virunga Mountains. "How about some lunch, sugar?" she coaxes, offering the plate of plantain, rice and beans to the boy with dull-brown eyes, who is probably in his early teens, judging from his height. She resists the urge to reach out and hold him close, assure him everything's going to be okay. That's not true and she won't lie to these kids, not after all they've been through by the time they land here. The boy is so thin, practically swallowed up by her wicker rocker, as he considers his bare feet, toes digging into the bamboo mat.

"Well, I'll leave your lunch right here on the table while I check on those cookies you smell baking." Her new ward cuts a glance toward her and she grabs the opening, leans a bit closer. "Personally, I'm torn between cocoa, peanut butter and cardamom," she confides, "so I mix up all three in my secret recipe." Lillian takes a minute to arrange a full set of silverware on a cloth napkin in front of the boy, pulls a few droopy petals off the vase of rainbow-colored wildflowers, and then wipes a powdery veneer of pollen off the mahogany tabletop and rubs a thumb across her fingers. Spring has finally come to the Rift Valley after a long, dry winter. This is her favorite time of year; filled with tiny miracles.

A knot of black-masked vervet monkeys perched in a nearby acacia tree chatter heartily as Lillian opens the screen door. "Don't you worry about them, all talk and no action," she says, waving a hand toward the little bandits who are too shy to come down and swipe the boy's food. They're more likely to give up in a few minutes and go raid the pea patch at the side of the house. She keeps watching the boy—nobody at the hospital could get him to reveal his name—from the front hallway, out of his sight. He keeps an eye on the monkeys, slides his chair closer to the plate and grabs handfuls of food, ignoring the silverware. Lillian smiles triumphantly. Sometimes that's what it takes, her up and leaving, before a child trusts the bounty is actually for him, accepts that there are no strings attached.

Out of the corner of her eye, in the mirror above the coatrack, Lillian spies a flash of pink barrettes. She pretends to startle and then reaches behind to catch nimble fingers latching onto the back pocket of her dungarees. "Rosie, I swear," she chides, "you're quiet as a leopard cub. I'm going to hang bells around your neck so you won't be able to slink up on me." The culprit falls into her, a curtain of shoulder-length black braids cascading across her wren-like face, snorting laughter through her nose. Lillian pulls her gently into her arms. How can

13

this child who spent the last week in bed, so listless she couldn't lift a spoon to her mouth, now be so strong? Another miracle.

Rose cranes her neck over Lillian's shoulder and wriggles out of her arms. "Who is he?" she asks. Lillian wipes a dab of honey from a shiny, cocoa-colored cheek. Rose has sprouted up during the past year, but she still looks closer to age six than eight. Some days, all she'll eat is Mama Lilly's special super-power cookies, packed with protein, baked especially for her. She's always been a finicky eater, ever since she was an infant. Lillian suspects it's because she never had the opportunity to nurse at her mama's breast.

"What's his name?" Rose persists. "Did Tucker find him in the mountains?"

"Tucker brought him from the hospital in Kigali," Lillian says crisply, to short-circuit a surge of sadness. "His mama can't take care of him anymore." She doesn't like keeping the truth from the children, especially when it's her own emotions getting tangled up.

Daniel Tucker first appeared on her front porch with Rose seven years ago, dressed in filthy jeans and a bright yellow UCLA T-shirt, a red bandana slashing across his light brown forehead. African-American, but there was no mistaking that he was more of the latter. He could have been a young backpacker in need of a shower, stopping in Mubaro to get water before heading into the Virunga Mountains to track gorillas. But there was that squirming bundle he held to his chest, wrapped in a dirty pink blanket. And then, there were his meticulously squared nails rimmed with dirt-encrusted cuticles: the hands of a surgeon in a war zone.

Lillian held out her arms instead of asking questions. The first time she holds a child, the feel of their body, if they settle or squirm, look up into her eyes or away, it's all-telling. The baby girl nestled into the crook of her elbow and sucked mightily on her pinky finger. Even with a film of dust on her brown fuzzy head, she still had a honey-and-milk baby smell. "You're a beauty," Lillian cooed, and then asked Tucker, "What's her name, son?" He shook his head as if confused, sadness pooling in his eyes. "We'll call her Rose for now," she said, guiding him inside her home. He's been staying here off and on ever since, providing medical care for the orphans as well as families who live in the mountain villages between Mubaro and the Uganda border, about fifty kilometers north as the crow flies, much longer by Jeep winding up and down dirt roads.

Lillian reaches out for Rose but the slip of a girl is too darned fast. "Sugar, wait!" The new boy doesn't need her asking his name, pestering him. Let him settle in for a bit first. But Rose is already on the front porch, introducing herself, talking to—no, wait, *with*—this child who Lillian hasn't been able to drag a blessed syllable out of during the past two hours. Within minutes, they're pointing at the monkeys still in the tree and giggling like old pals. Well, that's how it is with the kids she takes in, only three or four at a time now. They have an unspoken bond. They can reach each other when adults have done too much damage to be trusted.

A faint *ding-bleep-bleep-ding* becomes louder as Lillian heads toward the kitchen. Two brothers, Thomas and Zeke, are still in their school uniforms of khaki shorts and blue polo shirts, huddled at the table with Tucker. All three are mesmerized by the portable computer that was a birthday gift from Tucker a few months back. Lillian still can't get comfortable using it. She's gotten by with her Smith Corona for nearly forty years, a high school graduation present from her folks.

They worked hard to make sure their daughter was the first family member on either side to attend college. The look on their faces when she announced her intention to teach at an orphanage in Africa was nearly unbearable. To Mama's mind, Kenya may as well have been Jupiter. It wasn't the first time she had disappointed them. But it was the first time she didn't allow them to talk her out of *a terrible mistake*, Daddy's reference to most of the decisions she made on her own.

Lillian stands behind Tucker, who's hunched over the keyboard. "See?" he says to the brothers, tapping away. "This game's a cinch. Just keep your little dudes cruising through the maze, gobbling up dots to get points. The cherries are the real mother lode."

"Ten more minutes, then it's back to homework for a while," Lillian reminds all three of them, running her hand over the tightly cropped curls on Tucker's head. She sighs. Only thirty-two and already a smattering of gray.

It's this place, so beautiful and full of promise. Rwanda, the people and the land, draw you in, take everything you have and make you dig deep within your soul, willingly, to keep searching for more. Lillian squeezes Tucker's shoulder; it gives her such joy to see him cheering along with the boys as the blinking smiley-faces gobble up musical dots. The children nourish him. She could see that on the first day he arrived, his voice a monotone tenor as he reported that the Hutus had attacked the main hospital in Kigali, where he worked. The Hutu militia had been raiding Tutsi towns, burning homes and murdering entire communities since the Belgians left Rwanda in the late fifties. Nothing new there. But this was different: organized and premeditated. The terror spreading throughout the country was palpable, like the pulsing dots of color multiplying on the computer screen. Aid workers and foreign diplomats began trickling out of the country. Lillian canned corn and peas, and stockpiled potatoes in the cellar. Tucker hitchhiked from Kigali to find what he thought was a safe home for an infant whose mother was murdered before she could hold her baby to her breast even one time. There was no stopping what was being put into motion and would come to a head six months later.

The slaughter. That's what Lillian calls it. Genocide is far too polite.

"Lillian, you've got email," Tucker says. "Probably from Nadine. Check it out."

"Ten minutes," she repeats, giving him her best stern librarian look. He knows full well she's not keen on conversing through a machine. Computerized letters are too light and breezy: *Dearest Maman, dashing off to classes so just a quick note with all my love.* And, way too easy. *Maman, a bit of bad news. I'm afraid I failed my first college algebra quiz despite best efforts.*

Lillian hums the chorus of an obscure Nat King Cole tune that's been stuck in her head for days as she peers into the oven. Something colored sky... It's no use; she can't get rid of the itchy urge to check that blasted screen. She grimaces, the squeaky oven door setting her teeth on edge.

"Sorry, was gonna oil that..." Tucker jumps up from the table, shifting the laptop toward Thomas. "Now, don't let the ghost dudes catch up with your guy or it's all over. And make sure to let your bro co-pilot after a while."

"The oven can wait." Lillian motions for Tucker to sit and keep playing with the kids. It's good for all of them to have some fun. A few minutes later, she places a plate of warm cookies on the table, a sense of accomplishment washing over her. Tucker's hand is over

Thomas' fingers, Zeke pointing at the screen. All three of them cheer as the *bleep-ding-bleep* gets louder. "Mama Lilly, we got another cherry!" Thomas shouts.

"We won, we won!" his little brother chirps.

"So I see," Lillian lies. The screen is a mish-mash of blinking lights and nonsense. "Go ahead and shut that thing off, now. Time to get back to homework."

Tucker hovers the pointer over the glowing mailbox icon and Lillian's pulse ticks a bit faster. "I'll be in the gathering room in a few minutes," she says, corralling the boys away from the table and toward the door. "Thomas, you help the young ones with their addition and subtraction if they need it."

"It's from Nadine." Tucker gets up and offers his chair.

"If that child's smart enough to get a scholarship to the university in Nairobi, she can surely figure out how to dial a telephone," Lillian says.

"See that envelope? Click on it, and then hit the reply button."

"I'll try later."

Tucker rummages through the cabinet above the stove for a canister of grease. "The other email too," he says quietly. "It's been a month. She deserves an explanation."

"Believe me, that gal doesn't want to hear what I have to say."

"Which is?"

Lillian shrugs, a brief reminder of their agreement not to discuss certain topics. Henry Shepherd is at the top of the list. She hears the clunk and clang of tools that Tucker most likely doesn't need.

"Something," he grumbles. "That's all I'm saying."

Lillian fills up the deep metal sink with soapy water, though there's only a spatula and cookie tin to wash. She watches iridescent bubbles rise over her wrists and plunges her arms in past her elbows. A small luxury, a sinkful of warm bubbles popping on her earth-worn hands and quenching her skin, but one she can afford occasionally if she lets the dishes pile up the next day. Her mind wanders into deeper waters, places that are murky with desire and longing, places she can't afford to go.

Thirty-seven years…seems like yesterday that she first laid eyes on the tall, skinny white boy at the back of Ebenezer Baptist Church. She shakes her head; at seventeen, it had seemed like the bravest thing in the world to turn in her seat, look right past Daddy's stern stare from the pew behind, and hazard a slight wave on a dare from her girlfriend Deirdre, sitting beside her. Such a small gesture, but it had felt dangerous. Not as adventurous as Deirdre's plans to get on the bus to Selma, but certainly risky. She wanted her parents to see that she wasn't a little girl anymore but a woman with a mind of her own. *Follow the rules, mind your own business, and tend to your family*, Daddy was fond of saying. *That's the recipe for a good life.* But she wanted so much more. Things were going to be different now that she was accepted at Spelman. No more sitting in her room stuffing flyers into envelopes instead of attending rallies. She and Deirdre had already signed up for the Student Nonviolent Coordinating Committee.

Lillian dries her arms with a dish towel, the bubbles all settled into a dull sheen on the water. She sniffs once and refocuses her mind. She hears Rose across the hall, introducing the new boy as Robert, explaining to Thomas and Zeke that he likes soccer and monkeys. He'll fit in just fine. That's what matters, the children. She can't afford to let her mind wander back to the rooftop of Henry's cheaply furnished studio apartment, not far from Spelman, where they spent many nights making plans to raise a family of their own. They would use the money they were saving to move to Kenya, where it wouldn't matter that the color of their skin didn't match.

"I'd tell that poor gal to forget him," she says, so softly that Tucker might not hear her over the squeaky oven door he's busy plying with grease. Surely, Rachel Shepherd doesn't want to know the story of how Henry showed up here nearly a decade after they stopped pretending they were immune to the small-mindedness and violence; they were in love. Surely, she doesn't want to know her father was quietly dying inside while he took photos of pretty women oohing and ahhing over household appliances for advertisements. And the last thing Lillian wants to tell that gal is how her father deserted his family here, just as he had done to her and her mother. That wouldn't do anyone any good.

The computer beeps menacingly. Lillian aims the dish towel toward the sink. That seals it, the unwieldy gadget is going back onto the top shelf of her bedroom closet—or, better still, Tucker's closet. But first, she can't resist clicking on the bright mailbox and opening the note from Nadine. Even though she's practically grown, Lillian still thinks of her as a child sitting on the back patio and playing her wooden flute, or feeding crusts of peanut butter sandwich to the monkeys while her parents helped out running this place.

Enoch and Dahla kept her from making silly mistakes when she first came here, worked long hours even when there was no money to pay them. When Nadine was born, it seemed only natural Lillian would be named the child's godmother, felt right to become her legal guardian after she became an orphan during the slaughter. Naddie started calling her Maman. That was her idea; Lillian would never try to take Dahla's place. They were all family.

Dearest Maman, I know you are not fond of email but I had to let you know right away: my algebra teacher allowed for a make-up quiz and I earned a "B"! Of course, my music classes are going well. Opera is my favorite.

I'm sorry not to answer your phone calls the last few days, but I've been so busy with studying and friends. Still, I miss you. Please give my love to Tucker, Rosie and the other children. Je t'aime – Nadine

Lillian searches the screen for the reply button; it's one of these on the right. She sighs, rubs her eyes. Not quite a month since Naddie's been gone, just feels like longer.

Naddie, I'm so proud of you, earning a scholarship and going off to school in Nairobi. I know your folks are looking down on you, smiling hugely as they listen to you singing and learning more about music. God gave you a beautiful voice, although not the gift of solving algebra equations easily! Keep studying, you'll do fine.

I miss you too, more than I can say. I'll call you on Saturday right after supper—and you will answer your phone. I'll work at learning computerized mail, too. Everyone sends much love. Remember, the holiday vacation will be here before we all know it. Je t'aime très fort – Maman

"Oven's fixed." Tucker squeezes Lillian's shoulder. "I'm heading into Kigali for my shift at the clinic. Be back after the weekend. Anything else you need?"

Lillian places a hand over Tucker's, fastening his fingers onto her shoulder. She listens to the hum of the children in the gathering room across the hall. "Truth is," she says, patting his hand before letting him go, "I have every blessed thing I need." Why then, she wonders, clicking open Rachel Shepherd's email again, does this note stick with her, impossible to delete? It's as if Henry himself is reaching out for help.

Dear Ms. Carlson,

First of all, I hope I'm not bothering you. I'm trying to get in touch with my father. My mom recently passed away and he's all the family I have left. I want to tell him he's going to be a grandfather in three months. Maybe he'd want to know.

Henry Shepherd worked for the St. Augustine Record for a few years out of college, and one of his photos wound up on the cover of Life magazine. It was beautiful: a girl standing in the light of a stained glass church window, this fierce determination on her face. You're that girl, aren't you? Have you kept in touch with my father? Do you know where he is now?

Lillian pushes away the warm silver keyboard. That's the problem with this contraption, it only stirs up trouble. Questions that should be left alone. She still has the yellowed newspaper clipping dated March 25, 1965 with the same photo Henry later sold to *Life*. It originally took her a few seconds to realize it was *her* face staring back from the front page, right next to Reverend King, his fist in the air as he stood at the pulpit. She still remembers his booming voice, encouraging folks to walk the talk and join him in Selma. *Now is the time to take a risk.* The headline of the *St. Augustine Record* read: Making Dreams Come True.

You're that girl, aren't you? Lillian squints at the screen. Is she? Everything happened so fast as the sermon ended that day, a crowd of folks heading up to the pulpit to shake hands with the now infamous Reverend King. He had been preaching alongside his father for years at their neighborhood church. Daddy pushed her aside, the look on his face telling her he wasn't simply in a hurry to join the others. "All right, that's enough," he boomed, the echo of his voice able to draw a shiver up her spine even now. "Go on, take your camera and get out."

Lillian couldn't believe her eyes: That white boy was on one knee in the aisle, snapping photos. Snapping photos of *her*. She saw Daddy's hand drop onto his shoulder, yank him to his feet. Henry looked straight at her, his dark eyes wide and sparkling. She could have sworn he asked her a question and she held his gaze as if making a promise, counting the beats of her heart—*one, two, three, four*—to steady her nerves. Time seemed to slow down as the crowd pushed forward toward the pulpit, Daddy trying the best he could to fight the tide, strong-arming the intruder back up the aisle. The boy spun around, nearly dropping his camera, and Lillian snapped open her purse. She slipped her high school ID into the camera case hanging from the boy's shoulder. She wouldn't need it anymore.

That girl in the church window had been her inspiration for years, especially when she first came to Africa and was teaching English at a mission near Nairobi to children who needed shoes and a full stomach far more than prayer. She wanted to help change the world, and stayed at the mission for four years until she was *certain*—in a naïve way that living here has cured her of—that she knew how to really make a difference. Sometimes now, she stares into the mirror, not at the silver sheen on her black hair, not at the fine lines becoming deep grooves like a roadmap of her troubles hanging onto Kwizera, but searching for the light that was in her eyes in that photo. The certainty. Was it trick photography? She used to tease Henry, but it was true: he did spark the light in her eyes. He made her believe, even after Reverend King's assassination, that she could make a small but real difference in the world. She's done that for forty-eight orphans over the years. She could do it for one more abandoned child now, couldn't she?

She has the words set just right in her mind. She'll tell that gal about the man who helped her turn ten acres of clay and rocks into a farm, and a brick building with a leaky tar roof into a home for dozens of children, off and on for eighteen years. She'll say that Henry never forgot her. It's the truth, but a version that might bring some comfort. Satisfy her.

What comes most easily, as Lillian's fingers roam slowly over the keyboard, is a list of the things she loved about Henry: His sense of adventure, the way he'd go off for weeks or months at a time in search of mountain gorillas and golden monkeys. His generosity, giving her most of the money he earned shooting nature footage for TV commercials and nature films, to keep Kwizera going. His booming laugh, it was contagious, the way he made the children giggle at his preposterous stories about talking animals.

Your father sat for hours on the bank of the river that winds through the forest fringing our backyard, watching and waiting with his trusty camera. His theory was that if he sat there long enough, his body became like another appendage of the thick tree trunk he leaned against, his scent blended in with the smells of eucalyptus and pine. Eventually, a shy aardvark or okapi might show up to drink, or a herd of majestic kudu with their twisty antlers and slashes of white—like war paint—under their eyes.

Lillian stops typing and absentmindedly rubs her index finger on the spot at the nape of her neck where Henry could set off a cascade of shivers down her spine with his light touch. Sometimes, they would take a picnic to the tall mopani tree at the bend in the river—their special spot—where a window of sunlight opened up for an hour or so midday. Her heart quickens as she calls up the breeze rustling the leaves above, Henry's low, soothing whisper in her ear. *Lilly, my sweet Lilly.* Reminds her of the rush of the water. That river's been silent for years, choked with blood and bones, broken glass and garbage. Tears.

It's mesmerizing, how the words disappear backwards as her finger presses the backspace key until the screen is a blank slate.

Dear Rachel, I wish I could help you, but I haven't seen your father in two years. He lived here for a while, but I don't know where he is now. What I do know is that he loves you, always has and never stopped. I sincerely hope this gives you some comfort to know that. I'm afraid it's all I have to offer.

Lillian closes the computer screen. No, she isn't the girl Henry Shepherd photographed in Ebenezer Church. She hasn't taken that photo out of the old metal suitcase in the attic for two years, and she can't afford to start looking back now.

THREE
{ September 15, 2000 }

RACHEL SMILES AWAKE: A TINY FOOT, DEFInitely a foot, arcs across the interior of her belly. Serena's three a.m. calisthenics. She tugs at the waistband of her pajama bottoms. "Tell you what," she whispers. "Let me get a few more hours of sleep and then I'll finish that story about the kickboxing ballerina who flies to the moon with a spacecraft full of animals." The movement stops and Rachel imagines a miniature palm pressing against her own hand, slapping a high-five. It's crazy, this connection that's been growing right along with her baby during the past month. So different than the first pregnancy: ten weeks of expecting, waiting to feel like a mother. And then, nothing. Nothing at all.

She scooches closer to Mick, picturing the baby rolling along like a synchronized swimmer. And then, it's an older girl she sees in her mind's eye, seven or eight, who has her fair skin, a barely visible dusting of freckles across high cheekbones. Hopefully, Serena will inherit Mick's blond hair and athletic prowess, her eyes the color of pecan shells and love of music. She stretches an arm past her protruding belly and over her husband's chest, slows her breath to match his. Their daughter will be the best of both of them.

It seems like moments later when conflicting scents nudge Rachel fully awake. Definitely strawberries, green tea—God, how she misses coffee—and a tinge of something sharp that makes her nose wrinkle. She peels open one eye, looks at the collie splayed out at the foot of the bed. "Well, Louie?" She's almost afraid to see what her husband scrambled into the eggs today. "Spinach?"

"Nope, kale," Mick shouts from the bathroom, the buzz of his electric razor clicking off. "More iron. I checked online."

Rachel hoists herself up, bulldozes the pillows into a backrest with her elbows, and then reaches past the tray on her bedside table featuring green-flecked eggs—old tennis shoes, that's the smell—for something more appealing: her new iBook, a consolation prize from Mick for making it through a full month of bed rest. Tangerine orange, lighter than her clunky PC and, best of all, instant Internet—no dial-up! How it works is a mystery but she doesn't miss the screech-and-clang DSL soundtrack, like a train wreck on acid and it took forever to get online. Now, she imagines there's a genie inside who magically connects her to the world she's mapping out on the screen.

Colorful islands of icons dot the upper right-hand corner, chat room icons (parenting, music, and local happenings) have their own archipelago nearby. The upper left is AOL Nation: Instant Messenger, mailbox, and a folder of saved emails. Across the bottom are files of clip art, news items and music reviews she's written for a few e-zines to add to her GeoCities web page. It used to be devoted to the New York music scene, but now she's moving more toward a mommy-and-baby theme. She hovers the cursor over a folder labeled "recipes." Kale? Maybe not. She opts for the mailbox, lit up like the North Star as the email program kicks in.

Her pulse ticks up, a message materializing before her eyes. "Mick, check it out. Lillian finally wrote back."

Her husband strolls into the room knotting his tie, brow creased. "Rwanda Lillian, my father's..." Rachel waves her hand, unsure what this woman is or was to Henry Shepherd, and scrolls through the brief email.

Mick reads over her shoulder, and then kisses the top of her head. "Sorry, babe. Looks like a dead end."

"He lived at her farm," Rachel murmurs. Was Lillian her father's mistress? Wife? "Wonder why he left. This sure doesn't tell me much."

"That's probably the point. She's telling you to leave it alone."

"But why?"

"Maybe your dad's not such a great guy. Merilee certainly didn't think so."

"True," Rachel says softly. Her mom couldn't say enough bad things about Henry Shepherd. Always was irresponsible. No big surprise that he up and left, leaving her with an eight-year-old girl to raise alone. Never sent the full amount of child support. He didn't bother to send a birthday card or Christmas present after the first year. And yet, Rachel remembers racing home from school to check the mailbox, excited and hopeful... When did she stop hoping?

"Ray, I know you're going stir-crazy stuck in bed," Mick says.

"Sign up for that Accounting 101 class, or real estate, that's another great part-time career. Read the new baby books my mom sent. Finish knitting that blanket—"

Rachel raises her hand. Point taken.

Mick sits on the bed and pats her shoulder, like he can't reach his arm around her. Rachel surveys the dark blue expanse of the computer screen, the icons where she can set anchor for an hour or two and then move on, to fill the long days alone. If only he *would* reach around her. Hold her. Stay home for a day or two.

He pecks her cheek. Discussion over. "Don't forget to turn on the IM so I can check in quick between meetings. And take it easy today, okay?"

"Scout's honor." Rachel raises her hand in a three-finger salute. How much trouble could she get into, marooned in bed?

Why? THE QUESTION PROPELS RACHEL through the morning as she explores the hinterlands of Alta Vista, excavating bits and pieces of information to populate a newly discovered territory. Smack in the middle of the screen is a green folder labeled with bold letters: RWANDA. Her eyes keep darting back to Lillian's email, like a compass, open in the corner of the screen. Why did her father wind up at her farm? Why didn't he come home again? Why won't Lillian help her to find him now?

This isn't the first time Rachel has searched for signs of her father online over the past five years, since a handful of search engines opened up the borders of the Internet. Other than a few photo credits in nature magazines, she's come up empty. It's as if the man she

29

vaguely remembers building campfires in the backyard and sitting on the edge of her bed as she fell asleep at night entered the Witness Protection Program. He simply disappeared. But now she's discovered a new way into his life: Lillian. The fact that Henry Shepherd's mistress or wife—or whatever—is pushing her away only makes Rachel more determined to figure out what she's hiding.

One web link after the next reveals snippets about Lillian: Guest speaker at Ebenezer Baptist Church in Atlanta. An Op Ed piece in the *International Herald Tribune*, titled "Is Forgiveness Possible?" A note of thanks on the website of a Rwandan woman who grew up at Kwizera, and is now studying at the London School of Economics. But no photos. That's what she really craves. What does Lillian look like?

"Jackpot!" she says, an article from the *Jacksonville Times* popping up on the screen. There's a thumbnail photo: a petite black woman sitting on a bench in front of a field of sunflowers, surrounded by children. She's wearing a traditional African batik skirt and matching green T-shirt, her hair in a soft shoulder-length bob, the same head held high and chin jutted out as the girl in the magazine photo. Rachel imagines that her father took this photo, perhaps also wrote this news story about a brave woman from Atlanta who built a home for the youngest victims of Rwanda's tumultuous history of civil war. The brief article with no date brings up more questions.

"Maybe if I ask her some specifics." Rachel scratches the furry canine belly sprawled out beside her. Louie wriggles closer, like he's actually interested, while she pulls up Lillian's email again and hits the reply button. She quickly types the questions her mother has forbidden all these years: Why Rwanda? What was he searching for? And, what exactly did he do there? She stops typing, erasing the words as

Merilee's pat explanation comes back to her: *He has a new life now. Believe me, we're better off without him—forgetting him.*

Rachel studies the grainy online photo. There's a glint in Lillian's eyes, a knowing, as if she's sharing a secret with the photographer. A wonderful secret. Perhaps, the matriarch of Kwizera, like Merilee, is also still trying to forget the man she never stopped loving. "Lillian, is it okay…if I call you?" She tries the question aloud, fingertips clicking on the keyboard, "if I call you? One phone call and I won't bother you again." Fair enough, right?

By the time Mick returns in the evening, Kwizera-land is populated with a half-dozen articles about Lillian and several images of wildlife with her father's name in the photo credits. "It's not much, but this is the first real evidence I have that he even existed after leaving us," she says, showing her husband a photo from *National Geographic* dated 1983: a family of gorillas climbing a hillside blooming with purple and yellow wildflowers. Several in the clan appear to be youngsters. One gorilla, likely the mother, is carrying a baby on her back. A huge silverback gorilla glances over his shoulder, his arm raised, as if inviting the photographer to come along on their adventure. Rachel imagines her father waving back to the animal, running up the hillside after them.

Mick shakes his head as he reads the email. "You can't send this, Ray."

"Because?"

"She already said she can't help you. There must be reasons."

"I don't accept that." Rachel taps the send button. "He's my father. The last living relative I have." Her husband's face crumples. "Blood relative," she adds.

Mick heads toward the bathroom. "You know my family is *your* family. At least, they want to be." There's the sputter of water, the snap of the shower door, but her husband's still talking.

Rachel leans back against the pillows with a heaving sigh. They've had this discussion before: trading their East Village loft for a historic bungalow with a big yard and a view of the Catskills, his mom just around the corner. She'd definitely give them some starter furniture, there's a ton in the basement. Rachel places a hand flat on the art deco bedside table with a marble top and bear-claw feet. She scrounged it from an estate sale in Park Slope and refinished it herself. Mother O'Shea's taste runs more toward dark and somber Early Americana. Where the hell does she fit into her husband's perfect life?

"My sisters have this great system worked out where they work part-time and trade off babysitting so they don't need to pay for daycare," Mick says. "You could get in on that deal."

"I'm pretty much set on getting my accounting degree at NYU," Rachel replies, although the only job she really wants is full-time mom.

THAT NIGHT, AS RACHEL FLOATS on the cusp of sleep, Mick's weight shifting in the space next to her, she imagines her father's shadow perched on the edge of the bed, watching over her. Louie dispatches a dreamy grumble from his sentinel post on the rug. She reaches down toward the collie, her stomach tight and achy, and pats his head in appreciation: her protector. Suddenly, her stomach knots as if the baby is grabbing hold with a tight fist, a message she is unable to decipher.

After a hike to the kitchen for a glass of milk, she heads into the nursery, fully painted with Bumblebee Yellow walls and hip-high shelves lined with chubby books meant more for gnawing on than reading. She reaches into the crib, buffered with Goodnight Moon bumpers to remove the afghan-in-progress stuffed into a Macy's plastic shopping bag. She settles into the sliding rocker, and then rolls out the half-finished blanket across her lap. Tucked inside is a gold cardboard box in surprisingly good shape. She carefully opens this final gift from her mom. An ivory beaded necklace is nestled in tissue paper, a menagerie of wooden animals dangling from it: a leopard, zebra, elephant, and giraffe. The notecard reads, *Happy thirteenth birthday, Cricket.*

"Jesus, Mom," Rachel whispers. She brings the necklace to her chest, the other hand reaching for the snow globe on her desk. Her father's footprints in the snow. He called her Cricket, teased that she was always chirping away or something like that. Had he been sending her gifts all along? Letters too? She looks to the mountain trapped in a whirl of paper snowflakes, as if for answers.

As a child, Rachel worried about what happened to the oversized Florida Gators jersey that used to hang in the front hall next to her blue windbreaker. The fridge seemed empty without the huge bottle of Dr. Pepper her father would swig from on the top shelf. She spent entire afternoons playing detective, searching each room of the house for evidence that he had been there at all. The travel magazines that used to fan across the coffee table, the shaving kit in the bathroom, the chipped coffee mug that was always in the kitchen sink in the morning… *World's Best Dad.* All of his things were gone. And yet, these are the things Rachel still remembers about Henry Shepherd.

She leans back in the chair, closes her eyes and clutches the necklace so tightly that sharp zebra ears and a rhino horn dig into her palm. *Happy birthday, Cricket.* What did her father sound like when he spoke her name? And his laugh; he was always cracking lame jokes. At least that's how she remembers it. He used to sit on her bed at night and tell stories, this much she knows for sure. She loosens her grip on the necklace and brushes her fingers against her shoulder. He must have rubbed her back, or placed a hand on her head as she fell asleep. Maybe he sang… No, he would make up stories. Wouldn't he?

She hears her mom, loud and clear, in one of her more generous moments: "He loved you, and me I suppose, the best he could. I'm afraid," Merilee sighed, "he simply didn't have it in him to be a good father. Not everyone does." But the dad who sent the snow globe and necklace, he loved her. He did. And the young man with slicked back curls in the wedding photo, holding his new bride close…

"When?" she whispers aloud. When had the trouble started between her parents? Maybe it was before she was born. Had Merilee gotten pregnant with hopes of saving her marriage too?

Rachel always assumed Merilee's mercurial temper was to blame for their troubles, imagined her father trying to calm her down. Of course he loved her, only her. Coming downstairs to breakfast was always a gamble. Some mornings, Merilee sang along with Sinatra records, tapping a gold slipper on the linoleum as she cooked grits, fried tomatoes and poached eggs. Other times, a box of Lucky Charms was on the table, her mom nowhere in sight. Rachel vaguely recalls her father pouring cereal—memory or desire, she's not sure—shushing her. *Mommy's having one of her black days.*

Rachel circles her arm under her belly. "What was Grandpa really like, Serena?" she wonders aloud, a sadness unraveling from someplace deep within. It's a barren place where the missing pieces of her father—the stories he told, the jokes they shared, the trips to the park or the zoo they surely enjoyed together—used to fit snugly. Was he a good father?

He simply didn't have it in him.

A chilling thought shoots through Rachel's fingertips, her hand springing away from her stomach. Does she have it in her to be a good mother? She goes back to the kitchen and opens the laptop on the counter to check her email box. Nothing, of course there's nothing, it's too soon for Lillian to have responded. She shuts off the computer and walks back across the hall, slips into bed beside her husband. She'll check again after Mick leaves for work. Lillian has to help her find Henry Shepherd so she can reclaim these memories, not only for herself but also for her daughter.

FOUR

{ September 15, 2000 }

T HE CRACKLING *CHIRP, CLASH, BANG* OF the Internet connecting through the phone line is a symphony to Nadine's ear, her entry into a world where she's in charge of the information funneled to her instead of being forced to study math and economics. She flips through the algebra book next to her pillow and then lays her head close enough to smell the musty pages, as if she might figure out what linear equations are through osmosis. All she really cares about is music. She keeps an eye on the minutes passing in the corner of the computer screen perched on her desk: 2:01, 02, 03... She groans as the line goes silent and clicks on the dial-up button again.

Some nights she doesn't sleep more than a few hours, instead researching the world of music beyond Mozart and opera that isn't covered in her classes. Lately, she's been obsessed with American punk rock of the late 1980s—the anger and raw emotion is unlike anything allowed on Rwanda radio stations, where Madonna is considered cutting edge. There's a code that a boy, likely trying to impress her, revealed to bypass the Internet security settings of the university. Supposedly, they are protecting students from pornography and other unnamed evils floating around online, but escaping into her computer is far safer than sleeping. The nightmares are worse here, especially since the attorney from Kigali called last week, asking questions there's no use in answering. *What happened at the church? What did you see? Who murdered your friends and family?* What possible good will it do to speak of these things? She learned long ago that staying quiet is the way to stay safe.

While waiting for entry into the World Wide Web, a fairytale land she never had access to before coming to school in Nairobi, her gaze drifts to the neatly made twin bed across the room. Most girls would be happy for the privacy, a roommate who practically lives at her boyfriend's apartment, but the empty bed brings up unsettling thoughts. She shared a room with her older cousin, Sylvia, for nearly five years, after Sylvia's family was murdered and their land in a nearby town seized by the government. She remembers the feel of her cousin, soft and round, scrunched beside her on a bed like this one. They read with a flashlight, the same book, *A Wrinkle in Time*, over and over, Sylvia nudging her gently when she was ready to turn the page. The static finally clears. The first thing Nadine does is check email for a return message from Tucker. He'll know what to do about the attorney, and she can trust him not to tell Maman. Sure enough, there it is. The subject line reads: No worries.

Hey, Princess,

First of all, I need to tell you Rosie says, "hi." She's been practicing her mancala game with Zeke, so be forewarned. By the time you come home for the holiday break next month, they'll both give you a run for your money. Next on the agenda: the attorney from Kigali. I'm assuming she's with the United Nations International Tribunal, although you didn't say. They're pushing to expedite more trials of genocide crimes because of criticism by the new government. That's a good thing. But I can't blame you for being hesitant to testify. You have to tell Lillian. You know that, right? We'll figure this out when you come home. And listen up: Do Not Worry! I have a plan. You just concentrate on your studies. Check out the new Star Wars movie with your friends.

Nadine clicks link after link, trying not to think about everything. The attorney. The exam she's surely going to fail. Going home. How will she tell Tucker and Maman the truth, that she's lonely and quite possibly going to be expelled from university if she doesn't pass the algebra midterm? And Tucker's right, of course, about telling Maman the attorney called.

During waking hours, she does not think of her cousin Sylvia beside her in the cramped rafters, where Baba made them stay after the killing began, pulling up the rope ladder and replacing the false ceiling after each time they came down for food or to use the toilet. She does not think of Sylvia's hand clamped over her mouth as they heard gunshots, her father shouting and then only Umama sobbing. She does not think of her father's blood that stained the living room walls. She does not think of the false hope they clung to, walking through town with their suitcases to the church. Hundreds of Tutsis, wondering where all of their Hutu neighbors were, the men who had been guarding their homes for weeks, making sure they didn't leave.

She does not think of what happened at the church. At first, she had believed that Rahim Kensamara, the precinct leader, was sparing her life out of kindness. They were neighbors. He had often shared bottles of *urwaga* on the back stoop of their house with Baba and other men in the neighborhood, Hutu and Tutsi alike. *Some must be left to tell. Maybe you, maybe not.* This was all Rahim Kensamara would say when she asked if he was going to kill her. Being kept alive was a punishment worse than death, for the girl his youngest son sometimes protected at school.

She shuts down the computer and tries to study, but all she can think about is the attorney. *You must tell, so that justice can be served. It's your responsibility.* No, she will not tell anyone about the massacre at the church that Rahim Kensamara and the others called the Hutu glory. She will not remember, at least not during the daylight. But late at night, when she becomes so tired it is impossible to stay awake even with the Internet, that's when the punishment begins all over again. There is no controlling what comes to her in dreams.

FIVE
{ *September 15, 2000* }

RACHEL IS SUSPENDED IN ALMOST-SLEEP, the wooden hippos and giraffes solid and comforting around her neck, mooring her in place. She'll find Lillian's phone number online, call her tomorrow. What's Lillian going to do, hang up on her? Or, maybe Mick's right and she should leave it alone. If only her mom was here, she would have to come clean now. Rachel places a hand on the necklace. Wouldn't she?

She dreamily recalls her last visit with Merilee: leaning over her bed to plant a soft kiss on a heavily rouged cheek. A bright scarf. A flash of smooth scalp. A slash of coral lipstick. *Doing her face* several times daily became one final way of fighting back against the hideous disease. Another image comes to mind: the larger-than-life headshot of Merilee propped on an easel beside her grave. Her young bright face, bare shoulders dusted by sleek finger-waves of auburn hair. She's at the beach, of course, her favorite place, against a background of sparkling ocean and sky—a deep blue that mirrors her eyes. She's gazing into the camera Henry Shepherd is surely holding. So sensual! This is the woman Rachel wants to remember, before the cancer turned creamy skin rough and papery, and drained the light from her eyes.

"How's our little Rockette today?" Merilee asks from somewhere both close and far away, part dream and part memory. Rachel rubs her abdomen, a dull ache reminding her that her mom will never meet Serena.

"My little girl, a mother." Merilee sighs, and then closes her eyes and begins to hum *You Are My Sunshine*. "I sang, your father told stories. Sometimes I listened from the hall. Tired…so tired."

"What was he like?" Rachel asked quietly that day at Seaview Estates as her mom fell asleep. Was he smart, funny? Was he the one who helped her learn to read, ride a bike? Questions she had never dared to bring up as a child.

When Merilee awoke a few hours later, Rachel tried again. "You used to listen when Dad was tucking me into bed," she said, holding a mirror for her mom to assess her afternoon face after applying a fresh coat of make-up. "What did he say?"

"Oh, it's so silly."

"What, Mom?"

"I thought…" Merilee sighed, frowning at her reflection in the mirror. "I thought I might hear him telling you things."

"Things?"

"You know, *we* used to talk. Well, mostly I'd listen to Henry going on about how he wanted to travel the world, take photos of important places and people."

"Sounds exciting."

"He was never satisfied, not with me, his job, our life." Merilee traced her sagging jaw with a finger. "Me," she repeated softly.

"So, did you hear him telling me important things?"

"Fairytales about those exotic places he used to ramble on about. At the time I didn't think they were important, but now…" Merilee shook her head and pushed away the mirror, kneading her bony fingers against the hem of the sheet. "When you were older, you two would chatter away in your room for hours, making up stories together."

"Tell me," Rachel prompted.

Merilee recalled a scientist hunting for fancy black orchids in the Amazon jungle. An island with soda-pop rivers and gumdrop trees. A magical place with zebra and caribou roaming around the backyard.

Now, Rachel tosses in bed, clutches the animal beads around her neck. *Kwizera.* Her father told her stories about Kwizera. Had he been in contact with Lillian all along? Loved her? "Mom, it's okay," she whispers in her dream state. Back in the nursing home she sullenly asked her mother why she never joined them. What was holding her back?

"I'm ashamed to admit it, but I was jealous," Merilee confessed. "Of you and him, both. The two of you."

Perhaps Merilee knew all along about Lillian. That would explain why she was so bitter. Her mom's hands were clenching the sheet, the skin mottled and papery thin.

Rachel reaches out, now more awake than asleep. Why didn't she take those frail hands in her own? Her fingers go rigid on her stomach, tamping down a pulsing, uncomfortable heat. She always blamed her mom; it was so easy to believe that the bitterness was what drove her father away. The best she could do in that hospital room was to bite her lip and try not to say anything hurtful.

In her bed, lying beside her husband, she squeezes her eyes shut and tries to rewrite the past in her dreams. She curls onto her side, the heat in her abdomen radiating through her body. If only she could go back in time and change the way she sat frozen in the chair next to her dying mother's bed, afraid to touch that fragile version of the tough woman who raised her. So afraid her mom would leave her. She remembers how she watched, horrified, paralyzed for long moments before pressing the call button, while Merilee slipped into a coma.

Now, slipping back into the dream, she holds her mom in her arms and rubs her back. "Remember our pact?" she soothes. *Nobody leaves.* They used to whisper-promise in the dark, her mom lying beside her as she fell asleep.

Merilee pulls away and looks straight into Rachel's eyes. "He called."

"I know, that first Christmas—"

"No, after that too."

Rachel takes a few deep breaths, trying to shut off the hot pain shooting through her so she can listen carefully. Is that what her mom was trying to tell her as she slipped away? At the time, she assumed morphine-induced guilt had made Merilee remember things differently. "Tell me," she mumbles, kicking off the sheets, her skin too tight and warm. Did he really call?

"Don't hate me, little girl," Merilee says softly, the dream fading away.

"Mom!" Rachel yells, the pain ripping through her throat.

Nobody leaves.

Suddenly, she's falling somewhere dark and bottomless, clinging to the mattress, sinking under water, ropes of seaweed pulling her down. "Mom," Rachel gasps, throwing an arm across the bed, struggling to untangle herself from sleep. *Don't leave, please don't leave.*

Mick flips on the lamp. "Hey, just a dream."

She freezes as her hand lands on the thick stickiness oozing down her right thigh. "Mick!"

"Jesus, don't move, just don't move."

Rachel lies perfectly still, barely breathing, locking onto her husband's eyes. He's perched on the edge of the bed, as if afraid to touch her. "Yes, damn it, this is an emergency," he shouts into the phone, and then quieter, "It's okay, Ray. The ambulance will be here soon."

It might be minutes or hours later; Rachel's floating somewhere beyond time. She no longer feels the ache in her abdomen, the stickiness on her legs, the weight of her body as she's lifted onto a canvas slab. "Are you cold, ma'am? Need another blanket?" a woman's voice asks. Rachel doesn't answer. She can't. She's no longer there. *It's okay, baby girl, I'm here.* She echoes Merilee's voice in her head, blocking out the stab of a needle, the waxy oxygen mask slapped onto her face, the siren wailing.

Rachel awakens at three a.m. out of habit, anticipating the tiny kicks of Serena's early morning calisthenics instead of the throbbing in her womb. A soft blue light falls across her shoulder and she adjusts her eyes, at first confused to see a railing at the bedside. The needle taped into her forearm comes into focus, and then the tube running to a clear bag suspended in air. Beside it, a monitor shows the steady up and down line that verifies life. She watches the screen and smiles with groggy satisfaction, rubbing a hand over her belly. Her fingers freeze, grazing the sticky edge of a bandage. "Serena," she shouts, but all that comes out is a hoarse whimper. Her husband's arms wrap loosely around her—too loose. She's weak and exhausted, wants to sink safely into him but can't shake the dizzy sensation of falling. Falling, falling, as if she'll never again land on solid ground.

"Easy now, it's going to hurt for a while," Mick says.

Rachel looks blankly at him.

"They put you under for the C-section. The doctor thought it was best."

"Best?" Rachel searches her husband's face: his skin is ghostly pale, purple-black under his eyes as if bruised. "No," she says thickly, pulling at the bandage. "Too early."

"Ray, there was so much blood. You must've felt…" Mick's voice breaks into a sob. He presses knuckles against his forehead, hiding his face. "Earlier today, didn't you feel something? Something wrong?"

Rachel raises a hand toward her husband. He seems impossibly far away. "Make them bring Serena. She needs her mother."

Mick looks up, a flare of confusion rising from his neck to his cheeks. "Don't you remember…" Rachel hears faint stray words, as if they are being blown around by a high wind: *ambulance…umbilical cord…detached*. And then a nurse is standing over her. *Hysterical. Medication.*

She pulls back the sheet, needs to get the hell out of bed. A sharp pain slices through her, as if ripping her daughter away all over again. "You'll bring Serena," she says weakly, resigned to letting the nurse tuck her back into bed, too tired to keep fighting. So tired. Of course, the baby is sleeping. They'll bring her when she wakes up. Everything will be okay then.

THE NEXT TIME RACHEL AWAKENS, sunlight is flooding the room and a woman with flowing auburn hair is arranging flowers on a little table. "Mom?" she whispers, blinking awake, shading her eyes against the glare.

"I'm Molly," the nurse says. "You've been asleep for quite a while, most of the day."

Rachel blinks fully awake and sees that Molly's hair is more brown than red. She sits up, fingertips cautiously grazing her stomach. The bandage. Her mom admitting that her father called. Mick sobbing. The ambulance. Was it all only a horrible dream? "I need my husband. Where is he?"

"He'll be back soon."

"My baby?"

Molly smoothes the blanket. "I'll have a doctor come in."

A few minutes later, an intern is explaining how the placenta separated from her uterine wall and caused all the bleeding. He's so calm it's unnerving. Rachel keeps nodding, as if to lob the words back at him, keep them from sinking in and becoming real. *Initial tear so small it doesn't show up on an ultrasound...blood clots can form behind the placenta and hide the tear...* "Ms. Shepherd, nobody knows for certain what causes this. You wouldn't necessarily feel the rupture when it occurred. Sometimes, if the placenta hasn't attached correctly from the beginning, lots of movement can progressively cause the separation over a few weeks or sometimes only days."

"I should have known."

"It's nobody's fault. The ultrasound showed that everything was normal. This just happens sometimes. How could you have known?"

Rachel looks up to see her husband standing in the doorway and searches his eyes, waiting for him to agree with the intern. He's just standing there. "Mick…" she reaches out her hand, keeps it there although her arm is weak and shaky. The way he's regarding her hand, eyes narrowed, is frightening. It's like he's trying to decide whether or not to take it. "Stay with me," she whispers, her throat parched.

Nobody leaves.

SIX
{ October 15, 2000 }

LILLIAN STABS A SHOVEL INTO THE RED CLAY and stomps a foot on the rusty metal head to get some leverage. For weeks she's been working on this patch of land alongside the house, a few inches at a time. The morning sun shines generously, and then the roof throws a protective shadow in the heat of the afternoon. It's perfect for the dahlias Nadine loves. Tucker bought peat moss and fertilizer in Kigali a few weeks ago, and he's buying rosebushes in Nairobi to plant when the rainy season ends in December. Phlox, wild pansies, and ferns from the forest will have to do for now. At least this patch of land will look like a real garden when Naddie comes home for the holiday break next month. The perfect early Christmas present. She's uncomfortable receiving gifts, been that way ever since first coming here to live. Always giving away her toys and clothes to the other kids. The only possessions that child's protective of are her flute and a few photos Henry managed to recover from her folks' house in the foothills on the other side of town. Those foothills were charred and barren for years; this is the first spring since the slaughter that they're blanketed with white-blossomed coffee bushes again.

The shovel clangs against a patch of rocks. Lillian kneels, grunting as she heaves them aside. Anger is good fuel for doing something productive. She gouges her fingers under a stubborn slab of limestone, sweat dripping into her eyes.

"Hey, watch where you're throwing those things." Tucker approaches, a hand raised as if to fend off an attack. "A more paranoid guy might think you're trying to bean him."

"Not you," Lillian says as he kneels beside her to study the boulder. "Rachel Shepherd sent another email yesterday. Poor gal had a miscarriage. She's hurting bad. The baby. Her father. It's all mixed up, and she wants me to help with the untangling."

"She's the one you're tossing rocks at?"

"No, of course not."

Tucker takes the shovel and cautiously nudges the ground, as if he's exploring an open wound. "Henry might still be shooting travel videos for that outfit in London. I could give them a call."

Lillian continues churning up the clay under the limestone with her fingers. If only it was that easy. Simply call. For eighteen years, Henry was here far more often than not and she never asked him to stay. Never asked him to come back, except for the one time. Vowed never to ask anything of him ever again. She turns away to wipe the sweat and something else that's stinging her eyes with a kerchief tucked into the elastic waistband of her dungarees. Tucker pretends not to notice. He keeps poking around with the shovel until he finds a sweet spot where the earth gives a little, and wheedles out the thick slab.

"I'll get that." Lillian heaves the rock out, ignoring her grumbling lower back. He's always been like this, trying to fix things for everyone. Sometimes it gets under her skin, the way he won't give up. The way she lets him take care of her.

Tucker stands and brushes the dirt from his khaki pants, looks at her as if waiting for instructions. When she doesn't give him any, he starts stacking the scattered rocks to make a wall on the side of the garden away from the house. "I'll nail some barbed wire on top to keep out the monkeys and other rustlers."

"Good thinking," Lillian says. She hands him a good-sized chunk of limestone. It's not his fault he believes there's a fix for every problem. She could forgive Henry; to Tucker's mind, it's that simple. But he's never been in love, not really, not in the entire six years she's known him. Every relationship has stopped a bit shy of serious. As far as she can see, that's his choice even though the woman is always the one who walks away. Always. He never allows them close enough to risk true loss. It's not her place to bring up this observation though, just as it's not on the table for him to comment on her feelings for Henry. A fair trade.

Eighteen years… Of course she still loves him. Misses him. Even when he was away for weeks at a time filming gorillas in the mountains, or shooting a commercial in London to pay for help with the spring harvest, she always felt him right beside her. He became a part of her, at first comfortable and then necessary. She never blamed him for leaving. In fact, she admired him for refusing to go when the Red

Cross evacuated all foreigners. She still appreciates that he stayed until the Tutsi rebels took back the government in Kigali and ended the slaughter. Truth be told, she takes equal responsibility for the way things went wrong between them. The itch to roam, sometimes without the excuse of an assignment, and booze had always been easy escapes for Henry. She could have demanded more of him sooner, instead of telling herself he would ask if he needed her help. Now, Rachel Shepherd is asking. But it's not the same. It's not.

"Prime real estate for planting now." Tucker offers a hand to help her up. She accepts it.

"Don't mind this stormy spell. I'll get over it."

"At least give Henry's daughter his mailing address in London. Hell, he might actually answer."

Lillian squeezes his hand. She stopped looking for letters not so long before the emails started coming from Rachel Shepherd. Tucker's still hoping one will show up. "Walk with me," she says.

They head away from the house, past the grassy hillside where a few goats and a cow are grazing, and then across the gravel front yard toward the clinic. Lillian stops to point out a pair of gray cranes flying overhead, their golden crowns shimmering in the sunlight. The cranes disappeared during the slaughter, along with most of the other animals except domesticated dogs and cats, and the baboons. The wild animals could smell danger and death in the air, even the birds.

"They mate for life," Tucker says and Lillian squeezes his arm, a gesture he mistakes for encouragement. "Rachel should write directly to her dad, not to you," he rushes on. "Henry will want to know she's asking about him, right? Henry will want to know she came all the way here to look for him, right? He'll be psyched."

"That's all true."

"Think about it. Wouldn't it be good for Nadine, for all of us if—"

"Tucker," Lillian says gently, "No." Henry won't come back. He can't. He made that clear two years ago, during her last visit to London. That was the one time she asked him to return, not for herself but for Nadine. It still makes her angry, the thought of the International Tribunal subpoenaing a child to testify in a courtroom filled with hundreds of people, reporters' cameras flashing, expecting her to relive the trauma of the church massacre where thousands of Tutsis from the region were lured with the promise of sanctuary. Naddie could have used Henry's support to face Rahim Kensamara, her former neighbor, who was finally on trial along with six other Hutu men who had been in jail for four years.

Lillian can't pretend to imagine what happened at the church to steal the light from Naddie's eyes and render her practically mute. For months afterwards, the only person she would speak to was Henry. It was hard to believe this was the same thirteen-year-old girl who had spent countless afternoons on a stool in the kitchen, stirring cookie batter and singing made-up songs while Dahla, her mother, baked and cleaned. Even four years later, Naddie wasn't much use at the trial in the international court in Arusha. She was unable to testify, paralyzed with fear.

"We can't give up," Tucker says. "At least, I can't."

"I never gave up," Lillian says. "It was Henry's choice to stay in London. Naddie needed him. I needed him." What choice did she have but to give him an ultimatum? No more visits. No phone calls. No letters. What choice does she have now but to keep it?

Lillian's spirits lift as they approach the Kwizera clinic. There's already a line at the front door, and inside a doctor and a nurse who sometimes drive up from Kigali to help Tucker. Lillian shows a stethoscope to a young boy who's afraid of needles and needs a measles vaccination, and then models for several other kids how to open wide and say, "Ahhh." All the while, she writes a letter to Henry in her mind. She tells him how proud he would be of Tucker. The wooden shed they built has grown into a three-room clinic where parents from Mubaro bring their children for free vaccinations or to get a limb set instead of taking the bus to Ruhengeri, thirty kilometers away. She asks him what she should do about his daughter. Is there a choice she's not seeing?

That evening, after all the children say goodnight and Tucker retires to the tent at the edge of the forest where he sleeps far more often than his room in the farmhouse, Lillian climbs the steps to the second floor. She pretends that going into Naddie's room and kicking off her shoes to lie on the purple satin quilt is purely an act of missing her daughter. She lays her head on the pillow and looks up at the dreamcatcher overhead, hanging from a nail on the wall, white feathers swaying slightly in the breeze from the open window. Henry made this with Nadine. He assured her that the web of yarn and twigs would catch nightmares, even though they all had seen too much to ever again believe that dreams might be peaceful and safe. Henry slept on the floor of this room for months, holding onto Naddie's fingers draped over the edge of the bed.

Lillian's eyes dart around the room: There's a bookcase lined with sheet music, books about birds—nature's musicians, Henry told Naddie—and a full set of encyclopedias he used to teach all of the children English. On the wall there's a Florida Gators baseball cap on a hook, hanging right next to a warrior headdress of crane feathers Naddie's aunt and uncle brought from Swaziland when they visited a few months after the slaughter. They wanted to take her to live with them, but by then Kwizera was her home. Lillian reaches out to the bedside table crowded with photos, and plucks out one in a wooden frame imprinted with hearts: Henry is bent over Naddie, showing her how to use a camera. He is everywhere in this room, more so than any other place in the house. He loved Naddie, as he surely loved his own daughter. Does he think about them, love them, still?

Lillian glances up at the dreamcatcher, and then closes her eyes. She could use some sifting out of the images that come to her at night. She answers the emails from Rachel Shepherd in her dreams. The girl's questions unearth memories, not about her life with Henry at Kwizera, that soil's too fresh and soft—she might sink in completely if she treads there—but Atlanta. Back then, being brave was as easy as smiling at a white boy and slipping him her high school ID card, at least at first. There were months of talking on the payphone in the hallway of her dorm at Spelman. Henry had a steady girl in St. Augustine and Lillian was dating Samuel, a boy she had grown up alongside. But it didn't matter; she and Henry weren't dating—merely talking.

Henry came to Atlanta several times over that summer of 1965 to take photos at the Student Nonviolent Coordinating Committee rallies against segregation, where a handful of white students were now showing up. Things were changing, slowly and not everywhere, but hope was palpable in Atlanta. There was a handful of restaurants in Sweet Auburn where they could eat dinner without catching stares and a fine jazz club, the Peacock, where music was all that mattered. In retrospect, it was the possibility of change, being part of making the world a better place, that made their budding relationship so exciting. She still remembers their first kiss at the Peacock. Muddy Waters was singing about getting his mojo workin', begging his baby not to go.

Henry moved into a studio apartment near Spelman in September. During that year, Lillian spent more time in that one room with a pullout couch and hot plate than her dorm or her parents' house. She and Henry built their own home, and laughed at the small-mindedness of folks who judged a person by the color of their skin. They could do better. The world was changing and they could wait.

The cold breeze of early morning awakens Lillian. The photo of Henry is still in her hand, on her chest. He never wanted to be a hero, never pretended he was changing the world, not during the year they were together in Atlanta, not when it came down to choosing her or a safe and comfortable life back in Florida with Merilee. Not here. Changing the world was *her* gig, he half-joked. He was along for the ride, enjoying the adventure of helping her. She replaces the photo on the table. She truly believed he would do the right thing when she asked him to come back for Nadine. What makes Tucker think he would come back now, because Rachel's looking for him? Would he? She reaches up to pluck the dreamcatcher off the wall, and then places it on a hanger in the closet. She can't afford to consider the possibility. Can't afford to hope.

Downstairs in her bedroom she lights the kindling in the fieldstone fireplace, but it's no use: the cold is emanating from her bones. She reaches under the bed where the computer is stashed, her hands trembling as she opens it to read the email from Henry's daughter for the third or fourth time since yesterday morning. The last part is always where her eyes linger: *My mom didn't like to talk about my fa-*

ther, except to say we were better off without him. He became this larger-than-life mystery that could never be solved. Now, I need to find a way to reconnect with him—or at least my memories of him. Maybe the best I can hope for is to pack him away in the past and move forward with my life. Lillian, you're the only one who can help me. I'm hoping that if I mine your memories, I'll recover my own.

Lillian's fingers rest heavily on the keyboard, her throat thick and dry like the clay in Naddie's garden. When Henry first came here, the farm was falling apart. She was falling apart. She told him he could come and go as he pleased, in fact she preferred it that way as long as he helped her to keep Kwizera going. It was this place—the children—that kept her strong and rooted. It was this place she depended on, this place only, for years. Having Henry around was supposed to be a bonus. She never meant to grow to rely on him, didn't realize how much until he told her he was leaving for good after the slaughter. She couldn't accept it.

Was she wrong for going to see him in London every few months? Three years of pretending he wasn't drinking too much, him pretending that's why his hands were too shaky to take photos. Was she wrong for trying to force him into returning to Kwizera, where his family could help him? Where *he* was needed to help them. She was fool enough to believe that the past could be selectively forgotten, the parts that hurt blotted out and good parts kept intact. Henry insisted he had tried. *Try harder. Go see a therapist. Keep trying.* Now, she believes him. She can't afford to risk the memories, not even the good ones that Rachel Shepherd should hear, can't afford to risk the emptiness of losing him all over again.

The whir and final click of the computer going blank isn't as comforting as Lillian hoped it would be. Walking briskly upstairs to Tucker's room, she consoles herself: Never asked for this machine, he can keep it or put it away in the closet or give it to Nadine. Better yet, throw it in the trash. These emails that come out of the blue, they're too much…can't be responsible for them anymore, just can't do it. She walks slower on the way back downstairs to her bedroom. Rose. Nadine. Thomas and Zeke. Tucker. They're all counting on her. They're her family—not Rachel Shepherd. Not Henry, not anymore. Besides, she's doing the right thing, protecting that poor gal. Protecting Henry from disappointing all of them again.

SEVEN

{ October 15, 2000 }

RACHEL SLAPS SHUT THE MEDICINE CABInet, palms the bottle of sleeping pills and slides it into her robe pocket as Mick swings open the bathroom door. It's like he's trying to catch her breaking the promise she made: one month, not a day more. But even with the pills, she wakes up every few hours and presses her abdomen, searching for the painful reminder of her baby girl.

"Good morning," she says, offering her husband a kiss so he'll stop staring at her with that are-you-okay look where his thick brows caterpillar together. One month. As if there was a timetable for grief. Ridiculous, how she bargained with Mick. He would hardly ever pop an aspirin, how could he possibly understand?

"Say," he quips. "The flurry we got last night dumped a ton of snow up in the Poconos. I'll call and see if that little inn we stayed at last year has a room…" His voice trails off as Rachel attempts to unset the scowl on her face. This isn't the first time he's suggested a romantic getaway, implying it's their one-and-a-half bedroom loft—tiny now, although it used to be cozy—or the noise of the city that's the source of the tension between them.

"It's only been—"

"Four weeks. Exactly."

Rachel looks down, following his gaze to her pocket. Busted. She pulls out the bottle of pills and gives him a sly smile, the kind that used to trump his sternest poker face, have them rolling around in bed, forgetting whatever the hell they were fighting about. "Sorry," she mumbles, exchanging flirty for humble. "I guess I'm still not ready."

"All I'm asking is that you try." Mick turns to leave, adding under his breath, "The least you could do."

Rachel stands over the toilet bowl, shaking the bottle of pills like dice, but then places them back in the medicine cabinet. A compromise. She steps into the shower for the first time in three days and rotates the knob with extreme effort. What if she could disappear into the steam? She leans her head against the tile, shoulders slumped into a shell, until the hot water's tapped out. *Try. Damn it, try.*

A plan, that's what she needs is a plan. Clearing the clutter out of her bedroom closet is a good start, and then the one in the hall, after that the kitchen cupboards. She's energized, filling the box marked for Goodwill with things that should have been tossed instead of hidden on shelves out of sight. Mid-morning, she finds herself in front of the closed nursery door, the knob cold and metallic in her hand. A thought pulses in her vacant womb. She should clear out the nursery.

Clear it out for good. Instead, she retreats back across the hall, her energy drained.

The apartment is dim with late-afternoon light when Rachel awakens. She runs a hand through snarled curls and her tongue over fuzzy teeth. A groan escapes as she squints at the open bottle of pills on the bedside table, and then remembers the Goodwill box. Hauling everything in the nursery away isn't the answer, that won't make things better with Mick. She swings stiff legs over the side of the bed, and then shakes the cotton loose from her brain. This isn't helping either.

Water, lots of water. She fills a tall glass for the third time at the kitchen sink, her body like a sponge. She flips open her laptop on the counter and scrolls quickly through a handful of emails: *Lunch? Meet for coffee? Are you and Mick okay? Ready for a weekend shift?* The thought of facing friends or, worse yet, mixing martinis for couples on dates, sends her back to the bedroom. The jumble of sheets and blankets looks so inviting as she pulls on jeans, a cable-knit white sweater and her favorite black high-top sneakers. A short walk in the snow is exactly the thing to snap her awake before Mick comes home. A make-up dinner of fresh pasta and cannoli from Balducci's, some flowers to brighten up the place. He'll see she is trying.

The forward motion of walking, soft snow melting against her cheeks, is exhilarating. She strolls right past Balducci's and the market that has yellow roses year-round. Before long she's at Rockefeller Plaza, sitting above the ice rink and watching the sun-drenched stage, mothers and nannies with little children scattered around the outer edges. A young girl's carefree laughter rings out like the bell at recess and Rachel turns to track it. And then, it just fades away. She stuffs her hands deep into the pockets of her down parka, wishing for gloves, fingers searching for the twinge of the still-tender scar. Had Henry Shepherd grieved over losing her, this same way? She hugs her stomach, a wave of queasy fear washing over her. What if one day the pink scar toughens and fades away into nothing at all?

Rachel returns home empty-handed. A dress and mascara, and a reservation at that new sushi place down the street will have to suffice. She stops to get the mail: a few bills, an invitation to a holiday party, and the usual weekly letter addressed only to Mick from Mother O'Shea. *P.S. Say hi to your lovely wife.* There's a bubble envelope with a promising heft, no return address. Rachel prods the sticky seal while climbing three flights of stairs, but doesn't tear it open until she's behind her apartment door. She sits on the leather couch with her parka still on and pulls out a packet of postcards tied up with brown twine. The note reads: *Your dad wrote these but never mailed them. There are more of his things here that you may want to see some day. Hope this helps.*

"Kenya, Tanzania, Morocco." Rachel flips through the cards, fifteen in all, mostly animals and landscapes. How many cards and letters had he written? Sent? Maybe her mom's deathbed confession that he had called wasn't just the morphine talking. She remembers Merilee digging up the white tulips her father planted in the front yard; it seemed crazy even to her eight-year-old self. Was it so far-flung that she might also have destroyed letters from him?

She peels off her parka and lays out the pictures like Tarot cards on the coffee table, trying to extract some meaning: two decades, ten countries in Africa and Europe. Always coming home to Kwizera. "Home," she says aloud. Kwizera was his home for all of those years.

I'm taking photos for a commercial in a spooky old castle on the Rhine River that could be straight out of one of our bedtime stories. You should see it, Cricket.

This is my second week shadowing the mountain gorillas. I sure could use you as an assistant, it gets lonely out here. But I can't complain. I'm shooting footage for a TV show—just like ol' Walt Disney!

Not one mention of coming back for her. It's more like he's inviting her to visit his new home.

She picks up a postcard of a lion sunning on a rock:

Dear Cricket, it's funny how I came here searching for one thing and found something totally different. Here's a bit of wisdom from your old man: It's the search that really matters. The adventure of living your life. You can quote me on that.

What was her father searching for? And what did he wind up finding that kept him from coming back to her?

Hours later, Rachel startles awake as Mick tosses his coat next to her on the couch. "I didn't hear you come in." She glances at the grandfather clock on the mantle: nearly midnight.

"Didn't want to wake you." He reaches for a postcard on the coffee table: a field of red roses with a snow-peaked mountain in the background.

"Don't." Rachel grabs his wrist, and then quickly lets go.

"They're obviously in some kind of order. My mistake."

"No," Rachel says. "Really, I…" *I'm sorry.* So damn lame. It seems like they're alternately fighting and apologizing lately, with no middle ground. "I want to show you something. This is my father's life, they're from him. Actually, from Lillian."

Her husband sits on couch arm to get a better look.

"He wrote these during the years he lived in Rwanda but never mailed them," Rachel continues. "I'm not sure why Lillian sent them now. I'd given up on her answering my emails."

Mick squints at the note accompanying the cards. "May I?"

"Yeah, sure."

"Looks like she's had a change of heart. Maybe she's inviting you to visit."

"Or throwing me a bone so I'll stop emailing."

"Why now?" Mick asks, and then answers his own question. "Maybe she wants to use you as bait, to lure her straying husband back home."

"Or, how about this," Rachel counters. "She might be trying to get some closure, too."

Mick picks up the postcard of Mt. Kenya and reads the back. "Impressive." He picks up another of a silverback gorilla in a tree. "That would be something to see, right? Not like you could go."

"I don't know about that," Rachel bristles. The way he said it, a fact not a question. What if Lillian *is* inviting her? "Mom left me three thousand dollars. That's probably enough for plane fare and some time in Rwanda. It can't be that expensive there."

"You're kidding right? It's not that long since millions of people were slaughtered there. Isn't it dangerous?"

"No, I mean yes, but…" Rachel shakes her head. It feels more dangerous not to go, to just stay here and pretend her marriage isn't falling apart. "I'll be safe at Lillian's farm."

Mick taps the postcard against his palm, like some weird code she should understand. Rachel raises her eyebrows.

"Nothing."

"Mick, it's late. I'm tired."

"No, why not?" He drops the card on the table and wipes his hand on his pants, as if rejecting something grimy. "Go ahead, risk your life on a wild goose chase to find this shmuck—"

"Hey, he's my father!"

"Henry messed up, ruined everything with your family. He left because he was, what, bored? Didn't really want a family? Wasn't ready?"

"Wait," Rachel says to her husband's back as he heads down the hall toward their bedroom. Like hell he's talking about Henry Shepherd. "Damn it, that's not fair."

Mick slams the bedroom door. So much for trying.

THE NEXT MORNING, RACHEL FINDS a note taped to the bathroom mirror: *Racquetball. Back after lunch. Love you.*

She's actually relieved Mick's gone to blow off steam, leaving her with more time alone. She brushes her teeth and splashes water on her face, without a thought of opening the medicine cabinet, and then settles on the couch, computer on one side and her dog on the other. She studies the postcards on the coffee table and chooses a tranquil image of deep green water dotted with giant lavender lilies. On the back, her father wrote: *Lake Kivu, the most peaceful place to canoe in the world.* "Louie, where do you think Lake Kivu is?" she asks while initiating a Google search. The screen fills with similar images of the lake in northern Rwanda.

"Can you imagine…" She absentmindedly scratches Louie's ear. How did Henry Shepherd drift here from their suburban Jacksonville home? *Peaceful.* Did he find what he had gone searching for, at least for a while?

These questions, and so many more, pull Rachel out of bed the following mornings. She can't bring back her daughter, but it might be possible to rediscover her father—without leaving home. She spends her days wrapped in a fuzzy brown blanket, studying the postcards and writing down thoughts in a notebook, and slowly begins remembering more than just the pain of her father leaving. She also accesses snippets of the times when he was there for her.

On Saturdays, her mom's beauty parlor date, they would drive to one of the less touristy beaches up the coast with all the windows of his sedan rolled down. She can still taste the citrus-salty breeze. One time, a birthday, he took her on a boat ride in the Everglades. She remembers that his camera nearly fell in the water when a gator emerged right in front of their boat, jaws snapping the air. Asleep on the couch one afternoon, Rachel dreams of sitting at a sidewalk café on a bustling block of Little Havana, drinking spicy hot chocolate and eating Cuban pastries filled with guava and cream cheese. A large Haitian woman with two gold teeth in front who claims to be a gypsy offers to read her father's palm. When he opens his hand, Rachel snaps awake. Was he planning on leaving for months, maybe years? Or, was it impulsive and unavoidable? Destiny.

Who is Henry Shepherd, really? Mick could be right about him being a carefree travel bum, unable to commit to the responsibilities of a family. But she has to believe there's more to the story. Over the next few weeks, she becomes consumed with solving the mystery of Henry

Shepherd's life; it's so much easier than dealing with her own confusing, messed up world. Meanwhile, her husband seems equally content to avoid their problems, their apartment—*her*—spending long hours at work. They practically float by each other in the hallways, barely touching as they lie side by side in the dark at night. They're like amiable ghosts sharing the same haunting ground. *Tomorrow,* Rachel vows silently each night before falling asleep, not exactly tired but fully drained from the energy it takes to avoid her husband and their unspoken grief. *Tomorrow we'll both try harder.*

RACHEL SQUINTS TO MAKE OUT her reflection in the smeared subway train window, and tucks a strand of hair behind her ear. Can people see she's not actually occupying this body? Her first shift since the miscarriage, a short one but it seemed endless. For the past four hours, she's repeatedly been checking out the mirror behind the bar, putting a hand to her face to make sure she's smiling. It's exhausting, the concentration it takes to listen to the drink orders so she doesn't screw up, the balding man with a sweaty scalp who's on his third martini complaining about his ungrateful kids, the waitress who must be making a joke because she's laughing. Damn it, she is trying. But her mind has been at home, studying the postcards from Lillian, jotting down more memories and imaginings about her father in her notebook. When she stops thinking about him, the sorrow of losing Serena oozes in, threatening to carry her away to the dark place where she wants to give up altogether and simply sleep.

The apartment is dark when Rachel arrives home. She follows a slice of light down the hall, and then taps open the door to the nursery. Mick doesn't look up. He's sitting on the floor under the window, leaning against Clifford the Big Red Dog. Chunky books still line the shelves, the walls are still Bumblebee Yellow, and the crib is still decked out in "Goodnight Moon" themed soft bumpers and pillows. And yet, this room feels totally different without the promise of a baby. Empty.

"Hey," Rachel says. Mick barely nods. He's examining a plush cow jumping over a Swiss cheese moon, staring at the mobile as if it's broken. Rachel slides down next to him, takes the mobile and winds it. She tilts her head onto his shoulder as a bright, tinny version of *Twinkle, Twinkle, Little Star* begins to play. They listened to this song over and over, pasting Day-Glo stars on the ceiling above the crib. "What're you thinking about?" she says, wanting so badly for Mick to hold her, not knowing how to ask anymore. She doesn't want to have to ask.

He pats her shoulder and then removes his hand to rewind the mobile. Rachel inches away. He doesn't know how anymore, either. "It'll get better," she says, mimicking the calm resolve of a nurse. "We just need to give it some time—both of us."

Mick looks at her, his face gray in the dim light. "How much time, Ray? A few months more? A year?"

"We'll try again."

"When?"

Several sentences line up in Rachel's throat. *We'll try again, as soon as the doctor gives the green light. Next time, everything will go smoothly. Next time.*

"That money from your mom?" Mick prods. "We could use it for another round of IVF. Or, there's always adoption."

"No," Rachel says, too loudly, and then softer, "First, I need to know more about my father. I emailed Lillian again to ask if I can come visit." Mick stands abruptly and grips the side of the crib, turning away from her. "We could both go, an adventure," she rushes on, the words spilling out. "This trip could change everything."

"The danger aside, you're setting yourself up for huge disappointment if Henry doesn't show up. Come on, Ray, admit it. That's what you're hoping for."

"You're wrong," she says. "I don't expect him to show up for me—not anymore. What I'm hoping for is someone to answer my questions." Someone who might reassure her that Merilee was right: Henry Shepherd loved her the best he could, but didn't have it in him to be a good father. He was the one who was broken—not *her*.

Mick pounds his palm against the rail, as if trying to jostle loose words. Rachel gets up and smoothes a hand down his spine. "I need to do this for us, not for him," she says. "Get some closure. Before we try again. You get that, right?"

"I can see," he says slowly, "it's got to be rough. The shots and mood swings, the doctors poking and promising, the waiting."

"Yes, yes, exactly."

"And then things can still go wrong."

"And then, even more can go wrong after the baby's born."

"You're scared."

"I want to make sure—"

"Ray, I know you tried your hardest to do everything right," Mick continues, facing her now. "Both times. So, then, what went wrong?"

Rachel sits down fast, as if she's suffered a blow. Does he expect her to answer? To know?

"Last year," he says, "the embryo didn't take or something. I get that. But this time, our baby was kicking, doing somersaults. She was perfectly healthy one day—"

"Mick, no," Rachel says. "Don't go there again." The night of the miscarriage, at the hospital, she reached out for him—how could he blame himself?—and he moved out of her grasp. Now, she places a protective hand on her stomach.

"I shouldn't have let you talk me into going to work," he says. The look on his face—the splotchy crimson of anguish and anger—she's seen it only once before.

Last year, she came back home from the doctor's office, the ache of the D&C still fresh, and hauled nearly everything in the nursery down to the basement storage unit. Mick returned from work that night to find her disassembling the crib. He stood in the doorway, surveying the near-empty room as if a hurricane had blown through. "Jesus, Ray, why didn't you wait for me?" he asked, and then asked again, much louder. She couldn't respond. She couldn't say why getting rid of all reminders of the baby, as quickly as possible, had seemed like the logical way to erase the pain.

Now, Rachel rubs her arms. "You don't blame me," she says, the chill of her fingers penetrating her blouse. "Do you?"

"I'm just trying..." Mick pounds the rail of the crib with his palm. "I'm trying to make sense of it all."

The sound of rushing blood floods Rachel's ears as her husband keeps talking. Maybe if she had stayed in bed. He should have hired a nurse. Her head's light; she might faint. All he had to do was say *no, I don't blame you.* She leans back against the big stuffed dog for support, her head in the vice of her hands. "Stop, please stop. Just go," she says.

Then, there's the flick of lights, the click of the nursery door shutting, and she's alone. She lies down on the alphabet rug, a shaft of frosty light from the streetlamp sending a shiver through her. Flakes of snow fling themselves against the window and melt away.

Her mom never cried, at least not in front of her, not even the time she slipped on a slick patch near the stove. Rachel jumped up from the kitchen table where she was working on multiplication problems, alarmed to see her mom crumpled on the linoleum floor, holding her wrist. Merilee's face was waxen, lips pursed tightly, as if crying would be the worst possible thing—worse than the pain. The same waxen mask was on her face the morning after her husband left and for many days to come. Each morning, Rachel tried to forget the knot in her stomach by picking marshmallows out of her Lucky Charms, one by one, and counting them aloud. Who was she to cry?

A few weeks after her father had left, it occurred to her for the first time that he might not keep his promise to return. Merilee was across the table, sipping coffee and tapping her pencil tip against the *TV Guide* crossword puzzle. If she saw the shameful tears welling up, she didn't acknowledge it, an act of kindness—of love—Rachel thought at the time. She squeezed her eyes shut. *Twenty-four marshmallow half-moons, thirteen stars.* It worked. The tears seemed to back up into her chest and turn to ice.

Now, lying here in the darkness, her entire body is icy, mind numb. And yet she distinctly feels something brush her cheek. A feather falling. She places a finger to her skin and traces the soft imprint, following it down to her heart. A memory. Her father at the kitchen table, hunched over, shoulders shaking. She is afraid for him, wants to comfort him, now as then, but she was only a child. She stood on the stairs and watched, helpless and terrified. She holds her fist to her chest. The warm tingling path from her cheek turns dull and then it's gone.

A chilling thought replaces the warmth: What if this unbearable empty space, cold and barren, is where the memories of her father once lived, a missing piece of her heart that Serena had briefly shaded in, translucent and fragile? Too fragile.

The air is thick with the unnatural silence, a noxious gas that propels her out of the nursery. She shuts the door tightly, as if the danger can be sealed in this room but only if she never re-enters it. Her hand slides from the knob. What if it's not only the memories of her father she has lost, but also something intrinsic to her future happiness? Something only Lillian Carlson can help her recover? Perhaps if unlocking the place where she remembers her father might repair the piece of her heart that knows how to love, really love. Like a daughter. Like a mother.

EIGHT
{ November 1, 2000 }

Dear Lillian,

Thanks so much for the postcards from my father. It means a lot, know-ing he was thinking of me. I always thought he forgot about me after he left. After a while, I gave up on him coming back. You opened the door to a chance to get to know him. I'd like to come to Mubaro for a few weeks and stay near your farm. We could talk at your convenience. You said there are more of his things there. I'd love to see them. I know it's a lot to ask, but can you help me figure out where my father is now? I need to at least try and reconnect with him.

Dear Rachel,

I can see you're hurting. There are things you want to tell him. Need to say.

Tucker stops typing, flexes his fingers like an animal protracting his claws before a fight. He hasn't seen his own dad since he dropped out of the residency program at UCLA nine years ago and came here.

You might have been a great surgeon someday. Such a waste of an education. One final diagnosis by the renowned Dr. Daniel Tucker, Sr. No charge. It still hurts like hell when he calls his mom every few months and she tells him the stubborn son of a bitch is performing heart surgery, teaching a class, off somewhere at a conference accepting another award. Sometimes, Tucker hears—or quite possibly only imagines—the tease of a violin in the background and the rustle of a newspaper. Tchaikovsky and the *Los Angeles Times*.

He wipes a thin bead of sweat from his upper lip with the back of his fist, and then deletes the email. Who is he to bring Rachel here, raise her expectations of a happily-ever-after reunion? But she sounds so desperate, just like Lillian sounds sometimes. Although, Lil would never admit she still misses the guy. Still loves him. And then, there's Nadine. Henry can help her this time. He'll make things right and testify at the new trial. It's a win-win-win.

Tucker starts over, typing quickly before he loses his nerve: *I've thought it over and I agree: you should come here. The best way to get to know your father is to get to know Rwanda, the land he loved. I can send a letter to the last address I have for Henry, a PO box in London, but I can't promise anything. I haven't heard from him in years. As long as you realize that, I'll try. Let me know your flight information and send a photo. I'll pick you up. It wouldn't be wise to wander around the Rwanda countryside on your own.*

Tucker hits "send" without signing the email, and releases a breath he hadn't been aware he was holding. He has to at least give it a shot. Lillian will be glad once Rachel arrives. She's got to forgive him—eventually. Hell, she may even forgive Henry if he does man up and come back home.

NINE
{ November 1974 }

THE HUM OF THE PLANE ENGINE VIBRAT-
ing through Henry's body is rather nice, like those fancy
massage beds he's heard that some hotels in Miami have.
He stretches his legs and takes a long pull of Johnny Walker, his belly full after a chicken dinner that wasn't half bad. He's never been
on an airplane before, always imagined the ride would be bumpier.
But this... He sighs. No phones jangling, no meetings where people
blather on. No laughter in the halls, jokes he's rarely in on. At work,
he just keeps his head down and gets his job done. Eats a sandwich at
his desk for lunch and reads his paperback mystery. Up here, there's
no tense silence that meets him every night when he gets home. It's
like he's always supposed to be apologizing to his wife for something
he's done wrong, something else he's forgotten about. She sure as hell
wasn't happy about this trip, but it's something he has to get out of his

system. He'll be more attentive to his family after this one adventure, like Merilee is always telling him he needs to be. A month isn't so long. He'll send postcards to Rachel every day, or at least twice a week. He'll be a better husband and father when he returns. She'll see.

Henry presses his forehead against the cool window and squints, like he's activating X-ray vision. The plane will be landing in a few hours. There could be anything on the other side of this sea of clouds below.

Anything at all.

A decade ago, he drove to Atlanta in a beat-up Skylark: no radio or air-conditioning, a wall of thick August air that smelled of car exhaust and fast food, but none of that mattered. It was his first trip across the state line except for a bus ride to the nation's capital back in high school. At first, Atlanta didn't look that much different than Jacksonville, less than an hour from his hometown of St. Augustine. But walking into the red brick building that could as easily have been a courthouse as a church, he felt like a foreigner. In all his twenty-one years, he had never seen so many Negroes assembled in one place. Women in starched summer dresses swooshed by him like he didn't exist, greeting each other with the exuberance of long-lost sisters. Men in shiny suits, some sporting fluffy hairdos that would guarantee an ass-kickin' back in St. Augustine, regarded him with a semi-tolerant nod as he strode toward the wooden doors of the sanctuary. He kept his eyes on the camera at his chest, not so different than the way the elderly black grocery baggers at the Piggly Wiggly lowered their gaze and mumbled *Yes'm*, while young white ladies with a kid or two perched in the front seat of their grocery carts curtly reminded them to double bag.

There was a knot of photographers, mostly white and considerably older, plastered against the back wall. Nobody moved to make room as he sidled in between a gray-faced guy who smelled of mothballs and a tall kid with a massive Adam's apple bobbing up and down his neck while he snapped spearmint gum. Henry loosened his narrow black tie and tried to blend in, polishing his camera lens with a chamois cloth, at the same time blotting moist palms. He had been hired as a junior photographer for the *St. Augustine Record* straight out of high school. After two years of shooting car accidents, fires, and cats stuck in trees, this was his big break. A road assignment! *You only get one chance, Shepherd,* Dick Cromwell, the photo editor, had warned him. *Don't blow it.*

Henry settles back into his seat, lulled by the hum of the plane. Used to be that everything changed as the camera met his eye; he controlled the view and the rest of the world faded away. He's missed that old surge of confidence coursing through his veins like a drug. That day in the church, there was only the hunt for one perfect shot, the shot that would wind up on the front page of the *St. Augustine Times*. The shot that would propel him one step closer to New York City and the magazines with luscious photo essays that had fueled a longing for adventure since he was a kid.

He still feels the taut thread of excitement that connected everyone in the congregation as the preacher approached the podium. *People in St. Augustine want to know what all the fuss is about,* Cromwell had said. *Show us why this King fella is so magnetic.* The surprisingly diminutive man seemed to make eye contact with every last one of the hundreds of people crammed into pews, capturing their attention—drawing Henry up the aisle, his camera clicking away—as he began to speak. Reverend

King's low voice rumbled like the roll of thunder paving the way for an impending storm: *One of the great tragedies of life is that men seldom bridge the gulf between practice and profession, between doing and saying. Now, it's time to bridge that gulf.*

A wave of emotion swept everyone to their feet, the air punctuated with chants of *Yes, sir; Say it, now; Make it plain.* Henry's blood seemed to speed up in his veins, his senses sharp, hands steady as he scanned the crowd through the lens, knowing that his shot—his big chance—was somewhere in the audience, not up onstage.

Now, his breath catches deep in his chest, a private and protected place, as he spots her once again in his mind: the girl in the third row, dressed in a prim navy suit, her hair in a perfect updo, who had waved to him—a brief flick of her hand—before the sermon began. He sees her as she appears in his dreams: in profile, face tilted up toward the podium, neck craning gracefully forward, full lips parted. She is beyond beautiful, the light streaming through the stained glass window above reflecting slightly gold off her dark skin. Henry sees his younger self standing beside her, his heart beating so loudly he barely hears a man in the pew behind her grumbling, "It's not right, Estelle, that's all I'm saying. Not proper."

He bent down on one knee, as if proposing marriage. Through his camera lens Lillian seemed to be pulled closer to him. Pieces of sunlight aligned around them, creating an insulated bubble, a moment in time that might last forever. And then, the man he would later learn was Lillian's father clamped a thick hand on his shoulder and spun him around, pointed him back up the aisle. Later that night, when Henry cleaned out his camera case, he discovered a high school ID card.

The pilot announces that they're beginning the descent into Nairobi. Henry pulls the plastic photo ID out of his wallet and runs a finger over the girl's face. That took real chutzpah, as his gramps used to say. How did she know he would track her down at Spelman and call? They talked not so much about the lives they were living but their future selves, like they were also real flesh-and-blood people. Lillian's enthusiasm was as good as a blood transfusion that pumped energy into his dull existence.

Lillian made him believe he could escape from the house that hadn't been a real home, just someplace to sleep and eat, since his mom split when he was fifteen. He didn't have money for his own place, let alone college, and his dad was no help, blowing his meager cop's salary at the greyhound track, certain that the next race would turn his luck and make him a winner. Lillian encouraged him to move to Atlanta, a pit stop on the way to New York, and take photos. The year he spent in the heart of the civil rights movement, people laying down their lives for change while others were fighting equally hard for their world to remain the same, was as exciting as anything he had seen paging through glossy magazines. During that time, he became bigger than his small, dead-end life in St. Augustine. He looks for a hint of his reflection in the window, somewhere in the clouds. What the hell happened to that guy Lillian had so much faith in?

The solid thud of wheels hitting pavement lands in Henry's gut. The plane whizzes along, the rumble mixing with the blood pounding in his head. He presses a hand to his chest, unsure where the shakiness of the plane ends and the waves of jittery excitement skittering across his skin begin. For a moment it seems possible to break through some invisible barrier, into an alternate universe. The plane stops abruptly, and he waits for the ding of the bell signaling it's safe to get out of his seat. His fingers form a fist around the pink soapstone heart hanging from a silver chain around his neck, as if protecting the locket that holds a photo of his daughter from whatever happens next.

HENRY FIXES HIS EYES ON the silver numbers of the payphone as the line goes dead, his pulse pounding in the receiver in his hand. Flashes of brightly dressed passersby and words punctuated with exotic accents swirl around him like water swiftly circling a drain. Okay, he gets that Merilee's still ticked off, but to outright hang up on him? For chrissakes, she could at least have let him talk to Rachel. He slams his palm against the phone and replaces the receiver in the cradle in one motion, and then heads toward baggage claim. Man, it's not like he *left them*, not like that at all.

One month away, one measly month. Is that too much to ask for a guy who gave up on his life's dream to take care of a family that caught him by surprise? *Creative Director*. The title sounds like something Uncle Jerry made up, just to give him a "real job" at his ad agency in Jacksonville. He was twenty-two years old, still living at his dad's house on a reporter's salary, and Merilee was six months pregnant. He walks faster. Nothing creative about what he's been doing for the past eight years. And the money for the plane ticket was as good as a gift—a fluke. Money that, in essence, he had earned before everything that was his became Merilee's too.

After Reverend King's assassination, he mailed a handful of his best photos from Atlanta to a few magazines on a needling dare from his former self. *It's not too late—take a risk!* That hopeful voice in his head became louder and more buoyant when a photo editor in New

York called. He splurged on a bottle of genuine French champagne when the contract with terms of payment arrived. A cover photo for *Life* magazine! Payment? Holy Moses, he told Merilee, the bubbles making him bold, it could have been Monopoly money they were offering. Then again, it could be just the beginning, right? Merilee looked at him funny, and then laughed. Twelve hundred dollars for one of his photos? Of course, he must be joking. Of course. Henry spent two hundred bucks on a new dishwasher and rangetop stove for his wife, and socked away the rest in a savings account all his own. A "Someday" account, for what he wasn't sure. That was six years ago.

As he waits for his luggage, he checks his camera bag, making sure there are extra batteries and the lens didn't get scratched during the bumpy plane landing. He'll prove to Merilee that this trip isn't a boondoggle. *Father Morton. Teaching orphans. Can see Mt. Kenya from the schoolroom window.* That much he remembers from Lillian's letter. It's a sign that she wrote to him, after all these years. The *Life* photo editor said he would be interested in seeing some follow-up shots of the girl so inspired by Martin Luther King, Jr. that she devoted her life to caring for orphans in Africa. He had to go for it. Why can't Merilee see that? He'll fix things with her but he can't just turn around and go home, not yet. How often does a guy get a second chance?

{ *November 1975, Uganda* }

The tall elephant grass skirting the kidney-shaped lake is the perfect place for Henry to hide, not close enough for the herd of water buffalo sloshing around to see him or feel threatened by his scent. He snaps a few photos, sits back and waits. He has learned to be patient over the past year. Discovering this spot, a tip from an Aussie photographer he picked up thumbing a ride in Tanzania, was worth the wait.

According to the Aussie, only the locals know about this wetland in the middle of a forest. The Batwa people have been living here for centuries in huts of sticks, mud and banana leaves, hunting for berries and small mammals in the impenetrable thickets of trees, moss and vines. Henry hadn't even been certain he was on a real trail as he stumbled over mossy bamboo roots, a flashlight in one hand and a compass in the other, under a sun-mottled canopy of leaves. And then, suddenly, the jungle opened up on a clearing with a handful of huts surrounding this painter's palette of a lake. He widens the lens and shoots: pink flamingos, blue-black starlings, lavender-breasted rollers and yellow finches all in one photo. That's got to be worth some decent money. The perfect backdrop for a perfume ad. Good ol' Jerry, throwing him some freelance work, even though it's on the condition that the check is deposited directly into Merilee's bank account. Fair enough.

Henry flips up the collar of his corduroy jacket as the sky turns purple-gray with dusk. This is when the real action begins: armor-plated rhinos and twisty-horned kudu, two kinds of zebra, and sometimes the rare okapi. You never know who's going to show up for Happy Hour. The gorillas come after dark, ambling down from the Virunga Mountains that straddle Uganda, Rwanda and Congo, at least that's the rumor. But it's been a month, and still nothing. That's okay, he can wait. Henry settles into the nest of tall grass and sips a warm beer. The bitter liquid releases a heavy sigh; the divorce papers Merilee sent last month to the PO box he keeps in Nairobi made it clear he has all the time in the world. *Integrity. Intention.* She used both of those words several times, apparently they were tools of her transformation, said he should try them sometime. He can't blame her for giving up on him.

The thing of it is, it's not like he ever planned on staying away so long. One month turned into three, and then six; the adventure has become a new life during the past year, driving from Reverend Morton's orphanage near Mt. Kenya, through Tanzania and Uganda, with only a vague notion of finding Lillian and photographing her farm. *Somewhere in Rwanda.* That's all the preacher knew, or would say, about her whereabouts. Exploring this rugged and varied terrain, sleeping in his Jeep most nights and taking photos during the day— good photos, judging by the sales he's made—he has rewired his brain to view the world differently. For the first time since Atlanta, he sees all the possibilities. And yet, it came with a high price.

Henry's heart quickens as a small ripple breaks the smooth surface of the pond, and the spiny back of a crocodile floats by. Other than that, it's surprisingly quiet tonight. His mind wanders, the calm water a screen. He replays the delight on his daughter's face as she opened her birthday present just weeks before he left, a real camera now that she was a big girl of eight. The two of them spent one Saturday after-noon at the zoo, the next at the botanical garden, Rachel following him around with her little point-and-click Brownie, snapping photos when he did. The water turns murky and dark. Will he ever see her again?

He pulls a pen and postcard out of his camera bag: a lion sunning himself on a rock. Rachel would get a kick out of that. Writing to his daughter every so often is the only real habit he has that connects him with his old life. Not that he mails these cards anymore. A few came back to his PO box in Nairobi, and he wouldn't be surprised if Merilee tossed the rest of them in the trash. But it seems important to keep writing, saving these connections with his daughter in the photo album he's keeping for her.

"Dear Cricket," Henry says as he writes, "it's funny how I came here searching for one thing and found something totally different." He came hoping for excitement and, instead, found peace. Tranquility. "Here's a bit of wisdom from your old man: It's the search that really matters. The adventure of living your life. You can quote me on that."

A thick gray fog settles on the lake and still no gorillas, so Henry heads back to the two-room hut made of sticks and a banana-leaf roof where he rolls out his sleeping bag on the dirt floor, instead of under the stars, when it rains. His hosts are a Batwa couple, eighteen or twenty years old, who looked at him in confusion when he offered them money. So, instead, he gave away his Swiss army knife, a blanket, and several jars of peanut butter they use sparingly and keep wrapped in newspaper on a high shelf.

Neither Alia nor her husband, Jahi, speak more than a few words of English. They watch solemnly as Henry deposits the postcard of the lion in a shoebox. "For my daughter," he says, pointing to the baby Alia balances on her hip.

"Daughter." Alia smiles, holding out the squirming bundle swathed in a diaper of antelope skin. Henry brings the little girl to his chest, stroking her fuzzy halo of hair. These postcards are a Someday account of sorts for Rachel. Someday, he'll give them to her. He likes the idea that she might use these scenes of his life as cairns to follow the path of her own dreams.

Outside the hut, Henry heats up a pot of coffee over a small fire that keeps animals away. He rubs his stomach and offers a tin mug to Jahi. "Good."

Jahi grunts in agreement as he takes a sip. He points to Henry's rucksack to begin their nightly ritual. Henry pulls out a map and a red felt-tip pen, runs a finger slowly over a thick red line starting at Mt. Kenya. Jahi points to a spot on the path, a little farther than the one he pointed to the previous evening, saying a few words that need no translation.

"Ah, Tanzania. The Kikulo Plateau," Henry says. How can he explain the two weeks he spent capturing images of dozens of varieties of rare orchids in God's Garden, as the locals call it? He digs in his rucksack for photos of sturdy little white-faced flowers splashed with purple and yellow war paint. "These are my favorites."

Jahi studies the photos, and then points at the map again, glancing toward his hut. "You," he says. "Where you."

"Home," Henry says, the word landing tenderly, somewhere deep in his soul. Where is his home? He sweeps an arm, palm outward, around them, embracing the lake, the rustling grass, the glittering night sky, closing his fist as his hand lands on his chest. And yet, there's a hollowness there.

Later, lying under the stars, Henry can't sleep. He throws a fresh pile of sticks on the fire, searches through his rucksack and pulls out a plastic bag with some sticks wrapped in a slipshod web of blue and white yarn: an art project gone wrong that he's going to fix for his daughter by the time he returns home. He starts untangling the yarn but it's frayed and knotted. He's only made more of a mess with his efforts, not even sure what the hell a dreamcatcher is supposed to look like anymore. He sighs. Maybe he'll start over from scratch.

Next, he slides the unsigned divorce papers out of his bag. *Freedom.* Merilee's filing for divorce on the grounds of abandonment. No custody rights, but plenty of freedom. That's the trade-off. Isn't that what he has wanted all along, the desire for which he has been apologizing to her throughout their entire marriage? So then why, whenever he thinks about signing these papers, does a kind of vaporous panic release from his chest, expanding into his limbs? An untethered buoyancy sets in, as if without a home and family he could too easily float up toward the stars and disappear into the darkness.

He packs up his camera, sleeping bag, tarp and few other belongings, and leaves his tin plate and silverware for Jahi and Alia. If he leaves now, he can get to Rwanda by sunrise. It's time to go find Lillian's farm, take the photos he came for and head back home before it's too late. It's not until months later that he realizes he left the dreamcatcher on the rocks near the fire.

TEN

I T'S TOO WARM TO BUILD A FIRE IN THE backyard, but Henry's daughter insists. Her second grade class is studying Indians—No, *Native Americans*, she keeps correcting him. He has to admit it's been fun spending all day digging a little fire pit, listening to Rachel chatter away. It's amazing how her mind works, flitting from imagining what it was like to live in a tee-pee, to what she might give her friend Margie when she turns eight next week, to asking again if she can pretty please have a puppy. They roast hot dogs that could be venison and make gooey s'mores, feeding twigs into the fire. Now, Rachel sits beside him on a log at the edge of the pit, the flames curling up like smoke signals into the twilight sky. She's busy twining blue yarn around a web of sticks that are supposed to be some kind of Native American artwork he found a picture of in the encyclopedia.

"What does this do again?" she asks skeptically.

"Catches dreams—the bad ones, so they can't slip into your head," Henry says, absentmindedly fiddling with the clasp of the pink soapstone locket on a chain around his neck. A gift from Rachel last Christmas that he wears on the weekends to make her feel special. In his other hand is the light blue airmail letter he has practically memorized since it arrived at his office yesterday. He still can't believe Lillian wrote to him after nine years. He glances from his daughter to the letter, a bittersweet warmth washing over him as he starts reading.

Dear Henry,

Where to begin? I've started this letter in so many different places. This is what I most want to tell you: I remember. I remember seeing my photo on the front page of the newspaper, right next to Reverend King. That's when I knew, without question, that I had a responsibility to do my part in changing the world. I remember how you encouraged me to pass along the gift of my education and teach children who have nothing. I remember every day of the year we spent together, especially you standing beside me at the student rallies even though not everyone agreed with the reverend's stance on nonviolence and including white folks in our fight for equality. Thank you for all of that.

Rachel makes a sound like a frustrated colt. Henry looks up and takes the dreamcatcher, unwinds the yarn from around the sticks. He has tried, over the years, not to think about Lillian, as if that might qualify as cheating on his wife. But this letter gives him permission to wander back in time, back to April 1965 at Ebenezer Baptist Church. He sees the shy smile as her hand fluttered in a wave and then went to her hair. He hears her voice over the phone, the first time he called. She listened—really listened. Of course he would travel around the world, photographing people and places that mattered, things folks should see. She had always dreamed of going to Africa, never told anyone, afraid it sounded foolish. No, it didn't sound a bit foolish to him. Heck, they might even meet up there someday.

What if he had chosen the other path?

"Dad," Rachel whines, one long drawn-out syllable of defeat. "I can't do this."

"Now, Cricket, you just keep wrapping yarn in between the four sticks." He takes his daughter's hands in his, guiding her fingers as he retraces his steps during the fall he moved to Atlanta, after a summer of talking on the phone with Lillian. He took the first job he was offered: photojournalist for a weekly alternative newspaper. It wasn't a magazine in New York or even the *St. Augustine Record,* but he was happy, particularly in the evenings up on the rooftop with Lillian in his arms. She called that cement square—barely big enough for two corduroy cushions from his pullout couch—their own private island.

He feels the gravitational pull of that world: just the two of them, time seemingly suspended by the stars. Many nights, they fell asleep on the roof—just slept. It was the dawn of the sexual revolution, people hopping into bed together simply to prove they could, but Henry appreciated that Lillian was saving herself for marriage. Besides, he was a little afraid of the way that folks—black and white—cut them nasty glances or sometimes downright stared as they walked hand in hand. Lillian never seemed to notice.

In hindsight, he sees it was the danger that made their relationship so exciting. He had been dating Merilee since junior year in high school, never questioning whether or not they were truly in love. Certainly, he had never fought for their right to be in love. Daily, he and Lillian proved that the bond between them was stronger than the whispers loud enough for them to hear. Their love was stronger than the quiet disapproval of Lillian's parents at the Sunday dinner table. Stronger than the police brutality, burning crosses, and angry faces he photographed. That entire year, he felt as if he had magically stepped out of his life, stopped the clock from running. He and Lillian were so certain that *they* were the future. The rest of the world simply needed a bit of time to catch up.

Henry touches the scar on his temple, less than an inch from his eye, the doctor's words throbbing in his head: *Split...twelve stitches... lucky there's no damage to the cornea.* It all comes back to him: The screech of tires, the glittery explosion of glass on the sidewalk in Sweet Auburn where he and Lillian had been window shopping; a trickle of something sticky-sweet running down his face, into his mouth. Cola, he had thought, as he sank to the sidewalk. Blood smeared on Lillian's plaid skirt, that scratchy wool against his cheek. Blood on her fingers that he saw out of the corner of one eye, his other eye swollen shut. An ambulance siren. Screaming. All of it mashed together, like an alarm he couldn't shut off. Afterwards, he couldn't sleep and developed a tic that made it impossible to take photos.

Roland Carlson came to visit one night shortly after the bloody drive-by, while his daughter was waiting tables at a nearby restaurant. He didn't say much, just handed Henry an envelope and mumbled something about hoping it was enough for a plane ticket. Best for everyone if he went on home. Henry deposited two hundred dollars, all the money the groundskeeper at Spelman could scrape together to try and pay him off, into the savings account he and Lilly had started. He didn't want to embarrass Roland by returning the money, and he sure didn't need any convincing that leaving was the best thing he could do for Lilly as well as himself. It was, in a way, a relief, as if Lillian's father was giving him permission to return to the safety of his own world.

But when did *safe* become synonymous with a kind of uncomfortable restlessness, a restlessness that is sometimes tamped down into his gut by pouring a finger or two of whiskey into his coffee mug? A restlessness that made him send a few photos he took in Atlanta to *Life* magazine in the first place. A restlessness that this letter is riling up as he reads the rest of it.

Henry, I apologize for taking the long way around to getting to the point of why I'm writing now. I finally made it to Africa! I should back up a bit: Four years ago last December I married a fine man named Samuel. We had been dating before I met you and then took up again after you left. Samuel was heading off on a tour of duty in Vietnam, so we went and got married at City Hall—just the two of us. The big family affair could wait, but we couldn't. A month later, my husband's plane was shot down in Vietnam.

A year later, I was still having a terrible time getting on with my life. I decided to use some of the life insurance money from the army to try and forget about my own sorrow by helping others. Reverend Morton came to talk at Ebenezer Baptist about a school for orphans that his mission was starting in Kenya. I was only going to stay for a few months, but the children here grabbed onto my heart and wouldn't let go. And every day I was strong enough to teach them and help care for them, we all healed a bit.

You know how people say, God works in mysterious ways? I believe that's true. I recently spent the rest of Samuel's life insurance money to buy a small farm somewhere you've probably never heard of: Rwanda. The country has a bloody history of the two main tribes fighting for power, but there's a new government and it's relatively peaceful now. People are hopeful. I'd like to do my small part and provide a family for four or five orphans, more in time. I thought it would please you to know I'm using the check you sent to supplement whatever money I can raise through the church to fix up my new home once I move in. For now, I'm staying on at the orphanage for a bit so Reverend Morton can teach me how to apply for grants.

Henry folds the letter back into the airmail envelope and places it beside him on the log. They'd agreed that they could wait for the world to change, or they would travel to Africa together. Either way, they were in no hurry as long as they were together. A month after the drive-by attack, a year to the day after he had first moved to Atlanta, he mailed Lillian a check for nine hundred dollars. All the money in the savings account they had built up for their future. Their Someday account. He included a cryptic but honest note: *I'm sorry, Lilly, it's too hard. I can't wait any longer.*

"Cricket," he says, an idea crystalizing, "what if…" Over the past six years, since receiving the unexpected check from *Life* magazine, he's been squirreling away ten or fifteen dollars each paycheck, not enough to squeeze the household budget but enough to make him feel like this existence is temporary, his real life waiting for him somewhere. Someday.

"What would you think of going away together?" he asks.

"Just you and me?"

"Sure. We could have a great adventure." There's a pull in Henry's chest, like a heavy door cracking open. "We'll go over summer vacation."

Rachel frowns at the tangle of sticks and yarn in her lap. "What would Mom do?"

Henry brushes the bangs out of his daughter's eyes, and then lands a noisy smooch on her forehead to unravel the creases of concern. "Mom might want to go on an adventure of her own." Merilee has been talking about visiting her sister in California, the two of them going to some self-actualization spa. The time apart might do them both good. "She'll be fine."

The slam of a door startles him. Merilee appears on the back porch. That's his signal: time's up. "Well," he slaps his thighs. "Ready to hop in the tub?" Saturdays are father-daughter time; it's understood, like they share custody.

"Five more minutes?" Rachel pleads.

He sighs heavily, takes the dreamcatcher from her and unwinds the yarn to find a beginning point and try to salvage it. Fact is, Rachel is about the only thing he and his wife have in common. Both of them expected so much more from their marriage, from each other. From love. Merilee has accused him, more than once, of having affairs. That would be so much easier than the truth: he simply doesn't love her, not the way he loved Lillian—maybe still does.

"Dad," Rachel says in a high, squeaky voice. "You didn't really mean it, about us going away without Mom. Right?"

"No, of course not." Henry picks at a knot that refuses to unravel. Who is he kidding? The two of them going to Africa? Not likely. "Just a silly idea."

Henry, I wish you could see my new home: A white clapboard farm-

house with a wraparound porch, nestled into the foothills of the Virunga Mountains. It's beautiful! The rich soil is perfect for growing vegetables, banana trees, and flowers that I can harvest and sell to local restaurants and at the Saturday market. The sunflowers, golden stalks of sunlight, are my favorite. Zebra, impalas, and caribou are frequent visitors. They graze in the yard, and you can hear the occasional snarl of a panther or roar of a lion at night. I can't wait to move in and start my new life.

Henry returns the dreamcatcher to his daughter and takes her hand in both of his, kneading her palm to warm his icicle-like fingers. Lions roaring…just like the Disney movie he and Rachel watched on TV a few Sundays ago. Man, what he wouldn't give to take photos of animals that aren't behind bars at the zoo. "What I meant," he says, his voice floaty and soft, "is that I have a new story to try out on you. There was this guy who woke up from a long sleep."

"Like Rip Van Winkle?"

"Kind of, but this guy was only asleep for eight years instead of twenty. When he awoke, he found a canoe that could take him anywhere. Somewhere he could be happy, like before he fell asleep."

Rachel scooches closer, her face squinched in concentration. "This boat must be under some kind of spell. I'll bet it takes him to a magic castle."

"Kwizera," Henry says, the word tingly on his lips. *I'm calling my place Kwizera.* "It means hope in Kinyarwanda, an African language." *That's what I wish for you, Henry.*

He stares into the sprays of light in the fire pit and imagines finding the kind of happiness Lillian has discovered. His mind starts snapping photos of the places he visits while dreaming up bedtime stories with Rachel, and the movies they sometimes watch: Creepy moss-covered castles in Europe where Dracula or Frankenstein might live. Egypt's mystical pyramids and Lawrence-of-Arabia-style deserts. Sand-crusted kasbahs and those crazy marketplaces in Marrakesh. Why should he wait any longer to actually go and see those places? Sure, that's a good use for the money he's been socking away, an investment in finding himself—like Merilee is doing with her EST self-help stuff.

"Dad!" Rachel's shrill cry breaks through Henry's thoughts. Smoke. That's the first thing he sees. Sparks flying. For chrissakes, it's that mess of sticks and yarn. He lunges toward his daughter.

"Hold still," he orders, so she'll stop jumping up and down, flapping her arms. "Drop the dreamcatcher. Now!" But, instead, his daughter twirls around as if she's trying to get the damn thing airborne. Orange and gray embers float around her, settling on her windbreaker and in her hair. Henry scoops her into his arms and rolls to the ground, away from the fire. "You're okay, you're okay," he repeats over and over, shielding her from the showering sparks.

She's crying but not hurt, probably just scared, looking up at him for a cue. "Okay," Henry says, forcing a smile. "Let's get you in that tub."

"Rachel? My lord, little girl, my lord!" Merilee is running across the lawn, stocking-footed, a hand clasped at the collar of her housecoat. She swoops in, yanks their daughter away and pushes Henry aside.

"Daddy, I'm sorry. I didn't mean—"

"It's not your fault." Merilee throws a sharp glance at Henry.

Rachel nods fervently. "I was trying to save the dreamcatcher. I dropped it."

Henry's eyes follow to where she's pointing: the rocks surrounding the dying fire.

"I saved it for you, Dad." Rachel holds out the dreamcatcher, broken and charred.

"That's good, real good." It's all Henry can do not to run and grab the slip of light-blue ashen paper on a boulder, an edge still glowing.

"Well, it's over." Merilee takes Rachel's arm and marches her toward the house.

"But what about the story?" Rachel whines.

"I'll come upstairs and finish it after your bath," Henry promises, ignoring his wife's final glare. He picks at the singed letter with the tip of a shovel and salvages a few scraps. With each shovelful of dirt he dumps on the embers and sticks, a heavy thud reverberates in his chest along with a single word: Kwizera.

"YOU AWAKE?" HENRY WHISPERS. RACHEL kicks the covers off with a grunt.

"The story," she says sleepily. "I've been waiting."

Henry kneels by her bedside, strokes her hair while he weaves a tale about the two of them searching for an ancient kasbah where ghost-like genies called jinns have stashed stolen treasure, riding atop their trusty camel and trekking over mountains of sand.

"Are these good or bad genies?" Rachel asks. It's an important question for an eight-year-old, one that Henry considers carefully.

"The thing is," he says, "jinns aren't all bad or good. Sometimes they help people but you have to help them too. They've hidden this treasure for the two of us, and we won't know what it is until we get there. We won't know what they want us to do. We can't know, it's a mystery." And then he stops, can't finish the story, his throat gritty as if coated with sand.

"Is it over?" Rachel asks, disappointed.

"We find the treasure chest…" Henry's voice breaks. He clearly sees himself driving to his office in the dark, taking down the photo of the girl in the church window hanging on the wall and removing the savings account booklet hidden in the back of the frame. The excitement of the adventure has been sucked dry, the jewels in the treasure chest turned to dust. "No wait a sec," he says with a phlegmy laugh that sticks in his throat. "Like I said, this story's a mystery. There isn't an ending, not yet."

"We'll figure it out." Rachel yawns and snuggles back under the sheets.

"Soon." Henry kisses his daughter. "I promise." He clicks off the bedside lamp, ruffles her hair. Sure, they'll figure out the end of the story when he comes back. He turns to leave, and then as an afterthought picks up the soot-covered dreamcatcher from where his daughter dropped it on the floor. He'll finish wrapping the yarn on the plane ride and mail it to her from Africa to hang over her bed.

ELEVEN
{ February 1976, Rwanda }

FROM THE ROAD IT'S HARD TO TELL IF there's a farmhouse at the end of the gravel driveway; all that Henry can see is the dense forest. Eucalyptus and pine, from the smell of it. In the distance are the towering Virunga Mountains from Lillian's letter, so dark they appear almost purple against the gray clouds. But where are the banana fields? Vegetable garden that Lillian harvests for the Saturday market? All he sees is a balding red clay field sprouting tufts of leaves that could, he supposes, be attached to something edible underground. He pushes open the gate with his index finger, and notices scratchy letters engraved in the driftwood-like sign nailed to a tree trunk: KWIZERA.

It's instinctual, the way Henry raises the camera to his eye, searching for clues as he walks slowly up the winding path. He snaps a few photos of an oasis of banana trees surrounded by a moat-like irrigation ditch, a ballet of starlings flitting in and out of the water. He stops in the front yard, pivots and shoots: a busted fence, a few scrawny goats grazing on patchy grass. A sleepy-eyed baboon watches from the tin roof of the house, scratching his balls dispassionately. Hadn't the letter mentioned something about caribou and zebra? Pivots and shoots: a few tall sunflowers to the left of the porch reach up, as if gasping for air, from a jumble of thorny vines. Pivots and shoots: crumbled limestone steps, a torn screen on the front window. Where's the wrap-around front porch? He had imagined Lillian sitting on the top step with the children around her, singing songs like Julie Andrews in *The Sound of Music*. He walks briskly around the back of the large but dilapidated stone house to explore. Okay, maybe he's built up his expectations too much. This sure as hell doesn't look like anything he'd send to the photo editor at *Life*, unless maybe he wants to publish a story about another shattered dream.

The backyard, if you can call it that, is more of the same: a slash of red dirt and scrubby bushes with some kind of irrigation ditch trickling down the center like a tear. But it's not totally hopeless. There's a tall stack of lumber to one side, a rusty green tractor that may or may not work, and an assortment of shovels and rakes splayed on the ground. Two monkeys sit atop the tractor, examining a purple gardening glove. One flicks his tongue at it like a child might test the flavor of a lollipop.

"May I help you?" a distant voice calls.

Henry startles, doesn't see a living soul but the monkeys, and then turns toward the forest. A woman—at least he thinks so, from the baggy clothes it's hard to tell—is heading toward him, balancing a shovel over her shoulder like a rifle. One of the monkeys scurries past with the glove, makes a break for the trees. She runs after him, shouting, her straw hat flying off. Definitely a woman.

Henry squints into the sun. It's been ten years, but Lillian appears nearly the same. Nearly. Now, the perfect flip of smooth hair falls in soft curls around her face, short but not boyish. The stylish but prim pleated skirts and short jackets she used to favor have been traded for Levis and an oversized denim work shirt over a white tank top. She leans on the shovel, catches her breath, waves the glove as if she just scored in flag football. Well, she's still the most beautiful woman he's ever seen. Henry's mind flashes on holding her in his arms on the rooftop of his apartment complex in Atlanta. Their private island. How could he ever have left it, left her? The scar on his eyebrow seems to fade away.

Lillian walks closer, recognition lighting up her eyes, and then something else. "You came," she says, like a question.

"Took me a while, but I finally made it."

"Yes…" She's standing right in front of him now. "You did."

Henry is spellbound by her face: a light sheen of sweat on her forehead, a curl that begs to be swept from her cheek. He could—what, hug her? How he wants to kiss her. He punches his fists down into his pockets. Some of the best months of his life took place when his photos began selling at a few galleries and he could afford to take Lillian out to nice restaurants and jazz clubs, sitting right in front of Miles, Muddy, and Thelonius instead of ordering in pizza and listening to their records. He was earning a reputation for capturing the emotions of the turbulent mid-sixties. Folks actually wanted to see the world through his eyes. Tent City in Lowndes County, where Eldridge Cleaver was organizing rural blacks to vote. The rubble of a church that was bombed one Sunday morning not long after the march in Selma. One photo of a young white boy helping an elderly black woman onto a bus sold for more than he earned in a week at his steady gig at the alternative newspaper.

"How?" Lillian asks. "How did you find me?"

"It wasn't easy. Took me a few months to find that orphanage in Kenya, and then all Reverend Morton could tell me was that you had left for Rwanda. I was too late."

"There were so many children here who needed a home."

Henry's eyes flick from the tractor, to the ditch that smells of sewage, to the tin-roofed house. Are there any kids here? Not likely.

The light in Lillian's eyes fades into embarrassment. "I never thought you'd come," she says, kneading the purple glove in her hands.

"But the letter," Henry says. She had practically invited him here, hadn't she?

"I needed someone to believe I could turn this…" She sweeps her hand toward the house, and then drops it to her side. "I needed someone to believe in me. But I never thought, not in a million years, that you would actually show up."

Henry digs his hands deeper into his pocket. He must be the worst kind of schmuck, coming here to take photos and profit from her pain. Goddamn how he wants to kiss her, hold her, tell her everything will be okay like he means it. "I came to see what you did with the money. Our Someday account."

"Never spent it. Didn't seem right without you."

Henry nods, an idea sparking. He could still take photos for *Life* and give her some of the money he earns. They could both make their dreams come true.

"And now, you're here," Lillian says, her voice lilting with hope. "You came."

"I came…" The camera around Henry's neck is heavy, the strap digging into the back of his sunburned neck. They spent hours on the rooftop, making plans for their Someday account: they would keep saving ten dollars each week. They would wait until it was legal for them to marry, safe for their children. How might things have changed, he wonders, if he had found the courage to grab onto what he really wanted instead of being satisfied to make plans for someday? Instead of giving up, begging Merilee to take him back. "I came to help," he says, taking the shovel from her.

{ *February 1978* }

Henry slathers whitewash onto the new fence, three thick boards bound with barbed wire to keep the occasional lion and elephants out and the baby goats in, the sweat drenching his skin with satisfaction. He makes a mental list of what needs to be done before he takes off on a freelance assignment to film footage of the spring mountain flowers: The sump pump is acting up again. The baboons made a mess of the storage shed where Lilly keeps her gardening tools. And then, the toilet in the bathroom shared by two teenaged girls who recently moved in needs a new thingamajig so it flushes every time. Rahim Kensamara, who owns the hardware store in Mubaro, will know what it's called. The last stroke of paint—he slaps it on with a flourish, like an artist signing his name. Rembrandt and Picasso have got nothing on him.

The first year was rough, between scouting out work from ad

agencies in London and Johannesburg, and making the ramshackle farm into a real home. That year, they spent down their savings account and the investment has paid off. He waves at Lillian, sitting on the sturdy steps of the front porch—wooden now. It's not *The Sound of Music*, but she is weaving baskets with Marie and Keza. People from town are starting to ask if she has room for more kids, not just orphans but children of parents who simply can't afford to take care of them since the Hutu government has cut back on jobs that Tutsis can hold and taken most of the rural farmland. Lilly really is making a difference with these kids, and she's able to pay Enoch and Dahla a decent wage. She seems, overall, happy.

Henry stops painting to survey the agricultural masterpiece he has created with the help of Enoch and a few men from town. The corn's knee-high already and the root plants are budding nicely now that they have a working tractor to properly till and fertilize the land. The banana trees that fan out nearly to their neighbor's property will be ready to harvest by the time he returns in a few weeks. If he can sell footage of the gorillas as well as the wildflowers, maybe they can afford to hire some help with the fall harvest.

And then there's his surprise Christmas present for Lilly: a blueprint for the farmhouse she's been building in her head, going over the details as they lie in bed at night. The older children—at least fifteen of them—will sleep in the main house, and they'll build a nursery off their master bedroom in the farmhouse for two or three cribs. Ten older children and two in the nursery, Henry thinks, but he lets Lillian dream for now.

Man, Merilee's Uncle Jerry sure was right about cable TV booming. Ted Turner is a genius in Henry's book. And, others are catch-

IN THE SHADOW OF 10,000 HILLS

ing on. There's talk of more than one thousand channels eventually. Ad agencies that only produce television commercials are looking for nature footage in exotic locales. He has more freelance video work than he can handle—no time for shooting still photos anymore. That's okay, at least for now. What's important is Lilly's dream is coming true. She deserves this, and so much more.

He walks toward the shed to put away his tools and get a can of diesel to fill the Jeep. Tomorrow is Tuesday. He knows what day it is only sometimes: Friday is when Dahla hangs wash on the line, Saturday they go to the market, and Tuesday morning Lillian sends him into Kigali or Ruhengeri early to pick up barbed wire, batteries, fertilizer, whatever supplies they'll need for the week that can't be found in the small town of Mubaro. It's a good life, not perfect but damn good.

There's a secret sadness that flickers in Lillian's amber eyes sometimes, gray and smoky like a candle being snuffed out. It's there in the way she cringes a bit when he kisses the back of her neck, forgets that she doesn't like to be touched unexpectedly. He watches her with his own sadness some evenings when the children are busy with homework, and Dahla and Enoch have gone home. Lillian tends to the sunflowers and dahlias in her own private garden, working by moonlight. Sometimes, until after Henry turns off the lantern in their bedroom and pretends he's asleep.

Their sadness blankets both of them as she sleeps at the edge of the bed with her hand on the nightstand. Henry keeps waking himself up so that he doesn't roll toward her in his sleep. He doesn't touch her on these nights or the next day, tries not to take it personally—at least not anymore. But she's fine with the children, hugging them, linking arms as they walk. Protective.

These past two years, he has figured that she needs someone to protect her. He's done it without asking questions, without needing answers. He just wishes he could protect her from whatever she's hiding from him.

TWELVE
{ February 1978 }

ILLIAN SITS IN HER FAVORITE SUMMER SPOT, a narrow bench atop the hill that overlooks Kwizera and the forest beyond. The sunflowers thrive here; green leafy fingers tickle her arms. From here, she can take in so many blessings: The field behind her is more green than brown; the corn is nearly ready to harvest, golden rods of teff not far behind. The slope of patchy grass is finally thick enough to support a small family of goats. Down the hill is a red brick house with five real bedrooms, two beds in each, that has a tile roof instead of the tar that oozed a gooey mess onto the kitchen floor last summer during the heat wave. Across the yard is a white farmhouse that still smells of fresh lumber and paint that she and Henry share. At the side of the farmhouse, near the gardening shed, two teenaged girls, Marie and Keza, the first orphans who came to live here last year, are hanging laundry, fresh from a new washing machine—no more dragging a basket of clothes to the river.

Dahla calls from the front porch of the brick house for breakfast. Marie and Keza run over to the bench, each claiming one of Lillian's hands. Her arms swing back and forth as they walk, sweeping away the heaviness from her steps. She stops on the porch, tells the girls to head inside without her and looks out toward the mountains, offering a prayer of gratitude. Henry's making good money and a few small grants have come through, enough to bring in several more children within the year and pay for high school for the older girls. She has so much to be thankful for. So much at stake to lose.

Her fingers coil around the cold metal cylinder in her jacket pocket. *Dear Lord, give me strength…* She purchased the Colt 45 at a beer house in Kigali months ago, and has been hiding it in a toolbox in the gardening shed, trying to summon the courage to use it. Her heart beats faster at the thought of what needs to get done today, while Henry's off filming gorillas.

"Come now, eat some breakfast," Dahla calls in a motherly tone, even though she's barely into her twenties.

"In a minute." Lillian runs her thumb over the knoll of the trigger, testing the weight it would take to pull it. The trigger jiggles and her hand flies out of her pocket. Her stomach clenches as if a bullet has been released. Instead of going to the kitchen, she walks across the yard to the farmhouse and waits.

A few minutes later, a tall man, who Lillian briefly considered handsome when they first met, walks up the driveway. He's buttoning and unbuttoning the jacket of his navy suit. His hair is smooth and glistening, his teeth white and pointy, like cat teeth, Lillian thinks as she opens the door. "Good morning, *cherie*," he says.

"Gahiji," she says, acknowledging their agreement. She doesn't return his bow, stands perfectly still, except for a thumb rubbing the barrel of the gun in her pocket.

"A pleasant day, yes?" he inquires, as if this was a casual visit from a neighbor out on a stroll. As if he hasn't stood on this porch, or met her at a hotel in Ruhengeri when Henry was in town, the first Tuesday of every month for the past two years. How has she let it go on this long?

She first met Gahiji Kayibanda at the government headquarters in Kigali, while requesting a permit to open an orphanage. The deputy seemed to pull the three thousand US-dollar figure out of thin air, but Reverend Morton had warned Lillian that bribery was a common business expense here. She paid with Gahiji's guarantee that this would, of course, be a one-time fee. But he showed up on her porch a few weeks later. An additional two thousand dollars was needed for a construction permit, a farming permit, and a business permit. The cost of being an outsider. She had already met many people—Tutsi and Hutu alike—whose land had been seized by the Hutu government.

Most of Samuel's insurance money was gone, and using the Someday money that Henry had sent wasn't an option. Not for this. There was some seed money that Mama had collected at the church, but it was strictly budgeted for food and other essentials while she applied for grants. Gahiji feigned sympathy, an arm around her shoulders that set her skin crawling. "Perhaps we can work out an arrangement, one not involving money," he practically purred. "I do think we could enjoy each other's company."

Now, Lillian leads Gahiji around to the back of the house, doesn't want him in her front hallway where guests hang their hats and coats. He is not a guest. They walk down the hallway, past the bedroom she shares with Henry, to another bedroom nobody uses. There's a desk in the corner, scattered with papers so she can tell Henry this is her office. Gahiji slides by her, doles out what he must think is a come-hither smirk, an eyebrow cocked in a practiced way that she used to consider comical. Lillian's lips form a thin line as she recalls that same look on his face, at the café in Mubaro where she and Henry sometimes wait out the hot afternoon sun with a glass of iced tea and a beignet. A few months back, Gahiji approached their table and flashed his teeth as he offered Henry his hand. Shortly afterwards, he started demanding money again.

Her fingers curl around the gun; she could shoot him in the back and be done with it. But the blood, how would she explain the stain on the floor to Henry? She waves a hand toward the bed. She can use the sheets to muffle the discharge and then wrap him up in the blanket. She begins to pull the gun from her pocket, but her hand won't stop trembling. It was one thing aiming at tin cans on tree stumps in the woods, but what will Gahiji do if she only wounds him—or misses altogether? What will happen to Kwizera? Her kids? "I can't do it, just can't," she whispers, letting her coat drop off of her shoulders and to the floor, the thud of the gun reverberating in her chest.

Gahiji stands behind her, his hot stale coffee breath in her ear. "If it helps, *cherie*, think of the *mzunga* I share you with."

Lillian steels herself as he unbuttons her shirt, and then his hands cup her breasts. She mentally wraps herself in the rough sunflower leaves for protection against his slippery touch, her entire body tensing into this thick second skin. While he's on top of her, purring and petting, she keeps telling herself this is her choice. She is not a victim. This is far easier than murder.

After Gahiji leaves, Lillian sits at the desk and pulls open the only drawer with anything inside of it. She withdraws a purple velvet box that holds the memory of New Year's Eve 1969, several weeks before Samuel was scheduled to begin his tour of duty in Vietnam.

"You should have a ring," her fiancé of several months said. "It's not much—"

Lillian hushed him with a quick kiss. She couldn't take her eyes off the silver band etched with delicate flowers. Elizabeth Taylor's big ol' diamond couldn't have made their love any more real. She threw her arms around Samuel's neck so he wouldn't see the tears. A year apart seemed like a lifetime. How was she supposed to wait that long to become his wife?

Now, her thumb caresses the velvet bed where the ring once rested as her mind sticks on the matching band Samuel wore: a rope of vines that twined around his thick finger. She shudders. *His hands.* So strong around her waist as they kissed good-bye at the airport. Three short months later, those same hands appeared waxen and cold, crossed over his chest against a blue army uniform. His wedding ring appeared much too large, as if his hands had somehow shrunk. She had the strong urge to reach into the coffin and rub his fingers, warm them. What stopped her were his nails: an unnatural bright pink against dark skin. She tucked her own wedding band into the breast pocket of Samuel's stiff shirt.

Standing under the shower, water hot enough to draw Gahiji's scent out of her pores, her skin is slick with a combination of relief and shame. And then, there's something else. Is she a coward for not following through with murdering Gahiji? Or, is she due just a bit of pride?

Long ago, she made a commitment to nonviolence, a vow that was mightily tested by Reverend King's murder. His assassination was as good as a broken promise; all bets were off. Lillian's entire world became an angry, mistrustful place. The Student Nonviolent Coordinating Committee dropped the "nonviolent" and became allied with the militant Black Panthers. Henry was attacked and moved back to Florida, marrying his high school sweetheart not long afterwards. Samuel chose the Army, a controlled violence. Deirdre moved to Oakland to become more involved with the Black Panthers and started carrying a pistol in her purse. Despite all of this, Lillian held strong to her belief that nonviolence was the only way to secure long-lasting change. It was a show of faith. Now, it occurs to her she's being tested again.

She examines her face in the mirror: star-like lines crease the corners of her eyes, lips that were once soft and pink are now dark as the ochre clay. She brushes her ruddy cheek with calloused fingertips. Would Samuel even recognize her now? Four years at the orphanage in Kenya had not prepared her for the hard work of restoring Kwizera. The former owners, a Belgian couple, had given up on growing coffee here and left the place a shambles. At first, the work was therapeutic. She didn't mind the sunburn and blisters, falling into bed at night one hundred percent achy. Every morning she awoke fully refreshed. But it soon became clear that the men from town she hired on didn't take orders well from a woman. They stared blankly at her as she told them the day's chores, and then did little work. She needed someone to rely on.

Henry arrived here six years after Samuel died. Six years and her grief was still tender. The farm was falling apart. She was falling apart. Henry was a godsend. And, it was plain to see he had found his way to Kwizera for the same reason she first came here. They both needed a place where they could cultivate a home. They worked hard and became stronger together. She is proud of the strength of character grooved into the landscape of her face. This farm has become part of her, the dust of the soil on her skin even fresh out of the shower. If she uses the Colt 45, she will not become stronger, only tougher. Something inside of her will harden, as Deirdre hardened after she moved to Oakland and took up with the Black Panthers. If this is another test of her faith, she will have failed miserably.

Lillian peels the sheets off the bed, bundles them with the dungarees and blouse she wore this morning and throws on her jacket, the gun smacking against her hip as she walks. She'll find a way to keep paying Gahiji, maybe sell the pearl necklace that belonged to her grandmother, a gift from Mama when she turned eighteen. Gahiji will tire of her soon, when the creases around her eyes and mouth deepen.

She deposits the sheets in the washing machine in the shed, places the gun back inside the tin box where she used to store her gardening tools, and pockets a pointy-tipped hand shovel. Then, she heads deep into the woods, to the bend in the river marked by the mopani tree with butterfly-shaped leaves. There's a patch of sunlight on the riverbank where delicate purple and white pansies grow. She carefully, lovingly, digs up a hefty clump of wild pansies and then digs a bit deeper. She deposits the metal box, heavy now, and then replants the flowers where they belong. They need the mossy, stream-fed earth, would never survive in the hard clay of her garden near the house where she will claw at the earth with the trowel, working furiously, until all that's coating her skin is her own sweat.

THIRTEEN
{ New York, September 1985 }

ENRY SLIDES ONTO A PLASTIC STOOL, fingers drumming the silver-rimmed black Formica bar littered with overflowing tinfoil ashtrays, smudged glasses and crumpled napkins. The place is nearly deserted. Looks more like a warehouse—cement floors and faded brick walls—than a nightclub. His mouth waters as he considers the bottles lining the shelves against a mirrored wall behind the bar. He shakes his head at the bartender, a young guy in a strategically torn black T-shirt, a mop of stringy blond hair flopping over one eye. "I'll wait," he says, fingers closing around the soapstone locket, solid against his chest, with Rachel's picture inside. Where is she, anyway?

Two nights ago, he made the mistake of coming here after the band was in full swing, the base pumped up so loud that the floor shook and some god-awful gal jumped around onstage, screeching like a chimp in heat. Henry sat on this stool, nursing a whiskey and watching. Watching as his daughter offered a smile, a smile just for him, but only because it was too loud to actually hear his order. He pointed toward the bottom shelf of bottles. It had taken Rachel three tries before her hand landed on whiskey, not Johnny Walker but he didn't even care, the way her face lit up when he gave a thumbs-up that she'd guessed right. When the glass landed on the bar in front of him, he nearly seized her hand. She stood there, expectantly; he imagined she was waiting for an explanation. Why now, after eleven years?

"Three bucks," she shouted. Henry reached toward her, his fingers trembling, and deposited a ten-dollar bill in her palm. "Keep the change."

Last night, he swigged from a bottle in his hotel room and dialed the phone number of the one person who might be able to tell him what to say to his daughter. Holy Moses, she hadn't recognized him sitting right across the bar. "You'll be happy to know," he slurred, squinting at the harsh lights of a theater marquee directly out the window, "you were right. She didn't have a goddamn clue who I was."

His ex-wife sighed but didn't sound happy. Exasperated was more like it. He had been floored when a letter arrived at Kwizera last month with Merilee's return address. Liver cancer. She was at the top of a transplant list but it made her think, nonetheless. She didn't want their daughter to be alone in the world, without a family.

"Tell her you're back for good, or at least a while," Merilee said. "That's what she wants to hear."

"I can't say that."

"Well, you never were a liar. I'll give you that much."

"No, I never lied to you." Henry hadn't wanted to get married or have children, at least not right away, she knows that's true. After moving back from Atlanta, he took a job as a photographer at her uncle's ad agency with the idea of saving money to move to New York, or maybe travel around Europe by train for a while and build up his portfolio. Merilee had been, not exactly enthusiastic, but at least game to tag along. And then, three months later, she delivered some news of her own: her period was late. He has never been certain the pregnancy was an accident, but then what did it matter? He volunteered to marry her and to take care of her and their child, of course he did, that's what a stand-up guy does. He was faithful, despite her suspicions, but looking back he could see that wasn't enough. Of course she was bitter; who wouldn't be? Married to someone you knew wanted to be somewhere else.

"I'm sorry, Merilee," he said into the phone, the marquee lights blurring.

She laughed. One sharp crack, like a slap. "Henry Shepherd, don't you dare apologize to our daughter."

"For chrissakes, Mer—" His throat closed around his wife's name. Couldn't she give him a little credit for travelling halfway across the world to make amends? "I *am* sorry."

"I know, Henry."

"I want her to know."

"Sure you do. It'll make you feel better."

"Rachel, too."

"But how do think she'll feel, seeing you walk out the door again?"

Henry opened his mouth, but nothing came out.

"Go home," Merilee said. "Go home to your family."

HENRY HEARS RACHEL BEFORE HE sees her at the other end of the bar. Her laugh is light and airy, almost musical. The notes float over clinking glasses, thin lines of smoke marking the air. He startles, as if awakening from a dream; she's right in front of him with a beer for the guy on the next stool. How long has he been sitting here, staring? She must think he's a stalker, a creep, she must think—

"What can I get for you, sir?" she asks. He points toward the bottom shelf, his voice stuck in a hard shell in his chest. Rachel puckers her lips a bit to one side and then a smile starts in the crinkles around her eyes, exactly like when she was a kid.

"I remember you," she says, snaps her fingers at him. "Whiskey, neat."

"Yeah…yeah, right!" Henry nods vigorously, as if his daughter has miraculously guessed his birthday or weight. Or his name. "That's been my drink since…" He takes a breath that turns into a sharp laugh. "Can't remember—since before you were born."

Rachel's face turns soft as she studies him with…what? Recognition? He takes a bandana from his pocket to mop his face. Tears. Sweat. Bloody hell, he can't stop laughing like a crazy person. "I'm sorry, it's just…I'm sorry."

"It's cool, you're fine." Rachel leans toward him. "Tell you what, I'll give you a double. No extra charge. Looks like you could use it."

She's saying something, maybe about the band coming onstage again soon, but Henry can't hear over the roar of blood crashing behind his temples. It's not recognition he sees on her face but pity, just fucking pity, that's all it is. She seems to pour the amber liquid in slow motion. The exchange of the drink for three dollars will take less than two minutes, and she'll be on to the next customer. And then, this moment will forever pass.

He swallows hard, the shell in his chest now a solid lump that will not dissolve. He can't help but think of the tumor growing in Merilee's liver. A donor, that's what he needs. Someone to give him what it might take to be a real dad to this young woman who doesn't look a thing like him except for the wild curls, but he would recognize her anywhere. Maybe it's a missing gene, or something he learned—didn't learn—from his old man. But he could change everything right here and now. He could tell her that he came back, not just to apologize but to stay for a while.

His lips are dry, the lump in his chest throbbing as his daughter slides the glass toward him. What if he walks away and says nothing?

Lilly knows his shortcomings and loves him anyway. She allows him the freedom to come and go as he pleases. And each time he returns, his life at Kwizera is whole and intact. Nothing much changes there. If he walks away, Rachel will still be smiling and laughing, flirting with that guy, a guitar slung over his shoulder, at the other end of the bar. If he walks away, right now, nothing will change for her either. Who's to say that if he were to reveal himself it would be for the better, anyway? Would she accept the apology of her selfish old man as easily as she poured a crazy guy a double shot? And what if she can't forgive him, what then? It's not like he can go back in time and do things differently.

Henry jangles the ice in his glass, buying time while Rachel heads toward the guy with a guitar. He studies his face, gray and sagging, in the cloudy mirror behind the bar. Suddenly, there he is, grinning proudly in the front row at his daughter's high school graduation. His face turns stern, grilling her prom date, and then patient as he sits in the passenger seat of a Buick and explains how to parallel park. He sees the two of them gluing together a seventh-grade science project of ping-pong balls that revolve around a tennis-ball sun. He closes his eyes and imagines her floating next to him; snorkeling in the Bahamas, he's always wanted to learn; or fishing off Key West like he did with his dad a few summers, before his mom left and Roy Shepherd stopped doing much of anything with him.

His stomach turns sour with the memory of switching off a snowy TV, and then reading and rereading the same grimy comic books in bed, praying that the bastard would stumble home too plastered to come into his room. Sometimes, Roy Shepherd would sink to his knees, sniveling and begging for forgiveness. But more often he already had his belt drawn, cussing Henry out as if he had been the one responsible for smacking his mom around for years, until she finally got the hell out of there. Henry kept his mouth shut, and kept a baseball bat by his bed. He was big enough, at fifteen, for the football coach to keep trying to wheedle him into playing instead of taking photos from the sidelines and, anyway, Roy Shepherd preferred beating up women who couldn't fight back.

Henry cuts a glance at Rachel, still at the other end of the bar. She gives him a quick smile, raises her eyebrows: Anything else? He opens his mouth but his lips are gummy, the sour tang of whiskey now on his tongue. He shakes his head, places his hand flat over his glass. No, nothing else. Nothing at all.

Outside, the sidewalk is slick, snow crunching under Henry's feet. He walks at a clip toward his hotel, chin tucked into his coat collar, the bitter cold at odds with the whiskey sloshing, burning, somewhere between his gut and his throat. He races down an alley, braces his hands on a dumpster and pukes. One final heaving shudder rocks his body, the smell of his own self-loathing more rank than anything emanating from the garbage bin. He sees Roy Shepherd, smugly leering at him from the mirror behind the bar as he slipped a fifty-dollar bill under his glass and slunk out the door. There was a reason his old man regarded him with such disdain, a secret they shared: Roy Shepherd was a fucking coward at heart, even with the police badge and the gun. *Yeah, boy, we've got something in common all right.*

FOURTEEN
{ November 15, 2000: Nairobi Airport }

A WARM CURRENT OF BODIES SWEEPS RA-
chel down the narrow hallway leading from the plane and
into the airport, ebbing out into the terminal, leaving her
exposed and alone. She's exhausted, unable to process the blur of signs
on the surrounding shops, and stops to get her bearings through smell:
curry, strong tobacco, pizza, a swirl of floral perfume, coffee. Definitely
coffee. She follows the aroma into a nearby café and instead orders
tea to settle her stomach from flying. It comes dark and thick with a
creamy skin, more like a latte, and is sweet and soothing going down.
She double-checks the contents of a manila envelope in the front
pocket of her daypack—boarding pass for Kigali, passport, email from
Lillian, and the postcards from her father—and then heads back into
the terminal, ready for the last leg of her journey.

The international transit lounge is a labyrinth of people sprawled out on cracked beige chairs. The floor sucks at the soles of her black high-tops as she searches for a seat. She glances at a light-skinned black man whose soft features are almost boyish except for the grooved parentheses framing his mouth. He's obviously check-ing her out, his sunglasses dark but plenty transparent, bobbing his head slightly as if listening to a song only he can hear. American surf bum, she decides: the faded yellow UCLA T-shirt and Reef sandals are giveaways. Probably waiting for a buddy he's meeting up with to chase waves in Morocco.

"Go ahead, sit," he says, swiping a book off the seat next to him, a little too eager.

"That's okay…" But the computer bag on Rachel's frozen shoulder slides off, like it has a mind of its own. Her abdominal muscles tense protectively, out of habit, as she bends to secure the bag between her knees. It's been two months since the miscarriage, but she still some-times feels the echo of tiny kicks against her ribs. The lounge is eerily quiet except for a cough here, snoring there. She glances at her watch. Did she reset it in London? Is it six or seven hours later in New York?

"My husband," she says, producing her phone from her jacket as evidence that she's not in the market for a travel buddy. "He'll be ex-pecting—"

"No, yeah, sure," Surfer Dude interrupts. "He'll want to know you arrived safely. Go ahead, call."

Rachel curls into the wall for privacy. Her heart sinks into the place where she knows Mick's not remotely expecting to hear from her. He stoically drove her to the airport, like it was his duty, both of them quietly studying the traffic. The polite patter of flat optimism had tapped out weeks ago. *We'll work it out. After the New Year. We both need time. Time to think. Heal.* The thought of six weeks apart was a relief. And yet she stood at the airport curb, her fingers warm on the spot where he had pecked her cheek, moments after he drove away. A part of her had hoped he would ask her to stay, not because he wanted to try and have another baby but because he wanted *her.*

Surfer Dude is eyeing her, so she presses the call button. "Honey, it's me," she says brightly as voicemail picks up. "Well, I made it to Nairobi. My flight to Kigali doesn't leave for three hours, so call me back when you get this. Whenever. Or, I'll call you from Rwanda." She snaps shut the phone and places it to her temple. *Call me.*

Surfer Dude clears his throat. "You can call on a landline from Rwanda. No cell reception," he says, as if listening in on her conversation is entirely acceptable. "Still using walkie-talkies."

Rachel begins rifling through her bag for the latest *National Enquirer*, a guilty pleasure reserved for sick days in bed and plane rides. Surfer Dude is either flirting or simply killing time, she can't decide which one as she leafs through the magazine. She studies him out of the corner of her eye. He's handsome in an off-handed way, lanky frame but not exactly tall, square jaw, a bump on the bridge of his nose that seems like an afterthought. He's staring into space, tapping a finger against his knee. Probably keeping time to that song in his head. His smell makes her glance up: something sweet. Bright in contrast to the stale, dank room. "Have you been?" she asks. "Rwanda?"

He smiles, seemingly grateful for the opening. "I'm on that flight to Kigali. I live there."

"Live there?"

"Going on nine years."

"What brought you there?"

"I went to volunteer with the Red Cross, one thing led to another..." He shrugs. "Long story. You got three hours?"

Rachel flips shut the magazine and holds out her hand. "Yeah, I do. Rachel Shepherd."

"Daniel Tucker."

"Nice to meet you, Daniel."

"It's Tucker. Daniel is my dad."

His grip is firm and reassuring. Rachel reclaims her hand, eyes dropping to his UCLA T-shirt. "So...Tucker. You're from California?"

"No. I mean, yeah, but that was a long time ago." He removes his glasses, his eyes are a soft green. Sad.

Rachel makes her own eyes vacant, fumbles in her bag, a hand landing on her CD player and headphones. "I really need to rest before our flight, time change and all."

"Sure, we can talk on the plane. I'll watch your stuff while you catch some Zs."

"Thanks, I'll just listen to a song or two." Rachel clicks on Ella Fitzgerald and tips back her head against the wall. The song's barely begun though, it seems, when someone gently taps her awake.

"Excuse me, miss," apologizes the agent who checked her into the transit lounge earlier. "Boarding for your flight to Kigali begins shortly."

Rachel snaps wide awake. She spies the Updike book that Tucker was reading on the vinyl chair: both he and her computer bag are gone. Shit. "The guy who was sitting here..." Stupid, stupid, stupid, trusting him. She locks onto the agent's placid eyes as the room becomes louder, the air thicker. "Tallish, thin, a blue bandana. Have you seen him? He took my bag."

"You have two options, miss. Board your plane, or go to the security office and file a stolen property report. The next flight to Kigali leaves tomorrow at the same time."

An oily film slicks over Rachel's face as she gets up and tugs at the suitcase wedged under her seat. *Take all the time you need.* Mick's voice was so quiet when she first asked if six weeks away was too long. A white flag of defeat. The quietness settled into their relationship, like a deep unnatural sleep. The suitcase wheels seem to catch on each groove in the tile floor. "C'mon, damn it," Rachel hisses. She's not ready to give up. Lillian will be waiting for her in Kigali. She'll confirm that it's Henry Shepherd who is somehow broken, couldn't make his marriage work or be a decent parent. He's the broken one.

She squints bleary-eyed down two flights of steps leading to the main corridor, rubs her aching shoulder. A gentle shove is all it takes and her luggage loudly thumps its way to the landing below. She runs down the stairs, kneels to assess the damage, and then looks up when someone calls her name. Tucker is leaning over the railing.

"It kind of got away from me," Rachel says with an edge. "Hey, my computer!"

Tucker bounds down the steps two at a time, an orange duffle slung over one shoulder and her slim canvas bag on the other. "I went for coffee, came back and you'd split. Your bag was at the end of the row where we were sitting. Sorry, no laptop."

Rachel unzips the too-light bag and shakily pulls out the manila envelope, relief draining her of the strength needed to hang onto it. The contents scatter across the dirty tile floor. She scoops up the postcards, holding them to her chest.

"Let me help." Tucker offers her his hand. *Roses.* Weird, but that's the smell. Rachel takes a deep breath as her fingers interlock with his.

"The plane to Kigali," she says shakily, "I have to get on it. I'm meeting someone."

"I know." Tucker squeezes her hand. "I'm your ride to Kwizera."

RACHEL IS THE LAST ONE off the plane in Kigali. She stops on the metal staircase down to the tarmac and hangs onto the rail, momentarily dizzy from the bright sun and balmy breeze. Real air! After thirty-six hours of planes and airports, it's intoxicating. She inhales long, greedy breaths and surveys the surroundings. For an international airport, it's surprisingly small: a single runway lined with scrawny palm trees that look sadly out of place. The sunlight is trapped above the silver belly of clouds that forecast rain, but in the distance there's some patchy hope: the vague outline of reddish-brown rolling hills. She shades her eyes to scout out Tucker, who disappeared from his seat next to her shortly after the plane took off. He said he was going into the cockpit to chat up the pilot, a friend of his, and would meet up with her when they landed.

She doesn't see him at the gate or while going through customs. Funny, she thinks while waiting for her checked bag, she's usually the one asking questions, in bartender-shrink mode whether pouring drinks or not, but Tucker got her talking about moving to New York by herself straight out of high school. She had wanted to escape from staid suburban Jacksonville, loved the energy of the city, the possibilities, even though it meant sharing a one-bedroom walk-up with two other women. She knows hardly anything about Surfer Dude, except that he sometimes lives at Kwizera and knew her father, but not well. When she asked for details about Henry Shepherd, all he would say was, "That's Lillian's story to tell."

Tucker is leaning against the hood of a green Jeep parked at the airport curb. Rachel drops her bag a few yards away and studies him: His face is tilted toward the sky, eyes closed, elbows winged out. His skin has a light coppery glow compared to the dark-skinned Africans milling about, his features more closely resembling her thin European nose and lips. She rubs her bare arms, feels almost naked. There's a hushed hum as people walk by and stare: *Mzunga…* White person. That much, she understands. It's unnerving to think Surfer Dude is the closest thing she has to a friend here.

"Over here!" Tucker waves, and then slides behind the wheel. Rachel doesn't budge. "How do you know Lillian?" she asks. "I mean, why did she send you to get me?"

Tucker looks genuinely confused.

"It's just…well, you could be anyone."

"So could you." Tucker leans over to open the passenger door. "Tell you what, let's do this twenty questions thing on the road. If we don't get going now, we'll be driving in the dark. Trust me, not good."

Rachel is met by a lush wall of perfumed air as she gets into the Jeep. There are a half-dozen thorny bushes in the backseat, dripping with red buds. "Roses," she says. That's what she smelled in the airport. Mystery solved.

"Lillian's a nut for all kinds, and you can't find American Beauties in Rwanda," Tucker says. "My friend let me stash these in the cockpit."

American Beauties. Rachel makes a mental note. "What else does Lillian like, besides flowers? What's she like?"

"She's…" Tucker tilts his head one way and then the other. He gives up with a shrug.

"So, how do you know her?"

"That's at least twenty questions rolled into one. The short answer is that Kwizera is my home when I'm not working in Kigali. The longer version requires a bottle of banana gin and a lime."

There's a single paved road leading out of the airport, with a sign pointing toward Kigali. Tucker turns the other way. The land is cracked and dry, with few hints of green in the yards of the intermittent compact cement and brick houses. Rachel runs her fingers across the pane of the window, as if that might erase the dust clinging to other side. "How's Lillian going to keep those flowers alive?" she wonders aloud.

"The land's different up north, away from the city," Tucker explains. "There's still clay but you can break it up, mix it in with richer soil from the mountains."

"The volcanic ash," Rachel says to show she's done her homework.

"That, and the bodies."

The warm air turns thick and hot; Rachel can't get enough into her lungs. He's talking about the genocide, of course. Hundreds of thousands of bodies. Her father left during the genocide. *Disappeared.* That's how Lillian put it. "Some people escaped, didn't they?" she asks.

"There's only one road, through the mountains, that leads into Uganda and the Hutus had it locked down tight," Tucker says. "There was a stream of people—entire families—mostly walking. Anyone with a Tutsi ID, or without any ID at all, was shot. The Hutus hunted them down like animals in the forests and the rivers, where people hid underwater breathing through reeds."

Rachel cracks her window and cups a hand over her mouth and nose, but the dust sifts through her fingers; it's everywhere. Her eyes, her mouth. Lungs. The smell of roses is now cloying, almost nauseating, in the heat. What did her father find here? What kept him here? What finally made him leave? Her eyes sting; she wipes the grit off her lips with two fingers, rubbing smooth the dry cracks. This is the question she most wants to ask Lillian: How did her father disappear? And Tucker keeps right on talking. Bodies stacked like firewood along this highway that runs from Kigali north into Uganda…people hiding under the dead…nobody escaped.

"Slow down a little?" she asks weakly as Tucker takes a hairpin turn, quite possibly interrupting him. She barely hears her own voice above the rumbling of the Jeep, or maybe it's just the pounding of blood in her ears.

"Yeah, sure." Tucker offers a slight smile and takes a hand off the wheel. His touch on her bare shoulder, barely a brush of his fingers, is jolting. She feels exactly how tense her body is. Like a spring trap. He squints through the dusty windshield as if searching for something to say. "The land, the people…despite everything, it's all so beautiful. Still." And then he's quiet, either lost in his thoughts or he figures there's nothing else that needs to be explained as the Jeep rattles into the steep foothills.

He's right, the landscape changes dramatically as they continue to climb, turning from brown and gray to a palette of greens, some hues that Rachel has never seen before, mixed with sienna-red clay, amber grass, the light and shade of the clouds passing overhead. The dust dissipates and there's a slight cool undercurrent in the breeze, so she rolls her window completely down and takes in the scenery: tiered foothills ribboned with banana trees, and lower bushes thick with white clusters of flowers that must be coffee or tea.

Women wrapped in swaths of colorful fabric, faces shaded by

wide-brimmed straw hats, till the earth or fill baskets. Some have babies swaddled to their backs; all have children working by their sides. The younger children shout and wave as the Jeep chugs by, the older ones stare, and the women continue working. Rachel imagines her father, camera to his eye, capturing all of this.

An hour later, the road flattens out into the first real town they've come across since leaving the airport. The houses are made of mud plaster with sticks woven into the walls. Young children chase each other through narrow yards of dirt and scrubby grass, weaving past women hanging laundry on low wooden fences and stirring metal pots over fire pits in front yards. Other young mothers sit in groups of two or three in the patchy shade of tiny porches, babies squirming in their arms. Rachel leans out the window to inhale something spicy and sweet in the air. She so wants to be swept away by all this, as her father surely was.

The Jeep stops and a handful of children approach, calling *"Muraho*, Doctor Tucker, *Muraho!"*

Tucker opens his door to high-five each of the kids. "There's no hospital in town so they come to Kwizera," he explains. "I run a little clinic there a few days each week with a doctor and a few nurses from the clinic where I work in Kigali."

"So, you're a doctor," Rachel says skeptically. From surfer dude to doctor—didn't see that one coming.

"I was burnt out after the first year of my residency at UCLA, took a break to come here and volunteer with the Red Cross." Tucker digs through a paper sack he grabbed from the back seat. "I finished up my residency in Kigali. Never did figure out a reason to go back." He produces a handful of small wooden giraffes and hippos for the children, who regard him as if he's a magician. He leans toward a bold boy who has stepped forward. "Go ahead, take one," he says, and then to Rachel, "I kind of cleaned out a shop at the airport."

She places a hand to her throat. The necklace she found in her mom's things had animal beads just like these.

The other children step forward, one at a time, to accept their gift from Tucker and bow. Some deposit a swift kiss on his cheek. The last one, a small girl, leans into the Jeep to hug him, giggling as if on a dare, and then the group scatters.

Tucker starts to put the bag in the back seat, and then stops. "Maybe you can give me a female perspective on something." He pulls out a bundle of white tissue paper and carefully unwraps a necklace with tiny porcelain butterflies fluttering on a delicate silver chain. "Do you think a seven-year-old girl would dig this?" he asks. "Seems sort of cheesy, but my Rosie's a sucker for butterflies."

"It's perfect," Rachel says, brushing pastel wings with her finger. "Any little girl would love it. Rosie. She's your daughter?"

"I like to think she's mine." Tucker loops the necklace over the rearview mirror. "Not by blood, but by everything that really matters. Y'know?"

"Of course." Rachel's hand goes to her stomach, as if to catch the threads of sadness unspooling throughout her body.

"I'm sorry," Tucker says, "about your loss. The baby. I can see why it would bring up stuff about when your dad left. Losing him. Finding him."

"Lillian told you?" Rachel asks. "Wait...my emails. She showed you?"

Tucker fumbles with his keys in the ignition.

"Those were personal." Rachel pinches the bridge of her nose. The words weren't meant for Tucker, not even really for Lillian. They were meant for her father. There's a tap on her windowsill: the girl who hugged Tucker is holding out her palm, offering the carved hippo.

"For you, *Madame*. Bien?"

"*Merci. Très bien*." Rachel squeezes the girl's hand as she accepts the gift, and then looks at Tucker. "Sorry I blew up. I'm sure you were simply trying…" What? She's not sure.

"Not a problem. My bad." He offers the girl another figurine and turns the key in the ignition. "Tell you what, I'll make it up to you. I know a place not far from here that will blow your mind. Guaranteed."

Tucker pulls off the road, onto a dirt path that Rachel would never have suspected leads anywhere. The winding path descends, the hills rising steeper, and the houses are spread farther apart. In some of the scrubby front yards there's a single goat tied to a post or a cow so thin it would hardly be worth slaughtering. The Jeep stops at the edge of a marshy field; an emerald lake reflects the surrounding emerald hills. "This is it," Tucker says. "Lake Kivu."

"Well, you've succeeded in blowing my mind," Rachel says as she gets out of the Jeep. It's the same lake that's depicted on one of the postcards from her father. Pink-winged geese glide among oversized purple lilies that bow over the water like ladies-in-waiting. She can practically picture Henry Shepherd paddling in his canoe.

"Come on." Tucker's already heading toward the field. "Sometimes there's a boardwalk leading to the lake. Hasn't been raining much lately, it should be here."

Rachel follows him out onto a succession of thin wooden planks, jumping over oozing mud from one section to the next, her heart beating fast as she loses her balance and grabs his hand. Halfway across the boardwalk, Tucker stops abruptly. "Bingo, zebras at ten o'clock," he whispers, pointing to three large animals and two smaller ones approaching the lake. The family is so close that Rachel hears their hooves sloshing through the mucky grass. She starts to crouch, but there's nowhere to hide.

"Relax," Tucker says. "They don't know to be afraid of us. Just keep a polite distance."

The air vibrates with a series of high-pitched beeps and whistles as a spray of vibrant green and orange parakeets arcs overhead. The zebras, startled, lope away as quickly as they appeared. "That was a bonus," Tucker says, shading his face with his hand as he appraises the sky. "Welcome to Rwanda."

Rachel stands still, barely daring to breathe and disturb the magic around them, this vortex of energy that dozens of tiny wings have stirred up. This is what her father discovered in Africa, what he fell in love with here. She knows it. For a brief moment, she knows *him* again.

FIFTEEN

"YOU'VE GOTTA BE HUNGRY," TUCKER SAYS, slowing down like he's looking for a restaurant in the middle of nowhere among the mud-brick houses with tin roofs. She keeps insisting she's not hungry, not tired, not scared out of her gourd to have the tables turned and be the one whose skin color turns everyone's heads as they drive by. "It's not that they're rude, just honest," he says as they pass two boys trying to herd a steer down the road with sticks. They don't return her wave, but instead wear their frank curiosity in a squint and a frown. "They're easy to read. No bullshit."

He glances at Rachel. She has a pretty convincing poker face, but he notices her hands: one tightly fisted around the phone in her lap, not that her husband can answer her SOS. That thing is worthless here. The other hand grips the door handle, prepared for a quick escape. She's nervous. Guarded. Has no idea how easy she is to read.

When he first came here, he wore the same frozen half-smile that's precariously clinging to her face. He was terrified people might see how completely unsure he was of what he was supposed to be doing at the hospital in Kigali where the Red Cross placed him as a medical technician.

Growing up, Tucker had heard the story of his father's success, a story that made Horatio Alger look like a slacker, innumerable times. Daniel Tucker, Sr. had busted his ass to pull himself out of Watts in the early sixties and earned the UCLA trifecta: pre-med and med school scholarships, and then the first black residency in cardiology at the prestigious university. It had always been expected that "little Tucker" would follow in his dad's footsteps, like yet another reward or reparation for all of the dude's hard work and sacrifice.

You have no idea, his dad would say, wagging his head. Clearly, his disappointment in his only son saddened him beyond words. Tucker's dad seemed to want him to struggle, like he had, even though their split-level in Brentwood was a million miles away from Watts. Struggle was the last thing that Tucker wanted. He kept his mouth shut, his grades up, and his room clean. He followed the rules, except for a brief stoned and stupid period in high school. He just wanted to be fucking *good.* Isn't that all every kid wants? Isn't that what his dad wanted of him?

It wasn't until the last year of medical school at UCLA that Tucker began to question the gift of this life his dad had given him. After a full day of classes and studying into the evening, instead of sleeping he would drive to Playa del Ray, away from the city lights, and climb up a lifeguard tower. He spent hours in that hard wooden chair, surveying the silver-crested waves rolling in and crashing against the boulders at the far end of the sandy strip. He tried to imagine who he might be if it were his choice, and always came up blank. He didn't have a clue. The question haunted him. And then, a year into his residency in cardiac surgery, the question paralyzed him. He stood over a steaming warm body, staring at a human heart pumping blood, frozen by the knowledge that he wasn't sure why—or if—he wanted to be a surgeon or even a physician.

He couldn't quit. Daniel Senior didn't raise a quitter. His mom assured him that the uncertainty was merely a phase, they didn't need to bother his dad. Three months later, after an incident involving stolen supplies donated to a free clinic, Tucker's chief resident requested his departure. He suggested that the pressure of being a surgeon wasn't for him. Tucker did not disagree. He signed up with the Red Cross and came here, to the heart of struggle, to find out not just what kind of doctor he wanted to be but what kind of man.

"Shouldn't we skip lunch and head straight to Kwizera?" Rachel says. "I mean, Lillian's waiting for us. Right?"

"There's a café back this way a bit." Tucker waves a hand evasively out the window and turns onto the main road, back in the direction of Kigali. He needs time, just a little more time, to let Lillian digest the phone message he left from the airport payphone. *I'm coming home with a guest, Rachel Shepherd. We'll be there around sundown. It's the right thing to do. You'll see.*

He can practically smell the tension as Rachel asks why he's turning back—she's just said she's not hungry. "It's around here somewhere," he mumbles, slowing down even though they're still miles away from anything resembling a town. The Jeep lurches as they hit a deep pothole. He reflexively makes his arm a safety bar between Rachel and the dashboard.

"You'll like this place, it has character." Tucker offers a smile and she returns it. She wants to trust him, needs to trust somebody. Who else does she have? He suspects the phone in her lap wouldn't ring, even if there was cell reception.

The butterfly necklace hanging from the rearview mirror has slid down against the window, the ceramic beads clanking together. Rachel reaches up to hook it back onto the mirror. "Wouldn't want your little girl's necklace to get chipped," she says. "What does Rosie like besides butterflies?"

"She's got this lion, Kingston. He's raggedy and is missing an eye, but she won't go to sleep without him."

"I had a stuffed dog, Old Gold. He was my protector."

"Rose needs lion-sized protection. Between Kingston and Lillian, she has her bases covered when I'm in Kigali."

"Sounds like a pretty tight family."

"Yeah, it is." Tucker cuts a quick glance toward Rachel. Maybe he's not giving her enough credit. She might understand why he brought her here. "I owe Lillian a lot," he says. "She took in Rosie when she was an infant. Hell, she took me in too."

Rachel lets go of the door handle and turns her full attention toward him as he recalls how he and a nurse delivered the premature baby together. *Solange.* He still can't say her name aloud.

He hasn't even told Lillian that Solange was his fiancée and they thought of the baby as their own for two months, but it seemed like much longer. They fed and bathed her, cared for her, while her mother lay in a hospital bed with an oxygen mask over her face and fought a losing battle against tuberculosis.

He clenches his fist, tightening the thick watchband made of leather that Solange's father tanned himself. It had taken Tucker six months of Sunday dinners at her family's farm, on the other side of the Virungas in Uganda, before Moses allowed his only daughter to go alone on a real date with him. This watch was a present from her for their first anniversary as a couple. He flexes his hand and clenches it again. Next April marks seven years since she died. He still hears her heartbeat in the ticking watch.

"You have to trick her into sleep," Solange chided, taking the fussy infant from his seemingly too-big hands and humming, holding the unnamed baby girl to her chest. "The vibrations, that's what does it."

Tucker sat next to his fiancée, his head on her shoulder while he rested his eyes. "Lucky baby," he murmured.

It wasn't UCLA by a long shot, but he could take on as many patients as he could handle and specializing wasn't an option. He did everything from setting bones, to advising new mothers how to keep their babies healthy, to cardiac surgery. That was both the upside and downside of staying here to finish his residency after his two-year contract with the Red Cross ran out in 1993. There were always more bodies that needed stitching up, especially later that year when the mass murders of Tutsis across the border in Burundi began spilling over into Rwanda.

At that time, Radio Rwanda began stepping up their hate-laced broadcasts. They fervently warned that the Tutsis were preparing to take back their power, threatening the livelihood and well-being of their Hutu neighbors. Tucker was worried about the increase in attacks against Tutsi communities in the rural villages surrounding Kigali. The wounded were filling up medical centers all over the city. But all four of Solange's brothers were training to be soldiers in the new Hutu militia, the Interahamwe. Surely they would warn her if she were in danger in the city.

"We never named her, as a vote of confidence that her mom would pull through," Tucker says softly, lost in his memories, barely aware of Rachel beside him in the passenger seat. Solange gave each newly born baby two gifts: a smooth, round river rock, thought to hold the blessing of the Rwandan god Imana, and a white crane feather symbolizing a long life. In the end, it wasn't tuberculosis or AIDS that killed Rose's mother. It was an attack by a small group of soldiers, blowing whistles and swinging machetes. All of the medical staff and patients who could jumped out of windows and ran like hell. Those patients tied to their beds with respirators and tubes were murdered in a dress rehearsal for the countrywide massacre that would ensue five months later.

What Tucker remembers most is laughter. Crazy-ass high, unhinged laughter that he sometimes hears in his sleep. It could almost be jackals except for the cruel edge. Definitely human.

The same five guys arrived every few days. The hospital on a hillside where Tucker and a handful of other Red Cross medics worked was their beat. They blew whistles, waved machetes, and yelled as they walked through the halls. *Tutsi cockroaches, give yourselves up peaceably. Don't force us to hurt innocent people.* They never touched the staff; maybe that's why nobody fought back—not that they could have. At least, that's how they consoled each other while the soldiers checked patient ID cards, pulled out IVs and dragged the Tutsi men out to the courtyard, the women to the basement where their screams could only be imagined.

This one soldier carried a rifle, the only one of them who wore an actual uniform: camouflage fatigues and a black beret. Tucker asked how he decided who to shoot and who was hacked to death, not really expecting an answer. "Easy," the guy said, "whoever has money for ammunition." He laughed shrilly, clapped a hand over his mouth. That's when it hit Tucker: this soldier wearing a beret and a clip of bullets over his shoulder was only a kid. It all could have been a fucking video game. It still scares the shit out of him to think how every few days, with the arrival of the soldiers his limbs became noticeably heavier. A dusty film settled deep into his joints. At night, Solange's tears fell on his skin, rejuvenated him.

"How did she get her name?" Rachel startles Tucker, touching his arm. It's probably not the first time she's asked.

"Lillian," he says. "Someone from the Red Cross knew about Kwizera. When we showed up, Lil looked at Rose like she recognized her—already loved her." He was convinced that some force stronger and smarter than he was found both the baby and him a new home. He and Solange promised each other they would build a family for Rose. That promise is what keeps him here, keeps him sane.

TUCKER PARKS RACHEL AT ONE of the two white plastic tables on a thin slice of sidewalk and goes inside a cinder-block storefront that looks more like somebody's home than a bar: a single room with cushions on the floor and a white fridge smudged with fingerprints against the wall. There's a guy sitting at the only table, making cheese sandwiches in what appears to be a George Foreman mini-grill.

"Deux fromage," Tucker says, taking two clear bottles of home-brewed lager, probably made from corn, from the fridge. He looks at the payphone on the wall for a long moment and takes a swig from his bottle, before picking up the receiver and dialing. He glances out the window at Henry's daughter. What can Lillian do but like her—at least accept that she's here?

Two elderly men are playing mancala at the table next to Rachel, but nobody's moving the colored marbles while they talk in low voices and cut glances toward the pretty white woman with long curly hair piled atop her head. *Her hair.* It looks windblown even in the still air, tendrils curling down the nape of her neck. "We'll be there soon," Tucker says to the answering machine. "Don't worry, she's cool." One of the men motions for Rachel to join them, and she moves her chair toward their table. "Just give her a chance. Tell her a few stories about her dad, that's all I'm asking. Give Henry a chance to show up for both of you."

Tucker stands by the window and waits for his order, the luke-warm lager soothing his nerves. There's no use rushing this dude. He fiddles with the radio, trying to tune in a fuzzy Madonna song, while flies bounce off the slices of bread slathered with a glossy substance that could just as easily be car lube as butter. Laughter floats through the open window: the old men are showing Rachel how to play mancala. She points to a pocket of marbles on the wooden board and the guy with no visible teeth claps his hands while his opponent groans. It's obvious who she's pinch-hitting for. She sees Tucker and gives him a thumbs-up. He returns the gesture, for the first time really believing it wasn't a mistake inviting her here. There's something about her; Henry had it too, a warm, open smile that starts in her eyes and pulls people in.

Tucker offers Rachel a beer and a greasy cheese sandwich wrapped in wax paper. "Did you get hold of Lillian?" she asks, gives the sandwich a cursory sniff and sets it aside.

"Not exactly."

"But she knows we're on our way."

Tucker unwraps his sandwich, inspects the glistening bread. "I left a phone message at the airport, and then just now."

"So, she's expecting us. Right?"

Tucker takes a bite of the sandwich, chews slowly but can't seem to swallow.

Rachel leans forward. "Tucker, she invited me here. She must know—"

"Technically, I invited you here."

"Technically? As in you answered my email for her?"

"As in, she didn't even see your last email. Trust me, it's better this way."

"Because…" Rachel gives him a wide-eyed, are-you-fucking-nuts-or-an-asshole stare.

"It's better this way. Lillian will like you, once she meets you."

She's still staring, her eyes narrow, definitely considering the nutjob or asshole theory.

"Look." Tucker taps his palm. "For starters, you're Henry's daughter. And I like you, that counts for something." She's smiling now, kind of, so he rushes on. "She'll love that you chucked your suitcase down the stairs at the airport. Really, you two aren't so different. You'll—"

"I see." Rachel pinches the bridge of her nose.

"I'll try the shortwave." Tucker escapes to the Jeep and holds up his walkie-talkie for her to see, and then pretends to press the contact button. It is better this way. Besides, it's too late to turn back now.

SIXTEEN

THE WOODEN STAIRS MOAN AS LILLIAN climbs up into the attic, loose slats jiggling underfoot. She stops at the top and bats away a cloud of downy particles that seem to be magnetized to the dim light bulb. Her eyes sift through the shadows, landing on a silver-framed photo atop an old VCR that nobody's used since Henry left. This photo is where her mind went, listening to Tucker's phone message. *It's the right thing to do, you'll see.* "Coward," she mutters. Calling from the airport. He could at least have told her face-to-face before leaving for Nairobi, given her time to…what? Prepare?

She wipes off the frame with the hem of her batik skirt. Such a handsome couple: Henry wearing a brown suit with blue pinstripes, she in a silk tunic a shade of purple Henry had thought matched the wild pansies carpeting the riverbank in the forest. The extravagant clothes were an impulse buy at a boutique in the Nyamirambo district of Kigali, where the diplomats' wives shopped. They were in Kigali for the day, just to have lunch and window shop. They were celebrating. The farm was finally paid off.

She holds the photo firmly in both hands. Their wedding photo. March 7, 1985, twenty years to the day since they had first laid eyes on each other in Ebenezer Church. They bought a small bottle of Pernod in Kigali and spent that night making love, making plans, and writing commitment vows. Early the next morning, she awoke to find Henry sitting on the edge of the bed, dressed in his new pin-striped suit. "I was thinking all night and it finally came to me," he said. "The perfect place to recite our vows."

She pulled the sheet up to her bare collarbone and edged closer to Henry to give him a long, deep kiss. "Right here is plenty perfect."

"Save it for the honeymoon," he teased. "Now, put on that fancy dress, before the kids wake up."

Henry led her deep into the dark forest and stopped at the mopani tree that marks the bend in the river. He spread out a blanket on the flat area between two roots that held them like thick sturdy arms. They watched as the sun rose, pink light filtering through the distinctive leaves shaped like butterfly wings. They stood on the riverbank, no one to witness their vows except a few curious baboons chewing on seed pods high in the trees. Neither one of them had words written down. There was no need.

I, Henry Shepherd, promise to love and cherish you, Lillian Carlson, every day of my life. I've loved you since the first moment I saw you, standing in the light of the church window. Now that I've found you again, I promise to walk beside you and carry you when you get tired. I'll be your partner, your strength during the times when you're running low. I'll help to complete what you've started here, just as you complete me.

"I, Lillian Carlson," she whispers, her hand on the photo, "promise to love and cherish you, Henry Shepherd—" She licks her dry lips, tastes the salt and tinge of champagne on his lips. "I am so blessed that you showed up exactly when I most needed you. From this day forward, I'll be your light when there is darkness and comforting shade when the world is too big and bright. I'll be your muse and your faithful disciple in this amazing adventure. I'll always be your home, and you mine."

Lillian replaces the photo in its rightful spot, just so. There was no pastor, no ring, no wedding cake; they didn't need those things. Just as she rarely feels the need to come up here and peruse the pictures of their life together, hundreds of them in boxes on shelves and frames leaning against the walls. Henry is embedded in the mud-plaster he used to cement together the stones and beams of this place. He is in the land they tilled and harvested together. She steers back toward the stairs, negotiating a maze of boxes bulging with rainy day art projects and school papers stockpiled over the past twenty-four years. She pats the top of a filing cabinet as if greeting an old friend. It holds letters and photos from the children, now adults with broods of their own.

Henry has been her strength all along, so that she could be strong for all these lost children and give them a family. Kwizera has been their commitment to each other, not a small symbol—a ring, a piece of paper, a white dress and veil. That's why it hurt so deeply when she asked him to return for Rahim Kensamara's trials and he couldn't— or wouldn't.

Lillian stops and looks around the small jam-packed room with its sloping ceiling, her hand on the frayed string that will turn off the light. The truth is, she feels Henry beside her, day in and day out, in these walls and the land. She needs him as much as ever, even though he's been gone for two years. How could she possibly keep this place together alone? And now, Rachel Shepherd will be here soon, looking for what Henry might have left behind, what she might take for herself, the pieces to shore up her own home. No, there's no preparing for that.

SEVENTEEN

A PEACEFUL STILLNESS WASHES OVER Rachel as the Jeep turns down a path leading through an expansive banana field, no houses in sight, only the craggy Virunga Mountains hugging the horizon. The sun dips behind the dark mountains, the sky brightening in preparation for one final, spectacular moment before nightfall.

"Back when Lillian bought this land the farm was trashed," Tucker says. "Abandoned and ransacked. She brought it back to life."

"You spoke with her, right?" Rachel asks.

"Not since we stopped for lunch."

"When you left a message."

"She knows you're coming. Relax."

"Relax?" Rachel repeats, glancing pointedly at Tucker's fingers drumming on the steering wheel. She looks down at her own hands, clenched in her lap around her phone. There's a medicinal taste creeping into her mouth: Malarone sloshing together with stomach acid. She should have eaten more of that sandwich at lunch, skipped the beer. "I should stay in town," she says. At least get a good night's sleep. Call Mick.

"The nearest hotel is in Ruhengeri, about an hour away. Besides, if you want to learn more about your dad's life, this is the place."

"And, he knows I'm here?"

"I sent a letter to his post office box in London, but no answer yet," Tucker says, and then adds quickly, "Don't worry, I have to go to London next week to see an immunologist about Rose. I can track Henry down if he hasn't gotten in touch."

"Thanks," Rachel says hollowly. Why wouldn't he answer? Need to be tracked down? She rolls down the window to take in the cool night air. A layer of glowing lavender-gray clouds blanket the sky, like smoke lingering after a forest fire.

The Jeep rolls to a stop. "The Virungas erupted twelve million years ago," Tucker whispers, as if not to disturb the rustling banana trees. "You're looking at the oldest wall of this stretch of the Rift Valley. Spending time here, in the mother of all valleys, keeps everything in perspective for me."

They watch in silence as the sky turns deep blue and the mountains blend in with the night. Rachel feels Tucker next to her, his reverence as the sun sets. He could be seeing this for the first time right along with her. "Ready?" he asks.

"Ready," she says, now glad that he's the one who picked her up at the airport.

Not far ahead, the Jeep stops again at two sections of whitewashed fence held together with rope. "This is it. Looks better from the inside." Tucker jumps out of the Jeep to open Rachel's door. He struggles a few minutes at the gate, unknotting the loops of rope. Silly, really, since anyone could climb right over the low fence. Rachel runs her hand over a thick wooden sign lit up by the car headlights, a splash of rainbow colored block letters. "Kwee-zair-ah," she says, pronouncing each syllable. "What does that mean?"

Before Tucker can answer, crunching gravel announces someone approaching on the other side of the now-open fence. A petite woman appears, carrying a basket of huge sunflowers that seem to light up her face in the dark. Tucker steps forward, arms open. His smile twists into a wince as she offers her cheek for a quick kiss. Or, maybe, Rachel thinks, she's simply turning away.

"I'm Rachel Shepherd, but you already knew that, right?" Rachel laughs nervously and offers her hand.

Lillian shifts the basket into her arms. "Welcome to my home," she says, sweeping her hand toward the driveway but not moving.

Rachel hugs the sunflowers to her chest. There's a distinct chill in Lillian's voice, despite the lilting southern accent. And there's nothing welcoming in those eyes that had been wide open and brimming with love in the newspaper photo. Lillian surrounded by children, flowers in the background, a Mother Earth of sorts. Rachel can't quite picture it now. "I'm sorry," she blurts. "I can leave in the morning, go to Ruhengeri."

"Nonsense," Lillian says, "you'll stay right here."

It sounds like an order. Rachel stands motionless, the basket between her and her father's…what? Second wife? Mistress? The girl in the church window, the woman she has been wondering about ever since seeing her photo in Henry Shepherd's office. And now, it's Lillian who is studying *her* like a photo.

"I'll take Rachel over to the house," Tucker offers, climbing back into the Jeep. "I cleared out some stuff from my room and took it to the tent. She can bunk there."

Rachel remains planted on the gravel driveway, and waits for Lillian to release her. She's staring, eyes narrowed as if casting a spell.

"I see so much of him in you," Lillian finally says.

"Really?" Rachel puts a hand to her thick, unruly hair that she pays big bucks to get straightened if her tips allow. As far as she can tell, it's the only feature of her father's she inherited. His face was broad and tanned easily, while she has her mom's fair skin and delicate features.

"There's something...I can't quite put my finger on it." Lillian shakes her head. "Let's get you settled."

Rachel walks quickly toward the open passenger door of the Jeep and gets in. Tucker's revving the engine as if preparing for a getaway.

"Tucker, why don't you put Rachel's things in Nadine's room? I'll show our guest around."

Rachel gives Tucker a please-stay look. The chilling edge surrounding the words *our guest* remains frozen in the air. He squeezes her arm, as if to infuse her with strength—or push her out the door.

The sound of gravel under Rachel's shoes is like a shovel slowly filling up the silence as she follows Lillian up the driveway. She looks around, her eyes adjusting to the dim light from a lantern Lillian is carrying. "It's beautiful here, in a desolate kind of way," she says, and Lillian gives her a polite but measured smile. Rachel's gaze drops to the ground: red clay, strewn with straw-like patches of grass. They walk past rows of corn, vines of peas, and other low, leafy plants bulging from the ground. "It's a miracle anything takes root here," she observes.

"Miracle?" Lillian stops and swings the flashlight toward her, looks at her as if she suggested that the moon is made of green cheese. "We irrigate, till the soil, plant things with thick roots that can survive if there's no water for a few days or weeks. It's a lot of plain, old-fashioned hard work. Hardly qualifies as a miracle."

"I'm not much of a gardener," Rachel says, her face flushed with frustration and exhaustion. "The best I can do is geraniums and mums on our sliver of a balcony. I tried planting dahlias in a pot last year, but it was too early. The frost…" She pauses, but Lillian's not helping, just smiling like you might at a babbling toddler's long-winded explanation of how to make toast. How is she supposed to get through to this woman who's the only link she has to her father? This woman who has nothing to gain from reconnecting Henry with his former family. Why would she help her now?

Lillian reaches out to touch Rachel's cheek; it's like a shock of static electricity. "Your eyes, that's what it is," she says, holding the lantern up to Rachel's face. "Not the color, of course…but, yes, I do see a lot of Henry in you."

Rachel brushes her fingers against her cheek, as if tenderly nursing a wound. "Tell me…" she begins. What was the *look* in her father's eyes? She doesn't remember, doesn't know what the hell that even means. "What does qualify as a miracle?"

"Your father showing up here," Lillian says. "Now, that was close to a miracle."

"No," Rachel says sharply, the word breaking loose, rough and brittle, from somewhere deep in her soul. "Ten years after he snapped your photo in the church. Ten years, and he never forgot you." She clenches her jaw. He stayed here for nearly twenty years. Never once contacted his own daughter. Some fucking miracle.

"I never asked him to come to Kwizera," Lillian says.

"Kwizera." Rachel hears her father's twangy Florida accent. The word sounds magical, an exotic land he made up for a bedtime story. "What does it mean?" she asks, looking for a clue. What was her father looking for? What kept him here?

"Hope. Kwizera means hope." Lillian turns to walk up the driveway. There's no choice but to follow.

It's a good ten minutes before Rachel spots a single-story cement building painted bright yellow with a red tile roof. "That's the main house where most of the activity happens during the day," Lillian explains. "I only have four children living with me now, but there's a full house after school in the afternoon, usually until after dinner. Their mothers work in Kigali or Ruhengeri, or out in the fields trying to keep their small farms going."

"And their fathers?"

Lillian shakes her head. "Widows."

They stop in front of the house, lit up with lanterns on the front porch. Rachel returns the waves of a group of a dozen young children sitting on the steps around Tucker. He's lounging with his elbows propped onto the top step, legs kicked out in front of him. So comfortable. So at home. "One, two, three," he prompts and the children shout in unison, "*Muraho*, Miss Rachel. *Karibu!*"

Rachel returns their greeting, and thanks Tucker with a smile. The children stampede down the stairs and gather around but don't touch her, as if she's a museum piece. They're politely curious. "Madame, are you American? Do you have children? Will you stay long?" They keep glancing at Lillian, whose smile is completely transformed: soft and warm. Genuine.

"Everyone wash up for dinner, now," Lillian says, herding two of the boys back toward the porch. "Give our guest a chance to settle in. You'll have plenty of time for questions."

Alone with Tucker and Lillian on the porch, Rachel feels the tension between them. She should have insisted on staying in Ruhengeri. "So…" she says, drawing out the single syllable, rubbing her hands together, trying to summon something to say. Anything.

"The farmhouse," Tucker says, answering her non-question. He points toward a white, two-story bungalow separated from the main house by a stone path. "That's where you'll camp out."

"In my daughter's room," Lillian says.

Daughter? Rachel's heart skips a beat.

"Lillian is Nadine's legal guardian," Tucker adds quickly. "She's home from college for two months; it's the equivalent of our summer vacation. She's studying music in Nairobi. We're all proud of her."

"That's great." Rachel takes a deep breath. "Really great." Her mom might have been wrong about her father having an entirely new family. Lillian is Nadine's guardian, not him. She's not even sure he and Lillian are married.

There's a commotion inside the house: children shouting and laughing. A statuesque young woman with black hair lacquered into a ponytail appears at the front door, speaking to Lillian in Kinyarwanda. She whispers, as if embarrassed, cutting sideways glances at Rachel. Tucker jumps up. "Nadine, meet Rachel Shepherd. Henry's daughter."

Nadine bows slightly, and then returns her attention to Lillian.

"Gabrielle, one of the girls from town, has decided to give herself a haircut," Lillian explains, already on her way up the stairs. "Apparently, she could use some evening out in the back."

Rachel and Tucker are left standing outside, waiting, listening as the house quiets down. "You okay?" he asks.

Rachel shrugs. "It's a lot…for Lillian too, I suppose." Her head is buzzing with exhaustion, her mind racing with questions she has harbored during the past thirty years. Not to mention all the new ones cropping up. And, there's no indication that Lillian's going to answer any of them. She stumbles, her vision blurring.

"Whoa, easy." Tucker eases her over to the porch steps. "You sure you're okay?"

"Fine." Rachel places her hands on her knees, gives in to the buzzing, letting it grow louder than the questions. "I just need some sleep. The travel took a lot out of me."

"This country can take a lot out of you."

"What about Lillian?"

"Yeah, for sure. Living here all these years has taken a toll. She's not as strong as she makes herself out to be."

"But, why does she…" Hate me. That's the first thing that comes to Rachel's mind. "Well, she certainly doesn't want to talk about my father."

The sound of Lillian's voice rings out from inside the house. "Everyone gather round, Gabrielle's going to model her new hairdo. *Keza*, beautiful. Right?" There are murmurs of approval and clapping, a few whistles.

"Another crisis solved." Tucker grins, rakes a hand through his hair. "The thing is, once you get under Lil's skin, she'll help you. She will."

"What makes you so sure?"

"Because she wants what you want."

Rachel sits on the bottom step, looks up at Tucker, the buzzing louder. "Which is…?"

He laughs softly, like it's obvious. "You both want Henry to come home."

TUCKER LEADS RACHEL OVER TO the farmhouse. There's a trail of red begonias winding through a trellis that frames the front porch and two big wooden chairs on either side of the front door. "Lillian and Henry built this place a few years after he arrived, so they could take in more kids," Tucker explains. "Lillian sleeps downstairs. Up-stairs there are a few other rooms—mine, which I hardly ever sleep in, Nadine's, and then the door at the end of the hall leads to the attic."

It's comforting, seeing her familiar duffel bag in the simply fur-nished room where she'll sleep. There's a full-sized bed with a sat-iny purple quilt enveloped in mosquito netting, a small wicker dresser where she places the basket of sunflowers, and a desk under a picture window. She can barely make out the silhouette of the mountains against a starlit sky. The only things hanging on the pale green wall are a blue and orange Florida Gators baseball cap and a headdress made of long white and gray feathers.

A single photo, set in a wooden frame with hearts carved into it, is displayed on the bedside table. Rachel goes to take a closer look and sits heavily on the bed, trying not to crumple completely. *Dad.* Her throat closes around the word, knocking the breath right out of her.

"I'll put these flowers in water, and get you a tall glass," Tucker offers, but Rachel barely hears him. Her father is kneeling beside a younger version of Nadine, showing her a camera. A Brownie camera, like the one he gave her for Christmas. Was it when she was five? Six? Rachel looks up at Tucker, lips parted. There's something she's supposed to say; she can't imagine what that might be.

"I'll be right back." He hastily pulls a giant sunflower from the basket and places it on the bed beside her. "Don't go anywhere, okay?"

Rachel can't help but place herself in the picture frame. *Cricket, you just look through that little square window, point at some pretty flowers, and click the button. Being a photographer is as easy as pie.* She has a vision of the two of them spending entire afternoons at the Jacksonville Botanical Garden, her father snapping photos while she sat on a bench and wrote in her Nancy Drew journal. Had that actually happened?

"You and Nadine didn't get much of a chance to meet," Tucker says, placing a glass of water on the nightstand. "The haircut debacle and all. But, no doubt, you'll get along great."

"My father, the way he's looking at her—it's eerie."

"Must be weird, like déjà vu." Tucker sits beside her, the thick-stalked sunflower between them, to examine the photo. "Dahla and Enoch, Nadine's folks, lived here for years and helped out in dozens of ways. They bought a place of their own when Nadine was born, but she hung out here all the time. She grew up here."

"What happened to her parents?" Rachel asks. The pained look on Tucker's face is answer enough. People hiding in the river. Bodies stacked along the side of the road.

"Enoch grew up in Swaziland and came here by himself as a boy. He was so proud when he could finally pay for a house and some land of his own in a village on the other side of Mubaro," he says, his voice sounding faraway and strained. "Most of Dahla's family lived in a village in the south that was wiped out in the late eighties."

"Her entire family's gone?"

"We're her family now. Henry's the one who found her in town shortly after the Hutus came storming through the region."

Rachel studies the frame, running her finger over the indentation of a heart. He rescued her. "Were they close?"

"All the children thought he was cool. He was the fun one, while Lillian was stricter. Nadine felt safe with Henry, after all she'd been through." Tucker takes the photo and places it back on the table. "She started calling him Papa Henry. That says a lot about the guy, right?"

"Yes, it does," Rachel says dryly. Henry Shepherd did find a new family. He even found a daughter to replace her.

"Nadine didn't speak for about a month, just stuck to Henry like glue," Tucker continues. "I remember, he used to tell her and the rest of the kids these fantastical stories. That's how he took their minds off the gunshots echoing in the mountains and all they had lost."

Rachel clenches her jaw, setting loose a rumbling in her temples. *All they had lost, all they lost.*

"It was beyond horrible," Tucker says. "But Henry made them feel better, he did. You can be proud of your dad."

Rachel pinches the bridge of her nose, hunching forward so that her hair hangs over her face. *Stop talking, just stop…* It's absurd, ludicrous really, the way he's trying to comfort her and is only making things worse. Her stomach clenches against the fear that she'll laugh; Jesus, she may very well throw up. She wants to be proud of her father, wants to feel something for these children he took care of, rescued, made to feel safe. But all she feels is sick. She bites her lower lip until the shaking subsides, until she can—well, not look at Tucker—at least take a deep breath.

"Sorry, just tired," she says, rubbing her eyes, relieved as he takes the hint and gets up. She opens her eyes, the toxic laughter flushed out of her system, replaced with a hollow loathing. He's standing right in front of her, just standing there. Why? "You must think..." she says, her voice ragged. Why the hell doesn't he just leave? She's an awful person, they both know it. Jesus, jealous of orphans.

Tucker hands her the sunflower from the bed. "I think you're extremely brave coming here. Lillian will come around; give her a few days. For now, get some rest."

A shower and a fresh T-shirt later, the jet lag has transformed into something like the coffee-and-donut buzz after a late bartending shift, when Rachel's past the point of tired and may as well stay up a few more hours to see Mick off to work. She checks her phone out of habit, but of course it still doesn't light up. Her eyes dart from the unpacked suitcase next to the bed to the wicker dresser, but it seems invasive to open Nadine's drawers. Instead, she lies atop the purple quilt, hoping to tempt sleep, uncomfortable crawling under the covers in this room that clearly isn't hers. Her ears strain for the comforting sounds of home: the 24/7 drone of traffic and sirens, Mick's steady breath beside her, and the yip of her dog, Louie, if he hears anything remotely suspicious. There's always someone keeping guard while she's unconscious. Finally, she turns on a fan in the corner of the room and lets the whir-click-whir rhythm lull her into sleep.

EIGHTEEN

NADINE LIES ON A MATTRESS ON THE floor, Kingston's tail dangling within reach, and sings the lullaby her grandmother made up, passed down to Umama and then to her. Now, it is her gift to Rose. The murmur of Umama's low voice resonates in Nadine's chest and somewhere deeper, trickling into the vacant spaces that sometimes make her feel floaty and unreal. The tempo is slow and mournful, almost painful, similar to the Brahms violin sonata she chose to examine for music theory class. The great composer culled the tender notes from his soul, when there were no words to express his sorrow over the death of his godson.

She sings quietly, *"Holl amrantau'r sêr ddywedant, ar hyd y nos, 'Dyma'r ffordd i fro gogoniant, ar hyd y nos."* Sleep, my love, and peace attend thee all through the night; Guardian angels God will lend thee, all through the night. As a child, she had believed in angels. She had believed in God.

When she was a small girl, perhaps age three, Maman Lilly gave her a leopard with green glass eyes that was supposed to protect her while she slept. When did the stuffed animal disappear? No matter. She has stopped believing that anything outside of her body can be of any protection or comfort. Umama's lullaby is embedded deep within her, an essential organ that enables her to breathe and move her limbs, even when she is afraid.

At breakfast this morning, Madame Shepherd said that she came to find her father—or at least her memories of him. *Reclaim,* that's the word she used. As if her father took something that belonged to her, packed up these memories in a suitcase and spirited them away. Nadine can't quite connect the girlish woman who arrived last night, who seemed like she was trying to disappear—hands retracting into the big sweatshirt she wore today and long hair that hung in her face—as being Papa Henry's daughter. He had filled the room when he walked in. Why is Madame Shepherd here, not in London where Papa Henry is living? Why is it that she does not want to find *him*?

It doesn't take long for Rose's breath to become deep and even. Nadine tucks Kingston securely between the sleeping girl and the wall before leaving. Down the hall in the dark kitchen, Tucker's computer glows on the counter next to the phone. She crosses her fingers as she opens the laptop, hoping the screen isn't blue and lifeless. The Internet has only been available here since last summer and the connection, when there is one, is slow, the screen freezing up often, impossible to listen to music. Thankfully, the Google logo cheerfully greets her. She feels like a spy, deceitful and sneaky, typing "Rachel Shepherd" into the search box. But there are questions she can't ask anyone: Why is Papa Henry's daughter here for so long? Why now? Is he in trouble?

Why didn't Tucker or Maman tell her there would be a visitor for the entire holiday break? All she wants to do is relax and have fun with her family, not deal with a stranger living in her room.

Google comes up with some links to music reviews on a few e-zines that Nadine scrolls through. *The Violent Femmes. Nine Inch Nails. Death Cab for Cutie.* The names are playful and ghoulish. Intriguing, but not what she's searching for. She makes a mental note to read some of them later. A marriage announcement in the *New York Times* from three years ago doesn't provide any useful information, but the photo is interesting. Madame is wearing a pale blue dress, rather informal for her wedding day, holding a bouquet of lilacs and daffodils. She appears uncomfortable, standing beside her new husband in his formal tuxedo. There's a noticeable gap between them, even though his arm is around her waist.

One tap on a Geocities link springs open Rachel Shepherd's life, but her website isn't at all what Nadine expected. There are recipes for organic baby food, photos of infants in ridiculous Halloween costumes, and a section labeled "Tips for New Moms." Nadine puts a hand to her mouth. Rachel doesn't look pregnant, but perhaps it's the big sweatshirt she was wearing today. Is that why she wants to find Papa Henry, to tell him he's going to be a grandfather? She clicks on the section labeled, "Serena's Diary." There are entries for every day in September. *Today Serena did a double flip. Happy six-month birthday. Second sonogram today—looking good!* And then, after the first week of October the entries stop.

Nadine closes the laptop, her hand to her throat. After her family was murdered, she didn't speak for a month Maman tells her, although it felt longer. She stayed in her bedroom, listening to the rustle of the pines in the forest that seemed to cry for her; the fear had drained her of tears. Most of the people in her village were dead. It was being alive, not the deaths, that was somehow shocking. Her existence seemed to be an accident of fate, her life spent waiting in this room in Lillian's home, this room that was not hers. She was paralyzed, waiting for the inevitable correction.

She still misses her family's home in the foothills that rise on the other side of Mubaro from Kwizera. Umama's sister and her daughter, cousin Sylvia, had come to live with them before Nadine started primary school. Their village in the south had been taken over by the government, the rich land given to Hutus. Mubaro, a small town edging the rugged mountains, was far from the capital of Kigali. For decades, the Hutus had no use for the coarse land or the people. Many Tutsis lived there in peace. They were inferior to their Hutu neighbors, that was a given. Less education, lesser jobs, and forbidden to relocate without government permission. But at least their homes weren't burned down; their families weren't murdered as Sylvia's father and two brothers had been. And then, during the course of one week, the second week of April 1994, the entire village disappeared. The Hutus either joined the Interahamwe or fled the country, and the Tutsis were sent to the church.

One day after the killings at the church, Maman Lilly brought a fresh notebook and a pen to her room, both scarce, valuable gifts. She told her to start writing a song or a story; it needn't have anything to do with what had happened during the past month. Nadine chose to write an operetta: a short story set to music. It wasn't very good, mostly ideas taken from the book, *A Wrinkle in Time*, that she and Sylvia had read together many times. But she needed something to make tomorrow and the day after seem, if not hopeful, at least purposeful. Perhaps, she thinks now, coming here is Rachel's purpose for tomorrow.

RACHEL'S FIRST DAY IN RWANDA has been pretty much a bust, spent mainly hiding out in her room with the excuse of recovering from jet lag except for a walk around the grounds with Tucker and the three boys who live here. "Tomorrow," she resolves, climbing under the purple quilt. She won't even mention Henry Shepherd to Lillian, just offer to help out in the fields or with the children...wash windows. Something to make both of them feel like she somehow belongs here.

There's a clang in the hall and she jumps out of bed to open the door: Nadine is retrieving a spoon from the floor. "Madame, I'm so sorry," she says, rubbing the spoon with a napkin.

Rachel kneels to pick up the tray that holds a pot of tea and a mug, and a plate with a few cookies. "I was surprised, that's all," she says. "A nice surprise."

It's not much past eight o'clock but everyone goes to sleep, or at least heads to their rooms, right after dinner. The girl is dressed formally, her nearly black skin luminous against a crisp turquoise blouse tucked neatly into white pants. Rachel fingers the frayed edge of her own shirt, vaguely recalls dipping the sleeve in her dessert on the plane ride from London yesterday.

"*Karibu*," Nadine says, and bows. She looks at the tray in Rachel's hands. "For you, Madame Shepherd. You didn't eat much at dinner. I thought you might be hungry."

It strikes Rachel that this girl looks much older than a college student. She's beautiful: thin and statuesque, hair confined in a barrette at the nape of her neck. Nadine's intense dark eyes are trained on her, but not Spanish Inquisition-style like Lillian. More like she's trying to intuit the answer to a question too impolite to ask.

"*Murakoze*," Rachel says, taking the tray. "That's 'thank you,' right?" There's only one cup for tea, but Nadine's peering in the doorway—of course, this is her room. "Thanks for the snack and letting me use your room."

"*Sawa?* The room is okay?"

"More than *sawa*. Awesome."

"Awesome. I know this word from Tucker."

"He teaches you English?"

"*Yego*." Nadine's hand flies to her mouth. "I mean, yes."

"*Yego*," Rachel repeats slowly, filing the word away.

"Well, Tucker tries, but…" Nadine makes a sour face. "He says things like, jammin' and groovy. Does anybody really call their friend, *dude?*"

Rachel laughs. "Only in California."

"I think Tucker's stuck in a time machine."

"A time warp."

"Yes, quite. Precisely!"

Rachel goes to place the tray of food on the bedside table and glances at the photo of Nadine as a young girl, holding the camera. She's looking up at Henry Shepherd with wide-eyed amazement. *Twelve years old when her parents were murdered.* "I'm sorry," she says.

Nadine gives her a puzzled look.

"I mean, about taking over your space," Rachel says. "Would you like to come in?"

Nadine's eyes light up, but then she frowns at the floor.

"I feel silly, asking," Rachel continues. "I mean, it's your room."

"Well, I do need a few things." Nadine glides past. She opens the closet and pulls a sweater off the shelf above a row of mostly empty hangers. And then, she pulls out something that catches Rachel's eye.

"That's pretty."

"Ah, yes, my dreamcatcher." Nadine shows her a bowed circle of twigs covered with white and blue yarn. "Papa Henry made it for me," she says and then quickly adds, "It's yours if you like."

"No, that's okay, it's just..." Rachel looks at the web of sticks and yarn. *Native Americans, not Indians.* "My father helped me to make a dreamcatcher in the second grade, for school." It can't be the same one. But the four white feathers hanging from it look like the egret feathers she used to collect at the pond near their house.

Nadine holds the dreamcatcher up to the light, twirls it as she blows a cascade of dust particles into the air. The sight strikes Rachel as childlike. Magical. "I remember him telling me," she says, "something about it having special powers."

"Wards off bad dreams." Nadine shrugs. "Or some such thing."

Rachel watches the slowly twirling web, mesmerized. "No, it catches them, like a spiderweb..." *But instead of bugs it catches bad dreams, Cricket. The good ones slide down the feathers and right into your head while you sleep.*

"It's a nice story." Nadine places the dreamcatcher on the bed. "I prefer to keep the dreams away altogether. You keep this, Madame Shepherd, and sleep well. We'll talk more, yes?"

"Please, it's Rachel. And, yes—*yego*. I'd like to talk more."

"Awesome. Goodnight, my new friend."

"Goodnight," Rachel says. Could she and her brand new sort-of-sister really be friends? It seems more likely than her and Lillian winding up pals. And Tucker's nice enough, but he has some kind of agenda that she can't quite figure out.

Rachel places the faded twine and twigs, wrapped in a blue bandana, by her pillow and climbs under the sheet for the first time. She hugs the pillow to her chest, conjuring up her childhood bedmate, Old Gold. She used to hold the stuffed dog close to her cheek, pretending that it was him crying, concentrating on the soft swish of her lashes against synthetic fur instead of the muffled yelling from the kitchen downstairs. In the morning, picking out the marshmallow charms from her cereal, she would reassure herself that it was all only a dream.

The whir-click-whir of the fan crackles slightly. A downy feather pokes through the pillow and tickles her ear. *The bad dreams stay in the net and melt away when the sun comes up*, her father's voice whispers. *You'll never even know they were there.*

He gave her egret feathers and blue string… They made a campfire in the backyard, now she sees it clearly: flames low enough to toast hot dogs and marshmallows, and fireflies sparking the air. Her mom thought it was a silly idea to dig up the grass, but that only made it more fun. An adventure she shared with her father. What ever happened to the dreamcatcher they made, anyway?

The fireflies fade and the fan goes silent. Rachel slips into the dark place where she's not sure if she dreams or not. This has never mattered; it's not like dreams are real. But the next morning she wakes up with the sadness of something found and then lost, something that slipped away just before she opened her eyes.

NINETEEN

LILLIAN STOPS AT THE HALF-OPEN DOOR TO Rose's room, hearing Nadine's voice, and puts a hand to her chest as if to fill it with the sight of the two girls huddled together on the twin bed. She's missed this while her daughter's been away at school. On the floor is a mattress where Tucker usually sleeps when Rose is having a rough night. Nadine laid claim to it when she came home last week, and will probably sleep there for the entire two months she's here, until after the New Year.

"Go to sleep now, little one," Nadine half-sings, snapping pink barrettes onto the ends of a dozen tight braids. "You need to rest and get stronger. Tucker's orders."

"I've been in bed all day and yesterday, too." Rose sits up straight and shakes her head, the barrettes clacking together. "How can he expect so much sleep to come with no playing?"

Nadine clucks her tongue against the roof of her mouth. She pulls the hem of the quilt under the child's chin as if to seal her in bed. "Perhaps a lullaby will help," she says. "The one your Maman used to sing."

Lillian closes her eyes. The rich, low Kinyarwanda tones of her daughter's voice could be evoked directly from the reddish-brown Virunga soil and the mountains, now dark silhouettes against silvery clouds outside the window. It's a melody that Dahla sang to Nadine, but Rose doesn't need to know that. She doesn't need to know her own mother never had a chance to sing her a lullaby. It's bad enough the child has to deal with inheriting a legacy of AIDS, the Hutu militia's favorite weapon.

Rose settles into a cocoon of blankets, arms crossed over the one-eyed lion that rises and falls on her chest. Lillian remembers well when this tattered king of the jungle was brand-new. Each child receives the gift of a friend they can set next to their pillow to help ward off bad dreams and, sometimes, vivid memories worse than nightmares. These leopards, lions and elephants are comforting, like the tales passed down from parent to child, about animal spirits who act as powerful protectors. Lillian gave Kingston to Rose the first day she arrived, and the scraggly beast still stays right by her side. Tucker has stitched him up twice: last summer, his tail split during a tug-of-war between Rose and Zeke, and another time those crafty baboons nabbed him off the back patio and littered his stuffing across the backyard.

Lillian hears Tucker puttering in the kitchen. She walks briskly down the hall to make a cup of tea that will likely keep her up late. He's at the kitchen table, a slab of mahogany etched with the names of every child who has lived here, flipping through a medical journal a tad too fast to be reading. "The girls are waiting," she says, doling out a brief smile before turning her attention toward the stove to heat up the teapot. What else is she going to do, stay mad for another four days? Rachel's keeping out of her way, mostly trailing after Tucker or Nadine. And, to be fair, it's not so terrible having her around. When Rachel laughs, genuinely laughs loud and generous, Lillian hears a smattering of Henry. When she rolls her eyes and groans at her own corny jokes, something warm and familiar runs through Lillian, like the lullaby Naddie sings to comfort Rose.

Tucker squeezes Lillian's shoulders as he slides past. She reaches up to pat his hand, turns off the stove and follows him down the hall toward Rose's room. They'll talk later. She's still riled that he sent Henry's postcards to Rachel under false pretenses. The children come first; it's always been that way, the thing that bonded them right from the start.

Not long after Tucker first came here with Rose, he was back with two young boys. It broke her heart, telling him she couldn't take in any more orphans for a while. She and Henry had set a limit, even if twelve was an arbitrary number. Why not fifteen? Twenty? No, they agreed on two or three beds in each of the four bedrooms in the main house, two cribs at the most in the farmhouse. Twelve. Period. They could never truly do enough. She didn't see Tucker again until five months later, a week after the slaughter began, when he showed up on her front porch with Henry and Nadine in tow.

Lillian stops in the front hall, just a minute to make sure the front door is locked, and tells Tucker to go on ahead. She peers out the rectangle of double-paned glass in the door, into the darkness. Back then, she had peeled back a corner of newspaper stuffed into an empty frame, the glass smashed with the butt of a gun, before unbolting the lock. They all stood there, staring at each other like strangers. This couldn't possibly be happening. Tucker kept an arm around Henry, who was carrying a child so frail, her eyes vacant... This couldn't be Dahla and Enoch's precocious daughter. Lillian reached out to wipe a streak of dirt off the child's face. A nearly inhuman moan, feral and guttural, rose from Naddie's throat, a sound that still chills Lillian to the quick of her bones.

"I found them in town, on my way here to help," Tucker said. "Bodies everywhere, dead and alive. Nobody's helping."

"You are," Lillian replied, taking his arm to guide him inside. They walked through the dining room to the kitchen, stepping over teenagers curled up on the stone floor. There were so many kids that the older ones slept wherever they could find space, leaving the back bedrooms for the young ones to sleep two or three to a bed. It wasn't safe to walk to and from the farmhouse. Henry wouldn't look at her, but she smelled the fear—sulfuric and bitter—wicking off his body. She bit back her anger. *Why?* Why did he have to go into town yesterday with that damn camera? The anger felt good, better than the dread that had kept her up all night.

Henry settled Nadine at the kitchen table. She stared at the cookie from a near-empty tin that Lillian placed in front of her along with a cup of watery powdered milk. The way that child clung to Henry's hand was unsettling, the way he stood right beside her, both of them with arms taut. It was as if the flow of blood through their veins depended on maintaining that bond. As Lillian thinks back, it was probably only a few minutes she stood at the stove that no longer heated up, helplessly watching the two of them, but the silence seemed endless. And then, a baby's cry rang out from the back of the house. A flash of panic crossed Tucker's face.

Lillian went to get Rose from her crib in the gathering room, and placed the squirming baby into the cradle of Tucker's arms. A smile melted the grim lines on his face and lit a glimmer of hope in her. "Our girl's safe here," she said, not at all sure that was true even though the Hutu soldiers who came to ransack her fields had assured her they had no interest in her bastard children. "We're all safe."

A SMILE TUGS AT LILLIAN's lips as she enters Rose's room. Tucker is muscling his way in between the girls on the twin bed against the wall. He's become like a son to her. How in the world is she supposed to stay mad?

"Hey, how are my two favorite princesses?" he inquires. Nadine elbows him playfully as she inches over to make room.

"I'm good," Rose pipes up.

Tucker brushes his fingers against her forehead. "Nice and cool, that is good."

"No hospital?"

"Nope, that's only for sick people. You'll be back at school in another few days."

"And no needles."

"Now, I didn't say that. I need to draw some blood to take to Ginny, that smart doc in London who's helping you to get better. Just a vial, maybe two."

Rose huffs out a sigh, rolling her eyes toward Nadine.

"He does enjoy being a nuisance and poking people," Nadine whispers loudly around Tucker's back, glancing clandestinely toward Lillian. "It's why he became a doctor, *yego*?"

Tucker grabs Rose's pillow and feigns surprise when Nadine

snatches it away, swiftly swatting him. He uses Rose, who's giggling and clutching Kingston to her chest, as a shield. "Hey, Lil, help out a poor outnumbered guy, wouldja?" he pleads.

"How is anyone supposed to sleep with this ruckus, right, Rosie?" Lillian takes the pillow from Nadine and returns it to the rightful owner. She nods at Tucker: yes, all is forgiven.

Tucker and her daughter have always jousted like this. It's how he coaxed her back from the darkness. After the church massacre, she wouldn't play with the other children, always sticking close by Henry's side. He was Naddie's protector, while Tucker was the court jester, cajoling her traumatized soul into being a thirteen-year-old kid again, even if only for a few moments of exchanging jokes. Now, the two of them clown around to help Rose forget that she's stuck in bed for sometimes weeks at a time.

"It's nice having you back home," Lillian says, wrapping her arm around Nadine as they leave Tucker to settle Rose into sleep. "Sorry if I'm hovering, but I enjoy taking in every moment you're here. It's a mother's right to hover, you know."

Nadine laughs softly, her breath warm against Lillian's cheek as she deposits a kiss. "I've only been gone a short while. Besides, Nairobi's not so far away." Nadine hums Rose's lullaby as they walk outside onto the front porch. Lillian leans over the thick wooden rail, her face tilted toward the night sky. She and Dahla sat out here many evenings, Dahla rocking her baby to sleep. Lillian got in the habit of reciting a Kinyarwandan prayer to the heavens above. "Lord," she says now, "may my children have the peace in their sleep that is not always possible during waking hours." This nightly ritual honors the memory of her friend, a moment that harnesses all the children of Rwanda—living and dead—

in a prayer. "*Amahoro*," Lillian says, eyes on the daughter she and Dahla share. Peace in Kinyarwanda. Amen.

"Look, the crocodile is out tonight, still chasing after the elephant whose eye is the North Star," Nadine whispers, as if trying not to disturb the twinkling animals outlined against the blue-black sky. She clucks her tongue. "When will the poor fellow learn?"

"And there's Kingston's big paw." Lillian points to the east. "Swatting at the moon so he can turn out the light and get some shut-eye."

"Papa Henry's ridiculous stories…" Nadine tips her head against Lillian's shoulder.

"Your stories, too," Lillian says. The two of them would sit for hours on these steps, wrapped in a single blanket, Nadine—or possibly both of them—mistrustful of sleep. Lillian sat in a wooden chair by the door and listened to their banter about the jungle animals twinkling above.

"The night Papa Henry left, I sat here alone and looked for a story in the sky," Nadine says dreamily. "I imagined him riding on the back of the elephant. I knew he would be gone a long time, and I was thankful he was in the company of the largest and wisest animal. I felt certain the elephant would take care of him."

Lillian wraps an arm around her daughter, remembering the night in mid-July when Henry told her he was leaving. The Tutsi-led Rwandan Patriotic Front had surrounded Kigali and the fighting was winding down. They were celebrating with neighbors. They all pooled their meager canned supplies, courtesy of the Red Cross, for a stew: chipped beef, tomatoes, carrots, and onions. It was, at the time, a feast after three months of boiled potatoes and flat, tasteless teff bread cooked over a fire in the yard.

After dinner, Henry drank banana beer and laughed with the men as if nothing was wrong. He washed the dishes while she dried, and together they tucked the children into their beds. After that, he packed his rucksack and left. Not a word for four months, when the phone lines were up and running again and he finally called from London.

Lillian pulls Nadine closer, listening to her hum as they both gaze at the stars. *I'm sorry, Lilly. I'm not as strong as you are.* It was Henry's pat explanation, and she had always accepted it. It had never been easy living here. The injustice. The disease. The heat. It's why he left every few months, even when he didn't have an assignment. He could only handle so much. They both knew it. She was stronger. What he never fully realized was that she drew on him for her strength. She depended on him. Nadine depended on him too.

"You knew," she says, squinting up at the sky. It still amazes and confuses her, the way Nadine wasn't a bit upset when Henry left or when he didn't show up for Rahim Kensamara's trial. "You knew he wasn't coming back."

Nadine shrugs. "My Zulu grandfather came to visit from Swaziland when I was quite small. He told me that his tribe believes the bull elephant's tusks are wisdom sticks, holding knowledge of the future. They believe the males know when it's their time to roam alone, and when it's time to come back to the herd. Papa Henry will return, but it hasn't been his time yet." She takes Lillian's hand, pulling her down the porch steps, to end the conversation Lillian suspects.

She follows her daughter across the yard, in no hurry to retire and be alone with her own thoughts, happy to listen as Nadine bounces from one subject to another: when to plant dahlias in her Christmas garden, the opera she's composing, what classes to take next semester. A girl in her jazz theory class, she's from Sudan, is nice and they recently went out to dinner at an Indian restaurant—a first for both of them. Perhaps she'll invite her to Kwizera for the holiday next spring. They could share a flat next year. Lillian rubs her arms as an uncomfortable thought crawls along under her skin. Nadine may need to miss next semester altogether if she's subpoenaed to testify at a trial. She's left two messages at the International Tribunal office in Kigali for Valeria Ogoni, the attorney who's been calling Nadine at school. Why the deputy prosecutor hasn't already issued a subpoena is a puzzle, but also a blessing. Maybe if she hears from another adult that Nadine doesn't remember anything about the massacre, she'll leave her alone.

They walk along the perimeter of the vegetable garden which butts up against a dirt soccer field. Lillian stops to adjust the bow tie of a button-grinned scarecrow that was more of an art project for the kids than any real deterrent to the birds and monkeys. "Naddie, we should talk about the trial," she says.

"There's nothing to discuss," Nadine replies curtly. "I don't remember any more now than I did two years ago." She clucks her tongue, bending to pull a large weed. "Looks like I have my work cut out for me before returning to school."

"The garden could certainly use your touch," Lillian agrees. It's not her call to press Naddie, to decide what she does or doesn't remember.

What Lillian will never forget is sitting next to the shaking seventeen-year-old girl at the high-profile trial of Rahim Kensamara and six other men. They were accused of serving as precinct leaders in the Hutu military, hired by the government to recruit eight or ten locals who would cleanse each of their villages of Tutsis. Nadine sat beside her, stiff and quiet, in the packed courtroom in Arusha, eyes fixed on

her hands, folded in her lap. She seemed oblivious to the witnesses
who took the stand: several Hutu women verified that Kensamara
and the others had recruited their husbands with the promise of great
pay and a plan to exterminate thousands of Tutsis from the region in
a matter of days. And then, an elderly Tutsi man from a town not far
from Mubaro told how he and his neighbors went to the church with
suitcases, lured by a supposed messenger of the priest with the promise of a safe haven. They were met by their Hutu neighbors wielding
machetes, guns, broken bottles and boards studded with nails.

"Why don't you ask the children to help with harvesting these overgrown squash and yams before the market on Saturday?" Lillian says.

"We'll make it fun." Nadine kisses both of her cheeks, the trial
seemingly forgotten, but they both know that's not true. It breaks Lillian's heart, seeing how hard her daughter's trying to be light and gay.
They'll invite the children from town, and have prizes for the fullest
baskets but every child gets some kind of reward.

"That sounds nice, sugar." Lillian feels her daughter's pulse in the
trembling hand, warm and moist, on her arm.

"I'll invite Tucker, of course," Nadine adds. "And Rachel, yes?"

Lillian bites back a sigh.

They walk back toward the house, and Nadine returns to the mer-
its of composing the music to her opera before the words. Perhaps
she'll take a drama class next semester instead of all music electives.
"Maman, what do you think?"

"Well, let's go over the pros and cons of each," Lillian suggests to
get her talking. Meanwhile, her mind sticks on the trial in Arusha two
years ago. When the priest from the church in Mubaro walked up to
the stand and swore on a bible to tell the truth, he looked straight at

Nadine. The child didn't look up but clutched Lillian's hand so tightly her fingers went numb. When it was Naddie's turn to testify, she froze. Her daughter seemed to leave her body, and Lillian imagined she had gone back to the nightmare of the massacre. She'll call again, first thing tomorrow, and every day until she gets through to Valeria Ogoni. There's no way she's putting her daughter through that again.

"You needn't worry," Nadine says, as if reading Lillian's mind. "School is good. I have my friends, my music. I'm happy."

"I'll always worry about you," Lillian says. She sent Nadine to a private high school in Uganda to keep her away from the ugliness after the genocide and then, thankfully, there was the scholarship to Nairobi. But she can't protect her daughter forever. "Mother's prerogative."

"Maman…" Nadine turns quiet.

Lillian stops and offers her full attention.

"Maman, I like having a friend here too."

"Rachel." Lillian has seen them talking on the porch, kicking around the soccer ball with the children. She assumed Naddie was merely being polite, entertaining her. "You two are friends?"

"I'm teaching Rachel to speak Kinyarwanda, and she teaches me what American teenagers say. What's cool."

"You're helping each other."

"Sometimes," Nadine says hesitantly, "I tell her about Papa Henry. Is that all right?"

"Yes, of course."

"We both miss him, Maman."

"Of course," Lillian says. It hadn't occurred to her that Rachel Shepherd might be able to help her daughter in some way.

AFTER NADINE RETURNS TO ROSE'S room to sleep, Lillian climbs the stairs to the attic. She keeps her flashlight trained on a silver glint in the back corner as she crosses the room. She kneels and runs her hand lovingly over the dented topside of the bulky metal suitcase. The lock is broken, and the handle fell off somewhere on the bus ride between Nairobi and Kigali, years ago. This old thing has carried a lot of weight over the years.

She snaps open the suitcase and carefully removes the purple tunic. Her wedding dress is light and airy on her palms, as if it might float away. She scans the items underneath: onyx candlestick holders, one with a walnut-sized chip in the base, which they used only on special occasions. A tattered gold-threaded silk scarf that Henry bought for her in Morocco. A crumpled poster of Van Gogh's Starry Night from the New York Museum of Modern Art that Henry insisted on keeping. A mancala board, the green and blue marbles missing, that they kept in the bedroom along with a scorecard of who was the reigning champion. These are the things they salvaged when the Hutus destroyed their home during the slaughter. The rest of it—broken dishes and pottery, splintered furniture limbs, the rugs soaked with urine and beer—could all be repaired or replaced.

Her hands shake as she removes a brown leather album, flips through the pages of photos, taking note of the yellowed cellophane slots where the postcards had been. There's a brief note on the back page: *Cricket, I think of you often on my travels. This album is for you.*

The words blur as Lillian reads and rereads the brief note. She closes her eyes, but the words are still there. On the night Henry left, he told her to mail this album to his daughter, an afterthought after he had packed it in the rucksack along with his camera bag and a few items of clothing. "It's better that you send it, even if you have to wait a few months until the post office in Mubaro is open again," he said. "You'll send it, Lilly." Tucker wasn't wrong to mail the postcards to Rachel, Lillian concedes that now. And she wasn't wrong to hang onto this album that didn't belong to her. It was a show of faith that Henry would return and mail it himself. At least, at first.

She closes the suitcase and places her palms flat on the cool metal. Mama had packed it with sweaters and thick socks for the snowy winter in Cleveland, where her sister's family lived. Lillian sat on her bed and looked past her mother, out her bedroom window at the stark branches of a beech tree in the front yard. She'll never forget that night; it was the first time she felt her baby kick, the happiest and saddest moment of her life. She knew he was a boy, would be strong and proud like his father. How would she give up her last remaining piece of Samuel?

Early the next morning, before her flight, she crammed into the suitcase a few books, her diary and a favorite pen, a shoebox filled with letters from Samuel, and a bottle of cologne that smelled like Mama. She was never coming back to her parents' house, would take her baby somewhere far away, somewhere safe where they didn't need much money to get by. She hung onto this plan until she awoke in the hospital three months later, her baby gone, her womb still and cold. "Your healthy baby boy is with his new parents," the nurse said cheerily. "You're so brave, miss, giving him to a family who can raise him right."

Brave. Lillian rubs at the dullness of a deep dent in the suitcase. She can never take in enough children, can never give enough of herself to them, to make up for not finding the courage to keep her child. So then, why can't she help the child Henry gave up?

TWENTY

SUNRISE ISN'T A TIME OF DAY RACHEL'S ENtirely familiar with, except sometimes passing Mick in the kitchen as she drinks chamomile tea to coax sleep, still jittery from work, and he's brewing his first cup of coffee before jumping into the shower. Now, she rolls over toward the window to admire pale pink fingers of daylight spreading over the banana field, both missing and not missing the constant drone of traffic on the streets below her Soho loft. New York has an artificial 24/7 day, no downtime, always something exciting going on whether she's restless at two p.m. or two a.m.

Over the past week, her body has become in tune with nature's cycle of night and day. There's not much to do after the sun goes down and the electricity is switched to "conserve" mode, so sleep comes early and easily after reading or writing in her journal. Sometimes, like this morning, she awakens with a hand on her stomach, searching for Serena turning somersaults. The ache was allayed by the predawn exuberant *wahoo-wahoo* chant of the male baboons in the forest. She stayed awake to listen to the symphony of birds that ushers in the first light of day. They all sound different, and she's determined to figure out their names. "Cu-coo-ah, cu-coo," she mimics. This one might stump Nadine, who has an incredible ear. A musician's ear. It's amazing how she spots birds the same color as the leaves, by their warble or whistle, before they take flight overhead.

THE SKY TURNS FROM PINK to orange, to bright blue, within a matter of minutes. Rachel stretches lazily. There's still plenty of time before the bakery in town that sells thick espresso and melty beignets opens at eight or eight-thirty. She opens the nightstand drawer to retrieve the journal dating back to months before coming here, and flips through early sparse recollections of her father that she had wanted to pass on to Serena.

Now, the notebook is nearly filled with details about Henry Shepherd. He has become almost a mythical character, this buccaneer who took Nadine and her cousin Sylvia on a camping trip into the mountains in search of rare golden monkeys, and taught them how to chat with the gorillas through grunts and gestures. Henry Shepherd helped to turn a rundown farm into a home in a hundred different ways; this much Lillian would share with her. Tucker has great stories about the two of them sharing beers with a local shaman for a year before the village elder finally agreed to teach them how to distill medicine from leaves, flowers and tree bark.

Mister American's daughter. That's what the people in town call her.

Everyone seems to have known the white man with the camera. They stop her on the street to reminisce about their friend with the big guffaw of a laugh who always had a story about some big adventure he had gone on or was planning. *Henry Shepherd.* Rachel can't reconcile this larger-than-life persona with the details that are shading in her own memories of her father: a quiet man who rarely smiled. He was usually gone before she got up in the morning. After dinner, she would peer out the kitchen window at his silhouette in the dark, or sometimes drag a blanket out to the yard and lie down on her back, next to his lawn chair, both of them staring up at the stars. It seemed forbidden to speak to him. He was there but he wasn't—like now.

Be patient. That's what everyone keeps telling her. But how long is she supposed to wait for Lillian to show her something more than the fence Henry must have mended a thousand times? How the hell long is she supposed to wait for her father to show up? He must have picked up the letter Tucker sent before she arrived. He must know she's waiting for him.

The light streaming through the open window turns bright. Rachel shoves the notebook under her pillow, throws an arm over her eyes as if sleeping, and listens to the sound of twittering giggles coming from the other side of the door. She imagines Rose and Zeke daring each other with seven-year-old bravado: *Go ahead, open it!* The door creaks open and she lets loose with a roaring yawn, stretching arms over her head, setting off a burst of laughter and the scurry of small feet running down the hall. Rose is braver than her friend, but not by much. The tiny girl dressed in a clean but faded pink dress, a cascade of braids falling to her shoulders, takes a half-step into the room. She clutches a tattered lion to her chest.

"Good morning, Rose. It's nice to see you and Kingston."

"*Jambo*, Madame," she whispers, eyes wide, chin on the lion's bright orange mane.

"I'm glad you're feeling better." Rachel swings her legs out of bed. Rose claps a hand over her mouth, laughter escaping through her nose, eyes darting from Rachel's T-shirt to the floor.

"I agree, pretty silly." Rachel stands so Rose can take a better look at Scooby-Doo, stretching the T-shirt down over Mick's pajama bottoms. "Scooby's been my favorite cartoon since I was even younger than you."

"Scooby?"

"That's this crazy pup's name."

Rose comes closer to see. Rachel notices bruises on her wrist, no doubt left from a needle too large for the twig-like veins. The last time she saw Rose, a few days ago, she was in bed hooked up to an IV. She reaches out to snap shut a loose barrette, her hand landing lightly on the girl's shoulder. "Scooby's a detective, but not nearly as brave as Kingston. Your buddy looks like he's been through a lot."

"He has the name of a lion Nadine's grandfather once knew," Rose says. "He was a hunter, but Kingston was his friend."

"Friends with a hunter? Must be a special lion."

"Yes, quite. He protects the animals in the forest who are not so big and need his help."

"Sounds like a good buddy to have on your side." Rachel pats the one-eyed beast's lumpy head, noticing where it has been sewn up at least once. "I bet he's had a lot of adventures in his day. I'd love to hear about how he lost his eye."

"That would make a fine bedtime story tonight," Lillian chimes in from the doorway. How long has she been standing there, watching, Rachel wonders, retracting her hand from Rose's shoulder. She steps aside as Lillian enters. Rose practically sprints down the hall upon hearing the news that it's time to get ready for school.

"It's her first day back in over two weeks," Lillian explains. "She'll go for months without a flare-up but then..." She pulls up the quilt on the bed and fluffs the pillow in one motion. "Well, it's no way to be a child."

Rachel feels like a kid herself, in oversized pajama bottoms and a cartoon T-shirt, watching Lillian tug a wrinkle out of the quilt. "You don't have to do that," she says, and then grabs her sweatshirt at the foot of the bed before Lillian can tuck it neatly into a dresser drawer. She hugs the sweatshirt to her chest. "I'm sorry, that came out wrong." It's all wrong, everything she says and does—even her clothes. Jeans are way too heavy; why didn't she think to bring a skirt? Lillian stands hands-on-hips and frowns at the bed, trying to scare the wrinkles out of the quilt, no doubt. She settles on smoothing her earth-tone batik skirt that match a forest green T-shirt, nearly the same outfit as in the newspaper photo from more than a decade ago. Her face is more deeply lined now, but not much, her hair still far more black than gray. Rachel admires how she doesn't wear a speck of make-up, so unlike her mom.

Merilee was insecure about her looks, as if that's all she had to offer and it wasn't enough, even after she came home "empowered" from the EST training in San Francisco the summer after her husband left. For years, Rachel thought EST was a religion her mom had joined, no men allowed. Merilee kept saying she *had* to divorce Henry; she didn't want to but it wasn't a choice.

Lillian's eyes dart around the room, and then she closes them briefly as if to reset something in her head. "I clean, it's what I do," she says, sitting on the edge of the bed, her gaze dropping to hands clasped in her lap. "Some people eat, or talk too much. I clean."

Rachel slips into the sweatshirt and fumbles with the zipper. Nervous? The Lady of Steel? Around *her*? The thought is like a crack of light under a heavy door she can't figure out how to open. "It could be worse," she mumbles into her collar and takes a seat next to Lillian. "I laugh—the more nervous I am, the louder it gets. So embarrassing."

"It has occurred to me that you possess an incredibly broad sense of humor."

Rachel glances up. Did the Lady of Steel crack a joke?

"You are funny," Lillian continues matter-of-factly. "Rose obviously thinks so. I also see your kindness with the children. I appreciate how difficult it may be, being here so soon after losing your baby."

"No, it helps." Rachel places a hand on Lillian's arm, without thinking, and then it's too late to take it back. Lillian pats her hand before getting up to dust off the dresser with her kerchief. It hits Rachel that she does consider them all her children, not just Nadine. As much as she still misses Serena, maybe Lillian feels that same way about every orphan who has ever lived in this house. About Henry Shepherd. "Thank you, for letting me stay," she says.

"My daughter enjoys having you here."

"I'm glad we've become friends."

Lillian turns from the dresser. "Nadine could use a friend."

Rachel sees the struggle on her face. Yes, it's difficult having her here as a constant reminder that the man she loves is gone. And, yes, she wants her to stay. She'll do it for her daughter.

"Since you'll be here a while longer," Lillian says, "we need to have an understanding."

"Anything."

"I can't go after him."

"But he'll come here."

"There's a good chance he won't."

Rachel rubs her left temple to stop the rumbling. Hearing the words she has thought, has feared, sets off an avalanche of questions. "He must know I'm here, right? Why wouldn't he come back?"

"He stayed here for as long as he could."

"Why did he leave?"

"I think the brutality became too much for him. There wasn't anywhere to turn away from it, so he left. I can't fault him for that."

"But you do blame him. For what?"

"I only asked him to come home once," Lillian says. "Two years ago, there was a trial in Arusha, Tanzania for the man responsible for the murder of Nadine's family and many others at the church. It was one of the first trials conducted by the International Tribunal for genocide criminals. Nadine was subpoenaed but couldn't go through with testifying. She was terrified and could have used Henry's support."

"He never showed up," Rachel says. Not for Lillian. Not for Nadine. Why would he show up for her?

Lillian shakes her head slowly, her face seemingly aging, the lines deepening. "I'm sorry. I can't go chasing after him again."

"I understand," Rachel says. She understands that it's up to her to find her father, a man who obviously doesn't want to be found. Either that, or go home.

A FEW DAYS LATER, NADINE awakens Rachel, coaxing her out of bed with a mug of coffee. "There's no time for breakfast before we leave," she says.

Rachel groans, still mostly asleep. "Leave?" The birds haven't even fully tuned up yet.

"We'll eat at the market. Lillian's gone ahead in the Jeep to find a good spot."

Rachel takes a few sips of coffee and then jumps out of bed, pleased that Nadine—maybe Lillian, too—actually wants her to come along.

Walking to the market on a Saturday morning is an event in itself, Rachel notes as Nadine grabs her hand and weaves through the crowd lining the main road: women with baskets of fruit and water gourds balanced on their heads on crowns of thatch; men pushing wheelbarrows piled with grains, tea leaves, and coffee beans; a handful of brave bicyclists ringing bells. She pulls at the waistband of the skirt Nadine lent her, a bit too snug but way better than jeans and nobody even seems to notice she's wearing black high-top sneakers, which she'll swap out for stiff new sandals once they get to the market. Nadine seems almost proud, stopping to introduce her to people she knows. "Meet my *inshuti* from New York." Friend. It's the first time Rachel feels like she fits in here.

A boy with a thin scar across his forehead nods tentatively as he approaches. Nadine looks through him, so unlike her. Rachel glances over her shoulder as they pass and watches the boy disappear into the crowd. "Before the genocide, we were best friends," Nadine says. "I lost many friends, both Hutu and Tutsi."

The road ends at a dusty field where people are setting up tables and spreading out blankets, staking out their territory at the market.

Rachel is swept up in the carnival of activity, unloading Lillian's Jeep and arranging baskets of the week's harvest on a card table she recognizes from many games of mancala in the gathering room at Kwizera. More and more vendors, mostly women, show up with colorful pyramids of fruit, beaded jewelry, spices, straw brooms and bamboo rugs, woven reed baskets of all sizes, embroidered blouses and batik skirts, carved mahogany boxes, and sticky beignets that pacify little ones while their mothers shop.

The marketplace fills up within the hour, people bargaining fast and furious. A young girl passes by carrying a bolt of magenta and gold batik cloth on her head, and sets it down amidst a rainbow of fabrics on a nearby table. "I've never seen quite that shade of purple," Rachel says, wishing she knew how to sew.

"It's from Egypt." Lillian plucks a few brown leaves from a bucket of dahlias. "Too expensive, if you ask me."

It doesn't take long before the baskets on the table are empty and Lillian goes to buy supplies. Rachel notices a group gathering at the end of the square, under a tall, knotty acacia tree. There's a man in a suit handing out flyers and answering questions.

"He's come from Kigali to explain the *gacaca* trials," Nadine says. "Our leaders have decided there are too many people in jail, too many murderers to ever prosecute them all in the slow government courts. Many of the judges and attorneys were killed during the genocide or fled to other countries. So, now the new president has a plan. Local judges will be elected, and then communities will gather to tell what they remember and pass judgment on their neighbors. There will be some test cases to see how it works, in Mubaro and several other provinces."

"Six years…" Rachel notices a woman balling up the flyer and tossing it on the ground as she walks away. "That's a long time to wait for justice."

"Most of us don't expect justice, not really."

"Then, what?"

"The goal of the *gacaca* is reconciliation and forgiveness."

"Letting go of the past."

"Not so much letting go as finding a way to live with it."

By late morning, everyone is packing up. Lillian counts and re-counts the money in a satchel tied around her waist. "Maybe I can get a few last-minute bargains," she says, eyes on a man hauling sacks of rice into his truck.

"Let me." Rachel reaches for the nylon pouch under her T-shirt. Lillian flicks a hand toward the money—nonsense, she couldn't possibly—and walks away.

"She really does want that purple fabric," Nadine confides. "Next week, we'll come back and buy some. She'll accept it as a Christmas gift from both of us."

Rachel snaps shut the pouch. Why does it sting so, the way Lillian still treats her like a guest? "Thanks for the tip," she says.

"It's cool, dude."

Rachel laughs. "Dudette. That's the official female terminology."

"Okay then, *inshuti*, we will be the dudettes of Kwizera. *Sawa?*"

Rachel nods. Very *sawa*.

AFTER LUNCH, WHEN EVERYONE HAS finally cleared out of the kitchen, Rachel sits at the counter for a while longer before dialing the phone. It's six hours earlier in New York, so Mick's probably home from racquetball by now. To her surprise, this phone call was Lillian's suggestion on the way back from the market. Her husband answers on the second ring. He sounds so close, just across town in his office.

"It's nice to hear your voice," he says.

"Really?"

"Really."

"I still feel terrible—"

"No need."

Rachel sighs. Maybe they both needed some distance. A little time.

"So. How's the search for your dad going?" Mick asks.

"Good," Rachel chirps, and then rushes to ask what she's missed during the past week. *Sure, the search is going just great, money well spent.* Her father hasn't even called and Lillian flat-out refused to help find him. She presses the phone to her ear while Mick gives her the highlights: three new clients, a garbage strike, and a snowstorm that's expected by Christmas. It's all so mundane; it sounds wonderful.

"How are things on the homefront?" she asks. Suddenly, she'd give anything to be calling to ask him to pick up fresh pasta and a bottle of wine from Balducci's for dinner. Six weeks now seems like too long to be away. "How's Louie?"

"Crazy mutt's been hanging out by the front door a lot. Waiting for you to come home, I guess."

"Nice to know I'm missed." Rachel waits a beat before asking about Thanksgiving. Mick has always spent the holiday with his family while she went to Jacksonville to eat turkey with Merilee.

"Ma had a big spread, the whole gang was there except for Aunt Irene and her kids. Baltimore was snowed in."

A pit forms in Rachel's stomach as he goes on about how, two days later, he's still stuffed. She was homesick, missed her mother so, on what was just another day here. Not even a mention of the holiday, except Lillian's declaring it an abomination, a celebration of the slaughter of the Indian Nation that she doesn't miss one bit. "I could come home early, for Christmas," she says. "It could be nice, just the two of us."

Mick laughs. "Yeah, right, like Ma would let us miss Christmas."

"Right," Rachel says. *Miss* Christmas? "I was thinking more like renting a cabin in Vermont and making angels in the fresh snow." She pauses, giving him a chance to chime in, and then continues haltingly, "We could buy a Charlie Brown tree. One that needs a home. String popcorn. Dried cranberries." Make paper heart ornaments with single word wishes written in green and red magic marker. Peace. Snow. Chocolate. Joy. Baby.

"Sounds nice, but…" Mick's voice fades into a silent no. "Keep me posted if you change your flight."

The phone is warm and moist against Rachel's cheek. "I should hang up," she says. "I don't want to…" Cry. Yell. "…rack up Lillian's phone bill."

"Ray, wait a sec."

She takes a sharp breath.

"I hope you find what you're looking for, I do. I'm just trying to get on with my life, too."

Rachel's knuckles are white against the receiver for long moments after hanging up. Time seems to stop and rewind. *Ray, wait. I miss you. Come home.* That's all it would have taken for her to book a flight on the next plane. But her husband didn't say that.

RACHEL HEADS BACK INTO TOWN, despite the stagnant mid-afternoon heat that has sent everyone else indoors for a few hours. The streets are nearly deserted except for the soldiers standing on corners, wearing green fatigues and bored expressions. The first few times she walked through town alone, she quickly passed by the soldiers, head down. Now, she meets their eyes, returns a proffered smile or else simply nods. A few exchange the local greeting with her: *Amahoro*. Peace.

There's a hole-in-the-wall shop, down the street from the bakery, that rivals the collections of kitsch at the thrift shops near her loft in Soho. It has tables laid out with everything from piles of tennis shoes to plastic dolls with too-red lips, to basic art supplies. It's a respite from the sun. She takes her time, filling a basket with loose crayons—pennies each—for Rose and Zeke, an unopened box of felt-tip pens for Nadine, a cool pen/flashlight for Thomas and one for Robert, and a new notebook since her journal is nearly filled. An idea forms as she stuffs these treasures into her backpack, and then plucks other items from the tables: colored notecards, silver tacks, and a thick black Sharpie marker. Her final purchase is a corkboard, so large she carries it with both hands, like a shield, back to Kwizera.

Later, after everyone has turned in for the evening, she sits on the floor of her room with the notecards and a pen, surrounded by the postcards her father never mailed, the transparent globe with his footprints in the snow, the animal necklace he sent for her thirteenth birthday, and the nearly filled journal, flipped to the beginning. She writes down snippets of memories on notecards with dates, and then tacks them onto the blank corkboard, which is propped up on the desk under the window with its view of the mountains.

She moves the postcards, notes and photos around, one way and another, trying to grout together a father she can love even if he doesn't show up. By the time the wick of the lantern is nearly burnt down to the quick, the corkboard is a haphazard timeline with too many empty spaces she can't fill in. Too much time has been lost.

There's a tap on Rachel's door. "I saw the light," Nadine says. She offers a tray with biscuits and two cups of tea. "I hope you don't mind."

Rachel opens the door wide. "Come in—please."

Nadine studies the corkboard on the desk for a few minutes, and then goes across the hall to Tucker's room, where she's been sleeping. She returns with an armload of framed photos and arranges them carefully on the bedside table, as if setting each one in its rightful place.

Rachel sits on the bed to examine the photos. She's drawn to a girl with braids who is smiling up at a statuesque young woman with short, smoothed-back hair. They look so happy, holding hands. And yet there's something foreboding about the photo, the sun filtering through the trees behind them, casting a net of shadows. "You and your mother?" she asks.

Nadine nods. "I was twelve. It was right before Umama died."

"You look a lot like her." Rachel takes her wallet from her purse and pulls out an old photo of Merilee, before the cancer settled into her skin. "My mom died last summer."

"She's quite pretty."

"People say I look more like her than my father—except for Lillian. She says we have the same eyes, she can see him inside of me. Something like that."

"Yes, I see it. A softness of the soul."

"Is that a good thing?"

"*Yego.* Quite good."

Nadine sits next to Rachel and tells her about the other photos: her seventh birthday party, children sitting around a table with cake smudged on their faces. The baptism for a newly-born nephew, a cousin's wedding that took place in the gazebo that used to stand in Lillian's backyard. There are photos of uncles and aunts, cousins, and grandparents. Now, all dead or moved away.

"Do you..." still go to church? Rachel wonders, picking up the baptism photo. Was the massacre at this church? Instead, though, she asks, "Do you still believe in God?"

Nadine shrugs. "People say God lives in the ten thousand hills of Rwanda. During the genocide, he became lost in the Rift Valley. He wandered for ninety days, tears so thick he couldn't see straight. It's a nice story, but I can't believe it."

"Your parents were Tutsis, right?"

"Umama never spoke of being Hutu or Tutsi. She refused to say, although I'm certain she was Tutsi. Baba came here from Swaziland when he was young. His family is Zulu."

"Ah, his father is the lion hunter. Rose told me about him."

Nadine smiles. "That is a story I tell only for Rose. He was *inyangamugayo*, a respected elder in the village. People came to him with disagreements and he made peace. That was many years ago."

Nadine gets up to take the Gators baseball cap off the wall and gives it to Rachel. "I miss Papa Henry, too," she says. "I share the love you have for him. I hope that provides some comfort for you, as it does for me."

Rachel's eyes dart to the corkboard. The soft longing in the girl's voice makes it impossible to hold her gaze.

Nadine picks up the heart-stenciled frame on the bedside table.

She removes the photo of Papa Henry showing her how to use a camera, walks over to the corkboard and places it over a bare space. "*Sawa, inshuti?*"

Rachel hands her a thumbtack. "*Sawa.*"

Nadine reaches for one of the blank yellow notecards from the pile on the desk and a pen, writes a single sentence and then pins it on the bottom of the corkboard.

Rachel reads the note once, and then again: *April 1994—Papa Henry finds Nadine at church.* She shakes her head. "Tucker found you both in town."

"No, *inshuti*," Nadine says softly, "Papa Henry came for me. He came to help me."

"How," Rachel says hollowly. "How did he find you?"

"Everything's mixed up. I'm not quite sure."

"But my father was there, at the church."

"He saved my life."

Rachel rubs her temples. Everything's mixed up for her, too. Tucker lied about her father finding Nadine in town. What else had he lied to her about? And Lillian… Jesus. "Does Lillian know he was there?"

"Please, Rachel, you can't tell Maman." Nadine squeezes her hand. "No one can know, especially not the lawyer from Kigali who is asking questions."

"About what happened at the church?"

Nadine's shaking now, swiping tears from her face. "I promised I wouldn't tell. I promised."

"It's okay, *inshuti*, I won't tell," Rachel soothes. Who did she promise—her father? And why? What exactly is the secret Nadine and Henry Shepherd share?

TWENTY-ONE
{*April 14, 1994*}

H ENRY SHEPHERD STANDS ON THE FRONT
porch of the main house taking photos of the mountains
against a backdrop of pink-and-orange streaked sky. He
likes to start the day with a few moments of reverence for the natural beauty that cannot be destroyed. He sets down his camera and
sits on the top step for another small luxury. He rolls an unlit cigarette between his fingers before lighting it, takes a long drag and then
carefully snuffs out the butt before returning it to the crumpled pack,
counting and recounting the four remaining cigarettes.

The sun will be up soon, waking Lilly and the children sleeping
on blankets, some only a sheet, in the kitchen, the gathering room and
the halls. He glances toward the low hill that separates the main house
and farmhouse from the fields; it's been quiet all night, after six days
of chaos. No gunfire. No screams. Not one plea for help on the short-

wave radio in the kitchen. He takes a few steps. If he's lucky, all he'll find out there on the other side of the hill is the last of the sweet potatoes or some over-ripe fruit the monkeys and Hutus have overlooked.

A rumbling startles him as a United Nations truck appears in the driveway. Two Belgian soldiers dressed in helmets and uniforms, carrying rifles they aren't allowed to shoot, jump out of the truck. "Last chance," says a well-built young man sporting a blond buzz cut. "There's a plane arriving at the Kigali Airport in three hours, turning right back around for Nairobi. It's getting too dangerous for flights to land here anymore. Miss this one and you're on your own."

Henry sweeps an arm toward the house. The soldier shakes his head; they had this conversation when he was here two days ago—not to fight the Hutu militia arriving from Kigali, but to evacuate foreigners. *Sorry, diplomats and aid workers only. No room for locals.*

"I'd appreciate a lift into town," Henry says. "We're down to dry oats and sugar." For the past two weeks, Lilly has been boiling water from the river over an open fire. Yesterday, the water was an unnatural, murky color.

The soldier cocks his head toward the bed of the truck, where four other white men are sitting, suitcases between their knees, heads down. "*Amahoro,*" Henry greets them as he climbs in, his camera around his neck. They don't even look up at him.

The main street of Mubaro is deserted except for a handful of looters rummaging through burnt-out storefronts with empty shelves and cafés with dirty dishes on the tables. Henry stands where the truck dropped him off, paralyzed, staring up at an orange-threaded sky: a black cauldron of buzzards is bubbling over, some swooping down around him. He doesn't know where to look, can't settle on a meaningful response to the corpses lying in the street. Repulsion. Sorrow. Horror. Nothing is enough.

For as long as he has lived in Rwanda, there have been spikes of Hutu violence against their Tutsi neighbors, but this...for chrissakes, it's surreal.

He's heard stories of Tutsis forced from their homes, their cattle stolen and their belongings burned in their front yards. A friend of a friend in Kibuye, near the Congo border, or someone's uncle in Butare down south. Tucker has horrible stories about the attack on the hospital in Kigali five months ago. But Mubaro has always been protected by the Virungas, just a few hours from the safety of Uganda. The trouble has seemed far away, merely stories. Until now.

He takes a few steps to lean against the scarred trunk of a eucalyptus tree, its ashen limbs scattered across the road like a disemboweled pachyderm. The smell of kerosene is still in the air; some of the branches were used as torches. He scans the ground for something to steady himself, and then stumbles toward a Florida Gators T-shirt he gave to a young man who works at the market where he sometimes buys hard candy for the children. He kneels to the ground, but there is no identifying the skin hanging from the bones of what was once a familiar face.

A kind of rigor mortis settles into his own body, forming a protective shell. He stands and photographs the rust-splotched logo on the T-shirt. Nobody should see these atrocities, and yet he feels responsible to serve as a witness. He walks zombie-like, stepping over bodies, taking more photos. He peers into storefronts to try and find food, water—something useful, if not hopeful, that he can bring back to Kwizera.

Heading through the banana field that leads home, a half-loaf of bread tucked under his jacket, Henry stops at the sound of footsteps behind him, a child calling out. He barely recognizes the kid, tall with a glistening red slash on his forehead. What was his name?

"Mister American, come," the kid says, seizing his hand. "It is something special only for the men. Papa sent me to get you. Good, you have the camera."

Henry's toes curl as if stubbornly digging into wet sand. Christian, that's it. Rahim Kensamara's younger boy. He sometimes busses tables at the only café that serves burgers.

"Come." Christian's voice is urgent. Commanding. No longer the voice of a child. "The girl Nadine needs you. Right away."

TWENTY-TWO
{ London, December 5, 2000 }

THE SMELL OF FRIED FISH AND THE ROAR
of a cheering crowd is deceptively inviting from the street,
and Tucker steps heavily down the stairs into a dark, near-
empty pub. A soccer game blares from the TV that occupies the entire
back wall. The bald dude wiping down the bar nods as he takes a seat,
and then turns his attention back to the game. "Norwich is up by one,"
he says. Tucker's more interested in the way the gray rag skims along
the veneer, a fat greasy streak dissolving and then immediately reap-
pearing as if the surface is alive and regenerating the grime.

"You okay, mate?" the bartender asks.

Tucker opens his mouth, his jaw slack, throat constricted like
a fish who doesn't know what to do with actual air. "Beer," he says.
"Whatever's on tap." *You okay?* Fuck. What the hell kind of question
is that anyway? The infectious disease specialist at St. Mary's asked the

same thing this morning, two or five times. She kept tapping his arm as he stared at the results of Rosie's latest blood test. Yes, of course he understood the numbers. What he couldn't fathom was *why*. The T-cell count was way down. Why isn't the expensive cocktail of pills he flies here for every four months working? Christ, Rose has been in bed for a week. Why?

You okay?

Fuck, she's an expert in pediatric AIDS, should have some answers. At least better questions. Her eyes filled with pity, handing him five bottles of enough pills for another two months, not four. "Let's add something new to the mix, see if there's any improvement," she said, ushering him out the door.

No, he is definitely not okay.

When the cloudy mug lands in front of him, he's sorry he didn't order a bottle. He swirls the beer, figures the alcohol will kill any major bacteria. "Thanks. Tommy, right?"

The bartender glides a hand over his smooth dome as if sweeping his mind to place Tucker's face. "You're Henry's friend."

"Yeah, right." Tucker cautiously sips his beer. Some friend. The last time he saw Henry was four years ago, June 1996, when the promising HIV protocol first became available in London. It was awkward at best, sitting across from him in this pub downstairs from the dingy flat he leased month to month. Henry kept looking out the window, as if waiting for someone he saw approaching from down the street. It was unsettling for both of them to be reminded of the bond they shared. "I tried his apartment. Nobody answered."

Tommy grunts. "Still owes me a month's rent. Haven't seen him in, what, must be a bit over two years now."

"Any idea where he went?"

"He was always going on about taking photos again, finding something to inspire him. I figured it was just talk."

"Thanks." Tucker takes a long swig of beer. Two years. Shit. Henry could be anywhere. His thumb twists the brass band that has left a slight green tinge on his little finger over the past six and a half years. *Solange my love, I'm afraid this time I royally screwed up.* Rachel hasn't even been in Rwanda two weeks and she's already talking about giving up, going home early. Who could blame her? Lillian's still not talking, not about Henry at least. And now, he's disappeared completely. Everything's falling apart.

The brass band isn't worth much. Solange didn't want him to spend a lot of money on a gold wedding ring. They were saving up for a little beach house in Zanzibar. They had never been, but the way Solange said it was mouthwatering, like a rich chocolate treat. It sounded like someplace extraordinary. A place where they could escape from Kigali for long weekends and recharge to the sound of the ocean and kids building sandcastles. Rose would have lots of friends to play with, and he'd teach Solange to bodysurf.

Tucker raises the mug to his lips again but doesn't drink. *Happy anniversary, my love.* Six years ago today, they were to be married. A December wedding, just after the rainy season ended and the entire country would be clean, lush and green. The air at this time of year is practically bubbly with oxygen, intoxicating. The animals are fat and healthy. Everything is so fucking alive. Every December, he fights the urge to clean out his savings account and go to Zanzibar, just disappear into the ocean. He might already have taken that one-way walk if it wasn't for the promise he made to Solange.

Lying on a narrow hospital bed together, Tucker sleeping with a foot on the floor to give Solange more room, they vowed to build a family with the baby they saved together. He thought bringing Henry back, fixing things between him and his daughter, him and Lillian… Somehow, Rose might magically… He weaves his fingers into a vice, elbows on the bar, and presses his thumbs against the waves of tension rolling in behind his temples. They would all be Rose's family. They would be her strength.

Tucker closes his eyes, giving in to the crashing waves. When he finally talked to his dad about his wavering faith in becoming a physician, Daniel Senior's advice was to choose a specialty that would give him direction. Define him. The problem was, unlike his namesake, he wanted to be more than a surgeon sewing up flesh and mending bones. Solange was the one who taught him to be a healer. She sat with patients and talked to them, held their hands until they fell asleep if they were scared. She held him when he was scared. He became, not just a better doctor, but also a better man during those first three years in Rwanda. A loving partner to Solange, a father to Rose, a son to Lillian. Family became more than just a responsibility to fulfill, and love—not work, as with his father—is still the primary commitment that defines him.

His eyes ache when he exhales, burning with a dry sorrow. Maybe he was wrong to trick Rachel into coming to Rwanda; okay, for sure he was wrong. Henry is probably off in Morocco or Spain, hasn't even seen the letters he mailed. He rubs his temples, as if to release something liquid and soothing, but instead his fingers are like ice picks to his brain, chipping away at the promise he and Solange made.

"Another beer, Tommy." He slides his empty glass across the bar.

Keeping that promise, fixing the family he found for Rose, is what he has hung onto during the past few months while her health has been deteriorating. This is what has defined him. Christ, it beats the hell out of the way Rachel beats herself up about losing her daughter and quite possibly her husband. And Lillian…sure, she still takes care of the children, but he sees how her heart has become scarred and tender. What if, just like Rachel's mom, Lillian's scars become irreparably tough, her heart permanently closed? He pays for the beer and then leaves the full mug to catch a cab for the airport. Maybe he can catch an earlier flight back home. There's not much hope that Henry will show up at Kwizera, he knows this. But it's all he has right now.

TUCKER CAN PRACTICALLY HEAR THE forest yawning awake as he dumps his backpack near his tent, shedding the weight of his trip. He heads into the forest, down a path winding away from Kwizera, away from the blue-black sky that outlines the Virungas like some medieval castle hovering over the place. Hazy beams from his flashlight bounce off the branches, catching a surprised possum or silvery eucalyptus leaves still quaking from the weight of a more agile animal that might well be tailing him. Lillian dubbed this place the Forest of Ghosts after the genocide. She doesn't allow the children to come here, not even with an adult, as if the graves he and Henry dug might open up and swallow them. Tucker finds it peaceful here. He turns off the flashlight. Rays of light strain through the canopy, but he could find his way to the clearing he and Henry made about a half-mile in with his eyes shut.

During the first two weeks after the Hutu president's plane was shot down and retribution was declared against the Tutsis, he and Henry found two or three bodies each morning in the fields that now grow corn and teff. Mostly children whose parents thought they would be safe at Kwizera. The local Hutus waited for them each night. It was Henry's idea to take the bodies into the woods so Lillian wouldn't find them. They dug a separate grave for each child, marked with a chunky headstone of mahogany and an identifying characteristic written with a thin paintbrush dipped in black dye made from a kind of boiled fungus.

Red shirt. Kitten barrettes. Green eyes.

There was no identifying most of the faces: some of the heads were severed completely. After the Interahamwe militia from Kigali rolled into town in a cavalcade of trucks, there was a period of several weeks when there were too many dead bodies to hide them all from Lillian or bury them properly. They dug a mass grave in a section of land that intersected Kwizera and two neighboring farms, one owned by a Hutu, where sunflowers now catch the light, growing tall and strong. The Interahamwe soldiers watched from a distance but never intervened. Lillian said it was because they still had a little piece of their conscience working. It gave her faith, like God might not have completely turned a blind eye on Rwanda.

Tucker knew what kept him and everyone at Kwizera safe: he sometimes tended to the wounded soldiers. It was his job to save them, part of the oath he took in medical school. While he set an arm or tended to a knife wound, these men reverted back into teachers and auto mechanics, boys he had seen playing tag in the market square. He had to switch off the part of his brain that held fresh images of hacked up bodies, sometimes picked over by jackals, hyenas, or hungry house pets whose owners had disappeared. And then, there was the irony that here he was stitching up some of the same soldiers who might have attacked the hospital where he had worked in Kigali. Killed Solange. What kind of fucked-up karma was that?

A silver-threaded fog illuminates the clearing. Tucker walks through the maze of headstones, stopping at each one to remove bits of dried leaves or animal droppings. He uprights a marker tipped over on its side. There are twenty-nine graves in all, including four children of Kwizera who died, but not at the hands of Hutus. Measles, tuberculosis, polio. He brings vaccinations from Kigali; there are antibiotics he scored in London, donations from three different hospitals, in his duffle bag now. But it's never enough.

In the center of the clearing is a massive stump that serves as the base of an ancestral altar he helped Nadine to construct to honor her family. On top is a cross they nailed together, wood recovered from the Neguro home in the foothills on the other side of Mubaro, draped with beaded necklaces and a purple scarf that belonged to Dahla. He stoops and takes quick inventory of the scooped-out stump, sealed with a brick to keep out rodents and curious monkeys: shards of china plates and crystal wine glasses that the Neguros only used for special occasions; a jar with the charred ashes of the house that Enoch's five brothers and father from Swaziland had helped him to build; a plastic bag with a miraculously preserved paperback book cover, *A Wrinkle in Time*. He counts the purple flowers around the stump: forty wild pansies that Nadine planted for her mother's fortieth birthday just before she left for school last fall. Everything's in order.

He starts to leave but instead heads to the river, not far away, and wistfully stares into the murky water. How long will it take for the river to run clear again, as it had before the genocide? He kneels, pebbles digging into his knees, rubs his hands together like sticks that might spark. Nadine sometimes comes to the altar to talk to her parents and cousin Sylvia. Once, not long after the massacre, he heard her ask for their forgiveness. Tucker interlocks his fingers to contain the heat in his palms. "Forgive me," he whispers. The words form an image of Solange, along with a sadness so hollow and brittle he is afraid it may break him. If he can't keep his promise, if he loses Solange and Rose both, then who will he be?

The sun is just cresting over the mountains by the time Tucker walks out of the forest. His neck and shoulders are stiff, his eyesight blurry from jet lag and just enough sleep to make him truly exhausted. "Home sweet..." he mumbles, pulling back the mosquito netting he's rigged up as a canopy over his tent and a platform. He stops short. Rachel is sacked out on one of two low-slung beach chairs on the platform, folded into herself, knees curled to her chest. How did she manage to fall asleep sitting up?

She blinks awake, and then stands squarely in front of him. "Where were you?"

"Good morning to you, too."

"The last three days. Where were you? And what do you know about my father going to the church? Was he trying to find Nadine?"

Tucker opens his mouth. *Give it a rest. Not everything's about you.* It's the dark circles under her eyes that get to him. "Yeah, he went there to find her."

"To save her."

Tucker nods; sure, it could be true. He never asked Henry why he went there with his camera. "And then, I found them both in town."

"Where? How did they escape?"

"Whoa, just…whoa." Tucker collapses into a chair. "Give me a minute. It was a rough trip. London. I went to see an immunology specialist about Rose."

"How is she?"

"Her white cells still aren't doing their job of fighting off infections, even with the expensive new protocol I have to fly to London to get my hands on." Tucker sighs. "I'm going to have to take Rosie to Kigali for another transfusion and some tests."

Rachel leans in and places her hand lightly on his, setting off a series of not unpleasant but surprising tiny sparks, like static electricity on a blanket fresh from the dryer. Tucker reflexively slides his hand away, examines his fingernails. "So, your dad. I did some poking around in London. Went to the last address I had for him. No luck."

"What was it like?" Rachel asks.

"Small—but, y'know, nice." Tucker frowns as he tugs at a strand of cuticle unraveling from his thumbnail. Christ, what else can he say? Rachel leans forward, waiting, her eyes a paler shade of brown than usual. Watery.

"It doesn't mean anything," Tucker blurts. "He could be in Europe, on assignment. He could be back in the States, he could be—"

"Tucker." Rachel raises a hand to stop him. "I'm sorry."

"Me, too. I wish I could tell you I found him, but don't give up. I'll keep looking—"

"No, it's okay." Her hand falls on his open palm. "I'm sorry about Rose. Don't you give up either."

Tucker closes his eyes, his fingers curling tightly around hers, his spine adhering to the c-shape of the canvas. Yeah, he can totally see how she fell asleep sitting up. Her hand goes limp in his and he moves closer so that her head falls gently against his shoulder. That blanket, now soft and warm with sunlight filtering through the trees above, falls over both of them. He fills his lungs with dew-soaked air, nourishing the place where he is grateful to be alive. He grants himself the small permission, just for a brief moment, to put aside all that has passed and what is yet to come. To rest.

TWENTY-THREE

T HIS IS LILLIAN'S FAVORITE TIME OF DAY, the early morning before breakfast when the sun's bright but not yet high enough to heat up the air, perfect for teaching the two older boys about how to take care of the farm. Thomas and Robert, who are both about fifteen although neither child knows his exact age, link hands as they run ahead of her to the banana field. Their sheer joy makes her smile. They could be on a treasure hunt, eagerly searching for fruit ripe for the picking. She watches with a bit of envy, walking slowly to favor the leg that gets cranky sometimes if she sleeps on it funny. "Be mindful to stay close enough for me to see you," she calls out. Robert waves but doesn't slow down a bit, as expected. That's fine. She trusts Thomas, who is used to looking after his little brother, Zeke, and Rose.

She stops to roughly rub out an annoying ache that starts in her thigh and shoots up into her lower back. It's hard to believe Thomas will be graduating from high school in another few years and there will only be three children left at Kwizera. Seems like yesterday that she and Henry were downright lonely with less than a dozen young-sters around the kitchen table. They were going to create the next gen-eration: a strong and fair group of men and women, Tutsis and Hutus, brothers and sisters. Henry always said this was her gig, he was just happy to be part of the adventure when he wasn't off in the mountains, shadowing gorillas—his other family. But they were a team; she was the engine and he was the fuel. Life moves slower without him here.

"Miss Lillian, come see," Robert shouts from the nearest row of banana plants, which cover a fenced-in square hectare along sweet potatoes, beans and sorghum. The six-foot-high metal mesh topped with barbed wire is an eyesore, but it keeps out the vervets and larger rodents.

"Color's the easiest way to judge," she says, reaching up to point out a bunch of unripe bananas. "See how dark these are? Light green is what you're looking for, with a hint of yellow. You want to make sure they've stopped growing, but if you wait until they turn totally yellow the baboons may beat you to it. Those crafty devils are smart. Sometimes they dig right underneath the fence or gnaw open a hole with their teeth."

Both of the boys stare at the fruit, no doubt making mental notes, clicking tongues against the roofs of their mouths in agreement. Thomas and Robert are both interested in farming. They assure her, as boys getting a glimpse of what it means to be men will do, that they'll stay here forever and take care of Kwizera. Take care of her. A kind and generous notion and she doesn't doubt their sincerity. But she won't hold them to it.

She lets the boys rummage through the broad leaves and search for more ripe fruit they can wrangle down and add to their basket. Meanwhile, she surveys the rows of vegetables that she shares with nine women from town. They'd call it a co-op back in the States, but here it's simply being neighborly. She stoops to inspect the red clay soil. Thankfully, the sweet potato vines are poking through the crusty ground even though the heavens have been stingy with rain for the past few weeks. The aunties, as the children call the genocide widows who sometimes come to help out with the young ones, depend on the rotating crops for their livelihood.

Lillian places one palm on the ground, another on her heart as she says a prayer. Thank God for this group of sisters who help plant and harvest, and sometimes sell crops and handiwork at the markets in Mubaro and surrounding towns. She doesn't have the time or energy to manage all this land by herself. She's not comfortable hiring folks to work for her, giving orders. That was Henry's department. He had an easy way about him, could get a job done without being too bossy. It was different back when Dahla and Enoch lived here and helped out. They were part of Kwizera. Family.

The widows have become family too, taking Lillian into their quilting group, coming over for holidays and the occasional potluck Sunday dinner. After Henry left, for months one or another of the women brought over freshly baked bread or whatever was poking up in their garden. It was as if they knew he wasn't coming back, long before that idea moved from a paltry agitation in Lillian's stomach, to a throbbing discomfort in her chest, and then settled heavily in her head.

How could he not come back? They had plans. They would grow old and content, never elderly, together on this land. They would hire on the older children who wanted to tend to the farm and save some money to buy their own property, start their own families. They would build another house as their community expanded, maybe two—plenty of land, even without cutting into the forest. But every last one of her forty-eight children who graduated from high school have moved on, most to Tanzania, Uganda and Kenya. Not that she blames them for leaving. There's been plenty of talk about reform, but Tutsis are still treated like second-class citizens, worse than anything she saw growing up in Atlanta. And then, there are the prisons crammed with tens of thousands of Hutu men and women—some innocent, no doubt—still waiting to be tried for genocide crimes. The new Tutsi president, that fellow, Kagame, comes off sincere enough. He's stirring up hope among some with talk of reconciliation and forgiveness. Lillian shares most of the aunties' wait-and-see attitude. They'll wait on passing judgment until after the first round of *gacaca* trials. A test run of sorts, one right here in Mubaro after the New Year. Meanwhile, she continues her mini-revolution, creating small but significant increments of change, one child at a time.

She's so very proud of her kids: teachers and shopkeepers, one's a dentist and another runs a charity that builds houses in the slums of Kigali. Of course she's proud! And yet, sometimes late at night she is awakened by a spark of fear that ignites worries more easily brushed aside during her busy days. How long will she be able to take in new orphans, like Robert, who has blossomed during the three months he's been here? Who will keep Kwizera up and running when she's gone?

A black Mercedes pulls over on the driveway, not a total surprise but Lillian wasn't expecting her visitor this early. "You boys run on ahead," she says. "Ask Nadine to kindly fry up some of those bananas for breakfast. I'll be along shortly."

Robert and Thomas amble past the sporty car, a rare sight in Mubaro, boggle-eyed but not touching. A tall, solid woman with coffee skin, from Nairobi or London judging by the sleek navy pantsuit and fashionable knot of hair atop her head, steps out of the car and greets the boys in French. Lillian smoothes back her own sensibly short hair threaded with silver strands. Is this gal old enough to have completed law school, let alone be a deputy prosecutor for the International Tribunal?

Lillian flashes back to her friend Deirdre, plumping up a fluffy Angela-Davis-style Afro, so proud she'd been accepted to law school. Stanford, no less. Her best friend had taken a sixteen-hour Greyhound ride to Cleveland, during the gray winter she spent with Mama's sister's family, to share the big news. She can still see Deirdre's face, a mixture of sympathy and awe, eyes on the watermelon-sized belly between them. *Can you keep a secret? I'm fixing on working for the Panthers, making some real change. I'm never going back to Atlanta.* Lillian chose another route out of Atlanta: Reverend Morton's orphanage in Kenya. She shakes her head at her younger self, so certain that none of the violence erupting in the States, or South Africa, for that matter, could touch her in the remote town under the watchful snow-lidded eyes of Mt. Kenya.

Three years later, a letter from Mama changed everything: Deirdre had been shot dead in Oakland during a Black Panthers riot protesting the arrest of Ms. Davis. Shortly afterwards, Lillian asked Reverend Morton to help her find a small farm to purchase someplace where she could do some good for a handful of children who needed a home. She didn't care about the danger to her own life. Deirdre was dead. Samuel, dead. They had each, in their way, followed Reverend King's call to action and taken a risk to make the world a better place. She had no grand designs on the world, but she could surely change lives. She saw that during four years at the orphanage in Kenya. Buying Kwizera was her way of taking her own risk.

"*Mwaramutse*, Madame Carlson." The attorney offers a manicured hand, nails polished clear with squared white tips. "I'm Valeria Ogoni."

"Thank you for coming," Lillian says. She's conscious of her own rough hand against smooth fingers, almost ashamed of nails cut to the quick so that no dirt can get underneath.

"So," Ms. Ogoni says, "I understand you have some concerns about my office calling Mademoiselle Neguro at school."

"I'm the child's legal guardian," Lillian begins, just as she told the curt secretary who finally returned her call yesterday. "Although Nadine is legally an adult, she's still vulnerable. She's still under my care, and I prefer that you come to me instead of calling her directly. Now, what's this about Nadine testifying at a trial?"

Ms. Ogoni is head down, rifling through a slim black valise, and produces a packet of papers. "Our office has reason to believe that some young men in Mubaro are guilty of more serious crimes than they were originally convicted of as juveniles during the genocide," she says, handing the packet to Lillian without meeting her eyes. "We wish to build one strong case against Nadine's former neighbor Felix Kensamara and set a precedent. We need Mademoiselle Neguro to lay the foundation for these charges at the pilot program *gacaca* trial here in January. This is an internal document. I can't give it to you, but I thought you should read it to explain matters."

Lillian's eyes dart from the attorney to the document as she scans the first page, searching for what these new charges are. Shortly after the genocide ended, there had been a trial in Kigali for dozens of Hutu boys from the region, including Felix and his younger brother, Christian. Most were charged with the vague crime of disorderly conduct and given a light sentence as a reward for not fleeing to a neighboring country. Besides, they were children; they were only doing as they were told. That was the reasoning. Felix, nearly a man at sixteen, was given a sentence of four years. Christian, only thirteen, was free to go live with relatives in Uganda.

"I have to tell you," Lillian says, "my daughter doesn't remember much about what happened at the church." She flips to the second and then the third page, wading through the legalese, in French no less, picking out words she can translate.

"That did appear to be the case at the trial in Arusha for Felix and Christian's father," Ms. Ogoni says. "Perhaps now that mademoiselle is older, she will remember more. Yes?"

Lillian glances up, eyes narrowed. She believed Nadine then, she believes her now. "These new charges…" She can't figure them out for the life of her, but then she turns the page: *Rape*. No wonder the attorney couldn't tell her; it's impossible to say the word aloud. "How much…" she says, reaching behind her only to find there's nothing to hang onto. She allows her legs to collapse and sits, knees to her chin, on the grass. How much can one child take? There's no use in asking, not after all she's seen. She can only hope that Naddie truly doesn't remember.

Ms. Ogoni leans down to offer a white kerchief. "Now you understand why this case is so important. There are countless women living silently with the shame of being raped before, during, and after the genocide. The world will be watching the first *gacaca* trials. Felix Kensamara's case could draw attention to the need to prosecute this crime more fully."

Lillian wipes her cheek with the back of her hand instead of the lacy kerchief. Yes, she's well aware that rape is a powerful weapon of war throughout Africa, the victims often ostracized by their families and communities. But why wouldn't Naddie have come to her? Did Henry know?

"Madame, we need Nadine to testify this time. We need proper justice—"

Lillian puts up her hand, and then lets it drop as the attorney sits beside her on the grass. There wasn't enough evidence to convict Rahim Kensamara or the other men he was tried with, so they were released. She's not proud to think of how she and the aunties agreed that justice was served when, within weeks, all of the accused were shot and killed, likely ambushed by Tutsi soldiers. A twist of nausea turns her stomach as she flashes on the gun that's buried in a metal box in the forest. She nearly carried out her own vigilante justice against Gahiji, the man who forced himself on her.

They sit in silence, Lillian trying to call up a prayer, but none come to mind. What does come is a series of numbers: More than 130,000 arrests during the months after the slaughter. About 4,000 trials in six years. The International Tribunal was set up by the United Nations to expedite cases of the worst war crimes, but so far the organization has prosecuted less than thirty men and convicted about half of them. The number of women raped during the genocide is estimated in the hundreds of thousands; nobody knows for sure because few of the victims are alive and even fewer come forward. She's only heard about a small handful of convictions. What's the point of subjecting Naddie to what may be months of sitting in a courtroom, interrupting her studies—her life? She's the one who will, without question, suffer. Lillian folds the lacy kerchief into careful squares and hands it back to the attorney. To this day, part of her wishes she had murdered Gahiji.

"This is difficult, I know," Ms. Ogoni says. "A crime that nobody wants to talk about. We are counting on you to help Nadine. She must be strong for all of the others who cannot."

The attorney's voice is soft and cool, but it's Deirdre's sharp words that Lillian hears. *We must take action. No more bowing our heads and taking shit.*

"If it were me, I'd testify…"

Do the right thing. It's a new day, a new generation.

But Nadine's just getting strong again, Lillian pleads with the voice in her head. Last time, even without getting on the witness stand, the whole experience nearly pushed the child back into the dark place where she wouldn't speak at all. She wouldn't sleep alone for months afterwards, wouldn't walk to school with the other children. The shame was clearly unbearable. To speak of it, unfathomable. Still.

"Madame Carlson," the attorney persists, "if we can show evidence of these serious charges at the *gacaca*, Felix Kensamara will be tried in the international court in Arusha. He will go to prison for twenty years and set a precedent for prosecution of rapes committed by juveniles as an act of war."

"Nadine will be back at school in January," Lillian says. She's happy now, with her music and friends. "I'm sorry, I can't put her through that again."

"But this isn't only about your daughter." The hard edge is back in the attorney's voice, as if Lillian's the one on trial. "Our records show there were at least fifteen girls, quite possibly more, held hostage in the storage shed behind the church."

"Then you don't need Nadine," Lillian says loudly to drown out Deirdre's disapproval.

"We found fingerprints, hair samples, teeth, various physical evidence—"

"Ask someone else."

"There is no one else. The others are dead."

By the time Lillian walks back to the main house, breakfast is nearly over. Nadine's imploring a tight-lipped Rose to try one more spoonful of oatmeal. "Take a look at your friend Zeke," she cajoles. "See how much he's enjoying his breakfast?" Rose gives the boy with cereal dotting his cheeks a dubious glance, and then pushes her near-full bowl away.

"We'll eat breakfast together on the patio, how about that?" Lillian smoothes a hand over Rose's sharp shoulder blades, like a bird's wings. "Some of my superpower protein cookies."

"Cookies?" Rose grins up at her. "For breakfast?"

"Special treat." Lillian kisses the top of her head. It's warm but only a little. A good sign. "Why don't you go wait for me. I'll join you in few minutes, after I make tea."

Lillian isn't hungry either. She waits for the kettle to boil, mostly just for a chance to steady herself enough to be fully present with Rose. The audacity of that brash young attorney. *Perhaps now that mademoiselle is older, she will remember more. Yes?* No. What good will it do, encouraging Naddie to relive the horrors of the past? She startles at the hiss of steam, and then practically burns her fingers as she swipes the kettle off the stove. The aroma of peppermint and licorice is soothing. Hopefully, it will settle Rose's stomach. It does the trick with Lillian's nerves as she waits a few minutes for the herbs to steep. It's not really the attorney she's angry with.

She watches her daughter, humming while cleaning up after breakfast. It would be easy to assume the child doesn't have a care in the world. Naddie keeps her hands busy washing dishes and then drying them, stacking plates on the wooden shelves above the sink, wiping down the white and blue tile counter. It's her hands that give her away; they tremble slightly. Lillian hears it in the prolonged clatter of each dish as it hits the shelf.

When Naddie first came here to live, Tucker taught her to play his guitar to steady her hands. At first, she strummed a few simple chords that eventually turned into songs. It was a beautiful process, watching her daughter discover the joy of creating music, and then finding her voice, a powerful instrument that moves folks whether she's singing an aria from an opera or a Kinyarwanda lullaby. Her daughter's voice is responsible for her scholarship to the University of Nairobi, and giving her a real future. The kind of future Lillian can't afford to provide. The kind of future Rwanda surely can't promise.

"Naddie, there's something I want you to consider," Lillian says, a thought forming as she takes the dish towel. What if her daughter were to use her voice, her beautiful voice, to create change?

She takes both of Nadine's hands in her own. "The attorney from Kigali was here this morning with some papers. Details about the charges they want to file against Felix Kensamara." Nadine opens her mouth to protest, but Lillian rushes on. "Now, hear me out. I said you didn't have to be involved with a big trial in Arusha, but the *gacaca* is different. It's your community, people who lost friends and loved ones like you did. It's a place where you can stand up and tell the truth about what happened at the church."

"What does it matter?" Nadine says sharply, withdrawing her hands to cross them over her chest. "Telling the truth won't change what happened."

"Standing up for what's right does matter," Lillian says flatly. She lived her life by these words for a long time, isn't sure that she still believes they are true. "Justice matters."

"Maman, my loved ones are dead. There is no justice."

"Oh, Naddie…" Lillian rubs at a speck of nothing on the counter with her finger, looks down so as not to reveal her own doubt. Deirdre was going to be an attorney. And Samuel, dear Samuel, died fighting a senseless war for his country in the name of justice. She remembers standing with both of them at rallies, Reverend King's rumbling voice moving the entire room to their feet, moving an entire nation. Reverend King. Murdered.

"I'm sorry to upset you," Nadine says. "I know you cannot be proud to hear me say these things. I'll consider testifying at the *gacaca*."

"Nadine Neguro, I'm always proud of you." Lillian looks straight into her eyes. "Whatever you decide to do." No, it's not the attorney or her daughter she's upset with. She has always been ashamed that she ran off to Kenya. She gave up on fighting for civil rights, and simply wanted to find her own personal peace after giving up her baby. Was that so wrong? Justice might be too much to ask for. Maybe, the best most folks can hope for is a little peace of mind.

TWENTY-FOUR

W E'RE ALMOST THERE, RIGHT?" RACHEL asks hopefully, both hands on the dashboard to keep from bouncing out of her seat as the Jeep kicks up dust and pebbles. If there's a road on the steep hillside, she can't see it, but there's plenty going on outside her window. Leather-faced iguanas sunning on logs barely blink as the Jeep rumbles by. White lacy moths are flushed out of the tall grass. A flash of blue and gold wings darts into the acacia branches above.

"If by *there*, you mean a plateau where we park and then walk two miles to the village, then sure." Tucker clamps a hand onto Rachel's shoulder as the Jeep hits a major pothole.

She grasps his wrist and redirects his hand back onto the gearshift. "You don't have to take care of me, or amuse me while I'm here."

"What makes you think—"

Rachel cuts him off with a sigh. "This morning before breakfast. I heard Lillian ask you to take me along." More accurately, the Lady of Steel had said she was his responsibility.

"Regardless, I appreciate the company. Keeps me from thinking too much."

Rachel places her hand on his, still on the gearshift. Rose's fever spiked yesterday and she wasn't awake before they left this morning. "Don't worry," she says, "Nadine's parked in a chair by Rose's bed, working on a paper for school. And I can guarantee Lillian's not going far."

"It's not that; I know she's well taken care of," Tucker says. "It's a friend's birthday today. Someone who was special to me and Rose. She was murdered during the genocide."

Rachel has never asked him about the brass band that's a constant fixture on his pinky finger. Now, she feels his hand tense beneath hers, fingers twisting the ring. Was he married? Engaged? "Tucker, I'm sorry."

"No worries," he says, eyes fixed on the road. "Today's just a rough one to handle alone. Let's talk about something else."

Rachel looks out the window, searching for something to fill the awkward silence. The rugged countryside is so unlike the soft rolling foothills that hug the road from Kigali to Mubaro. She hasn't seen a person or a hut for at least an hour, since leaving the outskirts of Mubaro. "Where exactly are we going?"

"A village so small, I doubt it has a name," Tucker says. "The land gets rich and green to the east, where there's a valley with a chain of lakes. These amazing wildflowers pop up after the rainy season. A sea of purple, white, red, orange, gold. I think God made the valley difficult to get to because she didn't want humans driving bulldozers over everything."

"She? You think God is a woman?"

"I never gave it any thought until coming to Rwanda, but yeah. The immortal entity or energy, whatever it is that watches over this country, is definitely female."

"How do you figure?"

"The women here, especially in the remote areas. They're strong and patient—spiritual. At least, I see them that way."

"You'd have to be strong to live out here in the middle of nowhere."

"Enduring. That's the word that comes to my mind."

Rachel surveys the desolate landscape: the exact opposite of the blur of constant motion she thrives on in New York. It keeps her mind activated. Busy. "It's so empty," she observes. "Lonely."

Tucker laughs softly. "This is where I come when I need to refuel," he says, and then recalls his first camping trip up here. He walked into the village they're heading to, and introduced himself to the women farming the fields. Most of the men went off at dawn to find day labor in Ruhengeri or Kigali. Several women pointed out huts where there were ill neighbors. "I fell in love with the people, the simplicity of life here, and began bringing vaccinations and medicine every month or so," he says. "They pay me with baskets of fruit and fresh-baked bread left outside my tent in the morning."

The end of the road is a plateau that overlooks terraced farm-land in dazzling shades of green spilling into the valley below. While Tucker gets his duffle bag from the back of the Jeep and then checks the air in the tires, Rachel sits on a log and takes in the view: the chain of small lakes sparkles like tiny sapphires set in an emerald necklace. A curtain of late morning mist breaks apart to reveal flat, dormant volcanoes in the distance. "If there is a God, she definitely hangs out here," she murmurs, thinking of what Nadine said about God living in the ten thousand hills.

The low clouds cast shadows over the patchwork of green hills; translucent, shifting shapes appear to rise out of the earth. It would be nice to believe in a higher power that watches over everyone. But the genocide... "How can people still believe?" she asks aloud. "Ninety days was a long time for God to take a leave of absence."

"The story goes, sometimes God hides in the valleys." Tucker sits beside her and shades his eyes, stares out over the hilltops nudging through the low clouds. "My guess is that it was too painful for her to watch what was going on. Or maybe she wanted to see how we'd take care of each other if left to our own devices."

Rachel follows his gaze. What is he searching for in the mist?

He stands and offers her his hand to help her up. "Either way," he says, "sometimes you have to look even harder to find God—or whatever. Something resembling faith."

Tucker leads the way down the winding path, carrying a duffle bag of medical supplies, tapping the ground ahead of him with a long stick to check for snakes. The grass is greener, the ground darker, than on the higher ground. Leafy eucalyptus trees signal that water is nearby. Rachel smells the lake before she sees it, and then a row of clay and grass huts shaped like mushrooms appear along the sandy bank. A young woman waves from a wooden bench in front of one of the huts. Two boys dressed in saggy shorts splash nearby in the clear water.

"*Mwaramutse*, Clemencia. Good morning." Tucker bows to the woman. The smaller boy runs up to encircle his legs. "This is my friend Rachel. We're hoping to check on your father today."

"He has taken to bed," Clemencia says. She reaches down to gently unwind her son from Tucker. "The diabetes has turned Papa's left foot quite swollen, but he refuses the medicine you brought."

"I don't get it. Joseph knows those shots, every day, are important. The medicine is keeping him alive."

Clemencia scowls. "The problem is our village healer. He believes Papa's ancestors are angry and the sickness is a curse. No medicine, he says, just wait for comfort in the afterlife."

"I'll go see what I can do," Tucker assures her.

Rachel pulls an old Polaroid Instamatic out of her backpack and aims it playfully at the children. "Clemencia, is it okay if I stay here a few minutes and take some photos?"

Clemencia moves over to make room on the bench. Rachel takes photos while the proud mother directs her sons to stand still and look at the camera. The boys giggle, shove each other and make goofy faces. Some things are universal. They all watch as the photos develop before their eyes, the boys in quiet awe. "Some of the elders believe that cameras are taboo," Clemencia says. "They steal a piece of our souls to make the pictures. I prefer to believe they preserve a bit of us."

"I like that." Rachel gives her the photos. She thinks of the sonogram tucked away in her wallet.

The brothers are back at the edge of the lake, the smaller one sitting in the water, letting handfuls of pebbles run through his fingers to make a waterfall. He stands up and, with a warrior's cry, raises a fistful of pebbles over his head to take aim at his brother. He glances at his mom, sees she's watching and releases the stones back into the water, laughing. "*Aiya*," Clemencia says with a weary smile. "Do you and the doctor have children?"

"Tucker's a great dad. He has a daughter, Rose," Rachel says. "My husband is back in the States."

"Forgive me, Madame. I thought, since you are travelling together…"

"No, it's fine."

"And you? Children?"

"Yes," Rachel says. The word rises out of her chest, as if it has wings. "A daughter."

Rachel walks along the rocky shore of the lake and stops at a hut where Tucker's voice drifts through the open window. He's standing over an elderly man's bed. "Joseph, you need to keep this nice and loose," he says, wrapping gauze around the patient's foot. "We don't want the bandage binding, but we need to keep the open sores covered so you don't get an infection."

"I am not afraid," Joseph says. "Death will come soon enough."

Tucker places a hand on his shoulder. "We've been friends for, what, three years now?"

"Nearly four. Since Clemencia gave me my third grandson. Long enough to speak the truth."

"From where I sit, the truth is that we all live with the pain of too many people who left us too soon. People who had no choice." Tucker places a fist to his chest. "Don't do that, not willingly, to your family."

Rachel watches as he finishes wrapping the elderly man's foot and gives him a shot of insulin. She can't take her eyes off the ring on Tucker's finger. Who was this woman whose name he can't say, who left a hole in his heart?

They make rounds to the other huts on the lake, some with eight or nine children lined up for exams, siblings as well as cousins from nearby villages. Tucker makes a game of taking each child's temperature, checking their hair for bugs, and listening to them cough. He's enjoying this as much as the kids. Refueling, as he said. Rachel keeps the waiting patients busy by demonstrating the medical instruments, letting them look in her ears and mouth, and giving them Band-Aids to count.

The sun's setting as they walk back up the hill. "You're a natural with kids," Tucker says. "You're going to be one hell of a mom."

"I don't know about that."

"Why would you say that?"

"My mom wasn't big on nurturing after my father left. I understand now, it's okay. She was hurting and shut down her heart. But when I became pregnant, I was clueless. Jesus, I had no idea." Rachel starts to laugh but it turns into a gasp. "I read tons of books on parenting, but they don't begin to explain how much you'll love the child growing inside you. How much—" She leans against a tree, her breath sharp and jagged in her throat.

Tucker's hand drops onto her shoulder. "It must hurt like hell to lose a child you never had a chance to hold."

"Serena was just six months along. She depended on me."

"You can't blame—"

"I don't, not anymore." Rachel shrugs off his hand and starts walking again, faster. It wasn't her fault, she knows this now. But why do people think that makes her feel better? Serena is still dead. "I'm fine," she says over her shoulder. Tucker doesn't budge.

"It's not about blame." The air in her lungs is a hot metal blade; she flashes on Mick pounding the side of the crib. *Damn it, Ray, how could you not have known something was wrong?* She stops walking and takes a deep breath. "I guess, if I'm honest, part of me will always be-

lieve I should have been able to protect her better. Love her better."
She waits for Tucker to catch up, tell her she's wrong and this will pass
with time. It's what people say, because they don't know—they can't.
They don't realize there is no making her feel better, and that's not
what she wants. And so, she doesn't tell the truth anymore. It's much
easier to insist that she's fine, easier for everyone.

One month. That's how long her doctor said she should expect to
grieve, like it was a fact. One month, and then Mick expected her to
toss the sleeping pills and go back to work. Get on with her life. If only
it was that easy to quell the pain that sometimes, unexpectedly, still
churns up into her chest, making it hard to breathe. *The least you could
do is try*, her husband kept saying. But Tucker's just silently standing
beside her, twisting the ring on his finger, both of them watching as
the sun begins to set over the valley, the sky changing to dusty purple.
It hits her: the something-like-faith he's searching for here. His struggle, trying to stay positive with Rose. His love, still fresh and painful,
for whoever wore the ring that he never removes. He's grieving, too.

Rachel turns to give Tucker a swift kiss on his cheek. He takes
a half-step back and cocks his head. She flashes an it-was-nothing
half-smile. A show of solidarity, nothing really. "We should go," she
says, rubs her arms like she's shivering because she's cold. "Rose will be
bummed if you're not there to tuck her into bed."

TWENTY-FIVE

RACHEL SKULKS ALONG THE PATH LEADING into Mubaro, hoping to catch the troop of vervet monkeys that patrol the fields. Nadine, less serious about subterfuge, follows behind, singing something that sounds like Christmas, shredding flat, ribbed banana leaves. "That's a pretty tune," Rachel says with a tinge of melancholy.

"There's no exact translation into English, but the Kinyarwanda words aren't so hard." Nadine sings the chorus, catches Rachel's hand and swings it in time to the rhythm. "*Inshuti*," she says, "we'll teach the children this song at the tree decorating party on Saturday."

"I'd like that." Rachel smiles down at their interlocked fingers. How can she break the news to her friend that she doesn't plan on being here for the Kwizera tradition of decorating the fig tree in the backyard on the Saturday before Christmas? Instead, she'll be picking out a Charlie Brown droopy pine in need of a good home with her husband.

She sings louder, making her voice bright. It's a good plan. Mick will be so happy she's coming home early; she'll spring the news— an early Christmas gift—when he calls this afternoon. They've been negotiating their differences by email during the past few weeks, using a practically new laptop Lillian loaned to her. It's so much easier communicating in writing than over the phone, carefully editing her words. Of course she understands how important it is to go to his parents' house for a big family holiday. And, he does miss her; he does want her to come home early. How could she have doubted his love?

Mick is her priority, she sees this clearly now. He's right, a month is plenty of time to give her father a chance to show up. The stories in her notebook and the corkboard of memories she and Nadine have assembled will have to be enough. It's not the loving reunion she imagined, but it is closure. Mick will be glad to hear she's finally letting go of her fantasies about reconnecting with Henry Shepherd.

Nadine stops to wave to Lillian in the distance, in the field with three of the aunties. "Maman gave these women a piece of land to farm after the Hutus took their homes and their families, and something more," she says. "After the genocide, we who survived were no better than dead inside. We could see no reason for tomorrow to come. Maman gave the widows in town a place to work, as well as a place to go where they didn't have to be alone with their thoughts. Some worked the land, others came here to make baskets and sew. Together, they found renewed purpose."

"Lillian has such a big heart," Rachel says. Why can't the Lady of Steel find room to let her in?

"Maman! Maman!" Nadine waves to Lillian, who is clearly too far away to hear her. "She may want some things from town," she says, already running off, calling over her shoulder that she won't be long.

"Take your time." Rachel sits on a boulder, smoothes the skirt Nadine lent her, a pale okra the same color as the grass that tickles her ankles, scattered with pink flowers. She's in no hurry here. So different than at home, where she's a clock-watcher even before getting to work. Here, the minutes of the day seem to evaporate into the air, seconds marked by the flutter of wings.

She inhales the sweet earthen aroma pulled up from the ground by last night's rain. It's disappointing, in a way, thinking of being back in Manhattan's gray slushy streets that overcompensate with gaudy lights and plastic Santas. Instead of decorating the fig tree in Lillian's backyard, she'll be pouring booze like courage for people trying too hard to be jolly, and drinking enough herself to stay moderately engaged at a round-robin of holiday parties thrown by Mick's firm and his clients.

She hums an approximation of Nadine's Christmas carol, shades her eyes and watches the aunties embracing her friend. They are all surrogate mothers to Nadine. Her own mom made her promise to bring the baby to Jacksonville for Christmas. Serena would be about a month old, just the right age to sleep through a four-hour flight. A small part of her believes this will still happen; she'll fight the crowds at Bloomingdale's to find the perfect gift for her mom, a cashmere sweater the exact violet-blue of Merilee's eyes. She smiles at the thought of searching for that sweater anyway and wearing it on Christmas, wrapping herself in the soft memory of her mother's eyes lighting up when they had talked about the baby.

The snap of twigs turns Rachel attention toward the path: two boys, around Nadine's age or a bit older, are heading toward her. She braces a hand against the boulder beneath her. There's the boy with the scar on his forehead who Nadine said was a childhood friend before the genocide. And she ran into his companion, heavyset with a clean-shaven head, a few days ago on her way into town. He had been sitting on this boulder, and he squared his thumb and forefinger, putting them to one eye, squinting shut the other as she passed by. He made a click-click sound with his tongue against the roof of his mouth, as if taking a photo, and then laughed. Obviously, a reference to her father. Now, she stands as the two boys stop in front of her, both wearing the same uniform of green fatigue pants and black T-shirts, and mirrored sunglasses even though there's a low-hanging blanket of clouds.

"*Mwaramutse*," Rachel says, her gaze sliding toward Lillian and the aunties. The field or the house, which is closer? Nadine's former friend holds out his hand. "I'm Rachel," she says, offering her own hand, and then immediately feels something between embarrassed and idiotic.

Shaved Head laughs harshly and nudges his buddy.

"Take it." Scarface shoves a folded piece of paper toward Rachel's chest.

"For me?"

The boy sighs loudly. "Read if you like. It's for the girl Nadine."

"Who should I say this is from?"

Scarface looks past her, as if her question isn't worth the time to answer. Or, maybe it's that Lillian is coming their way. "May I help you," she says in an icy too-sweet southern drawl. A "fuck-you-very-much" that Rachel rather admires.

"No, Madame." Scarface bows and turns to catch up with his side-kick, who's already well ahead of him.

Lillian sweeps a hand along Rachel's arm as if checking for broken bones, staring after the boys.

"They gave me this note for Nadine." Rachel unfolds the piece of lined paper and a book of matches falls out. Lillian takes a step back, as if an actual fire has been ignited, and then quickly recovers. She stoops to pick up the matches and snatch the note.

"Who are they?" Rachel asks. These boys who have the ability to pierce Lillian's armor.

"Cowards." Lillian shows her the note, written in English. *Nadine go back to Nairobi so no more bad comes. Your mama surely not want more bad for you. The trial not good for anyone. Only bad. Bad for our family. Bad for new family of yours.*

"I suppose," Lillian says, "the Kensamara brothers think we'll be scared and tell Naddie not to testify against them at the *gacaca*."

"Kensamara…" Rachel reads the note again. "Is Maura, the woman who owns the bakery in town, their mother?"

Lillian nods. "Their father, Rahim, was one of the men on trial two years ago in Arusha. Nadine was supposed to testify and couldn't."

"This morning, Maura invited me to their home to talk about my father. I could go—"

"No, that won't help," Lillian says, slipping the note and matches in her coat pocket as Nadine appears from the direction of the house. "That woman has no reason to tell the truth. She's merely trying to protect her family."

"Why…" Rachel stops at the sight of Nadine cresting the hill. Why would Maura lie about her father? And, why doesn't Lillian want her going to talk to Maura? What's she trying to hide?

Nadine counts off the grocery list on her fingers. "Flour, salt, currants, oats." She puckers her lips, tapping her thumb. "And one other thing that I noticed we're running low on. Milk?"

Lillian's squinting in the direction that the Kensamara brothers went, a hand worrying the thin silver chain around her neck. "Maman," Nadine whisper-sings, as if awakening a child or bringing someone out of a hypnotic trance. "Milk, yes?"

Rachel's gaze drops to the fist clenched in Lillian's pocket and then to her amber eyes, flecked with sparks of confusion and something else. "C'mon, Naddie, let's get going before the beignets cool," she says. "I'm sure the groceries can wait until tomorrow."

Lillian's lips part but no words come out. It scares Rachel to see the Lady of Steel this way. *Fear.* That's what is lodged in her eyes, in the sloped shoulders that make her suddenly appear old.

"We can pick up some supplies for the Christmas party on Saturday," Rachel adds quickly. "When I was a kid, my mom and I made cotton ball snowmen and strung popcorn to hang on the tree."

"That sounds lovely," Lillian says. She draws herself up tall and walks back into the field.

THE GOOEY SMELL OF BEIGNETS turns Nadine's stomach, knowing who is pulling them out of the oven. Madame Kensamara used to come to their home to make bread with Umama every Sunday after church, with some of their other neighbors. The women baked and the men sat on the front stoop drinking home-brewed banana beer and smoking cigarettes. The children played tag and jumped rope in the backyard. Christian Kensamara, Chrissie back then, used to protect her from other Hutu boys who were bullies, their classmates as well as his brother, Felix. But that was before.

"Are you sure you don't want to come in?" Rachel says, holding the bakery door open wide, as if this might tempt reconsideration. Nadine holds her breath, smiles as her new friend offers to bring her pastries, and then hurries down the street, past the burnt-out cement storefronts with boarded up windows and piles of rubble that used to be a pharmacy, a café, another bakery. She barely notices the soldiers, who stand on the street corners in brown uniforms, smoke cigarettes and stare dully as she passes by. The Tutsi soldiers have become part of the scenery during the past six years, blending in with the dusty, bland surroundings. Part of her longs to go back to school in Nairobi, with its tall gleaming buildings and people dressed in bright colors; but, even with all the sorrow and pain, Rwanda will always be home.

Stepping through the strands of blue and silver beads that hang from the door frame of one of the few rebuilt shops in town is always an adventure, far better than any shop in Nairobi. She surveys the large, dimly-lit room. Where to begin? A dozen wooden tables are stacked with paperback books and tennis shoes that look used, single pens and markers, backpacks and notebooks, cans of Campbell's soup and tins of sardines. You never know what you'll find in here. Nobody asks Monsieur DeGarr where he gets these luxuries. Perhaps it's true that he buys for a small price what the street children can beg from diplomats and aid workers or steal from bigger shops in Kigali, only an hour's bus ride away. This is not Nadine's concern. Her task is arranging for Rose and the other children to have an abundance of shiny materials to dress up the old fig tree in the backyard. Every Christmas, Maman makes sure there are presents under the tree before waking the children. How does she manage it, getting up even before Tucker to surprise everyone with boxes wrapped in festive paper she saves from year to year?

Nadine gravitates toward a table scattered with bright silk-like blouses, her fingers grazing the glossy fabric. Maman should have something luxurious she would never consider buying for herself. Something to make her feel special, if only for a few moments while opening a package. A hand drops lightly onto her shoulder, spinning her around. A small cry rises to her throat, where she must keep it.

"I didn't mean to scare you," Christian Kensamara says.

"So, now you follow me?" Nadine straightens, as if a steel rod has been inserted into her spine. She coolly regards the hand now on her upper arm but does not remove it.

"I'm sorry," Christian says, the softness taking Nadine off guard. For a brief moment, his touch is warm and reassuring again. The touch of her friend, Chrissie, who walked her home from school, one hand gripping hers, the other carrying a board with nails in it. "Please, *inshuti*," he says, "go back to school early. Don't talk to the attorney who visited your home yesterday. It is best, *inshuti*—"

"Do not call me that, Christian," Nadine snaps, shrugging off his hand. "We are not friends." She goes rigid, trying to control the trembling that begins somewhere between her stomach and chest. It is the place where she will always be that scared young girl at the church, the girl who looked out of a cracked door and saw her friend, holding perhaps a machete, she couldn't be sure. She doesn't remember except in the place deep within her that will always be afraid. He was guarding the door of the utility shed, making certain she did not escape. A spike of anger quiets the trembling; he begged her to believe that he was, in fact, protecting her, until Papa Henry could safely return.

"It's true," Christian says, "we are not friends anymore." He touches the scar on his forehead, made by his own brother's knife. Felix had tried to scare some sense into him when he, at first, refused to join the Interahamwe. "But it's also true that the soldiers from Kigali would have killed me if I didn't cooperate," he continues. "They would have killed me as easily as they did everyone else."

"My parents." Nadine says flatly. "My uncles and aunts. My cousins. Friends." She sees a distant image: she is standing on a chair to look fully out her tiny bedroom window. There, in the field where Madame Kensamara grows coffee, are Chrissie's father and other men she recognizes, some fathers of Hutu schoolmates, along with the men who came in a truck from Kigali to organize the local militia. They sit there all day, watching, making sure nobody—Tutsi or Hutu—leaves their homes. This goes on for a few days, and then a week. The food is running out in the houses that have been marked with a red "X." No water. No electricity.

She and cousin Sylvia slept in her parents' bed at night, and during the day they all sat in the gathering room. At first, Baba amused them with stories about growing up in Swaziland. After a few days he sat motionless in a chair, his face ashen, while Umama cleaned or knit. She and Sylvia played card games to pass the time. They all talked to Baba, but it was clear he had already left them. She could see it in her father's faded eyes. It was a small blessing, knowing that Baba's spirit was perhaps back in Swaziland when some of the men from the field, including Rahim Kensamara, pounded on their front door and beat him to death, making Umama watch. Nadine heard Umama moaning, begging them to kill him swiftly, while she and Sylvia hid in the rafters above their bedroom.

"You are happy in Nairobi, yes?" Christian says.

She shrugs, not wanting to give him any absolution. He went to

Uganda shortly after the genocide and didn't return for the trial of his father and the others who organized the massacre. Why should she believe he wants to help her now? He reaches out his hand, but stops short of touching her again. "Now that Felix has been released from prison," he says, "you need to go where you are safe."

"I am not afraid," Nadine lies. Her heart is pounding against her ribs like a parrot in a too-small cage. At the church, Felix Kensamara amused his friends by making a joke of her life, asking Chrissie if they should keep his playmate alive so she could tell what happened. Now, Felix is afraid she actually will talk. Is he still proud of what he did?

"Believe this, Nadine," Christian says. "You must go."

She waves her hand through the air as if to wipe away a foolish boy's useless threat. Her eyes briefly meet his. She sees the history they share. The fear.

"My brother will hurt you," he says softly.

Nadine freezes, her hand suspended in air. Felix used to sit on his back porch, watching her and Sylvia on the swing set and playing tag with their friends, with a look of bemused disdain. Felix was the leader of the older boys at school who didn't just call the Tutsi girls names but sometimes followed them after school, pushed them down hard and took their schoolbooks. Felix joined the Interahamwe, the Hutu militia, of his free will, months before the truck loaded with soldiers carrying guns and handing out machetes to Hutus came to their town.

Nadine turns to leave, but Christian blocks her way. "Promise me," he says. "You won't talk to the attorney. You won't testify at the *gacaca*. It's the only way I can stop him."

"I do not need your protection." Nadine pushes past him. "I am not a child anymore." A wave of nausea erupts and she rushes out the door. It's the smell of the shed: turpentine and ammonia for keeping the church clean, and something so vile that she kept a hand to her nose until she realized the disgusting smell was *her*. It was the smell of the stickiness on her body, the crusted blood, not just her own, and the filth. Dirt from the ground, dirt from the men who had lined up fifteen of the girls taken from their neighborhood, several as young as Rose, and ordered them to remove their clothes. Adia, Marie, Rashida. She remembers all of their names. Cousin Sylvia. She sometimes awakens at night, even still, to soak in a scalding hot tub. But it is not possible to ever be clean again.

It's all she can do to control the trembling as she walks home with Rachel. Alone in Tucker's room, her room while Rachel's here, she retrieves an impala-skin satchel from the top shelf of the closet. Holding the hide to her chest, waves of calm surge through her.

Nearly three years ago, on Umama's birthday, she was digging up wildflowers in the forest to plant at her family altar. Delicate pansies for Umama, tough spiky thistle for Papa, daisies for Sylvia. Her trowel clanged against something hard—a metal box—under the moss that grew along the riverbank, where the purple pansies thrived. There was something exciting about opening the box and unwrapping the plaid dish towel, as if she was opening a gift. She stared at the gun for a long time, sunlight warming metal, fusing it to her palm. Yes, she thought, it was a gift from Umama to give her the strength needed to go to Arusha and speak of things, in front of a courtroom full of people, that her body knew but her mind could not yet admit. Knowing the gun was hidden beneath the loose floorboard under her bed made her feel protected. It was comforting to know that, if need be, she could rely on something with more power than she had.

Now, she removes the gun from the satchel. It fits her hand perfectly. She checks the chamber: five bullets remain. She fired the sixth one into the forest on the day before leaving for Arusha, dropping the weapon with the force of the unexpected explosion, the shake of leaves on a nearby tree, the chastising screams of a chorus of monkeys. She vowed never to fire the gun again. She would give it to Tucker, not wanting to upset Lillian, after the trial. But the longer the gun remained in the satchel under her bed, the more she grew to depend on its existence. It protected her while she slept, kept the nightmares away, rather like how Papa Henry had explained his dreamcatcher.

Many nights at school, especially since the Tribunal attorney first called, she has missed being able to pull this gun out from under her bed to feel the coolness against her skin. Sometimes, she imagines the gun in her hand, pulling the trigger when the Hutu men forced their way into her family's home. *Umama, Baba, come quick! We'll go out the back window, run through the woods, down the hill to the river.* She dreams of her family walking at night, all night, hiding in the water and breathing through reeds during the day, for a week or as long as it takes to reach the Uganda border.

In her dreams, there are no gunshots in the front hall, no smell of fear on Sylvia's skin as they hold each other in the closet, no blood-soaked pale blue sofa where Umama holds Baba for the last time. Now, she inhales a sharp breath and nuzzles the nose of the pistol into the notch between the wings of her ribs, the place where the tremble begins. Her finger caresses the trigger with a knowing that is soothing. Freeing.

She startles at a knock on the door. "Sorry, I'm coming," she shouts, remembering her promise of a bedtime story for Rose and Zeke. She places the gun back in the satchel and cinches it tight. Could she actually use it? Could she stop the tremble forever?

RACHEL SURVEYS HER BELONGINGS SPREAD out on the quilt, and then the open suitcase at the end of the bed: definitely too small. She sets aside her favorite faded-white jeans, the blue and gold batik shirt Nadine gave her and a bulky flannel shirt to wear on the plane, but she'll still have to leave some things behind. The corkboard propped up on the desk, for one. It's bigger than her suitcase, even if she disassembles the pieces of her father's life.

She surveys the time capsule, a work of art, really: a cracked leather camera strap slung over one corner of the frame, the dreamcatcher over the other side. Dried purple daisies that Nadine collected from the soccer field are pinned in place throughout the collage of photos and notecards that the two of them have cobbled together over the past month. The centerpiece is her necklace of animal beads, pinned like a frame around the postcard of a lion sunning on a rock. She removes the dreamcatcher swiftly, as if tearing off a Band-Aid, and hangs it back in the closet. Nadine can keep this fairytale notion of protection that Henry Shepherd dreamed up. The rest of the board she'll take apart later, after Mick calls, and pack in a bag.

She picks up the phone in the kitchen on the first ring, anxious to share her good news. "I'm leaving on Sunday, your Saturday night," she tells her husband. "Either way, it's only two more days. I'll be home in time to go to the Catskills for Christmas." It is a good plan, good for her marriage. And yet a sadness rises, souring the sweetness of Mick saying that he and Louie will pick her up at the airport. It's not only her father she's leaving here. Lillian is finally warming up to her, actually confided in her about the Kensamara brother.

"I love you," Mick says.

"I love you, too," she says, but it comes out like a question. Her mind flashes to Tucker, who's at the hospital in Kigali with Rose. He wasn't sure they'd be back by Saturday for the party. How will she say goodbye to them? To Nadine?

"Listen, Ray, I know going to my folks' house for Christmas isn't your ideal holiday."

"No, it's fine."

"How about a low-key New Year's Eve? Just you and me, and a bottle of Dom Perignon. A new beginning."

"That sounds heavenly." Rachel sighs. Yes, a good plan.

"Some of the bluesy-jazz stuff you like. A little Ella, a little Coltrane."

"We can throw in a Springsteen album for you, but no Metallica."

"Deal."

The phone is warm against Rachel's cheek as they make plans for Christmas. They'll drive up into the mountains after the presents are all opened and make angels in the virgin snow, eat lunch at the diner that serves meatloaf and macaroni. Comfort food. It's been so long since they've been in sync, bantering playfully instead of negotiating like plea-bargaining attorneys.

"So, I talked to Ma."

"About?"

"A memorial service for the baby. She wants to do something special on Christmas Eve."

Rachel pulls the phone slightly away from her ear, a metallic buzz in the connection creeping in as her husband unfolds his own plan. A special prayer at Midnight Mass. Ma's already planted a fruit tree, pears he thinks, in the backyard before the ground froze. They'll each sprinkle some of the ashes under the tree. Aunt Somebody's coming from Baltimore with a silver urn. "It's been in the family for two generations."

"No," she says. "Just…no!" Didn't he get her last email? On New Year's Day, they'll take Serena's ashes in the box at the top of their closet and spread them in the fresh snow in Vermont. Maybe, the note was lost in cyberspace. Maybe, he just didn't get it.

"C'mon, Ray," Mick chides. "I want her buried at the cemetery in town with the rest of my family."

"That's not what I want," Rachel says. The buzzing on the phone line, or maybe it's just in her head, grows louder. "Mick? Are you still there?"

"Look, we tried it your way last time."

"My way?"

"You packed up the nursery, alone."

"I was in shock. I didn't know."

"You found a way to move on. Alone."

"I didn't know what else to do."

"No," Mick says sharply. "You made a choice."

Rachel inhales gingerly, as if she's been punched. After the first miscarriage, she was stuck in a lonely, timeless kind of hell. During the ten weeks she had been pregnant, she kept waiting to *become* a mother. She never felt different in any of the ways the books described. No mother's intuition, no dreams about the baby growing inside of her, no glow when she looked in the mirror. Not even morning sickness. She wouldn't have known she was pregnant except for a craving for chopped liver, was far from certain she knew how to be a good mother. She kept waiting for the metamorphosis she had always imagined, terrified it was merely a myth.

"Now, I'm doing what I have to do," Mick continues, "to move on."

"From me?" Rachel asks weakly, but he doesn't answer. Or, maybe, his voice has fused with the cottony buzz.

The first miscarriage had been, in a way, a relief. A horrible relief, the pain of it a thick residue on her womb that could not be sucked away. She was terrified it would infiltrate her blood, flow through her veins, turning her skin a sickly yellow shade of shame, terrified that her husband would see the putrid relief if they packed up the nursery together. But this time has been different, from the moment she felt Serena turning somersaults, jabbing her with tiny fists. She felt Serena growing stronger and bigger. She worried about her. Loved her. There was no magic moment of transformation, but now she is a mother. Still.

"We both need to put this behind us," Mick says. "This…thing we're stuck in."

"Serena's death," Rachel says softly, the buzzing replaced by a peaceful stillness. Have they ever actually named this thing? Said their baby's name aloud after the miscarriage?

"Don't be morbid," Mick snaps, and then apologizes. "Look, I want to save this marriage, I do."

"So do I."

"But, Ray, I'm not like you. I need my family."

RACHEL WALKS ACROSS THE YARD to the farmhouse, mesmerized by clusters of bright pinpoints of light emerging in the dark blue sky. The phone call with Mick is heavy in her limbs, weighing her down. *Ray, I'm not like you…* Funny, she had thought *she* was his family.

Lying in the grass, staring up at the hazy arc of the Milky Way, some one hundred thousand light-years away, there's the sense that she has been here before. The sky seems to tilt just a little.

She is on a blanket next to her father's lawn chair, making a wish on the North Star, wishing he would break out of his sad trance and show her the crocodile's tail and lion's paw twinkling above. She is staring up at the Day-Glo galaxy that canopies Serena's crib, on the night Mick implied that the second miscarriage was her fault and she knew their marriage was broken, quite possibly beyond repair. It all feels like the same supermassive black hole of grief.

The memory of Serena's tiny elbow or heel jabs at Rachel's ribs; she caresses her stomach. She doesn't want to move on. She'll always cherish those few short months when her baby turned somersaults in her womb, settled to the vibrating hum of Billie Holiday, and seemingly couldn't get enough of Balducci's cannolis and lukewarm chamomile tea. Nobody can take those moments away from her. It's the place where she will always love Serena, always miss her, always be her mother just as a part of her will always be Henry Shepherd's daughter.

Back in her room, the photos on the corkboard propped up on the desk under the window are bathed in starlight, bright and glossy but too dim to make out the images. She looks out the window, images of the past few days flashing before her: Felix Kensamara clicking his fingers like a camera, matches falling to the ground, the insistence in Maura's voice as she invited her for tea.

Branches from the jacaranda tree that obscure the moon form a web of shadows over a corner of the corkboard, like a photo-negative of the dreamcatcher she stashed in the closet still looms there, over her father's life. *Maura's merely protecting her family. She has no reason to help you, to tell you the truth.* What nightmares is Lillian keeping from her? Before going back home, she needs to find out more, not just the happy stories about picnics and the time a baboon chased her father into the river. She needs to find the real Henry Shepherd. The truth is, he's still part of her too. For better or worse, he is her family.

TWENTY-SIX

RACHEL DISMOUNTS NADINE'S GREEN HUFFY, and pushes it up the steep hillside leading out of Mubaro. The women and children working in the fields stop as she passes by, regarding her as a curiosity. The women stare, perhaps offer a nod but rarely smile, shush their young ones who point and giggle. She has become used to this, being an outsider, over the past month. The whispers of *mzunga*, the way the soldiers in town sometimes follow her for a few blocks or ask where she's staying. Mostly, as Tucker says, people are merely inquisitive about a white woman travelling alone, maybe even looking out for her. Their curiosity no longer unnerves her. But today, she courts any slight smile of reassurance, greedily stockpiles every hint of soothing vanilla and eucalyptus in the air. Near the top of the hill, she turns onto a gravel path, walking quickly, churning up a crunch-and-scrape below her feet that might scour away Lillian's warning that Maura doesn't have her best interest at heart.

A commotion in a nearby tree pulls up chill-bumps on her arms. Within seconds, a troop of baboons is assembled along the roadside, some snacking on green coffee beans and leaves as if settling in for a matinee. More likely, sussing out if she has any real food or means of defending herself before moving closer. She buys a little time to hop onto the Huffy by chanting the first song that comes to mind, loud enough to be a bit threatening but not so loud that the baboons go on the offensive. Funny, this Kinyarwanda Christmas carol that Nadine has patiently taught her over the past few days sounds far less foreign than the Destiny's Child and Usher that Naddie cranks up on her computer.

At the end of the road, there's a clearing with about a dozen identical brick houses. Each yard has a fire pit and some sparse landscaping, a fruit tree or two, and low beds of flowers lining a walkway. Rachel thinks of the neighborhood where she grew up in Jacksonville: tract houses dotting cookie-cutter yards, pipe metal playgrounds in the back. This is Mubaro's version of a suburban subdivision. Madame Kensamara is husking a basket of corn on the front porch, waiting for her.

"I'm so happy you came," the stout woman says, getting up with some effort. "*Murakaza, neza.* Welcome."

"I appreciate the invitation, Madame Kensamara." Rachel bows and places a closed hand over her heart.

"Call me Maura." The older woman returns the sign of respect, and then motions toward the front door. "I invite you into my home as a friend. Yes?"

"Yes, of course," Rachel says. They have, in fact, become friendly during her routine morning visits to the bakery, Maura fixing her an espresso or sometimes a pot of tea. It's possible that she invited her here to figure out a way to end the trouble between Nadine and her sons. Maybe Lillian's wrong. Maybe they all want the same thing.

The house is surprisingly sparse: a single sunlit room decorated with brightly striped cushions on the cement floor against one wall and a batik curtain that probably walls off a sleeping area. Maura pulls out a chair at a metal table in the tiny alcove that serves as the kitchen. "It's just me here now…" Her voice trails off into a sigh as she sits.

Rachel follows her gaze to the photos taped to the wall: two young boys in blue shorts and white button-down shirts, probably school uniforms, on a soccer field. A young mother cradles an infant in her arms. An attractive man with nearly black skin, the same thick features as Felix, sits at this table and lifts a glass of red wine in a toast. The entire family dressed in their Sunday best, arms around each other on the front porch of this house. It's hard to believe the ordinary-looking husband and father masterminded the massacre at the church, and enlisted his two young sons.

"You have a beautiful family," Rachel says, afraid Maura might be able to read her thoughts.

"Rahim was a good man."

Rachel keeps her eyes on the photos.

"A good father," Maura says fiercely. She stands and reaches to wipe some dust off a photo frame. Rachel can't help but stare at the scar on her forearm as the sleeve of her shirt inches upward.

Maura lifts her sleeve to reveal thick, purple-black rivulets that bubble under her skin. "I was lucky to keep this arm. The Tutsi soldiers held it to the fire in the yard, asking where to find my husband. Rahim heard my screams from the coffee field. He sacrificed his life for me."

"During the genocide?"

"After he was released from jail. Two years ago."

"I'm sorry you were hurt."

Maura blows out a puff of air and rolls down her sleeve. "My husband was murdered. One son put in jail and the other living in Uganda with my brother's family, afraid to move back home."

Rachel opens her mouth and Maura holds up a finger to stop her. "Rahim was guilty, I know this. But the Tutsi army has killed, too. Tens of thousands of Hutus—some guilty, some not. This hatred between brothers with the same great-grandfathers goes back hundreds of years, even before Europeans came and put the Tutsis in charge because they looked most like them. We were slaves to the Tutsis, not allowed to own land although Hutus were the majority. Did you know this?"

"No." Rachel's gaze drops to the table. Stupid, so stupid. How could she possibly understand the history of these tribes, the built up hatred? Lillian's right: she shouldn't have come here.

"*Aiya*, my manners," Maura says. "I invited you here for tea."

"It's okay, really. I should—"

"No, sit, sit. I go to heat water over the fire in the yard. American tea, no sweet milk, like in my shop."

Rachel's eyes dart from the open door, her escape route, to the photos of Maura's family that pin her to the chair. What the hell was she thinking? She would come here and chat with Maura about her sons bullying Nadine, as if they're schoolkids trading insults at recess? Jesus, they are still kids. Felix laughing, pretending to snap her photo with his fingers. A few mornings ago, Christian was in the bakery dithering over a chocolate croissant or cinnamon beignet like it was the most important decision of his day. Just one, Maura lovingly scolded. Six years ago, these boys were soldiers.

And then there's Nadine, who hums softly to herself and makes up stories for Rose, pretending their mothers are sister-angels who watch over them. They take the form of stealthy panthers at night and the ever-present yellow finches with their black-painted warrior faces during the day. Naddie makes wishes on flower petals scattered into the wind, skips with the contagious abandon of a young girl. Rachel clenches her fist. How does her *inshuti* forget for even a few moments all she's been through?

The photos on the walls seem to slant downward, casting admonishing stares, as if she has been caught in voyeuristic revelry, peeking into a forbidden window and witnessing the intimate, private moments back when this home held a family. She stands to leave and then freezes, overcome with a shame that stings her eyes.

"You are leaving?" Maura is at the open door, a teapot in her hands. Overlaid on her face lined with sorrow is the loving gaze, faded with years of sunlight, of the young mother in the photo peering down at the baby cradled her arms.

Rachel shakes her head slightly but doesn't speak, doesn't sit.

Maura looks past her to the photos and whispers something, or maybe it's just the heavy hiss of a sigh that Rachel hears. She goes to take the clay pot, her hand touching Maura's arm, the one with the scars. Maura is simply another woman—a wife, a mother—who has experienced unfathomable loss. Is that why she invited her here? Did Maura simply think that a woman travelling across the world to find her father would understand her own loss, her own pain? "I want to understand," Rachel says. She sits down again. "Please."

Maura sips tea, slowly, as if it's medicinal. "We are told not to talk about the genocide or the wars before that," she says. "The past has no place in today's Rwanda, our new president tells us. We can be fined for speaking of these things in public."

Rachel nods. That's why Maura wouldn't talk to her in the bakery with the soldiers posted on street corners within view.

"We are told to start over," the older woman continues. "But then, I am told my sons will both go on trial again at a community *gacaca* in January. Christian has quit a good job at a factory in Kampala to come home again. Felix was released from jail only weeks ago, and speaks of leaving in the night to join the Hutu army in Congo. I may never see him again. How can we start over?"

Rachel bites the inside of her lower lip. What they did... How could Maura possibly think it was okay? Then again, how could she sit here and even pretend to understand?

"Come." Maura leads Rachel into the backyard, to a wooden outhouse. She opens the door and stares into the dark shack, seemingly unaware of the stench. "My two nieces, Adanna and Eshe, hid here for several weeks. I made beds of blankets among the coffee bushes where they slept at night. They were five and seven. Still babies."

The smell of human waste is rancid and potent; it's part of the story. Rachel can't turn away. Out of the corner of her eye she sees wispy shadows glide into the grove of low bushes. There's the scratchy sound of something or someone scrambling through the brambles to find safety. She takes a step toward the bushes and then stops. Of course, that's not possible. It's just the gathering clouds churning up mist from the ground, the wind rattling branches.

"My sister was Hutu, her husband Tutsi," Maura continues. "They were desperate to save their girls. I knew to hide them well, for all of our sakes."

"They were safe here?" Rachel asks, the woozy answer forming in her gut.

Maura shuts the door. "Rahim and two other soldiers came home for lunch one day, unexpectedly. He did it quickly, one shot to the back of each girl's head, before the others..." She reaches out a cupped hand, as if to offer Rachel something or catch a handful of dew. "That night we buried the girls in the bushes, wrapped in blankets that had kept them warm while they slept. Never before had I seen my husband's tears, although I knew all along they were there."

Rachel studies the landscape of Maura's palm: dark valley-like creases; mounds of skin, ashen and rough like the Virungas. She tries to imagine the thickening moisture in the air forming rivulets in the bowl of this craggy hand, softening it. She flashes on Tucker, looking over the valley of lakes where God had laid low for ninety days. Searching.

"What your husband did was, in a way, kind," she says. Horrific, yet somehow loving. She wants to see this story the way Maura does. She braces hands on knees, her legs suddenly unsteady, unable to shake loose the image of a terrified girl with Nadine's features whose beloved uncle is aiming a gun at her head.

Maura drops her cupped hand. She turns to walk back toward the house. Rachel follows unsteadily, eyes on the ground. The light rain beads up on the cracked earth, just as on her bare arms, forming an icy slickness even though the air is dense and warm. Her hair is damp, T-shirt and jeans sticking like Saran Wrap. "The choices you had to make. Your husband..." she says. Even her words are thick and difficult to maneuver. "I can't imagine."

"Many, like Rahim and my boys, did not have the luxury of choice."

Maura turns to Rachel. "Your father was at the church by choice."

"To rescue Nadine."

"He came with his camera."

"He always had a camera around his neck. Tucker and Lillian, that's what they said."

"Did they say how he knew to come to the church? My husband sent Christian to get the American with the camera."

Rachel wipes the slickness from her face, but it only seems to smear. She bites her lower lip, but the questions come anyway. "Why would Rahim do that?" Why would her father go?

"The government ordered my husband and others to document the Interahamwe victories over the Tutsis," Maura says. "I know it sounds terrible now but every day, for months before the mass killings began, on the radio and in the newspapers, we were told this war against our neighbors was necessary. Justified."

Rachel's head is buzzing, nearly deafening, like the flies hovering around the pit toilet. Her eyes dart to the bike on the front porch; maybe she can make a run for it, escape Maura's words. People being chopped into pieces. Children raped. Her father snapping photos he could sell. Children like Nadine.

"I have to go...the rain." Rachel stumbles toward the porch. *Nadine.* Her father helped, he rescued her. It's this thought that keeps her feet moving even though her legs are heavy, her jeans wet and stiff.

"It is not so easy to judge the ones you love," Maura calls after her. "This is what you need to understand, to remind Lillian and Nadine. My husband and my boys did what was needed to survive. Henry Shepherd made a profit from the suffering. Who will accuse him in court? Who will lock him away in prison?"

RACHEL RACES DOWNHILL ON NADINE's bike, trying to outrun the gray clouds swirling above, trying to outrun Maura's words. *Your father was there by choice. Taking photos for Rahim.*

Did he really think he'd sell photos to magazines, like the glossy images of gorillas and orchids that Lillian showed her? How could this be the same man who felt sorry for the animals trapped in cages at the zoo? The same man whose proudest achievement was the weekend he spent in Atlanta, the images he captured of Reverend King and Lillian prominently displayed on his office wall.

The sky opens up with sharp droplets that pelt Rachel's back and arms. She stands on the pedals and leans into the wind to catch more speed, to dry her tears before they fully form. This wasn't the same man, the father she came here to find. It's this place. The genocide. *The injustice and brutality chipped away at your father. He drank a lot. He was depressed.* Jesus, Lillian tried to warn her; he changed. That's why she stopped visiting him in London, why she wouldn't chase after him. That's why she didn't want her to come here in the first place.

Rachel pedals faster. Lillian knew the version of Henry Shepherd she longed to find had ceased to exist. Why the hell did Tucker trick her into coming? Was he flat-out lying about her father rescuing Nadine at the church or just clueless?

Nearly down the hill, Rachel hears the low growl of a truck pulling up beside her, the driver commanding her to stop. Her brakes are no match for the rain-slicked road but she's more afraid of disobeying what could be a soldier's orders than falling. She jackknifes the bike into the grassy ditch, landing hard on her side. "Shit," she mutters, pushing the bike aside, rubbing her shoulder. A door creaks open and slams, and then someone is standing over her.

"*Jambo*, Rachel Shepherd," a familiar voice says. She looks up to see Christian Kensamara, rain plastering a black T-shirt to his thin frame. The driver revs the engine, impatient for whatever's going to take place.

"Tell me, why are you out alone so close to night?" Christian asks.

"Visiting a friend," Rachel replies, trying to mimic calm. Did Maura tell them she had been at their home? "Look, I just want to get back to Kwizera before dark."

The driver rolls down the window and yells sharply in Kinyarwanda. Definitely an order. It takes Rachel a minute to recognize Felix without his red-trimmed aviator sunglasses, squinting through the rain. Christian mumbles a response, and then to Rachel, "It's not safe here," he says, holding out his hand. "You shouldn't have come."

She considers his hand and gets up on her own, pain shooting through her shoulder. Felix cusses in English as he heaves his body out of the truck. He pushes past his brother to grab Rachel's backpack from the ground and dumps out the contents: a notebook and pens, a few postcards, a half-full bottle of water, Chapstick. Nothing she can't replace. He rifles through her wallet, takes forty dollars, and tosses the Visa card and some stray receipts into the ditch. He studies the plastic accordion of a dozen photos: her mom on the beach, her and Mick atop the Empire State Building, the sonogram of Serena. What possible value could these be to him?

"My passport," she says. "Please, leave my passport so I can get the hell out of here."

Christian takes a step toward his brother and grabs the passport, glances at Rachel like maybe he's actually going to give it to her, and then palms it. The two brothers get back into the truck. Felix tosses the photos at her and spits out the window for good measure. The truck peels out, splattering flecks of mud.

Rachel watches as they drive away, Christian waving her passport out the window. She tries to upright the battered bike, but instead, stumbles and lands in the ditch. Her shoulder is throbbing and her left cheek, too. She swipes water from her face and cringes, appraising fingers speckled with pebbles and blood. Her heart races as she sweeps a hand through the dirt and sticks, rescues the photos and then the Visa card as an afterthought. She pats the photos on her T-shirt and tucks them both back into her wallet.

Fuck, she can't just sit here. It's getting dark and cold. What's to stop the Kensamara brothers from coming back? She pushes herself up gingerly, tests her weight on one leg and then the other. The rain is letting up, which only makes her colder as she starts down the hill toward the specks of light in town. It will take a good hour at this rate, favoring her left leg even though that doesn't help her shoulder, to make it to the café where she can call someone to pick her up. But who? Tucker and Rose are in Kigali. Does Nadine drive? Lillian isn't an option; she'll think Henry's foolish daughter is screwing things up even more. She walks faster, pain zinging up her left calf with every step.

Two streaks of light on the road become brighter, bigger. She cuts a glance toward the brush on the other side of the ditch, but what if it's someone who might help her? Her legs go numb, arms dropping to her sides like a stunned animal.

"Rachel, what the hell." Tucker jumps out of the Jeep, almost before it stops, and whips his coat around her shoulders. The warmth brings up a spike of shivers as he dabs at her bruised cheek with a bandana. "Did someone do this to you?" he asks.

"The Kensamara brothers stopped me."

"They did this."

"No, they didn't touch me. Just wanted to scare me."

"Scare Nadine."

"I fell off her bike. It's ruined."

"But you're okay?"

The slight movement of a single nod seems to release every tensed muscle in Rachel's body at once. She collapses into the solidness of Tucker. The smell of him is surprisingly familiar. Soothing. He runs a hand along the nape of her neck and down her spine. Her back tenses—too familiar. And then his hands are on her shoulders, supporting her, as he looks into her eyes with a penlight. A doctor checking out his patient, of course, nothing more.

"I'm fine. Really." She shifts her weight from one foot to the other and back again, even though her ankle feels like it's on fire. "So, Rose… How was Kigali? The blood transfusion?"

"We'll have to wait and see. But Rose felt good enough to come home for the tree decorating party tomorrow."

"That's good."

"Yeah, she could use something to celebrate." Tucker clicks off the penlight and exhales a long, shaky breath. He grabs onto her, an unmistakable hug.

"I'm glad you're both back," she says.

IN THE JEEP, AS RACHEL'S nervous system resets, relief spikes into anger. "You lied to me," she says.

Tucker throws her a quick baffled scowl. "You'll have to be more specific."

"You said my father went to the church to rescue Nadine."

"True."

"Maura told me he went there to take photos."

"He always had a camera around his neck."

"He went to take photos for Rahim."

"I don't buy it."

"Not to rescue Nadine."

"But he did rescue her."

"No," Rachel shouts. That's beside the point. A fluke. "All he cared about was selling those photos, making money."

"Bullshit."

"He didn't care." Rachel gasps as Tucker touches her arm, a rush of air exploding in her lungs. "Henry Shepherd was a selfish monster, not—" A sharp breath cuts into her chest. Not my father.

"Rachel, listen, you've got it wrong," Tucker says, so evenly that at first she thinks he's angry. "All wrong. Things here aren't so clear-cut. Good or evil."

"Some things are just fucking wrong."

"Do unto others... The Golden Rule and all that?"

"I know it's not that simple."

"It's hard to wrap my mind around how the Hutu government twisted morality," Tucker says, his voice soft with wonder. "Over the past three decades, they pretty much fucked the Golden Rule, replaced it with the idea that God sanctioned the extermination of an entire tribe. Both Hutus and Tutsis came to accept that as the gospel truth. Can you imagine?"

"Truthfully? No, I can't."

"Isn't it possible that Henry taking photos of the massacre wasn't about doing good or evil, just trying to capture a version of morality gone mind-blowingly wrong?"

They drive through town in silence, except for Tucker drumming a finger in time to the tap of the windshield wiper. When the Jeep pulls into the winding driveway at Kwizera, he turns to her. "Maybe," he says, "your dad was simply a guy doing the best he could in an impossible situation. Could you accept that?"

TWENTY-SEVEN

THE FLAMES ARE NEARLY OUT BY THE time dozens of neighbors and friends start showing up, far more help than is needed to quell the fire in Nadine's little Christmas garden, but Lillian knew they would all want her to call. Folks show up with wheelbarrows and shovels to smash the last orange embers together. They show up with bowls of stew, loaves of bread and cheese, whatever they can spare from their own dinner tables. They show up with flowering plants exhumed from their own gardens. The men carry away shriveled plants and ash to bury in the woods, but they all know the acrid smell of petrol will linger for weeks. The women help Nadine dig up bulbs that might bloom again, advising her to keep adding fertilizer and turning the soil, give the land a few months to heal.

After the ground is no longer smoldering, they all hold hands around the demolished garden, swirls of petrol-tinged smoke lingering in the air. Lillian says a silent prayer of thanks: the damage is miniscule, everyone is safe. Foolish boys. All the Kensamara brothers have done is brought their community together and helped them to remember; the remembering is what keeps them strong. She looks around the circle of friends, into each face. Some acknowledge her with a somber nod, others softly chant, ensconced in their own prayer. And then there are those who stare past her, lost somewhere in time. *Six years ago. Eight. Twelve.* She knows when each of these Tutsi families lost their own crops and homes and had to rebuild, some with the help of the few brave Hutus here.

Thirty-two years. The candlelight vigil for Martin Luther King. A tragic loss, but it pulled folks together, blacks and whites. Their grief united them.

While people are setting up food on the patio, Lillian stands at the kitchen sink filled with cool water, trying to revive some charred lavender vines, sifting out those that are more purple than gray. She's relieved Tucker called; Rachel's fine, just banged up from falling off that rickety bicycle. The lavender will make a nice salve along with some eucalyptus to soothe the bruises—the ones on the outside. She has no idea how to heal the rest of Rachel's pain. Surely Maura told her about the photos that may or may not still exist. She's never seen them, never wanted to. Well, that's not quite true. She would gladly have endured viewing them at the trial for Rahim Kensamara and the others in Arusha two years ago.

It's a fine sight out the window: An impromptu band is starting up with someone strumming a gourd strung like a guitar. A group of teenaged boys, including Thomas and Robert, smack drums fashioned from upside-down plastic buckets, and several girls accompany

them on homemade wooden flutes. Nadine is laughing, loud and re-
bellious, dancing in a circle with Rose, Zeke and some neighborhood
kids, while others kick around a soccer ball in the yard. For just this
one night, all the house lights are on, inside and out, never mind the
electricity bill. Maybe Christian and Felix are out there somewhere
with binoculars, watching. Maybe they can see Nadine, or at least hear
the music.

Lillian strips purple buds into a bowl, releasing a heady aroma;
the healing herb is so much stronger than petrol. Tucker's Jeep rolls
into sight on the driveway. She plucks a few hearty branches from the
counter to arrange in a vase to place beside Rachel's bed. She'll see
that something survived the scorched garden.

"*Inshuti, inshuti!*" Nadine calls out, running over to help her friend
out of the Jeep. Rachel leans on Naddie as they head toward the farmhouse. Lillian smiles with pride; her daughter is resilient, more powerful than the fire. They all are.

LILLIAN MENTALLY CLEANS THE WHITE tile bathroom spattered
with mud, while she dabs antiseptic on Rachel's arm. The tub will
have to be scrubbed with bleach; Rachel's clothes in a heap on the
floor might come clean after a few washings… It keeps her mind from
wandering back to the Kensamara house, back to what could have
happened to Rachel when Felix and Christian found her.

"Now that you're cleaned up, I can distinguish the bruises from
the mud," she says evenly. "It's not so bad."

Nadine sits next to Rachel, kneading her friend's hand. She must
have apologized a dozen times. Of course Rachel doesn't blame her,

nobody does, but it's easier for Naddie to take on the responsibility for all of this mess. It gives her a sense of power in a senseless situation. That's why Rachel went to talk with Maura, too. Lillian's rather proud of her, trying to protect Naddie. She rolls up Rachel's pant leg to assess the swollen ankle. There's no standing between her daughter and the Kensamara brothers—people are only going to continue to get hurt. There's no protecting any of them from the past.

"How did Tucker know where to find me?" Rachel asks, wincing as she peers down at her leg. Nadine winces too, in solidarity.

"I had a hunch," Lillian says. "It's exactly what I would have done." She gently presses on the ankle bone, only a nasty sprain. "Not that I'm saying it wasn't foolish—"

"I know, I know."

"But I'm touched you were trying to help."

"You were hurt because of me," Nadine says. "I won't testify at the *gacaca*. I'll talk to Christian."

"You'll do no such thing," Lillian says, surprising herself. "This… what happened tonight, it won't stop even if you keep quiet and afraid. It won't stop if you keep blaming yourself…" She takes a deep breath. It's what the Tutsis have done for decades, accepting that they're second-class citizens, too afraid to stand up and fight. "Sugar, you need to tell the truth. Shout it."

"Yes, Maman," Nadine says unconvincingly, but Lillian leaves it alone and turns her attention to Rachel. Her ankle is badly swollen. "Let's get you into bed," she says, and then adds to Nadine, "Your turn in the shower, then off to bed. Both of you need some rest."

Lillian goes to the kitchen in the main building and finishes mashing the lavender with eucalyptus oil. All of the neighbors have left. Kwizera is pitch black except for a light over the kitchen sink and another in the farmhouse that she sees from her post at the window. Rachel's room, where Tucker is bandaging her ankle. That gal will surely have even more questions now. Lillian stops on her way back to the farmhouse, to sprinkle a bit of lavender on Nadine's charred garden. A small gesture of hope, her own try at gaining a bit of control.

The threads of Henry's life are unraveling and it's up to her to keep everything together, for Henry's sake as well as his daughter's. Or, perhaps, she can be a role model for Naddie and give Rachel pieces of her father's story that she can patch together into something warm to wrap around herself. That's what she came here for, isn't it? The trick is doling out bits of the truth without revealing the entire hurtful story.

She kneels to mulch a handful of purple buds over the dirt and ash. She spent hours tending to her own garden, her own pain, here on the side of the house where the sun hits just right all afternoon. What if she had told Henry about Gahiji, trusted him with the truth? Would things have changed between them? Would he have stopped running away every few months, chasing after the mountain gorillas that he joked were his second family, and stayed to protect her?

She has always maintained that they didn't need a marriage license or wedding rings, that she didn't mind his wanderings. The truth is, she never asked Henry for a real commitment because she was protecting herself from the pain of depending on him too much, loving him too much, and then losing him. Each time he left for a few weeks that might stretch into a month she was, in a way, training herself for the day when he would leave their family for good. She stands and brushes the dirt from her hands. Who is she really protecting now?

Thankfully, by the time Lillian reaches the farmhouse, Rachel is fast asleep. Hashing out what Maura told her can wait until morning; the fire is enough for one night. She pulls back the quilt, slowly, rubs the herbal poultice on the swollen ankle, and then redresses the bandage precisely as Tucker had it. The herbs will help, but that ankle's going to be tender for weeks. Travelling back to New York in two days won't be easy. Lillian massages more oil on scraped legs. The thought of Rachel staying while she heals is warm on her palms, the heat travelling up into her chest. She has become not only Nadine's confidante over the past month, but a part of Kwizera. Lillian smoothes the quilt under Rachel's chin; she has started to see her differently during the past few days—as family. Henry's daughter.

Rachel's body goes taut, a muffled cry caught in her throat, like she's trapped in a dream. "Maura…" She sits up and touches Lillian's arm tentatively, as if testing what is real. "She said horrible things about my father. Is it true? Did he take photos at the church massacre?"

"I honestly don't know," Lillian says. She has heard rumors but she does not know, not for sure, that Henry even went to the church. She never questioned that Tucker found him and Naddie in town. The three of them showed up on her front porch; they were safe. That was all she needed to know. "We'll talk tomorrow. You need your rest now, lots of rest." And time. Two days isn't nearly enough.

"I can't sleep. I keep thinking of him, taking photos." Rachel shakes her head, almost violently. "Tell me," she says, her voice ragged, "what did you love about my father? Please, I need to know."

"There were so many things."

"But what first attracted you to him?"

Lillian flashes on Henry standing at the back of the church sanctuary, so young and hopeful. The warmth in her chest turns searing and painful. "It's late. We'll talk tomorrow."

The high break in Rachel's voice as she says Lillian's name stops her from leaving. She sits on the edge of the bed. "Henry was handsome, even with the camera plastered to his face," she says. "But it was more than that. His excitement, snapping photos even before Reverend King came onstage, that's what caught my eye. The other photographers looked rather bored, leaning against the wall, chewing gum, examining their nails."

Lillian's heartbeat ticks up a bit. Henry's excitement was contagious, still is. "I tell you, that boy had such nerve, sauntering up the aisle while the others hung back. Imagine my surprise when he stopped right beside me. And then, the reverend came to the podium and started speaking about his plan for the march in Selma. He said it was time to take a stand. A risk. The entire congregation was on their feet, stomping and clapping. But I felt like this stranger and I were alone in our own bubble. I knew he longed to take a risk, do something grand with his life—just as I did. We shared a moment that was so powerful it united us for life."

Lillian moves closer, pulled by a force that is equally strong, connecting her with Henry's daughter in a way she doesn't quite understand. Before she knows it, she's telling her about Henry's airless studio apartment and how they spent most evenings up on the rooftop, him pointing out constellations and her falling asleep in his arms. She's laughing, recounting how they ate spaghetti every night for a week sometimes so they could splurge on a Saturday show at the Peacock. Bobby Bland, Dizzy Gillespie, B.B. King, Otis Redding. She's telling Henry's daughter about the Someday account, the money they scrimped and saved for their future. "Your father had the ability to see things, not as they were, but what might be possible. That's what made me fall for him." That's what has kept her loving him for close to forty years.

"My mom always accused him of being a dreamer," Rachel says. "Like it was a bad thing."

Lillian shakes her head. Daddy thought she was foolish, spending her savings to go to Kenya and teach for free. That's not what he had in mind, working hard to provide his daughter with a good education at Spelman. Henry was the one who encouraged her to dream, up on the rooftop while they counted stars. They would move to Africa together. She would teach and he'd take photos. They would have lots of children, build a family.

Rachel tugs on her arm, reeling her back into the story. "It couldn't have been easy for the two of you in Atlanta."

"We were in love. We thought that was enough."

"Why didn't it last?"

"We were too young," Lillian says. Too scared. She can still hear the screech of tires and the shatter of a bottle that was probably aimed at her. Henry's hand slipped from hers as he fell to the sidewalk in front of the store where they had been window shopping. A busy street in broad daylight; people stared, but nobody chased down the truck. Nobody offered to help. She sank to the sidewalk, hysterical, pressed her skirt against the gash above Henry's brow, so close to his eye. *Someone call an ambulance, call the police...* It was Daddy who finally showed up, someone had gone and gotten him. He drove Henry to the hospital, commanded her to wait in the car and then took her home. She rubs her fingertips together, as if Henry's blood is still crusted under her nails.

"But, it did last; he came after you," Rachel prompts. "He came here to find you. Why?"

"I sent Henry a letter not long after I bought Kwizera, not because I thought he'd come here but because I needed to remind myself that someone might actually believe I could pull this off. The place was a shambles. Nadine's folks and your father helped me to bring Kwizera to life."

"How do you do it? Stay hopeful. Stay here."

"The children," Lillian says. It's a reflex. They have always been her hope. "I'm sorry," she adds. "That was insensitive of me."

Rachel smiles down at her hand, cradling her stomach. "Once in a while, I still feel a little kick or jab of an elbow..." She looks up, her face questioning. "I never want that to go away."

"I admit, there was a time when I lost hope," Lillian says. "Several years after Henry left Atlanta, I became engaged to a man—a good man—who was killed in the Vietnam War. I was three months pregnant when Samuel died. Our folks all thought it was best to give up the baby for adoption. I wasn't strong enough to disagree. But I knew nobody could ever love that child as deeply as I did. It's not the same as a miscarriage, but I do understand the ache you still feel. The loss."

"You've helped so many children since then," Rachel says. "Lost so many."

"I had buried children before the genocide, but nothing could have prepared me..." Lillian shakes her head. At first, it was overwhelming. Henry and Tucker thought she didn't see them going out each morning before dawn to bury the bodies. She let them think that for a while, let them believe they were doing something to lessen the pain. But after a few weeks, she couldn't afford the sorrow. She was busy making sure there was water they could drink, hauling buckets from the river and boiling it over a fire in the yard, and food to eat, pooling resources with neighbors who also had a few vegetables or a cup of rice to add to a watery soup. There was no time to be slowed down by sorrow and it all became dammed up, stagnating inside of her like the putrid stream where dead bodies were dumped. But what is it that she truly wants to tell Henry's daughter? What will help her deal with her loss?

"After the fighting ended, I was completely drained. I needed help, but there was no one to help. Tucker took Rose and Nadine to Uganda to stay with a friend. Some of the other children had relatives they could live with, some stayed with families in town. Everyone was in shock, merely going through the motions. Bodies were buried. Trash was burned. There was no rebuilding, just clearing away the chaos. I had never been so scared in all my life. And then, your father left and things became worse. I was utterly alone." That's what broke open the dam inside of her. All the loss she had endured during the slaughter came pouring out, rushing through her veins, poisoning her soul. "The grief was so intense," she says. "I had to shut everything off. The pain. The love. Everything. Over time, it became clear to me that Henry felt the same way."

Rachel leans toward her and takes her hand. "It was like that after Serena died. I came here to find my father because I wanted to feel again. What did you do?"

"I went to my mother's home in Atlanta." Lillian stops, feels several sentences line up in her throat but can't coax them out. She's never told anyone about trying to find her son. The thought of finally seeing him was what gave her the strength to physically endure the trip back to

Atlanta. But it won't help Rachel to tell her that the adoption paper-work had been destroyed in a courthouse fire, so she skips over the part of the story where she couldn't drag herself out of the bed in her child-hood room for a full week. She had to find something—anything—to get her moving again.

"I spent a lot of time at the cemetery with Daddy and Deirdre," she says. Neither one of them would have stood for her wallowing in self-pity. "I had never taken the time to grieve for either one of them. It helped. I found a place to begin feeling again. A month later, I was ready to come home to Kwizera and start again."

"Was there a turning point?" Rachel asks. "How did you know you were ready to go home?"

"A newspaper photo," Lillian says. "There were lots of articles about the atrocities, photos of dismembered bodies, so many that I think people became numb. But this was a young woman sitting on the front porch of what was left of her home. Broken windows, the Kinyarwanda word for cockroach spray-painted in big letters across the front door. She was staring at her hands, folded in her lap. So defeated, like there was nothing she could do—not even whitewash her door. I saw myself in that photo. It snapped something back on, made me angry. Angry at myself—so many folks had suffered far greater losses. And, I was angry at Henry for leaving me alone with all that grief."

Rachel gets up gingerly and hobbles over to the desk to examine the corkboard jigsaw puzzle of photos, baubles, and notes that she and Naddie have spent so much time and love creating together. There's something missing from the right upper corner: the dreamcatcher. Lillian recalls taking it off the wall above the bed and placing it in the closet when Rachel's emails first set her mind down paths she didn't trust her footing on. It pains her that, apparently, Henry's daughter now feels the same way.

"What made you come back while my father stayed away?" Rachel asks.

Lillian shakes her head. It's a fair question, one she has often considered but never answered to her own satisfaction.

"He didn't care about the children," Rachel says, her voice high and wispy.

"Of course—"

"No, not the way you did."

Lillian stands behind Henry's daughter and studies the pieces of his life, trying to discover some new clue: dozens of images of gorillas, the river, orchids. Only a few of the children.

"If he did care," Rachel continues slowly, "then why..." She turns around, eyes moist with wonder. Lillian can see straight through to the place where the pain of Henry leaving has pooled.

"He loved you, sugar, truly he did," Lillian says, her chest swelling with all she cannot say. For years, she encouraged Henry to reconnect with his daughter, make amends with his ex-wife. She was the one who insisted that he go to visit Rachel after Merilee wrote to tell him about her cancer diagnosis and their daughter's whereabouts. Lillian agreed with Merilee: Rachel was going to need him. When Henry returned from New York and told her he had sat across the bar from his daughter, ordered a drink but hadn't revealed who he was, hadn't reached out and taken her hands... She couldn't fathom it. He told her he didn't know how to be Rachel's father anymore. Truth was, he didn't have it in him to stay and figure it out. That's what kept her from answering Rachel's emails; she told herself it was better that way. But now, Henry's daughter is looking at her, waiting for some kind of truth she can live with.

"He talked about you all the time," Lillian begins. "He wrote post-cards, the ones Tucker sent and more."

"Mom admitted he had called a few times during the first year after he left, but she wouldn't let him speak to me. He could have mailed letters that she destroyed."

"Yes," Lillian says carefully. "That is possible." But, perhaps, Henry never mailed those letters with a return address because it was easier that way. He could tell himself he was being a good father, writing to his daughter, without the responsibility that would come along with any letters she mailed back.

Rachel nods, hungry for more.

"He tried to find you," Lillian says, "in New York."

"When?"

"Shortly after Merilee became ill. She wrote to tell Henry you were attending New York University."

"Two journalism classes in three years. My main priority was bartending at clubs so I could listen to bands for free."

"Yes, I remember Henry telling me about a place he went to called the Mud Room."

"CBGB's—that's right!"

"He came home after five days. He couldn't find your apartment, the address Merilee gave him didn't exist... I can't recall exactly what happened."

"But he did look for me," Rachel says. "He wanted to find me."

Lillian hugs her tightly, before more lies can begin. "I'm sorry, so very sorry, that Henry hasn't come back," she says, feeling the pain, not of her own loss, but of the inherent cruelty of the truth, knowing that if she is entirely honest Rachel's face will forever change—the hope will drain right out of it—and she will be responsible for that.

HOURS LATER, LILLIAN SITS ON the floor in the attic, a brown leather photo album open on her lap. She has studied each page, each note Henry wrote, trying to memorize the words and images that have been hers to access whenever she's been lonely or simply needed to remember how to love him. Rachel's right: he didn't care about the orphans as deeply as she did. He loved them, in his way. But his passion was the images he saw through his camera lens, even when it meant ignoring what was right in front of him.

The night Henry left, Lillian sat on a mattress, the only furniture in the room that had been a storage closet before the slaughter began. She held baby Rose in her arms. She watched him pack his ruck-sack. It didn't take long; neither one of them had taken many things from the farmhouse after the Hutus ransacked it. She didn't ask him to stay; how could she? Rahim Kensamara had come to their home several times since the fall of Kigali a few weeks earlier, asking about some photos Henry had apparently taken in town and elsewhere. He was polite. He was scared. The new government was Hutu, but mak-ing arrests. Rahim kept saying he trusted Henry and believed he had destroyed the incriminating film, but he kept coming back. Earlier that night he had arrived with four other men, all carrying guns, who searched through closets and drawers, and examined the floorboards for one that might come up easily.

"They're good, Lilly, I know they're good," Henry said, holding up the black plastic bag with six rolls of film that had been buried in the forest for the past month. He tucked it away in the lining of his jacket.

"I'm sure," she said flatly. She also knew Henry would rather sell these photos than use them to put war criminals away, but she couldn't argue with him anymore. Now, Tucker was driving him to Kampala so he could rent a place and set up a darkroom, far away from the Hutus.

Henry took her face in his hands, traced her jaw with his thumbs. "If these photos are as great as I think they are, magazines all over the world will want them. We'll finally have enough money to hire more help—"

"I don't need more help," Lillian said. "I need you."

"I'll call from Kampala, or maybe London by the time the phone service is working here again. But don't worry. I'll call."

Lillian closes the album, smoothing her hand over the rough cover. Nearly four years of going to London, believing that, eventually, Henry would return. She believed in him, even seeing the well of his own faith subside, little by little, month by month. His skin seemed to develop a dusty film, his voice crackled, the moist light drained from his eyes.

Why did he accept her ultimatum so easily? It's been two years, not one phone call or letter. If she still had faith in Henry, she would have to believe something has prevented him from calling and asking for one more chance. Surely, he would beg her to come visit because he misses her touch, because without it he will turn to dust. It is also possible he has simply given up on their love. She does not know, not for sure.

She looks around the attic, her own corkboard medley of the pieces of Henry's life: the old VCR and box of movies they watched on Saturday nights, his paperback mysteries lined up on a bookshelf in the corner, and the hanging bag that protects the brown pin-striped suit he wore when they exchanged vows under the mopani tree. The uncertainty about why Henry hasn't contacted her softens the hard pit in her gut. The uncertainty makes her hang onto these cherished memories. But the uncertainty comes at a high price: Bitterness. Longing. Anger. She has had to replace her faith in Henry with a story that he gave up on their love, just as he had done in Atlanta and then in New York with his daughter, because it became too difficult.

Lillian clasps the album to her chest as she carries it downstairs to the room where Rachel is asleep. On the night Henry left, she told him straight out that she wouldn't mail this album to his daughter. At the time, she called it a show of faith. He would come back and mail it himself. Several years went by, and that faith became something desperate and petty. She coveted these photos and postcards that did not belong to her. The hard pit in her stomach moves up into her chest. She hasn't been protecting Rachel from the truth, not really. She's been protecting herself.

Depositing the album next to Rachel's bed is like unyoking a heavy weight from around her neck, a weight that has not been altogether unpleasant. This sudden floaty sensation is freeing; it is equally terrifying. What will keep her anchored now? She retrieves the dreamcatcher from the closet and places it atop the album. What she does know, without a doubt, is that Henry's daughter needs him to show up for her, perhaps in the only way he can, even if it means she must find a way to face the truth of the past six years. She must finally let him go.

TWENTY-EIGHT
{ London, August 1998 }

A T FIRST THERE IS ONLY THE CEILING above him: a gray stubble of dust laced with broken strands of web, the Rorschach of rusted water that could be the eye and tusk of a warthog skull or the handle of a machete. There are no grains of glass scattered across balding carpet that was once blue or green, but there is the familiar film of lime and ash and something astringent, more like turpentine than gin, that coats his mouth. There is the ache behind his eyes that keeps his lids half-shut against the gray light seeping through a grime-mottled window, his face sunken into the damp pillow that seems to exhale his sour breath. There is the pounding at his temples but no heartbeat, no arms or legs cramped from too much time spent in this bed, no bladder that needs draining. There are no thoughts, only a single word: *choices.*

Henry rises slowly onto his elbows, and then heaves one leg over the side of the bed, testing his footing. It has been two months—no, closer to three—since Lilly threw a bottle of banana gin against the wall behind the sofa bed to get his attention. *Damn it, Henry, you have choices!*

He used to measure time by her phone calls, Sunday evening at nine like clockwork, and her visits every two months. And then, at some point everything slowed down—became harder. Was it when his hands started shaking so badly he could no longer shoot photos? He stopped caring about most everything after that. Maybe it was two years ago, when he bought a plane ticket to Kigali that he never used. Or last year, when he quit seeing that shrink with rodent eyes who kept yammering on about visualizing the beauty before the genocide, as if that was somehow possible. He tried for a few months, and then he simply pretended to try for a few months more. When he quit therapy altogether, Lilly wasn't just angry. *Disappointed.* That's the word she used.

What is it they say about hindsight being 20/20? Looking back, he sees clearly that there was no specific event or two that he might be able to isolate, apologize for and expunge from his life. This slowing has been more of subtle shift since he left Kwizera. It's as if the plates of the earth have been moving apart over the past four years in a glacial manner, undetected, carrying him farther and farther from Lilly, their family, his old self. It became increasingly difficult for Lilly to get here every two months, and then ten or twelve weeks, but it wasn't only her doing, this fissure that developed between them. He began lying: he was travelling on assignment, too busy, even after he took a job at the bar downstairs because he couldn't keep his hands still enough to hold a video camera and shoot footage for commercials.

He gets to his feet, the debris from the gin bottle Lilly shattered in desperation no longer sharp, ingrained in the carpet or maybe in his skin; it's impossible to tell anymore. He pads gingerly toward the bathroom as if hot-footing it across sand. The mirror over the cracked porcelain sink is particularly unkind this morning. *Haircut*, a voice in his head says. His morning hygiene regimen is akin to the way a farmer might care for an old plow horse that has outlived its usefulness but he can't bear to send the old boy to the glue factory, not today. He runs a toothbrush over his teeth, steps under the shower for a few minutes, skimming a bar of soap from chest to thigh, and then tosses on the same gravy-brown sweatshirt and faded jeans he's worn for the past three days.

Coffee, the voice commands and Henry marches off to the kitchen. Caffeine is a necessity in the morning, food more of a chore that can be put off until noon, just before he heads downstairs for his shift. Tommy doesn't give him the evenings anymore, too many customers now that they serve chicken wings and stuffed mushrooms, too many fancy drinks. What the hell is a Long Island Iced Tea, anyway? He gets things mixed up, that's okay, Tommy says, let the waitress mix the cocktails. But it's not okay. Nothing is okay since Lilly left for good.

She stood right here in this kitchen, he's certain it was four months ago, sees it clearly now. *I've been patient for four years, but I can't pretend this is okay anymore.* She swept her hand around the apartment, landing on a bottle of gin on the counter between them. She had stopped asking him to come home and he had stopped pretending the therapy was working, but now she asked one more time. Now, she told him, the asking wasn't just for her. There was going to be a Tribunal trial for Rahim Kensamara and some other men in

September. Nadine had been subpoenaed to testify. *She needs you to come home and tell what you saw at the church,* Lilly said. *You were there. You can say the things she can't.*

Henry's heart quickens; he recalls a kind of panic rising as he placated Lilly. Of course he would come back for Naddie. How could he not? Four months was plenty of time to get himself together. He would contact that shrink with the rodent eyes again, how about that? He reached for the gin, thinking he would toss it down the sink. Instead, he froze. *Choose me, Henry,* Lilly said shakily. *Choose me, or I won't come back.* Now, he raises a similar bottle to his lips and then wipes at his eyes, the image of Lilly—right there in front of him—fading. For chrissakes, she was under the mistaken impression he had choices. He couldn't blame her for heaving the bottle against the wall. And then, she was gone.

Mr. Coffee sputters out a slick of black fluid that is slowly eating away the lining of Henry's stomach, along with the gin and greasy bar food. He tips a splash of gin into a cloudy coffee mug, swirls it around. How long will it take for time to stop altogether?

His eyes lock onto the photo above the sink: a close-up of a young girl's face, a machete at her throat, her eyes dull and resigned. A web of memories, fragile strands connected by this photo, momentarily paralyze him. The knife blade is also dull. He knows this because he saw Rahim Kensamara use the same machete to hack through tendons and bones, like a butcher at the market. At first, he could pretend he was also simply doing a job: taking photos that nobody else could take, photos the world needed to see. The chaos at the church was surreal at the time.

Months later, developing the film in Uganda where he could finally get his hands on some processing materials, it hit him: He had been wrong. No one should see these photos. He has kept the gruesome images as a reminder of why he can never go back home. All of them are buried in an envelope in the bottom desk drawer, except this one that he barely recognizes as Nadine, which he taped on the wall after Lilly left for the last time.

Mr. Coffee hisses and Henry pours black sludge into the mug, stirs it with a finger. The first gulp always burns going down. He winces, his eyes falling on the open drawer below the counter: chopsticks and crumpled take-out menus, keys that don't match any locks, a few forks but no spoons. He plucks out a serrated bread knife, tests the blade with his thumb. What Lilly doesn't understand, what he can't possibly explain, is that he didn't actually choose to leave Rwanda. He didn't choose the gin over her. It's not that he doesn't want, more than anything, to go home again. For chrissakes, who would choose this life? Who? If she had seen the photos, she would know there are no options. He had to leave, couldn't return, even if the Hutu soldiers hadn't been threatening him. But his last shred of solace is his one good choice: Lilly hasn't seen the photos. Nobody has.

Henry squeezes droplets of blood from his thumb onto the white tile counter, slowly, like seconds ticking away. There was so much blood; it was everywhere, soaking into the dry clay like rain. At first, when Henry showed up at the church, he had been relieved to see Rahim. But it soon became clear that this wasn't the same good-natured guy who had sold him new batteries for his camera at the hardware store in Mubaro just weeks earlier.

"So, Mister American, big-time photographer," Rahim said. "You want us to spare the girl Nadine? Then, make use of your camera.

Show the world the Hutu glory."

Henry fell to his knees in the dirt, begging for Nadine's life, for his own life, his voice quickly hoarse from shouting over the screams, warrior whoops, music blaring from a boom box somewhere. "Where is she?" he finally asked, taking a different tact. "Show me. I need proof she's still alive."

But there was something else Rahim wanted him to see. They went into the church and on the stage was a long line of women, waiting. Henry sat in the first pew and watched as Rahim and the others butchered them, one by one, like animals at the market. He tried to turn his head away to vomit and his neck met with the cool resistance of a blade. "We can add your head to the cabbage pile," a jubilant young voice said, setting off a round of jeers. "*Mzunga* cabbage. Tasty flavor with cockroach!" Henry glanced out a gaping hole in the wall behind the altar where a window had been busted out. Men in pink uniforms, Hutu prisoners bussed from massacre to massacre on work detail, were tossing cadavers into a dump truck and carefully placing the heads into big plastic garbage bags. Cabbage, that's what they called the heads; thirty cents each was the going rate. Henry shuddered as his stomach gave one mighty lurch, but nothing came up. There was nothing left.

"Take our photo, take our photo!" the men onstage chanted like some twisted church choir. A part of Henry, the part that had already left his body, watched with morbid fascination as his finger clicked on the shutter button. There was a reason the Hutus called the murder sprees their *work*. It was grueling; they were sweating. And the Tutsi women, for the most part, didn't even try to fight back. It was a given: they would die. It was the law. God's will. They had no choice.

Henry slams shut the kitchen drawer with such force that he takes a step backward, reaches for the counter to steady himself and instead lands a hand on the coffee carafe. "Shit!" he sucks at the scalded fold of skin between his thumb and finger, sinks to his knees as if praying to the girl in the photo with a machete at her throat. What kind of fucking choice did he have? And then it's another girl in a very different photo he sees: Lilly, the way she had looked at him as they stood side by side, two strangers enraptured by a commanding voice. *Now is the time to take a risk.* It was as if they shared a secret, back in that church in Atlanta: The two of them were up to the task. They were brave.

He pulls his throbbing hand to his chest. Lilly made him think he was brave, at least for a while. But by the time he came to Africa to find her, he had lost all illusions of taking photos that would change the goddamned world. He told Merilee he had to find himself, just like she was doing with EST—what a crock. Truth is, he only wanted to prove to her and to himself that he could be a big-time photographer.

Now, he just wants to find that younger version of himself who stood beside Lilly in Atlanta and truly was brave. Braver than the man who travelled all the way to New York and then couldn't face his daughter. Braver than the man who left Rwanda instead of turning the photos in his desk drawer over to the Tribunal two years ago. He untacks the picture of Nadine from the wall. He doesn't want to change the world now either, simply the fate of his family. Maybe, that's brave enough.

Two weeks later, Uganda

Henry has no idea how long he's been sitting here at the side of the road, hands frozen on the steering wheel, staring at the long line of trucks, the mesh fence, the young men with ammunition bandoliers draped over their shoulders like Boy Scout sashes studded with merit badges. A nearby sign reads: *Rwanda Border Crossing.*

The sun is barely starting to sink behind the Virungas. Two hours and he can be at Kwizera. Two hours, if he leaves right now. He places a hand on the pink soapstone locket around his neck that he used to wear as a good luck charm and has become part of his penance. The spring is jammed but he doesn't need to open it to see his daughter Rachel's face: a full-on grin, chin jutted forward and squinched-up eyes. This isn't just about making things right with Lilly and Nadine.

He pulls into the long line of cars—he can do this, it's not like the last time. Rodent-Eyes had it wrong: it's not about reimagining the past, or skipping over the nightmares and pretending they never happened. He has to go back and try to fix his mistakes. Maybe if he is able to take the photos in his backpack to the court in Arusha, then he can also find the courage to face his daughter again—not for himself this time, but for her.

TWENTY-NINE

TINY PARTICLES OF SOOT INFILTRATE through the cracked window, prickling Rachel's skin like a battalion of paratrooper no-see-ums. The eucalyptus was tingly and soothing when Lillian slathered it on not long ago, but now a gooey mess is oozing out from under the bandage on her ankle. She kicks off the blanket, but then rolls halfway back under the protection of the sheet, stuck in almost-sleep purgatory, eyes shut but blinking. Maura's words keep coming at her, rapid-fire: *Photos. Rape. Murder. Working for Rahim.* Did the genocide change her father or, as her mom maintained, was Henry Shepherd always a selfish man who didn't know how to love?

She should open the window to get more of a breeze, but the soot... Maybe, readjust the sputtering fan. No, that would mean opening her eyes and then starting the getting-to-sleep process all over again. She squeezes her eyes shut tighter and takes a deep, resolute breath: gasoline and lavender. The smell is at odds with itself, inviting and not, impossible to ignore. She wrinkles her nose and inhales into a memory. The smoky-sweet tang of her father's cologne. Sandalwood. It permeated the house: the living room sofa where he devoured paperback mysteries in the evenings, her bedspread where he sometimes dozed off during a story, and even the fresh towels. After he left, as that smell faded, their home became unfamiliar and bleak. It didn't help that her mom sold a lot of the furniture and kept the heat off, even on chilly winter nights, to make ends meet. Sometimes, it was warmer to sit by the fire pit in the backyard.

Rachel gropes for the satiny purple quilt, smooth and cool, and brings it to her cheek. That winter after her father left, she and her mom sat on a thick red-plaid blanket, feeding Christmas tree twigs into slow-burning flames. It occurs to her that Merilee might also have found comfort in the pop-and-sizzle of glistening pockets of resin sparking with the warm, earthy aroma of Henry Shepherd.

The smoky garden and forest beyond churn up the embers of memory; a dreamy fog fills Rachel's head. She is seven, sitting in the backyard on a log next to her father, the glow of a fire warming her face. Fireflies swirl around her, landing on the ground and her favorite blue windbreaker. She jumps up and waves her arms, but they are always just out of her grasp. She reaches toward the fire pit...the dreamcatcher that her father's helping her make for school is floating toward the flames. Suddenly, he shoves her to the ground. *Drop it, Cricket! Drop the damn thing!*

"No!" The force of Rachel's voice exploding in her lungs pulls her completely out of sleep. She's tangled in the sticky sheets. *Blood.* That's her first thought. She jolts upright, shaky fingers patting a moist thigh.

The heat is unbearable. What the hell happened to the fan? She tries to flip on the bedside lamp but it doesn't work. Her hand sweeps the table for a pack of matches, landing on something dry and skeletal: feathers and bones. Her heart pounds in her fingertips as she swats it away, sending the lamp and something wooden-sounding crashing to the floor.

Another power outage, that's all, she assures her younger self, a shaky hand reaching for the gas lantern hanging from a wire on the wall. She lights the lantern and examines her legs: slimy eucalyptus, no blood, of course there's no blood. Of course. Her gaze drops to the floor and lands on the dreamcatcher—twigs, not bones—that should be in the closet. She leans over the edge of the bed to take a closer look. Twigs, not bones, twigs. But how did it get there?

Rachel shines the lantern on a photo album splayed open: Henry Shepherd's round face smiles up at her from behind the wheel of a Jeep. His features seem to move a little as her fingers sweep away shattered glass crusting the yellowed cellophane. She could swear there's a flicker of light in his eyes, and his lips are parted slightly as if there's something he wants to say.

"Dad," she whispers. "Jesus, where the hell are you?" She waits, perfectly still, but then the cellophane puckers up again; his lips close. Once again, her father is merely a stranger in an old photo. Henry Shepherd.

Rachel excavates the thick photo album from the mess on the floor. The leather cover crackles against her fingers, like the trunk of an old tree. She pulls the quilt around her, a chill emanating from her bones, and flips quickly through the pages of desolate beaches, castles and churches, marketplaces swarming with people and yet there's a lonely quality in the mass of faces.

There's only a single photo of Henry Shepherd. It was as if after he left their home, he simply disappeared behind his camera. He was alone. Was he lonely? He had called and asked for her, Merilee admitted as much. She scans more postcards he never sent, evidence that he wrote to her, thought about her. There's a brief note on the back page: *Cricket, I think of you often on my travels. This album is for you. Love, Dad.*

He wrote to her. He thought about her. He missed her. Why doesn't any of this make her feel better?

The silence is suddenly deafening without the whir-and-click of the fan, the air thick, almost curdled with the smell of her own sweat. There's the low moan of an animal, wounded or maybe just longing for its mate. She goes to open the window wider and investigate, leaning out into the dark night; the sound is so close, so human-like it's eerie.

On the night of the campfire-gone-wrong, after her father had tucked her into bed, a faint noise seeped through the wooden slats of her bedroom floor. Her parents were arguing; she was used to that, hugging her stuffed dog, Old Gold, to her ear to muffle the sharp voices. But this was a gasping sound like a ghost might make, or a jinn in the bedtime story her father had just told. She crept downstairs with her stuffed dog and froze on the bottom step, stunned: her father was in the kitchen across the hallway, bent over the table, shoulders shaking. Sobbing. Maybe if she gave him Old Gold, maybe that would make him happy again. But he was the parent. It was his job to make *her* feel better. She turned around and crept back up the stairs. The next morning, he was gone.

The wind picks up, opening a black hole in the layers of shifting clouds. Rachel closes her eyes, face tilted toward the warm breeze. Why was her father crying that night? What was he looking at...

holding. The smell of the ashen garden below raises chill-bumps on her arms along with a memory: Blue ashes in the fire pit. Her father had been reading a blue letter—airmail, quite possibly from Lillian—while they were making the dreamcatcher. He was reading, not listening to her, not helping. She tossed the dreamcatcher into the fire to get his attention. The letter must have fluttered into the flames, too. She could see smudges of ash on the Formica kitchen table the next morning; it seemed to infiltrate her glass of milk, turning it gritty and sour.

She rubs her arms, but the chill is deep within her, somewhere she can't reach. Her father was crying over the blue ashes... No, it was something more. A flash of pink in his palm: the soapstone locket she had given him the previous Christmas. He was looking at it. He was choosing between her and the letter.

She walks back to the bed slowly, as if in a trance. Her father did love her and chose to leave anyway. He took photos of castles and exotic places she might enjoy, and collected them in an album. He wrote postcards that he never sent. *Cricket, I think of you often on my travels.* He missed her, but not enough to come home.

Lillian said that he did try to find her. He came to New York. She flips through the photo album and finds the close-up image of her father behind the wheel of a Jeep, traces his face with a finger. The man who left her a fifty-dollar tip at the bar. It was him. He did find her, and then decided to leave without so much as introducing himself. He didn't even give her a chance to turn him away or forgive him. She slides the album under the bed and steps into her sandals, has to get out of this stuffy room, out of the goddamned silence. Her mom was wrong: it wasn't that Henry Shepherd didn't have it in him to be a good father and husband. He simply chose not to be either one.

THIRTY

THE DARKNESS GREETS TUCKER LIKE A living thing with thick, meaty arms and rancid breath as he cracks open the door of Rose's room. He places the lantern on the floor by her bed and kisses her forehead: skin warm but not hot, smells more like seven-year-old-girl than the bleach and medicine of the hospital in Kigali. All good. She kicks at the sheets as if swimming in her sleep, arches her back and belly-flops away. "C'mon, Rosie," Tucker whispers, shaking the paper bag of pill bottles like a maraca. "Bottoms up, and then I'm outta your hair until morning."

"No." She lifts her head first, and the rest of her body follows into a sitting position. "Stay."

"Yeah, sure." Tucker pulls up the rocking chair that Lillian brought in from the porch and pours a glass of water from the pitcher on the bedside table. Eight different pills, every six hours. He used to cut the pills in half and place them in a Mickey Mouse Pez dispenser. Now, Rose takes the bag from him and lines up the bottles on the table. *I'm not a child anymore. You don't need to make a game of it.* Sadly, Tucker thinks as he watches her shake out one pill from each bottle, this is true. In the gray light of the lantern, she looks like a wizened old crone, body bent over the table, thin arms sticking out of an oversized Scooby-Doo T-shirt. He smiles; nice of Rachel to give up her favorite nightshirt for the hospital stay.

"Miss Rachel's back," he says.

Rose pecks his cheek. "Everything is good again."

"Totally." Sort of. He still doesn't know what went down at the Kensamara house. Rachel clammed up on the ride home. He can't blame her for being pissed off. He hasn't exactly told her the truth, not the whole story, about what happened to Henry at the church… Like he even knows what the hell that is. The guy took photos? What the fuck! At least that explains why he stayed away after the genocide. But what about now? Why hasn't he at least called his daughter? And where are the photos?

"One week from tomorrow," Rose says resolutely, and then downs all the pills in one gulp.

Tucker nods. He doesn't have the heart to remind her again that she might not be well enough by Christmas to go to church with her friends. He had barely kept it together when she wrote a letter to St. Nick during the car ride to Kigali, and that was the only gift on her wish list.

"Time for some shut-eye," Tucker chirps, slaps hands on knees as he gets up to leave. Rose seizes his arm. The darkness clamps onto his shoulders and shoves him to his knees. He's not fooling anyone. He stays there, eyes fixed on thin fingers curled around his wrist. Rose's other arm is hooked around the scraggly neck of the one-eyed lion that rises and falls on her chest. The lion that Lillian gave her for protection. He makes a fist, nails digging into his palm; how could he be so fucking stupid, imagining she would be immune from death here, convinced that Lillian would give her what he couldn't.

Rose's hand slips from his arm as she falls asleep, the brush of long, tapered fingers taking its place. Tucker shuts his eyes tightly against the warm memory of Solange's touch. It's the worst kind of torture, knowing he can't hold her, comfort her. He can't keep his promise. And then, her fingers go limp and cold. There is only the darkness, wrapping him in the memory that it was his idea to stay in Kigali to help the wounded instead of going to her family's farm in Uganda.

A month after the mass killings began, after all the Red Cross medics had left and the hospital closed down, he and Solange, a few other nurses and one doctor from Germany, snuck into the hospital through a broken window and pilfered what supplies they could salvage from the wreckage. They cobbled together a triage center in the basement of a nearby abandoned school, setting cracked bones and stitching up wounds, doing what they could without electricity or anesthesia. By the end of the week, patients were laid out on the floor, wall to wall.

Tucker was asleep in a room upstairs, Solange's head on his chest, when he heard the commotion: whistles blowing, people screaming, and the shrill giggle he recognized from the hospital. It was like a parade that had gone terribly wrong. A familiar face appeared in the doorway: Solange's twin brother Aaron, waving a pistol. "Run," he ordered, "before they find you. They'll kill you for helping, they'll kill you!" There was the sound of footsteps on the stairs, voices swelling in the hallway. Tucker smashed his fist through the second-story window and jumped out, thinking surely Solange would follow. He has always been thankful that he couldn't be certain it was Aaron's gun he heard firing as he hit the ground.

The darkness releases its grip and Tucker stands, woozy and unsteady. The lightness of his body is unsettling, as if the darkness has somehow sucked him dry and emptied him of vital organs. He drifts ghost-like out of the room.

Rachel's standing by the fuse box at the side of the house, where he left the toolbox before going to check on Rose. "Hey," he says, reaching for her and then gesturing toward her bum ankle. "You should keep your weight off that foot." His hands seem giant-like and awkward as he kneels to check her injury. The overwhelming relief of finding her at the roadside earlier in the evening comes back to him. The feel of her in his arms. He loosens the bandage and then tightens it again, stands and stuffs his hands into his pockets.

"Any idea which of these switches to flip?" Rachel stares into the fuse box, holding a screwdriver as if preparing to stab something.

"It's probably one of the cables buried in the ground that needs replacing. I'll take care of it tomorrow." Tucker hears the know-it-all doctor, a voice he became all too familiar with as a child, taking over. "Really, you shouldn't be out of bed."

"I just, y'know, wanted to help get the lights back on."

"No worries, I'll take care of it." Tucker winces. Thanks, Dad. "Let me help you back to your room."

Rachel offers him the screwdriver. "Thanks for coming after me. I was pretty awful, accusing you of lying. Sorry about that."

"No problem." Tucker takes the tool, imagines his fingers inter-locking with hers. He missed her during the past week. And she ad-mitted missing him too, right?

He taps the screwdriver against his palm, regarding it as if work-ing out a complex math equation. Right. But not like that. More like the guy who tapes up sprained ankles and fixes blown-out fuses.

"I didn't know about the photos,"he says. "But now, it makes sense why Henry never came back."

"I've been thinking I'll go look for him." Rachel grabs onto his arm, as if pulling him along. "Start in London and see where it leads me."

"No, I'll go."

"We could go together. Take Rose to see that doctor at the AIDS clinic."

"Rose would like having you along." Tucker's pulse quickens, Ra-chel's grip squeezing life back into the space emptied by the darkness. He backs away and starts fiddling with the toolbox. What would it be like, going to London with Rachel and Rose? Building a family with her? "You should stay here, in case Henry comes back," he says.

"My father's not coming back, even if you find him," she says. "Is he?"

Something in her voice, the questioning lilt, implies she's shel-tering a small flicker of hope. "No," Tucker says, dousing the flame. "I don't believe so." It's not fair to her, the hope. For years he looked for Solange in the crowded streets of Kigali. For years, he saw her in his dreams. Every morning, there was a moment before he was fully awake when he harbored hope. And every damn morning, he heard her scream his name as he opened his eyes fully and faced the hard, cold fact that he had to endure yet another day alone.

"I'm sorry," he says, "for bringing you here. I thought I could make things right for Henry and Lillian, for you. For everyone. But if he was going to come back, he would be here by now."

"At least I learned the truth," Rachel says. "For years, I thought there was something wrong with me. I mean, why wouldn't a father love his own daughter?"

Tucker opens his mouth to tell her she's wrong but she rushes on, her voice high and shaky. "And then, I thought he was the one who didn't know how to love. Now, I realize that he did love me. It's this place. The genocide. He had to stop feeling, stop loving because it was too painful, right? That's what turned him into a monster."

"C'mon, let me get you inside and take a better look at that ankle," Tucker says, letting her be right. She needs it. Besides, how can he tell her the entire truth about what happened to her dad without revealing the truth about himself? If anything, Henry cared too much. That's what destroyed both of them during the genocide.

THREE DAYS OF WALKING ALONG the highway, trying to get to the one place in the country where Tucker thought he might be safe. No one would stop to give him a ride. There was no room in the cars stuffed with belongings. No time. On the fourth day, he hitched a ride with a Hutu family heading for Uganda and got out at the dirt road leading into Mubaro. It was a moonless night, but he could smell the chaos as he walked into town. The headlights of trucks—one, two, and then ten—stabbed the road and he hid in a ditch. Men were standing atop what he thought were truckloads of logs. When they passed, the smell told him these were dead bodies.

He ran, his legs rubbery, Rosie and Lillian his only thought, but as he got to the main road in Mubaro something stopped him. One way was Kwizera, the other was a field at the dead end past the town square. The clouds parted and a slice of moon lit up the cross atop the church, just across the field. He was drawn toward the cross even though he hadn't stepped inside a church since he was a kid. He needed, for some strong but inexplicable reason, to pray before seeing whatever was to be found at Lillian's farm.

Take It Easy. That was the insipid Eagles' tune that he hummed over and over, placing one foot in front of the other, not thinking about whether it was a stick or a limb he was stepping on in the tall grass. Crossing the field between town and the church was surreal: abandoned luggage everywhere, some popped open and empty. At first, he thought the swatches of denim and batik, white cotton undergarments and silky flowered scarves, were all simply the contents of emptied bags strewn in the dirt. The skin and bones were already decomposing, blending into the rust-colored clay.

When he was nearly to the church the tinge of tobacco infused the air. He imagined a curl of smoke that he followed to the shack behind the church. There was Henry, sitting in the grass, leaning against the door, smoking a cigarette. He didn't get up, didn't so much as acknowledge Tucker until he was standing right over him.

"I figured, one lone guy," Henry said flatly, a sigh of smoke escaping from his nostrils. "Someone was either here to kill me or rescue me."

"We've gotta get out of here," Tucker said. "The trucks, they'll be back."

"I heard them loading the bodies from in there." Henry cocks his head toward the shack.

"How?" Tucker locked onto his eyes. How had he survived?

Henry took a final long drag off the butt, until the filter snuffed out the ember. "I was under a tarp, some cans stacked in front. Funny, they were so quiet loading the trucks. None of the singing and laughing. Maybe some of them realized what the hell they had actually done."

Tucker gave Henry a hand up, pulled him in close and clung to him. He heard a strangled sob and pulled away, horrified, a hand to his chest as if he might take back the sound that had generated there.

Henry tapped a finger to his lips. "She's finally asleep."

"Who?"

"The girl."

Tucker wiped his nose with the back of his hand, the runny mucus coating his throat, choking him with a gurgle that was repulsive to his ear. He looked at the ground. The glint of something shiny caught his eye. The blade of a knife. No, it was a single silver earring near Henry's foot. He bent down in fascination, and then jumped back. The triangle of silver was still attached to an ear. He took Henry's arm. "C'mon, let's go home."

Henry yanked away and opened the door to the shack. Curled up on the cement floor littered with broken bottles and garbage was, in fact, a young girl. Dahla and Enoch's daughter, who sometimes sang to Rose and played a flute. Nadine was wrapped in a filthy, too-big flannel shirt. Tucker noticed Henry was bare-chested under his denim jacket.

Tucker sits at the end of Rachel's bed after changing her bandage. A warm breeze carries the soothing smells of the nearby forest: eucalyptus and pine. He leans back, resting his head against the wall. "If I nod off, just wake me," he mumbles, but she doesn't answer. Probably sound asleep. That's good. He should go across the hall and check on Nadine. Make sure Rose is still asleep. He should go.

Suddenly, the wind shifts; the air is ripe with the smell of the dead bodies he and Henry buried among the ferns and moss. *Red shirt. Kitten barrettes. Green eyes.*

He takes a deep breath and sets his jaw, bracing for the next wave to crash over him, pull him under. It's not that he can't shut off the memories but he chooses to let them come, that's what he tells himself. In high school, during his stoned-and-stupid phase, he and his pothead bros hung out at the beach at night. They drank cases of Coors around a bonfire and talked trash about girls who wouldn't give them the time of day. They walked slowly into the ocean to play chicken with the waves. It was a rush, scary-exciting, proving he was a man to his friends.

Red Shirt. Kitten barrettes.

Now, this game of playing chicken with his memory is just fucking terrifying. What he's proving has become unclear. The worst part is, he's completely alone.

Green eyes.

Their faces haunt him, doll-like and innocent, eyes closed as if asleep and yet still seemingly staring up at him from the field. He saw all of their eyes as green: his own eyes, reflecting back at him. Every morning there were more children, more eyes demanding something he did not have the power to give them. He clenches his teeth, releasing a rumbling in his head to drown out the voices chanting his name. *Tucker, Tucker…* He curls into himself, rocking back and forth, palms clamping his temples like they're the only thing holding the bones of his skull together.

"*Tucker!*"

Solange. He heard her clearly among the screams and gunshot, that night in Kigali as he ran away. He couldn't help her. He couldn't help the children in the field. Rose… He moans, presses harder against his temples as if to shut off a thought.

"Tucker? Hey…"

"Sorry," he mumbles into his chest. Shit. Rachel's awake, probably thinks he's a lunatic. He should say something; he owes her some kind of explanation. Something. "Every morning," he says, "sunrise, before Lillian woke up. We went out into the field. Henry's idea. I sure as hell didn't want to go."

"Why did you go?"

"We had to find them, before Lil…" Tucker's throat constricts. He presses the heels of his hands against his eyes. They would look for the dogs, house pets turned wild, hunting for fresh kills. That's how they found the dead bodies.

"What were you looking for?" Rachel asks.

He shakes his head. Those eyes, wide open and staring, accusing, while they shoveled dirt over their bodies. She can't possibly want to know.

"Tucker."

The sound of his name, soft and imploring, like maybe he really could help her. "Children," he says into his hands. "Injured children." He keeps his head down as he explains how Henry helped him in the clinic. They repaired machete wounds, cracked skulls and broken limbs. It's true, some of them were only injured. What he doesn't tell her is how every morning for weeks, they took the dead bodies into the forest to bury them. Henry didn't want Lilly to know that children had been murdered trying to reach safety, trying to reach her. And then, there were too many bodies to hide. They buried them the best they could in the field where sunflowers now grow.

"Thanks for telling me that my father did something good," Rachel says.

Tucker's hands relax and fall to his sides, his head drops to his chest. "He's not a monster. Not perfect, nobody's saying that. Just human." So fucking human.

"It helps, knowing that he did care about the children."

"I should go." Tucker tries standing, too fast, churning up a cluster of stars as the blood drains from his head. He reels back onto his heels, the back of a knee meeting the edge of the bed. "Give me a sec..." There is the touch of Rachel's hand on his back, catching him, the cool pillow against his cheek, the breeze—warm and sweet again— and then, thankfully, there is only darkness.

THIRTY-ONE

RACHEL HALF-SLEEPS FOR MOST OF THE night, flat against the wall but not in an uncomfortable way, so there's plenty of room for Tucker's lanky body in the double bed. It seemed so natural to pull him back into bed and move her pillow so that his head landed on it. The smell of him, the weight of his body next to her, the slight sound of his breath…so satisfying. It feels a bit like she's cheating on Mick, even though there's a barrier of blanket between them. Tucker just needs a good night's sleep, that's all.

During the past year, Rachel has never allowed herself to consider what it might be like to wake up to the smell of a man other than her husband, actively pushing the thought away along with the crumpled receipt she found on the closet floor. Why had Mick paid for a hotel room on a Wednesday afternoon? She would have accepted most any explanation—an out-of-town client, or maybe he just needed a quiet space away from the office and home—hell, it didn't even need to make sense. So, why did he choose the truth? *Just the one time. It didn't mean anything.* Well, not exactly the truth. What sticks with her is how he came home, picked up the receipt from the coffee table where she left it for him to find, and presented it to her again, like maybe she hadn't read it carefully, hadn't noticed the date was exactly one week after the first miscarriage. It meant plenty.

Lucy. That was her name. Why the hell would Mick think she wanted to know the slut's name? A simple question, but he exploded. *Jesus, I needed something—someone. You sure as hell haven't been there for me.*

For months afterwards, she made her husband sleep on the couch, not as a punishment but because she couldn't fall asleep next to him. It was his smell, the uncertainty of his scent. It wasn't that he was wearing extra cologne. It wasn't that she suspected he showered before bed to cover up more than the smell of sweat from the racquetball club. His scent changed for her, the moment she realized that he wanted her to find out. He wanted to hurt her—to take something from her, although that seemed too cruel—the same way she had hurt him by packing up the nursery alone. At the time, she had thought she was sparing him pain; she had thought that's what a good wife would do. She still misses the smell of him, the way it used to coat her in a protective shell as she slept, breathing him in.

Now, lying next to Tucker, it's Rachel who feels protective. She wants to shush the symphony of birds tuning up for sunrise. She wants to cover him fully with the blanket, but is afraid of disturbing his sleep. He just needed sleep… No, she admits, moving away from the wall, he hadn't said it but he needed *her.*

I need you, Rachel. God, how she used to crave hearing those words whispered in her ear. At the same time, neediness has always struck her as almost lazy, a weakness of character. Her mom never came out and said it, but Merilee's extreme self-reliance after her husband left was as good as saying that depending on someone else—their help, their approval, their love—was a distasteful trait. Rachel could see the unattractive neediness of the men parked on barstools, nursing something strong on the rocks and serenading her with sad stories of being misunderstood by a girlfriend (never a wife), undervalued by a boss, dissed by a co-worker, screwed over by a cab driver or waiter. They spoke in the hushed tones of secret desires, the high pitch of possibilities, the bravado of bald-faced lies. She listened gratefully as she mixed generous drinks. These stories served as her menu of reasons that she remained unattached, unnecessary to anyone.

She's not proud to admit to herself that sometimes, before she met Mick, after a few shots of Johnny Walker toward the end of her shift and then later in bed, neediness had been a brief turn-on. It gave her a thrill—tenuous and fleeting, but still—that she could be somehow treasured. She could be powerful, like a genie who might choose to grant a wish. She could be, not exactly loved, but essential. This had seemed so much safer than love.

She studies Tucker in the first light of breaking day and places a hand lightly on his back. Her fingers spring away as if testing the temperature of a potentially hot surface. He has never made a move, not even after she kissed him while they watched the sun set over the chain of lakes in the mountains. He has never asked for a thing from her. And yet...

When he returned from seeing the immunology specialist in London, that morning at his tent, his love for Rose was so raw and tender. Reaching out to hold his hand was such a small gesture, but he gripped her fingers as if clinging to a mossy rock on a cliff. She sat next to him in that concave canvas chair for hours, his need making *her* stronger. Last night, his voice was scraped raw with the memories of searching for wounded children with her father. When he finally looked up, she wanted to swab the pain from his face with a soft cloth. Or, her lips. Now, she leans closer, just above his shoulder, close enough to kiss the nape of his neck. He needs her, yes he needs her, in some foreign and utterly desirable way.

And yet. A thought that started as a slightly irritating bump is now a full-blown tumor: she needs him, too. Her desire, something she's not at all certain she can—or wants to—control, takes her aback, propels her toward the end of the bed.

There was a time when she and Mick couldn't get enough of each other: in the shower first thing in the morning, his touch igniting a spark in the middle of the night. Sometimes, he would email her midmorning: *Lunch?* Their code for quick sex on the kitchen table or the couch. But their lovemaking turned scheduled and predictable. Date night. A box to check off on a to-do list. She hasn't felt this must-have desire for Mick in…how long, exactly? Before losing Serena, for sure. Was it even before becoming pregnant the second time?

Rachel slips out of bed, toward the door, feeling guilty as hell—but not about being in bed with another man. The first miscarriage, yes, that's when things changed between them. Was Mick right? Had she chosen to be selfish, packing up the nursery and grieving alone? What she feels now for Tucker, might she have shared that intimate bond with her husband? She'll call Mick, make this right. They'll have the memorial service with his family on Christmas, bury Serena's ashes and make snow angels in the Catskills—it doesn't need to be Vermont. Something stops her, her hand on the doorknob. Has she ever felt this magnetic ache, this longing, for Mick—for anyone—that makes it impossible to leave now?

She sits on the edge of the bed, next to Tucker, who is still sleeping soundly, brushes her lips against his cheek and then lies down between him and the wall. She tosses the blanket onto the floor and places her arm across his chest. Maybe it's not that her father took a piece of her heart when he left, but that she has chosen—without realizing it—to keep her distance from people. She has chosen to keep her distance from love.

THIRTY-TWO

E ARLY THE NEXT MORNING, THE SKY
breaks open with summer thundershowers that wash away
the remnants of ash and smoke. Rachel helps Nadine to
sweep off the patio and set up tables in preparation for the Christmas tree decorating party while Lillian is at the Saturday market. She
could nearly forget about the fire, except for the two guards Tucker
hired, patrolling the grounds with rifles slung over their shoulders.

In the late morning, dozens of children from town start trickling up the driveway and into the backyard, along with the aunties,
each woman carrying one or two cloth bags filled with shiny materials
to make Christmas decorations or baking supplies that will become
cookies and a dinner of goat stew and cardamom bread. Rachel sits at
a table on the patio with Nadine, where they have been directed to stay
put while most of the widows cook. Lillian is allowed in the kitchen;
she is one of them. "This is their party," Nadine explains. "Something

special they do for all the children."

It's clear to Rachel that this celebration is also a way the widows honor their own children who can't be here. She's surprised by how young some of them are: Sentwali, who can't be much older than Nadine, is stringing popcorn with Rose and a circle of her friends nearby, shooing away a group of bold vervet monkeys with the snap of a dish towel. Auntie Marie has set up a table on the patio with pinecones, and paint made from plants, berries, petals, and flour. Auntie Julia's specialty is stars stenciled on cardboard that the kids cut out and then wrap in foil. Over the next few hours, it's impressive how everyone works together to transform the gnarled old fig tree that looks like something out of a bleak Grimm's fairy tale with a raven perched on a high branch, into a glittering holiday vision.

Rose appears tired but happy as she skips across the patio with an array of popcorn-and-dried-fruit garlands hanging on her arm. She places one around Nadine's neck and then Rachel's. "*Sawa*," she says, satisfied, "now you both look ready for Christmas."

"*Murakoze*," Rachel says. "In America we have a tradition of holiday sweaters decorated with sparkly candy canes and reindeer whose noses light up. I should have brought mine."

"Like my Scooby Doo shirt?" Rose asks, climbing into Nadine's lap and handing her several barrettes that have fallen out of her braided hair.

"Kind of. I'll send you one for next Christmas." Rachel holds out her hand so that Nadine can deposit barrettes as she unwinds dozens of braids. Rose shakes her head, curls springing every which way. She plants a kiss on Nadine's cheek and runs off to spread holiday cheer to one of the guards, a handsome young man posted by the kitchen door. He declines the garland, but then glances over at Nadine and takes it when he sees that she's watching.

"You should talk to him," Rachel says. "Lawrence, that's his name, right?"

Nadine blows out a puff of air, clearly embarrassed, and turns to the line of girls that has formed in front of her. She claps her hands, signaling the next customer to climb up and get her hair styled. Rachel smiles wistfully, watching her friend untangle and rewind the girl's braids. "Do you want kids of your own one day?" she asks.

"Perhaps. Many children is a sign of great wealth in Africa, but it was not to be for our family."

"I was an only child," Rachel says. "Sometimes, it was pretty lonely. My mom worked all day as a secretary, and then at night she watched TV and went to bed early. She was lonely, too."

Nadine finishes braiding the girl's hair and convinces the others in line that they should go decorate cookies while they are warm. She reaches across the table and touches Rachel's arm. "My mother was with child when I was quite young. She became ill with fever and the baby arrived too early to survive. I remember the village healer telling Umama that her womb was cursed."

"Not being able to have children can feel like a curse, but that's terrible—blaming her. So unfair."

"Umama was never with child again. She said that God sent me as her only blessing and that was enough. He chose his most precious angel because she could only have one child."

"That's beautiful." Rachel watches the children playing. Her due date was last week, but Mick was certain they'd have a Christmas baby. "I miscarried not long before coming here. I think of my baby that way. An angel."

"Serena," Nadine says tenderly. "I looked at your website. I hope that's alright."

"Of course," Rachel says. The sound of her baby's name is so sweet. Comforting.

"You will be a mother again," Nadine says. "An awesome mother." She walks over to the glittering fig tree and adjusts a star here, a pine-cone there.

Rachel goes to stand beside her and admire the tree. That's when she notices the tears sliding down her friend's cheeks. She takes a tin-foil star from a branch and hands it to her.

"I cannot have children," Nadine says, eyes on the star in her hand. "A doctor in Kigali told me this when she examined me after..."

Rachel hugs her friend, smoothes a hand down her trembling back, once and then again. The church massacre. She can feel the fear crawling under Naddie's skin.

"Felix did this to me," Nadine whispers. "This is what they want me to tell at the *gacaca*. Maman does not understand it is still hap-pening. At least, it feels that way. My body sometimes hurts, terribly. I imagine everyone can see he ruined me."

"*Inshuti*, you should tell Lillian."

"I don't want to worry her."

"I'm glad you told me."

Nadine pulls away. "There is something else. This afternoon, I'm going to Christian's home to assure him and Felix that I won't testify."

"But what about the things you saw...your friends and family. Don't you want the truth to come out?"

"I'll always carry the sorrow of my loved ones who are gone. The *gacaca* won't bring them back to me." Nadine looks toward the ashen garden. "If I testify, this will not be the end of the violence. It doesn't matter if Felix is locked away. There are many others who will take revenge. Protecting my loved ones who are still alive, this is what is important now, my sister."

Rachel takes both of Nadine's hands in hers. Lillian was right: even if Henry Shepherd doesn't show up, she still has family here. "What's the Kinyarwanda word for sister?"

"*Shika.*"

"*Shika*, I'm not going home tomorrow. I'm staying right here."

"But your husband—"

"He'll understand." Rachel nods, hoping this is true. She'll call him later, in his early morning, and tell him to go ahead and bury Serena's ashes with his family, if that's what he needs to do. She will always carry their baby with her, whether her ashes are under a tree in the O'Shea backyard or scattered in the mountain snow. They'll find another way to honor Serena when she comes home, as originally planned, on New Year's Eve.

"Don't go to the Kensamara house," Rachel says. "I'll do it."

"*Oya*, definitely not. Even if I were to agree, Maman would never allow it."

"Then I'll go to the bakery right now. Lillian doesn't have to know I'm gone." Rachel's heart starts pounding fast at the idea of facing Maura again. "What should I say?"

Nadine leans forward, and glances toward the kitchen where Lillian is cooking. "Tell her what I told the attorney and Maman. Tell her what I've always said. I don't remember."

RACHEL STARTS OFF TOWARD THE path that cuts through the banana field, but the handsome guard with the popcorn garland around his neck stops her. "If you must go into town, I'll take you," Lawrence says. "The doctor's orders are that nobody goes anywhere alone."

When they arrive at the bakery, it's already closed. She directs Lawrence to drive up the hillside and park at the end of the dirt road leading to the Kensamara house. "I'll just be fifteen minutes," she says, getting out of the Jeep. "You'll be right here if I need you, right?"

Christian is in front of the house, bent over the open hood of a truck. Rachel stops. The same truck that nearly ran her off the road. There's a fast stab of fear in her stomach as the boy takes a step toward her, fist raised, but then he places his hand to his chest and bows. "Come," he says. "You are welcome."

The sign of respect takes Rachel off-guard and she returns it, but stays put. Close enough so that Christian can hear her but not so close that she can't outrun him back to Lawrence and the Jeep.

"It's okay for you. Felix is in Ruhengeri, seeing about a new engine. Maman has gone along with him."

"I have a message from Nadine," Rachel says.

"For me?"

"You and Felix. You win."

"Win?"

"She's not going to testify."

Christian's face clouds over with confusion.

"The fire?" Rachel prompts. "It did the trick. She's afraid that next time it won't only be her garden that's destroyed."

"*Oya*, Madame, *Oya*. I knew nothing of this."

"Well…regardless. It doesn't matter," Rachel falters. He looks sincerely upset. "Just pass along the message to your brother."

"Wait, Madame. Please, wait here."

Christian returns a few minutes later with her passport and a dusty-pink stone heart that has a chip on one edge. "These are yours. I'll give them to you in exchange for delivering a message to Nadine. Tell her I had nothing to do with the fire. It was Felix. Only Felix."

Rachel slips the passport into her pocket. She turns the carved stone over and over, examining the rusty spring, the cracks lined with dirt and time. "Where did you get this?"

"My mother keeps it in her jewelry drawer, but never wears it."

Rachel rubs her thumb against the spring, coaxing a memory. How does she know it's jammed shut? A Bic pen...the tip of the cap was a perfect fit, tripping the spring and opening the locket to reveal her own face smiling up at her. She had wanted to get her dad a plastic red heart with a troll inside for Christmas. A good luck charm. But her mom insisted on this one, instead. *I'll wear it myself if your father won't.* "Where did you get this," she says, her hand closing into a fist. "Was it your father?"

"*Oya*, Madame."

"Did he take it from my dad at the church?"

Christian's face softens. "You should go home, Madame Shepherd. Go back to New York. There's no reason for you to stay in Rwanda."

The pink stone is warm in Rachel's palm, seems to throb with a pulse all its own, as she walks back into town with Lawrence following close behind in the Jeep. Even if Rahim took this trinket from her father, that doesn't mean he's dead. She stuffs the locket in her shirt pocket. There's no reason to alarm Lillian or anyone else. And yet, Christian's words, the empathy in his voice, continue to haunt her.

THIRTY-THREE

LILLIAN SITS TALL AT THE SHINY, VENEERED dressing table she paid way too much to have shipped from Atlanta after Mama passed last year and tilts her chin upward, as her mother used to do while adding the final touches before church. The wide-brimmed straw hat is a bit plain, but a splash of red begonias that match her sundress will help. She dabs a blush of color along her cheekbones and tosses a silver tube of lipstick into her purse. Maybe later. Mama always said that Sunday was the one day each week when you put on your best face for church. It wasn't about vanity. *There are always folks who have it as bad or worse than you, and they don't go to the house of God to see your troubles,* she said. *If you're tired and beaten-down, that's between you and our lord. Part of the reason we go to church is to lift up others in the community. Don't let them see anything but your church face.*

"Okay, Mama," Lillian says into the mirror. "I'm ready."

She hasn't been to church since last Christmas, instead rooting her faith into the ground, wearing dungarees and sweating side by side with the genocide widows. They are her community. But once a year, she pulls out this red dress. Once a year, she sits on a hard wooden bench and reminds the children not to squirm or fuss with their good clothes which may be a season too tight. She does it for Mama and Daddy, both gone now, for Deirdre and Samuel, for the baby boy she gave away. She does it for the six orphans—two with measles, four with tuberculosis—who she buried at the foot of Mount Kenya. She does it for Enoch and Dahla, and the countless others who died at the church where she'll worship today. She does it for Reverend King, who never lost his faith in God.

Rachel's already waiting on the front porch. She gives a low whistle of approval. "I've never seen you in an actual dress and sandals with any kind of heel," she says. "Very chic."

Lillian buttons her white cardigan self-consciously. The V-neckline doesn't show much cleavage, but still this is church. "You look quite nice, too," she says, appraising the new peasant blouse with an embroidered bodice and long, flowered skirt from Nadine's closet. Henry's daughter could be a college student herself: hair swept back in a ponytail, orange and yellow beaded earrings that dangle nearly to her shoulders, a splash of sun-freckles across her cheeks.

"These aren't too much?" Rachel's hand goes to a dangly earring. "I bought them in town."

Lillian brushes a rebel curl out of Rachel's eyes. The lost look that was there when she first arrived is gone. She still reminds her of Henry, but not the broken man who had been afraid to return to his family after the slaughter. There's a glint of light, a sparkle reminiscent of the man who first showed up at Kwizera looking for adventure. "Beautiful," she says.

"I bought something for you, too." Rachel pulls a bolt of magenta fabric out of her backpack.

"You remembered." Lillian runs her hand over the mesh of glittering threads that attracted her to the fabric at the market.

"It's not much, considering everything you've done for me. I wanted to thank you for the photo album—for everything."

"You can thank me by helping to make some new kitchen curtains. And we'll keep enough material for a skirt for you."

The second gift of the day appears as Lillian enters the main house: Rose is in the entranceway, twirling to show off her satiny green dress, a hand-me-down from Naddie. Tucker looks terrible, wearing the same rumpled T-shirt and chinos from yesterday and quite possibly the day before. "Morning," he says, like he's not sure it actually is.

"What happened to Merry Christmas?" Rachel asks in a tone that sounds a lot like flirting. Lillian stifles a smile. She gives Tucker a long hug, trying to infuse some vigor into him.

"Deck the halls and all that," he mumbles.

"He doesn't sleep enough," Rose chides. "That's why he looks, well, not quite ready for celebrating."

"You, girlfriend, look marvelous." Rachel removes the pink scarf from around her own neck and drapes it onto Rose's shoulders. "This was my mom's. I'm sure she would approve of me giving it to you as a Christmas present."

"*Murakoze*," Rose murmurs. She pulls the scarf to her neck and looks to Lillian, who nods. Yes, she may keep it. "I'll wear it only to church, and then put it away."

"Hold on, there," Tucker says. "I thought we agreed that you and I are staying home to rest this morning."

"No, we did not agree," Rose protests. "I slept fine last night."

Lillian opens her mouth but then closes it when Tucker looks to Rachel for help, curious to see how this will play out.

Rachel kneels and tries adult logic, a weak first move with a seven-year-old. "You don't want be tired for the party later, right?" Rose sets her jaw tighter. And then, there's good old-fashioned bribery: "We'll make more decorations. Or, cookies! How about that?"

Robert and Thomas appear from the kitchen, handsome young men in blue blazers and pressed chinos, agreeing heartily that Rachel's plan sounds a lot more fun than church. They'll make more decorations for the tree, but no opening presents until later.

"Rose, honey," Lillian intervenes before things get too carried away and someone winds up in tears, "can you pick a few begonias that match my dress? And you gentlemen go find Zeke and wait for us by the Jeep, please."

When Rose is out of earshot, Lillian turns to Tucker, her other stubborn child. "It would be nice if we all attended church today. Rose can take a nap before we have lunch and open presents."

Tucker frowns. "I don't think church is a good idea."

"For her or you?" Lillian says. "I wouldn't ask if it wasn't important." She hasn't asked in years past. Nadine says it makes her stronger going to the site of the massacre, but not Tucker. It only reminds him of all he can't fix in the world. She kisses his furrowed brow. "We're still strong, a strong family. I want folks to see that the fire hasn't changed that. Nothing anyone does can change that."

"Yeah..." Tucker draws in a breath and nods, as if convincing himself. "Yeah, okay."

"Now, you'll take Rose and Rachel in your Jeep after you change into fresh clothes. Nadine and I will walk into town with the other children."

"Nadine's going?" Rachel asks, and then adds, "She should come with us in the Jeep."

Lillian starts to object, and then instead says, "You're right, good thinking. I'll see you there."

RACHEL LOOKS OUT THE WINDOW as the Jeep stops in a grassy meadow dotted with groups of people wrapped up in their Christmas best. It's surreal: How can this be the same place where thousands of people were massacred? The pink locket is a slight, constant weight against her thigh, nestled in the pocket of her skirt. She can't imagine what her father photographed here, doesn't even want to try. And Nadine, laughing with Rose in the backseat. Is she pretending not to remember for Rose's sake or has she truly forgotten, if only for a few hours, the atrocities that happened here? Across the field there's a red brick building with a tile roof, a huge gold wooden cross looming above. The house of God. Miracles. Maybe, as Lillian says, everyone here is summoning what's left of their faith, some praying and some only hoping that mankind's capacity for love is greater than the history of their deeds.

"Do me a favor and take it easy," Tucker says, opening Rose's door.

"Yes, yes of course." She pushes past him impatiently and runs off toward the church, Nadine close behind.

Rachel walks briskly after them, turns to say something to Tucker but he's not there. He's still standing beside the Jeep, watching her, his hand on the open passenger door as if adhered there by something stronger than he is. "People are heading inside," she says, running back to take his hand. She gently pulls him away, and then follows his lead around the back of the church, away from the crowd. They walk along a stone path, stopping in front of a granite plaque overgrown with purple and white wildflowers.

Tucker runs his hand over the engraved block letters. "Eighty-seven names," he says flatly. "These are the only bodies they could identify. An estimated two thousand people were murdered here over about a week. This memorial, this dilapidated shack, is all that's left of their lives. There are shacks, schools and churches with plaques like this one all over the country."

Rachel tries the door, padlocked shut, her hand freezing as it hits her: "This is where you found them. Nadine and my father." She walks around to the back and finds a small, barred window. A whiff of something harsh, like rotting meat, burns her nostrils.

"Nearly seven years later and still…" Tucker shines a penlight inside the cracked pane of glass. "I don't think the smell will ever completely fade."

Rachel reaches up for his hand and knocks the light away as she sees the wall of shelves lined with skulls. Below it, there's a row of suitcases. "They thought they were leaving. They thought someone would save them. They thought…" She holds a hand to her stomach, vile liquid churning up into her throat. Her father was right here in this shack—was he hiding or in plain sight? Was he judiciously taking photos or simply clicking away?

"No sane person would ever ask to witness what happened here,"

Tucker says quietly, as if reading her mind or maybe her face. "And yet being a witness makes it impossible to turn away. At least, that's my experience."

Rachel takes the flashlight and shines it on a shapeless, colorless mound in the center of the room. As her eyes adjust, forms and colors pop out: shirt collars, pant legs, belt buckles, the worn elastic bands of underwear. There's a small bear missing an ear atop the pile. The light turns shaky. When she offered to replace Kingston's missing eye, Rose gave her the strangest look and shook her head. It was as if she knew that a new eye wouldn't change what the tattered lion had seen.

"How can you stay, after all you've seen?" Rachel turns away from the window, doesn't want to see anymore. She understands why her father had to leave.

"It wasn't an actual decision, not really. Being here..." Tucker says. "My parents had disowned me. Finishing my residency at UCLA was off the table. Truth is, I was kicked out. There was an 'incident...'" He makes air quotes with his fingers. "I stole some bandages and meds for this homeless clinic where a friend of mine was working."

"Very Robin Hood of you."

"I was a kid trying to do the right thing, but I had no idea what that was. That's why I came here. Stayed here." Tucker looks at the ground, twists the brass ring on his finger. "I promised to do one truly good thing before I left. Still working on it."

Rachel grabs his arm. "How can you say that? You save lives."

"There's so much suffering. Most days, I'm not even making a dent."

"I don't think I could do it. Being so selfless."

"No, it's not like that. After witnessing so much suffering and violence, I couldn't go back to the States—for sure not California. Being here has become my reality. It's who I am."

"When is it enough?"

Tucker squints past her, into the dark, dusty tomb. "You'd better get going," he says. "The service should be starting soon. I'll stay here, try to summon some kind of prayer."

"I haven't prayed since…" Rachel shakes her head. The last time was when she was a kid. Her mom insisted they attend services for the high holidays every year to ask for absolution for their sins and then start fresh again on Rosh Hashanah. She grabs Tucker's hand and takes a few steps toward the church. Maybe, she thinks, it's more important than ever to believe in miracles—even if only for one day. "I know it's corny, but I want to see Christmas through the eyes of the children. Love, faith, miracles. All of it."

Tucker doles out a weary smile, but he doesn't budge. Rachel tugs harder. "C'mon. This will still be here tomorrow."

TUCKER CLICKS OFF THE FLASHLIGHT and places it back on the windowsill. He doesn't have the heart to tell Rachel he's given up on miracles and the jury is still out on faith and love. As they enter the dimly lit sanctuary, she points at the large, blue and gold stained-glass windows at the front as evidence that something beautiful and pristine remains in this room. All he sees are shards of light cast toward the altar, like dozens of tiny swords. His eyes dart around the room, trying to find somewhere blank and plain to land, and settle on his shoes. She doesn't notice the spackled ceiling where there were bullet holes, doesn't know these are brand new pews because the old originals were chopped up to burn along with the bodies. She doesn't see the decapitated statuettes of the Virgin Mary and Jesus that used to hang on the walls. Maybe some of the Hutus felt a sliver of shame. It's Christmas so he gives them the benefit of the doubt; maybe they didn't want any celestial witnesses to the evil they were carrying out in God's name.

Rose waves Tucker over to sit near her and her friends in the first row. He give her a thumbs-up, actually feels something lighten in his chest. She's no longer flushed; the new HIV cocktail from London is kicking in. The miracle of science. *That* he can believe in.

The church choir limbers up with a Kinyarwanda hymn, surprisingly cheerful, accompanied by an old man plucking the thin metal tines of a kalimba and a young woman playing a flute. Tucker's spirits rise as the children and adults alike sway in the pews. Sitting between Rachel and Rose, he wants to be swept away, wants to find evidence that God still lives in this place or at least is making a guest appearance today. A hush falls over the sanctuary as the reverend, a heavy man dressed in a long purple robe, seems to float across the stage despite his girth. He kicks off the service with a silent prayer in praise of a loving God. A generous God. Forgiving.

It's been a long time since Tucker has said a prayer, but he closes his eyes and holds Rose's small hand. *She looks good today. Thanks, Man. If you can watch over her, give her some extra time...* He starts to open his eyes—it's the best he can do—but then Rachel's hand brushes his knee. *One more request. Make her stay.* The thought is like a flash of bright light and he blinks open his eyes. For years, he has been so busy trying to save lives, fix the problems of people he loves, prove to himself that he's a healer, not just an MD. It never occurred to him, not until now, that he might need someone to help him heal. *Solange, forgive me. Forgive me.*

He lets out a shaky breath that unwinds a tight coil throughout his entire body. He looks down, brushing away the moisture from his cheek. Rachel's palm is covering the clenched fist on his thigh. For a brief moment, he does believe in miracles.

NADINE'S EYES FOLLOW A TWIST of smoke that curls up from a braided incense stick toward the stained-glass window and then dissipates into nothing. Her breath comes in a halting staccato rhythm; wispy fingers of myrrh and frankincense play upon her lungs. The fragrance of forgiveness, the reverend says as he begins his sermon.

Forgiveness. That has been the theme of the Christmas service for the past three years, since people began coming back to this church, Hutus and Tutsis alike. No one speaks of the former priest, the one who christened her and Sylvia both, who is locked up in jail still awaiting trial. Three years ago, when this new reverend—neither Hutu nor Tutsi—came from Uganda, the walls of the church were painted dark brown to hide the stains and brand new pews were installed. One might even believe the murders never happened. All of the evidence is hidden out of sight in the shed around back.

Nadine glances around, grinds the toe of her shoe into the floor. The reverend's voice is loud and fervent as he goes on about opening one's heart to the possibilities of the New Year. It is always the same. Merely words. She looks directly at Chrissie, sitting toward the back of the room. He has been staring at the back of her head, she is certain, but now his eyes avert to the floor. Nadine turns her attention back to the altar again as the reverend's voice careens up an octave. He's excited, talking about the country's first *gacaca* trials, which will take place next month, one right here in Mubaro, in the field between the church and the market square.

"May we open our hearts to the sweetness of remembering a time long ago, before the hatred began. Before the killings. Let us say a prayer for peace. *Amahoro.*"

Everyone bows to pray. Nadine fights the urge to turn around and smile at Chrissie. He returned Rachel's passport. Surely, Felix wouldn't approve. Maybe it's true that her friend didn't help his brother to set the fire. He might still be the boy who used to walk her home from school, a skinny boy who carried a stick that wasn't large enough to harm anyone. He couldn't really protect her from the boys who followed them, cackling like crows. *Filthy cockroach. Dung beetle girl.* They didn't dare to call Felix's little brother names, not with him right there with them. Felix was always right there. Had he been protecting his brother?

She quickly glances over her shoulder, scratching a hard-to-reach spot where there could be an itch. Yes, Chrissie is still looking at her. He lifts his hand to his chin, a thumb tugging at the corner of a smile. Nadine nods. Yes, she wants to forgive her friend. She wants, not to forget the past, but to remember. Before.

If only she can plant herself firmly in the place where Umama sang her to sleep as a young child. The place where she and Sylvia barely dared to breathe as they time-travelled through wormholes in space along with Meg and Charles Wallace, their trusty paperback as good as any tesseract or spaceship. The place where she and Chrissie had studied geography and it dawned on them that people sometimes left their homes, found new friends and created new families. Together, they made children's plans: They would move to London or Paris, Cairo or New York, someplace far away and full of all sorts of people living together. She would be a singer, not like on the radio but on a big stage, telling stories to music. Chrissie would design tall, sleek buildings with elevators that could transport people, in the time it took to count to ten, up into the clouds.

She bows her head and counts slowly, the incense filling her lungs. One... two... three... four... *Amahoro.*

THIRTY-FOUR

RACHEL STROLLS ACROSS THE FIELD TO-
ward town, in no particular hurry to try and win her bet
with Rose that she can make it to Kwizera on foot before
Tucker's Jeep gets there. It was the only way to convince the obviously tired child to accept a lift instead of walking with Lillian and
the boys. The landscape is dotted with a rainbow of sun parasols, but
there's no sign of Lillian's floppy straw hat, or Nadine for that matter.
Naddie disappeared after the service and is probably back at Kwizera by now, making sure the presents are arranged just so, wrapped
in batik cloth and ribbons with crisp bows, under the fig tree. Lillian
will take charge of the kitchen, appointing Tucker and the older boys
her sous-chefs while she prepares lunch. Nothing fancy, probably just
sandwiches since the aunties will be over later for a potluck dinner,
but it will still be festive. Zeke will set the dining room table, Rose by
his side straightening napkins and filling water glasses. Everyone has

their part in making sure that the celebration runs smoothly. It was nice of Lillian to ask her to be in charge of picking fresh flowers for the centerpiece.

She stoops to pluck a bouquet of button-sized daisies to set at Rose's place at the table, in between her and Nadine. Clumps of flowers cling to the patchy grass, soft drifts of snow on the ochre-red ground. A sadness unspools from her fingertips; there's probably at least a foot of powder in the Catskills. She misses waking up early on Christmas morning, as excited as a kid, to look out the window, hoping for fresh snow to make footprints in and secretly searching for reindeer tracks. Her tongue tingles with the memory of the aromas of strong coffee and apple strudel sprinkled with cinnamon sugar wafting through the floorboards of Mick's childhood room. At eight o'clock sharp the house fills with assorted shapes and sizes of O'Sheas who convene around the Christmas tree nestled in a bay window overlooking the Catskills, their plates piled high with eggs, bacon, and slabs of crusty confection.

She has her place in Mick's family, too. Everyone knows that the Barcalounger kitty-corner to the fireplace is reserved for her. She settles in with a mug of tea to watch the show. One by one, youngest to oldest, members of the O'Shea clan shake presents wrapped in red or gold paper that matches the tree ornaments, per Mother O'Shea's instructions. Mick brings Rachel her gifts and makes a show of bowing. It's a family joke: everyone always knew he would marry a princess, treat his wife like royalty. They all concur that Mother O'Shea raised her only son right. Rachel does not disagree. It would be petty to tell him that she feels like an outsider, not royalty. Just once, couldn't he have offered to go with her to Jacksonville for Thanksgiving, *her* family holiday with her mom and Aunt Carole?

Rachel removes the elastic band from her hair to wrap it around the wispy daisy stems. At least New Year's Eve will be just her and Mick. She considers the bouquet. What's her resolution for 2001?

She runs back across the field, around the back of the church to the shed, and deposits the white blossoms on the windowsill as if they might emit a fragrance that will absorb the dust of decaying bones and empty suitcases. She removes her father's locket from her skirt pocket and places it alongside the daisies, considers tossing it through the cracked window. What stops her is the image of Tucker gazing out over the valley of lakes, searching for faith or at least something to make sense of his life. She retrieves the chipped stone heart from the windowsill and turns to leave. Maybe Tucker's right: Henry Shepherd wasn't a monster, simply an average guy trying to negotiate an impossible situation.

She clutches the locket. The night her father left, he was sobbing at the kitchen table, holding this picture of her and the ashen remains of Lillian's letter. Agonizing. Was he torn between being a responsible husband and father, and following his dreams? Had he been trying to do his best back then, too? Is that what he's doing now?

Mubaro is practically deserted, everyone home with their families, by the time Rachel hits the main street. She quickens her pace. Lillian and Nadine probably have Christmas lunch on the table by now. She startles at the tap of a horn, a truck slowing down beside her. *Run.* That's her first thought when Christian Kensamara leans out the window and calls to her.

"I was on my way to Kwizera," he says. "Wait, we must talk."

"Unless you can tell me what happened to my father, we have

nothing to discuss. Is he still alive?"

"I promise you, I don't know."

"Did your father hurt him?"

"Please, Madame."

Something urgent in his voice makes Rachel stop. He stops the truck and opens the passenger door. "Come. I need your help."

"Me, help you?"

"No, Nadine."

Rachel steps toward the truck. "Where is she?"

"We don't have much time."

"Why should I trust you?"

"We must stop my brother. He's angry—"

"Didn't you tell him Nadine's not going to testify?"

"Felix believes it's a trick. He thinks you have the photos and plan on using them at the *gacaca.*" Christian starts the engine. "You must come with me, tell him it's not true."

Rachel is frozen with indecision. How can she trust this boy who took her passport in the first place, and quite possibly tricked her father into going to the church? "We'll go to Kwizera, get Lillian and Tucker," she says. They'll know what to do.

"There's no time, Madame. Felix is with Nadine at the church."

THIRTY-FIVE

N ADINE TILTS HER HEAD ONE WAY AND the other, imagining the pieces of light refracted onto the floor and walls through the stained glass windows are a fortress. Nothing can touch her. Umama's lullaby vibrates in her chest, just as it did when she was curled up under the blue tarp during the massacre. *Sleep my love, and peace attend thee all through the night; Guardian angels God will lend thee, all through the night.*

She breathes in remnants of frankincense and myrrh. Forgiveness. Reconciliation. Will the *gacaca* really make these things possible? Her family and most of her friends are gone, but Chrissie is still here. She needs her friend. She does want things between them to return to as they were before the day six years ago when everything changed. She squeezes her eyes tightly.

Before.

But this is what comes to her: crows screaming, circling above, the Greek chorus of something like a grotesque opera. She listened to the cacophony to distract her mind, confuse her body. Dust and pebbles coated lips that were not hers; useless tears turned to dust on the impervious clay ground. The pain in her groin, far worse than the blade at her throat, seemed to dissipate into the harsh cackles above. Hot breath in her ear faded into a wisp of wind as she floated away from the pain.

She watched from up high with the crows as Felix soiled her body and the other boys, some who she recognized from school, did the same to Sylvia and their friends. Afterwards, she lay with one cheek pressed to the ground, one arm under her body, palm sticky with oozing blood. She watched her other hand, which lay limp near her face, entranced by fingers shaking spastically. It was her hand but not; it was a large spider, legs dancing, body paralyzed.

"Get up, cockroach." Felix yanked her limp body from the ground, like he was hoisting a sack of teff. She fell against him, arms flailing, her legs seemingly unfamiliar with gravity. She clawed at his arms and neck, imagining that her body belonged to the lion her grandfather had befriended in the woods. Kingston would protect her.

Felix slapped her and twirled her around, a blade, sharper now, against her back.

"I'll do it," Chrissie said, suddenly beside her. He patted her bare shoulder, twice. A signal she couldn't decipher.

Felix grunted. "You are a child like she is. Her friend."

"Remember what the general from Kigali told us. First, you must kill a friend. After that, it is easy."

The tip of the knife prodded between Nadine's shoulder blades as Felix considered his choices.

"I want to be a soldier like you, brother," Chrissie said, his voice husky. "I want to be a man."

Now, Nadine's eyes open wide as she hears footsteps outside the church window. Her hand goes to the impala-skin satchel tied around her waist, presses the outline of the gun against her hip bone. She remembers the crows screaming. Felix laughing, shoving her at his brother. The sensation of falling, stumbling into her friend's arms. Felix taunting, "Look at you, afraid to even touch the cockroach. I promise, she doesn't bite."

She doesn't remember Papa Henry pushing Chrissie out of the way and wrapping her in a soft blue shirt that hung nearly to her knees. She only recalls staring down at his hands fastening the buttons, ashamed that he had seen her naked. He had seen Felix on top of her. She kept her eyes on his hands. "Don't tell Umama and Baba."

"No, of course—" His voice broke as he pulled her to his chest. A shudder that could have come from either of them ran through her and settled in her groin; the shockwaves of pain would never completely fade.

"Shhh… quiet now, Nadine," he whispered. "I'll be back for you. Just try to think of your mama's voice, maybe a song."

"Hey, Mister American, you want to go with them?" Felix shoved Papa Henry toward the shed. "Take some photos?"

Nadine began crying hysterically. No, she didn't want him to see any more.

"Back to work, *mzunga*," Felix ordered, "or I go tell my father."

"Nadine, remember what I said," Papa Henry shouted as two soldiers led him away.

"Stop crying, Nadine," Chrissie hissed in her ear. "You must stop or he will make me kill you, right here." And then, there was only the sound of the crows as her friend took her into the shed.

Nadine keeps her eyes on the sanctuary door as it clicks open, fumbles in her bag—Kleenex, bobby pins, a hairbrush, a cluster of coins—and grips the thin slab of steel. The door swings open. The orb of light surrounding her shatters. Felix steps into the room, his eyes darting around and landing on her. He looks nearly respectable, dressed in a white button-down shirt and black chinos, except for a thick number tattooed on the side of his neck. His prison identification number. A mark of honor for militant Hutus.

"I wasn't sure you'd come," Nadine says. She slipped him a note after the service, asking him to meet her when the sanctuary emptied out.

He shrugs. "What do you want?"

Nadine stands perfectly still, holds her breath. Maybe Felix won't see how badly she wants to run.

"What?" he barks.

"Leave me and my family alone."

He waves a hand through the air as if swatting away an insect. "No gacaca, no trouble."

"Christian, too," Nadine says.

Felix narrows his eyes. "My brother will do as I say. Besides, soon he will go back to Uganda, you to Nairobi, me to Congo. All of our troubles will be over. Forgotten."

"No." The word springs from Nadine's chest.

"Cockroach, we have no more business—"

"I remember," Nadine blurts. Maman is right. Staying silent has made her feel helpless and weak for too long. "I'm not scared of you anymore. Leave us all alone or I will testify."

Felix sighs loudly. "So, now you remember? Prove it."

The smirk on his face is cruel and pitying as Nadine tells him some, but not all, of the secrets she has kept to herself. It's too painful to recall aloud how she and the other girls had been ordered to strip in the shed and then line up outside, naked and cold, each one with a boy at her side holding a machete. "I remember your father telling you and the other Hutu boys that what you did to us was your right. Your blessed initiation into manhood," she says flatly. And the Tutsi girls' initiation into the hell they deserved. *Justice* is what Rahim Kensamara called it.

"If you remember so good," Felix says, "then tell me something. Why didn't my brother carry out orders and kill you?"

Nadine licks her lips. Why?

"Your brother slammed shut the door to the shed. He called me terrible names…" She remembers Chrissie frantically rummaging through the paint cans and shovels, kicking at clothing and trash on the floor. "He threw things at me." A pair of underwear. He couldn't find a dress or shirt that wasn't bloody or in shreds. He did find a large blue tarp and tented it over a stepladder in the back corner. *Sit here, under the ladder. Don't move until I come back, even if you hear the door open.*

Nadine places her hand to her nose. The smell of dust and turpentine, and something like rotting bananas grew so intense that she scraped a tiny hole in the tarp. And then, there was something odd: the faint smell of chocolate. A cruel trick of hunger; her last meal had been breakfast yesterday. Or had it been the day before? Sometime later, curled up in the dark, head to knees, she noticed a crinkling sound in the breast pocket of the flannel shirt Papa Henry had buttoned up to her collarbone. She ripped off the wrapper of the Snickers bar and devoured it, the intense pleasure on her tongue shameful, sucking the delicious gooeyness from her fingertips like an animal, not caring about the dried blood and dirt mixed in.

"Why?" Felix repeats loudly. "Why didn't Christian do as he was told?"

"Because..." Nadine's breath is hot in her lungs, her skin turning flushed and prickly. That day, Chrissie acted like a real man. He saved her life. He guarded the shed and told everyone he had buried his friend, and then went to find Papa Henry when it was safe. So why isn't she grateful? Why is she angry with him? "Because he was a scared little boy."

Over the hours, as daylight faded, she picked away at the hole in the tarp, making it large enough for her eye. She watched a spider weaving a web. All the while, she wondered why. Why hadn't Chrissie killed her?

"My brother was foolish," Felix says. "It might surprise you to know it was me who took him to our uncle's house in Kampala. The others wanted to kill him for saving your wretched life."

"Am I supposed to thank you for sparing your own brother?"

"You should be grateful to me as well as Christian, grateful you are alive."

"No, it is not so." A tremor begins in Nadine's jaw, igniting her entire body. When Papa Henry opened the door to the shed, it was nearly the second nightfall she had been there. He helped her up, her legs weak and useless. She saw, outside the open door, the bodies on the ground. Her stomach tightened with a convulsion that brought up putrid-sweet liquid and the memory of begging whimpers and screams. Her friends. To this day, the smell of chocolate makes her nauseous. While her friends were being murdered, she was eating chocolate and nuts, safely hidden under the tarp. What right did she have to fill her belly? To live?

"Why are you spouting all of this nonsense anyway, cockroach," Felix goads. "I don't care to hear any more."

"I needed to tell you." Nadine clutches the satchel. "I won't testify at the *gacaca*, but not because I don't remember." She looks at Felix across a chasm of light. She may find forgiveness for him, someday far in the future when time softens her memories and he becomes merely a stupid boy following orders. Not next month, though, it's too soon. And she may never forgive Chrissie, her best friend, for saving her life.

Felix takes a few steps toward her. "I didn't come to hear your sad story."

Nadine fastens her hand tighter on the satchel.

"Give them to me. The photos that *mzunga* Shepherd took that day."

"You are crazy."

"The woman Rachel, his daughter, your friend…" Felix takes a few more steps, eyes fixed on the satchel. "She came here with the photos didn't she?"

It all happens so quickly: his face twisted into sheer hatred. A tightness snakes through her lungs, as if the blade of his knife is once again pressed to her throat. She grips the gun, unsure how it got into her hand. A hot jolt of metal thrusts her backwards, the edge of a pew sharp against her thighs, a shattering rumble above. She shields her head as splinters of blue and gold glass cascade around them. Felix lunges for the gun but she's quicker, standing over him, both hands on hot metal, shaking but firm.

He looks up at her, a hand raised to his face but she sees the fear in his eyes. She lifts her chin. So, this is what it is like to have power.

"You're right," she says, "I do owe you." Umama and Baba, Sylvia and her friends. The screaming crows that wake her up at night. The filth under her fingernails that can never be washed away. She startles as the door swings open; another shot fires, but it's not Felix who cries out and then falls at her feet.

GLASS EXPLODES INTO THE SKY from the church window, showering slivers of sunlight everywhere. Rachel shades her eyes, as if looking straight at the sun. Christian runs ahead of her, into the church. Another shot rings out. "Nadine!" Rachel yells, pushing open the sanctuary door. She stops short: Christian's lying on the floor, clutching his shoulder, Nadine at his side.

Felix is standing over both of them with a gun. "Stupid girl," he says. "It's all her fault."

"We have to get your brother to a hospital," Rachel says, calmly she hopes, her eyes on Nadine.

"*Oya*," Christian gasps. "No hospital. They'll ask who did it."

Rachel kneels next to the boy to look at his shoulder. "I'll call Tucker on the radio in your truck."

Felix aims the gun at her. "No calls!"

"You can't keep protecting him," Rachel says to Christian. "You can't—"

"He's right, it's my fault," Nadine says. "I did this."

335

"No, *inshuti*." Rachel stands and holds out her palm as if offering Felix the pink locket resting in it. He raises the gun to her head but she doesn't move. "You started this," she says. "You can end it. Tell me where you got this."

"It belongs to my mother."

"No, I bought this locket for my dad's Christmas present. I was seven. There's a photo of me inside."

Felix glares at his brother, says something in Kinyarwanda, and keeps the gun trained on Rachel.

"*Oya*," Christian says. "No more killing, brother. No more."

"Nobody needs to die." Rachel steps sideways to shield Nadine. "We'll take Christian to Kwizera. Tucker will stitch him up. But first, I need the truth. Where did you get this? What happened to my father?"

Felix's eyes dart from his brother to the locket. "Henry Shepherd is dead."

Rachel closes her fist around the stone heart. Her legs buckle, her hand dropping heavily to her side. "You…" Felix killed her father. Now, he's aiming the gun at her chest. "You can stop this," she says. "Please, stop this."

Felix shakes his head, a flash of soft sadness crossing his face. "Madame, there is no stopping it." He cocks the gun and raises it slightly, and then Christian bursts forward with a roar of strength and grabs at his brother's legs. The two brothers topple as the gun goes off and Rachel sinks to the floor, blood pooling at her feet.

THIRTY-SIX
{ August 1998 }

H ENRY CROUCHES BEHIND THE THICK trunk of the old fig tree, close enough to smell the tang of sage and roasted goat meat in the air but far enough away not to be seen in the square of light that is the window above the kitchen sink. Inside, his family is sitting around the weathered mahogany table, Lilly holding Rose in her lap. No, that's not right; Rose is nearly three now, big enough to perch atop a pillow on a chair. He imagines that Lilly keeps the hum of conversation going by asking each child about their day. How did Nadine do on the math test she was tied up in knots about? Did Thomas resolve his squabble with a friend?

He squints at the square of light, picturing each of the four boys and six girls who were living here when he left. How many have graduated from high school and moved on? Have others taken their place during the past four years? Did Naddie get a scholarship to college?

Does she still play the flute? His gaze falls to his shoes. Lilly will be glad to see him, of course she will. She wants him back for the trial. But what happens after that? The uncertainty keeps him here in the dark where he has watched the window for the past several hours, trying to find a way to walk through the door to his home.

He pats his jacket with a shaky hand and extracts a blue pill from the lint and Kleenex in the breast pocket, lets the bitterness melt on his tongue. It had seemed like such a good plan: He would show up with the photos in his rucksack, be a hero for a brief moment and then take off again before daylight. He can't stay, the Hutus would kill him, Lilly knows this. But now, hearing the murmur of her and the children, the clink and scrape of silverware on plates, the clang of a pot on the stove as someone refills their plate… For chrissakes, he can't leave his family. Not again.

Henry gasps, his breath catching in his throat, as Lillian appears in the window, leaning over the sink, her upper body floating in the light. He stands flat against the tree to get a better view. She's washing dishes, talking to someone he doesn't recognize who's drying and stacking plates on the counter. The girl comes to the back door and looks up at the sky. Henry lets out a painful sigh. *Nadine.* She's a young woman now. Beautiful.

"Maman, come look," she shouts excitedly. "The crocodile's out tonight." Lillian appears in the doorway, wipes her hands on her apron and places an arm around Nadine. They're so close; Henry takes a step out of the shadow and then stops short, the force of something like a large hand flat against his chest. He thinks of this shape-shifting entity as a jinn who makes sure that he eats, bathes, craps, sleeps. It keeps him alive, but at a cost. That's the deal he made at the church. The only way he could snap the shutter button, take the photos that saved Nadine's life and his own, was to give up a piece of his soul.

Thirty-six photos. These images are the first things he sees when he awakes each morning—doesn't even need to pull them out of the desk drawer anymore—just in case he doesn't remember the nightmares. If he were to move back into the farmhouse, these images would, without a doubt, follow him there. He didn't realize that this was part of the deal.

The victims of the massacre live on in the part of his soul that became vacant as he snapped photos at the church. The place where he used to take photos of things that made him feel vital and alive: gorillas and orchids, Lilly and the kids, the shadows that shift over the green, tiered foothills as morning turns into afternoon, and then blend in with the dark night sky. All of the beauty he once loved about living here in Rwanda. Gone. He is truly alone.

After Lilly and Nadine go back inside and the light in the kitchen dims, the ceiling of stars seems to drop a notch closer. Henry lifts his hand, as if he might harness the bright jewel of light at the tip of the crocodile's tail. For a moment, he is at peace with his solitude.. He shades his eyes against the infinite glittering path of the Milky Way. The stars are the eyes of the dead... He read that somewhere. No, it was in a Disney movie about space that he had watched as a kid.

He never knew whether or not his dad was telling the truth about his mom dying in a car accident shortly after she left them. It seemed easiest to believe that was true. He would look up at the twinkling North Star, even years later in his backyard in Jacksonville with Rachel by his side, imagining his mom shining down on him. She was finally happy. Free. He imagines the piece of his soul that left him four years ago at the massacre is a shooting star, only it's heading back up into the sky where it belongs. What would it be like, to truly be free?

Henry walks into the forest and follows the river until he comes to the mopani tree at the bend, where he and Lilly spent many hours in the cradle of the thick roots, atop a blanket, sometimes with a thermos of lemonade. The ground is cold and hard. He digs into it with his pocketknife, and scrapes the clay with his fingernails. He takes from his rucksack a rusty metal box that he found last night, half buried with sticks and dirt, on the riverbank. It was the perfect size for the thirty-six photos of the massacre. Now, he places the box in the ground and tamps down the earth with his hands. He'll slip a note under Lilly's door, telling her where the photos are. Telling her he still loves her and he will always love her.

He walks out of the forest, his step light, and heads across the soccer field toward the farmhouse like he's simply coming back from a late-night stroll, will brush his teeth and splash warm water on his face before slipping into bed next to Lilly. For a moment, he can believe this is true.

He stops, his heart quickening at the sound of something stirring in the field of sunflowers behind him. A shadow of clouds seems to slip over the stars, darkening the eyes of the dead, and his mind goes momentarily blank. It feels surprisingly nice. Suddenly, the rustling becomes footsteps, footsteps of the children he and Tucker buried in the field, the shadow seemingly springing to life. He turns around and heads back toward the woods, slowly, to give the shadow time to catch up with him and draw it away from the farmhouse.

The shadow follows him, toys with him, as he walks through the forest, not so fast as to be suspicious. He wants, more than anything, to make it to the mopani tree. He hears a lion roaring, but that's impossible. There haven't been any lions, giraffes or elephants—not even zebra, caribou or impalas—in Rwanda since before the genocide. All the animals that didn't have the sense to flee were killed for food or poached. The national parks are now refugee camps for thousands of Hutus, genocide criminals who were extradited from Zaire by the Rwandan government.

When he gets to the mopani tree, he snaps the silver chain around his neck and drops it, along with the heart-shaped locket, under the tree where it will be easy for Lilly to find. At least she'll know he was here. Then, he walks to the riverbank and waits, thinking back on the important moments of his life: when he first showed up at Kwizera, and realized he couldn't leave; the wedding that only the baboons witnessed, right here. The first moment he saw Rachel squirming in Merilee's arms; making pancakes with his daughter on Saturday mornings; the way she dragged a blanket into the backyard and sat next to him at night, both of them watching the stars. Driving his blue Skylark to Atlanta; walking into Ebenezer Church, scared and excited at the same time; Lilly waving at him.

A shot rings out. He's frozen in time. There is the pulpit with Reverend King raising his hand like a witness being sworn in as he speaks. There are rows of dark faces, turning to stare at him as he walks down the aisle. There is the girl who waved at him; she looks like an angel through his lens, shards of light from the stained glass window encircling her. He stops beside her, wants to stand in the light with her, that's all he wants now. The light is warm and soothing; it washes over him. He falls into the light as his body sinks to the bottom of the river. Peaceful. Free.

THIRTY-SEVEN

enry Shepherd is dead. RACHEL ONLY SU-
perficially understands these words, keeps them at arm's
length while driving Christian's truck to Ruhengeri. Nadine is in the back, Christian's head cradled in her lap. Kinyarwanda
whispers of sorrow, love and forgiveness float within Rachel's grasp.
She collects these words, stitches them together into a patchwork
quilt of comprehension, along with the questions that remain. Why
did Felix murder her father? How? Where is his body?

She keeps her eyes on Tucker's Jeep straight ahead. Felix is lying
on the back seat, unconscious. In her mind, she sees a clear image of
her father. He is sitting in a lawn chair in the backyard, head tilted up
toward the stars. He is cold. Shivering. She longs to warm him somehow. She prays that Felix will make it through surgery. He's the only
one who can give her the final pieces of her father's story so she may
finally lay him to rest.

At the hospital, Tucker tells an admitting nurse that the unconscious boy now on a stretcher has lost a lot of blood. Felix is taken down the hall to the Emergency Room. Luckily, the bullet that Nadine shot only grazed Christian's shoulder. Tucker offers to dress his wound. The admitting nurse directs him to a room the size of the kitchen at Kwizera where about a dozen patients who have been assessed as stable rest on tight rows of cots.

Rachel tries to stand out of the way, doesn't know quite what to do with herself or how to help. Clearly, the hospital is short-staffed. She hasn't seen anyone remotely resembling a doctor since they arrived. A woman wearing a navy dress, who may or may not be a nurse, provides Tucker with a roll of gauze, tape, and an industrial-sized bottle of Tylenol. There are no medical instruments in sight, not even a thermometer. Tucker goes in search of antiseptic, a surgical needle and thread. Nadine kneels on the floor beside her friend's cot and holds his hand. Rachel offers to track down food and water, embarrassed to be encroaching on what is clearly an intimate moment even in the crowded room.

She heads outside, into a courtyard teeming with activity. The air smells of *ugali*, a sweet cornmeal porridge, coffee, and the harsh scent of bleach. In the center is a makeshift kitchen: one woman stirs a black kettle simmering over a low fire, another sits cross-legged on the cement and slices bananas into a wooden bowl. At the far side of the small square, several other women hang towels to dry in the afternoon sun on a crowded rope clothesline tied between two acacia trees. Babies and toddlers splash in a big trough of water where clothes are also being washed. More mothers and children nap on thin squares of blankets on the dusty ground under the trees beyond the courtyard.

Rachel nods at each woman she passes; there is a palpable exchange as their eyes meet. Nearby, a young woman, a baby in her arms, is struggling to hang a blanket on the rope line. Rachel takes one end of the blanket and clips it on with a clothespin, the child grasping at her hair. For a moment, she is connected with both mother and child.

"My son's papa is ill for many months," the woman says. "You? Why are you here?"

"My father." Rachel gazes tenderly at the curly-haired boy who is busily sucking his fingers. "Do you mind if I hold him for a bit? *Sawa?*"

She takes the child over to a nearby patch of shady grass, and sits with him in her lap. He coos and giggles as she shutters her hands over her face, and then removes them. The universal language of peek-a-boo. A few minutes later, the mother returns and offers a bowl of porridge.

"*Murakoze.*" Rachel takes the bowl, the warmth travelling from her hands throughout her entire body. She watches the mother and child walk away, a soft longing cracking open the place where her tears have been frozen for years. She sits under the tree and cries for her father. For her mom. Serena. She cries alone, and yet there is the sense of being held by this courtyard filled with mothers and their children. She takes a bowl of porridge to her newly discovered *shika*. For the next few hours, she sits with Nadine while Christian sleeps and Tucker observes Felix's surgery. No, she is not alone.

Dead. LILLIAN PRESSES THE PHONE to her ear, the fist of her heart pounding out the flat syllable. Tucker sounds much farther away than

Ruhengeri, the faint static-laced words barely reaching her as he relays Felix's confession on the way to the hospital. Henry returned and the boy shot him. When and where, he didn't say. But, she knew.

Her hand goes to the silver chain around her neck that she found under the mopani tree, not long before Rahim Kensamara's trial in Arusha. She knelt in the dirt and clawed at the ground. The heart-shaped locket Henry had always worn around his neck was nowhere to be found. That was good, she assured herself; the chain could belong to anyone. And yet she has worn it ever since, the weight of the phantom locket hanging like a small vial, cold and metallic, just below the dip in her collarbone. This is where she has secreted away her grief and love for Henry during the past two years, intertwined like this chain. It was easier to pretend that he had chosen to abandon her and the children. It was easier to be angry. But she knew. "Rachel," she says into the phone. "How is she?"

Tell me, what did you love about my father? Please, I need to know.

It was easier to believe she was protecting Henry's daughter from knowing him fully because it would somehow hurt her. The truth is, she kept not only Henry's photo album but also her own memories locked away to protect herself. If she were to unravel the love and share it, then the grief might also come undone.

Tucker assures her that Rachel seems all right. She's strong. But, of course, she's worried that Felix won't live to reveal what happened to her father. She needs to know. "Keep that boy alive," Lillian says before hanging up.

As the afternoon unfurls, the children opening Christmas presents, neighbors stopping by to exchange cookies and jars of home-made jam, Tucker's words fade completely away. There is only the vibrating thud of a single dull beat against Lillian's ribs, like sonar trying to locate a small vessel in a vast ocean. *Dead, dead, dead.*

By the time the aunties arrive for Christmas dinner, the throbbing weight has dropped down into her stomach. She tries a few bites of chicken and sweet potato casserole. Even a thin slice of the carda-mom-apple cake Julia brought for dessert is a chore to swallow. She imagines it would be a relief for the metal vial to crack open within her, a slight fissure from which drips something like mercury, hot and cloying, slowing down her heartbeat until it flattens out.

She prays it won't be like the last time she grieved for Henry, knowing in her heart that when he fled with the massacre photos to Kampala he wouldn't return. Her grief was unexpected, spilling out all at once. Days after he left, she finally removed his razor from the edge of the bathroom sink, tested the dull blade against her thumb and then tossed it into the garbage. This single action released rush of pressure, like a spigot in her chest had been violently wrenched. She doubled over in pain, and then there was nothing.

Nothing at all during the weeks she took care of everyone else, helping Tucker to pack and leave for Uganda with Nadine and Rose, making sure the other children who stayed at Kwizera during the slaughter all had somewhere to live while she supposedly cleaned up the farm. Nothing during the months resting at Mama's house in Atlanta, as if she had a terminal illness and couldn't care for her own needs. She searched for her son as a way to try and feel again, to find a way out of grief. Instead, when she hit a dead end, she discovered another antidote for grief: anger. That's also what she felt, looking at the newspaper photo of a young Rwandan woman sitting on the porch of her ravaged home, helpless and defeated.

Washing the dinner dishes beside Julia, Lillian looks out the window into the violet-blue dusk. The silhouettes of foil snowmen and stars are losing their shine as the sun goes down. Her hands suddenly go motionless in the tepid gray water. She could swear Henry is crouching just to the left of the fig tree, and when he sees her he moves out of sight. There's a slight tug in her chest, part of her straining to detach and follow him into the darkness. Instead, she reaches out for the anchor of her friend's arm. "Henry's not coming back," she says quietly, and then louder, "He's dead."

"*Oya*," Julia murmurs, as if she already knew. "*Oya, inshuti.*" Her touch, a brief gentle press of fingers on Lillian's hand, seems to release tiny granules of relief from the metallic vial. No, this is not like the last time. The aunties. Naddie. Tucker. Henry's daughter. This time, she is far from alone. The thought pearls into tears, but not for herself.

"Julia," she says, wiping the foam of soap bubbles on her hands briskly onto her apron. "There's somewhere I need to go. Would you mind looking after the children?"

Maura Kensamara is sitting on her front porch. It's no surprise that she doesn't stand to greet the Jeep, but she doesn't so much as glance up as Lillian takes a basket of food from the backseat. Surely, she must be curious; for six years, they haven't said a civil hello or even met each other's eyes when passing on the street. Lillian walks up the steps and places the basket beside her. "You need to stay strong for your boys," she says. "They need you strong."

Maura moves over, only slightly, and Lillian sits beside her to make a plate for each of them. They exchange a single word, a prayer, before they begin to eat: *amahoro*.

WHEN RACHEL RETURNS TO KWIZERA, without Nadine who's coming back with Tucker and Christian after Felix is out of surgery, the main house is dark and quiet. The electricity is off. Everyone must be asleep. She walks around back to the patio, looking for Lillian. A tiny tumbleweed of wrapping paper and tinsel scraps blows past her feet. It's surreal; only hours earlier, the matriarch of Kwizera was helping children to open cheerfully wrapped presents that teetered in stacks under the now-barren fig tree.

The kitchen door opens and Julia emerges, carrying a bowl of stew. "You need to eat, Madame."

Rachel sits at the nearest table, although she's not the least bit hungry. "Where's Lillian?" she asks.

"She has gone for a while."

"Gone?"

"Delivering dinner to someone in need." Julia looks pointedly at the untouched bowl on the table.

Rachel dips in the spoon and takes a courtesy bite. "How does Lillian do it?" she wonders aloud. "Take care of everyone else." Pretend nothing is wrong.

"We do what we must. We take care of each other in times of sorrow." Julia stoops to pick up a stray foil star and places it on the table before she leaves.

Rachel holds onto the ornament, her fingers smoothing out a bent edge, and watches Julia disappear down the driveway. The children. Lillian said they have always been her saving grace. *They keep me focused on what's important.* Perhaps it isn't that the Lady of Steel is as cold as she sometimes seems, but that she and the aunties have all been in a kind of survival mode just like the mothers in the hospital courtyard.

She hangs the misfit star on the lowest branch of the fig tree, the slight weight of the soapstone heart in her skirt pocket shifting. A silent wish starts as a warm ache in her chest, and then flows into tears. It's a wish she hasn't dared to name for many years.

RACHEL SITS CROSS-LEGGED, LEANING AGAINST the mahogany headboard, reviewing the photos and postcards her father never mailed, now floating around her on the satiny quilt as if adrift at sea. She leans down to reluctantly remove the last postcard from the stripped corkboard on the floor: a lion sunning on a boulder. The image that brought her here. She slots the card into a crinkled plastic sleeve in the photo album on her lap, her hand heavy with a kind of defeat. Another week, and then it's back to New York, mixing drinks and listening to other peoples' stories. Back to trying to figure out her own life.

She glances out the window: it's a clear night, the sky lit up with millions of glittering pixels. There's the crocodile that her father showed her, and the lion's paw. What was he really searching for in the images of the stars, sitting in his lawn chair in the backyard, night after night? Did he see Lillian's face? The exciting life he left behind in Atlanta? Did he come here trying to discover something more than the good-enough job and family he had settled for? Her own search feels incomplete.

There's a tap on the half-open door. Rose peeks in, Kingston nestled snugly under her chin. "Shouldn't you be asleep?" Rachel asks.

"I usually have a bedtime story." Rose sighs. "Julia gave me my medicine, and then Thomas read from a book that wasn't a bit interesting. I think it was something assigned for school."

"I've got a story for you." Rachel scoops up the photos and moves them to the bedside table. She pulls back the quilt for Rose to climb in. "Once upon a time, there was a genie who buried a treasure somewhere in the desert," she begins. The night her father left he told her a story… Where was the jinn's treasure buried, anyway? "Wait, let's start over." She flips through the photo album, searching for something to begin a new story. "This is about my dad, Henry. You're too young to remember him."

"Nadine's Papa Henry?"

"Papa Henry." Rachel points to the postcard of a field of red and yellow rosebushes with Mt. Kenya towering in the background. "He worked at a flower farm in Kenya for a while." Rose leans over her to get a better look. Rachel strokes her hair; she had wanted to tell her own daughter stories about her grandpa someday.

She weaves a story about how Papa Henry talked to animals and travelled in search of adventures, her hand going to the necklace of chiseled animals still hanging over a corner of the board on the floor. She drapes the beads around Rose's neck. "What do you think? Did Papa Henry ride a zebra or an elephant to work in the mornings?"

"Perhaps a giraffe," Nadine suggests from the doorway. Rose moves over for her to sit on the bed.

Next, Rachel picks up the photo of a silverback gorilla climbing the hillside. He's looking over his shoulder, as if inviting the photographer to come along. "Papa Henry had a best friend." Rachel taps the photo against her palm. "His name was Max." That's what her father called the old gray gorilla at the zoo. The sad-looking animal always appeared to be waiting for them—or something, anyway—giant fingers gripping the metal bars. "They went on long walks every evening," she continues, "talking about their day, my dad planting flowers and Max..." She looks at Rose. "What did he do all day?"

"He was magic, like that genie," she pipes up.

"Well, Max was a very special gorilla." Rachel flips through the photo album for the next piece of her story. She lands on a postcard of her father canoeing among the purple water lilies on Lake Kivu. "One day, Max surprised Papa Henry with a magic boat he made out of bamboo and banana leaves. He said it would take him wherever he wanted to go."

"Anywhere?" Rose asks, her voice squeaky with awe.

Nadine reaches over her to turn the pages: photos of castles on the Rhine, Moroccan kasbahs, white powdery sand dunes. "Anywhere at all," she says dreamily. She stops at an image of Lillian in the sunflower garden. It slides easily out of the cellophane sleeve and seems to come to life, the colors more vibrant against Nadine's palm.

"Where did Papa Henry go?" Rose asks.

"He got into the boat, and then Max gave him a shove off into the water." Rachel takes the photo from Nadine, her hand shaking. She thought her father was trying to be funny, leaning over the rail to console a smelly old gorilla, talking to him about what it might be like to roam free in the jungle. *You'd like that, big guy, wouldn't you? Get the heck outta here and pound your chest a little bit.* Now, it occurs to her that he related to the trapped animal. He left to find freedom. And yet, he stayed here with Lillian and the children for nearly twenty years.

"The gorilla waved from the shore," Nadine continues. "'Have fun,' Max shouted, 'and make sure to keep your eye open for a beautiful princess.'"

Rose nods in approval at the photo of Lillian. "She does look like a princess."

"And where do you think Papa Henry found his princess?" Rachel asks, shuffling through the photos on the bedside table of her father's life in Rwanda: Lillian surrounded by kids on the front porch, a single tiger-striped orchid, Henry showing Naddie how to use a camera, the craggy fortress-like Virungas, a family of gorillas splashing in a lake, a lone vulture circling in the sky. These are the treasures her father discovered here.

Rose snuggles into her side and yawns. "He must have found Maman Lilly at home. Kwizera."

Rachel turns off the lantern on the bedside table and lies down next to Rose, whose breath is already heavy. Nadine hums for a few minutes, and then there is silence as her *shika* also falls asleep. There is the gentle rocking of the mattress as someone sits on the end of the bed: Lillian. In the soft moonlight radiating through the window, it's hard to see at first that her cheeks are glistening with tears. "Tucker's home," she says. "Felix didn't make it."

Rachel sits up slowly, so as not to awaken Rose or Nadine, and moves toward Lillian. This news makes her father's death seem real. Final.

"How will I tell Maura?" Lillian asks. "How…"

Rachel holds out her hand, the heart-shaped locket in her palm. "I want you to have this. Christian gave it to me."

Suddenly, Rachel's hand begins to shake. Her father didn't leave her and Merilee for another woman, he left to find a piece of himself the same way she did. He came here searching for freedom, and what he found was something stronger that kept him here, bound him to

Lillian and his life at Kwizera. *Family.* That's what she wished for earlier, on the tinfoil star. How had he ever given that up?

Lillian unsnaps the silver chain from around her neck and slips the locket onto it, then places the necklace on the bed between them. "This doesn't truly belong to either one of us," she says.

Rachel hangs it on a nail above the mahogany headboard.

THIRTY-EIGHT
{ December 31, 2000 }

T HE SUITCASE SEEMS MUCH SMALLER than when Rachel unpacked it six weeks ago, even without most of the clothes she brought here. She doesn't have the heart to reclaim her Scooby-Doo T-shirt from Rose. It's tougher to part with her Knicks sweatshirt and favorite buttery Levis that took two years to break in, but Nadine wanted some authentic American clothes. She tamps down three batik skirts that were a fair trade, a filmy purple-green silk tunic that Lillian says doesn't fit her anymore, and an assortment of handmade embroidered blouses. The photo album will take up the bulk of the carry-on bag. All that's left on the bed is the album, a thin bolt of gold-threaded fabric left over from Lillian's new kitchen curtains and the dreamcatcher.

She tucks away the bolt of fabric in the top drawer of Nadine's dresser. Lillian will teach her how to sew during her next visit. Maybe if she takes on some extra shifts she can make enough money for a plane ticket by summer or next Christmas. Now that Felix is dead, the tribunal has lost interest in staging a *gacaca* trial in Mubaro in January, postponing it indefinitely and focusing on other more promising cases in Ruhengeri. Nadine is returning to school, Tucker is taking Rose to London for the upcoming school semester, maybe longer, to be close to the AIDS clinic... The truth is, she's not at all sure when she'll be back here. She places the photo album atop the dresser. Lillian may need it more than she does.

Nadine enters the bedroom with a gift wrapped in a slip of white tissue paper. It's so light it could be nothing at all. "For the New Year," she says. "I refuse to call this a going-away present."

Rachel unwraps a long silvery feather from a crowned crane. She smiles at Nadine. They have often watched these majestic birds that have resided in Africa for some fifty million years, and marveled that some things of beauty can't be extinguished.

"This morning, I went to visit Chrissie," Nadine says. "A large crane landed outside his bedroom window and stood there for quite a while, stamping, shaking his golden bristles. I think he wanted to make sure we noticed him. And then, he flew away. He left this feather behind."

"Maybe this was his gift for you and Chrissie."

"And now I am passing it on to you, *shika*. The crane is a symbol of *amahoro*."

"I like that. Peace."

"Yes, and something more." Nadine places her hand over Rachel's fingers. "I told Chrissie I cannot forgive all that has happened, but I am no longer angry at him. There is nothing he could have done to stop the murders, he was a child—as I was. But, these horrible things did happen. Felix and their father…and Chrissie was part of it, too. All this cannot be erased, cannot be changed. I want him to be my friend again, but it will never be the same. We held each other and cried for a long time, for the loss and the love that will bind us forever. *Amahoro*."

"Grief," Rachel says. She picks up the dreamcatcher, the last item on the bed, and replaces one of the ragged feathers with the silvery new one. She hangs the web of sticks and yarn on the nail where the soapstone heart hung, only now it's not there.

RACHEL HEARS THE COUNTDOWN TO midnight and the noisemakers that signify the New Year from where she is sitting on the bench atop the hill that overlooks Kwizera and the forest beyond. She twists her wedding band. It sticks at her knuckle, her hands falling into her lap. A few hours ago, she called Mick. *Amahoro.* She told him that's her wish for both of them in the New Year. They need to grieve together over the loss of their daughter—find peace—before moving forward in different directions.

She imagines going home tomorrow, the two of them peeling away the Day-Glo Milky Way from the ceiling, removing chunky books from the shelves and taking apart the crib. After everything is packed into boxes addressed to Kwizera for Lillian to use or give away, they will drive high into the mountains. They will find a tall, thick pine tree that stands alone in the sunshine. They will bury Serena's ashes in the snow. She imagines her father's footprints materializing in the ash, just as they seemed to appear in the snow globe he sent from Mt. Kenya, and then the ground turning clean and white again. Only snow.

She sees the Jeep's headlights on the driveway, in front of the farmhouse, and runs down the hill to meet Tucker. "I tried to make it by midnight," he says, a soft apology in his kiss. He pulls a bottle of banana gin out of a brown paper bag on the front seat. "I came prepared for the pathetic and dateless route, just in case you were already out making champagne toasts with some other guy."

"I'm glad you're here." Rachel looks down at the gold band, which now slips easily over her knuckle. She cups the ring in her palm. "I spoke with Mick. We agreed. It's over."

Tucker takes her in his arms and kisses her hair. "Rough night," he says. "Rachel, I'm sorry."

"We both knew..." She takes a deep breath and slowly exhales. Being apart during the past six weeks has made it clear that they've both been living alone, even while sleeping together in the same bed, for years.

Tucker sits on the bottom step of the front porch and offers her the bottle. "Here's to the many splendors of being single."

"Cold cereal for dinner, no worries about hogging the bed." She sniffs the gin—antiseptic and juniper, not at all sweet like bananas— and tips the bottle without putting her lips to the rim. The warm splash stings slightly, feels almost cleansing, as it goes down. She passes the bottle back to Tucker. "What else do you have?"

"Don't forget keeping the toilet seat up." He raises the bottle in a toast, and then takes a long swig. "As luck would have it, I have many words of wisdom for you about the joys of singlehood. At the top of the list is, of course, dating." He cringes as if dipping a toe into an icy pond, and then launches into tales of his numerous dating fiascos. At first Rachel smiles mostly for his benefit, but then finds herself actually relaxing, laughing as she dredges up a few of her own fix-ups gone wrong before meeting Mick.

Mick. They were good together for a long while. They loved each other the best they could. They did their best. She moves closer to Tucker. Now, she wants to do better.

"And then," he says, "there's the date *de résistance*. A few years ago, I gathered my courage and asked out this gorgeous woman who's a clerk at the bank I go to in Kigali. I was, of course, extremely smooth."

Rachel links her arm through the crook of his elbow. "Do tell."

Tucker clears his throat in mock annoyance. "Anyway, her father shows up at this classy restaurant in downtown Kigali with a cow and a goat, no lie." He puts a hand over his eyes and shudders. "He was bringing me a taste of his daughter's dowry. I was duly impressed; she was totally mortified."

"Stop, please…" Rachel shuts him up with a kiss. "Before you scare me into running off to join a convent."

"Ah, but there's more," he says. "We spent the rest of the evening walking with her father back to their farm—five miles in heels. The girl, not the cow. And then, I had to head back into the city again to retrieve my Jeep. I lost everything—the cow, the girl, the goat. A very bad date, indeed."

Rachel kisses him again, long and deep. "I don't want to date, that's for sure."

"What do you want?"

"Honestly? I don't know. I thought my marriage would last forever. Maybe I was expecting too much."

"No, you deserve more."

"We both do." Rachel follows his gaze down to the brass ring on his pinky finger.

"Solange," Tucker says. "Her name was Solange."

Rachel listens quietly as he tells her about a nurse at the clinic in Kigali where the Red Cross first assigned him to work. Solange slept on a cot in the maternity ward, a big room with ten or twelve single beds squeezed into it, not just to take care of the patients but also because she was sending her paychecks to her father and five brothers in Uganda. They were Hutus but none of them supported the Rwandan government except her twin brother, Aaron.

"I didn't know any of this for months after we met," Tucker says, "but I could tell right away that Solange was strong and brave, in ways I wanted to be. She completed me. The family we were going to have was everything to both of us."

"Rose," Rachel says tenderly. Solange must be the nurse who helped Tucker to deliver her.

"We were going to build a family for her."

"And you have."

"We would take care of her. Together." Tucker stands and takes a few steps, stops at the driveway as if waiting for someone to arrive. "The truth is, I can't do it alone. I need to take Rose to London, not just for a few months."

"But her family is here." Rachel goes to plant herself in front of him. "Your family."

"And you?"

"I'll come back." She places her hands on his shoulders, feels the tension as he cranes his neck to look past her. "Tucker, I'll come back for you."

"The AIDS clinic in London has a hospice for when Rose needs it."

"Then, I'll go with you."

The tension transforms into a tremor that begins between his shoulders and releases down his spine. She holds onto him tightly and the tremor dissolves into tears. Her tears and his. No, she thinks, he wasn't waiting for someone to arrive. He was watching Solange walk away. "Tucker," she says, "let me be your family."

THE STARS HAVE FADED, THE royal blue sky backlit by the promise of a sunrise. A new day; a new year. Rachel hears everything in the bright silence. She hears high flute-like notes that call across the soccer field: *Phew. Phew-phew.* A pair of Scops owls. She hears each step Lillian takes, the squeak of her swinging lantern, which carves a shaky path through the red clay. As they enter the forest, the pine trees seem to sigh, bristled branches heavy with dew. She hears the baritone grunts of groggy baboons not yet ready to start in with their wake-up wahoos.

Something snarls. Lillian shines the lantern into the trees. "Probably a baboon," she says, but doesn't move.

"We could go back," Rachel suggests. "Get Tucker."

"No." Lillian starts walking again. Rachel stays a step behind and hangs onto the older woman's rough hand. This walk was Lillian's idea. She woke her up and insisted, it had to be now. Early. Just hours before Tucker drives her to the airport.

Lillian leads her down a path that she hasn't taken on her daily hikes with Nadine. Or, maybe it's just that everything looks different. The gray-pink light now filtering through the thick canopy makes it difficult to see. Invisible wings brush her bare arms, silky booby traps of webbing cling to her hair. The shadows in the trees could be animals or simply her imagination. It even smells different this time of day; the earth is damp and ripe. Alive and not. *The forest of ghosts.* Tucker said that's what Lillian calls this place. She won't allow the children to come here. Why did she bring her here, why now?

They head deeper into the forest, the morning chorus building in waves: Black-bellied seedcrackers, waxbills, spurfowl and bulbuls. Go-away-birds, starlings, weavers and bru-brus. Rachel mentally catalogues each coo and cackle. Nadine will be so impressed.

Lillian finally stops at a clearing and turns off the lantern. The cloudless sky is now the palest blue, a crown of soft light collecting in the silvery eucalyptus leaves. There are dozens of chunks of wood arranged in rows on the mossy ground, all with scratchy lettering. *Red shirt. Kitten barrettes. Green eyes.* Rachel has the sense of wandering into someplace forbidden and spins around, looking for Lillian, afraid she has disappeared.

Lillian is kneeling, not far away, in front of a tree stump topped with a cross, picking dead leaves off a patch of pansies. "Dahla," she says softly. She runs her hand over the purple flowers. "I miss you, my friend." She looks up, her eyes soft and moist. "I miss them all."

Rachel offers her hand to help Lillian up, and then keeps holding on. They walk slowly, Lillian setting the pace. She stops and lays her hand atop each marker, whispers a name even if there's not one carved in the wood. "There will always be more children who died than headstones," she says. "It doesn't matter if the name matches the body."

"What matters is this place. The way you honored their lives."

"Not me. It was Tucker and Henry. They got up early every morning during the first weeks and went out to find the bodies in the field. Henry thought I didn't know. How could I not know?"

"He was protecting you."

"It's one of the reasons I loved him."

Not much farther, near the river, there's a mopani tree that towers above the other trees. Lillian steadies herself against the trunk as she speaks. "Your father used to claim these woods were enchanted. Magic flowed in the water, nourished the trees and animals. This was our special place before the graves. We said our commitment vows here."

"I understand," Rachel says. That's why Lillian never joins her and Nadine on their walks. She can't come here anymore. "Why did you bring me here? Why today?"

Lillian takes the soapstone heart necklace out of her pocket and lays it on the carpet of green and brown butterfly leaves between them. "I found this chain here on the riverbank, not long before Rahim Kensamara's trial."

"This is where Felix murdered my father?"

"We'll never know for certain, but I like to think his spirit is resting here. The locket belongs here, too."

Lillian takes a hand shovel out of her jacket pocket and digs up some dirt at the base of the mopani tree, in between the thick ropes of roots. Next, Rachel plunges the shovel into the ground with all of her might. It smacks something hard with a clang. She uncovers a metal box, offers it to Lillian, instinctually knowing that whatever is inside was meant for her to find.

Lillian raises her hand, like a shield. "I can't," she says.

Rachel opens the box and removes the photos inside, one by one, laying them on the butterfly leaves.

One...two...three...four...

She sees the horrific images but not. She sees Henry Shepherd behind the lens of the camera. His hands are steady, but his heart is pounding wildly. A paste of dust and sweat coats his hands, and he prays that the camera still works. If the shutter doesn't click, he and Nadine will also be murdered.

Eight...nine...ten...

She sees her father hiding these photos from Lillian, just as he buried the children's bodies in the woods.

Fifteen...sixteen...seventeen...

She sees what it cost him to stay away from his family, to have Lillian believe he was a coward. He was protecting her.

Twenty-eight...twenty-nine...thirty...

She sees that by the time he returned to Kwizera, it was too late to come back to his family. He had been living with these images for four years. They had become part of him. Changed how he saw the world.

Thirty-one.

Rachel grips the last photo. *Nadine.* Her hand shakes uncontrollably. Lillian gently loosens her fingers, takes the photo and places it back in the metal box. Rachel adds the stone heart with the broken spring that will never again open to the photo of the little girl with a squinty grin. She is no longer that child; she will never again love the same way a child loves. But what she has learned is how to love like an adult.

There's the distinct sound of water rushing even though the river is low and still. Rachel hears her father's voice, weary and smooth like tumbled rocks. *I need to go find that treasure chest. When I do, I'll come back and finish our story. Promise.*

Something cracks open inside of her, a warmth that trickles into the vacant space where Serena turned somersaults and the memories of her father still live. Nadine is right: there is no moving past this *thing*, as Mick once referred to grief. This is the new normal: love tinged with sadness that ebbs and flows with the passing moments. This is her own *amahoro*.

She retrieves her wallet from her daypack, her hand going to the accordion of photos where she keeps her sonogram, and places the translucent black-and-white image in the box atop the locket. Her grief over losing Serena and her father—and her love for both of them—are interconnected, like strands of DNA that constitute her soul. They are both intrinsic to who she is: a mother and a child.

GACACA
{ January 2004, Mubaro, Rwanda }

THE GRASSY FIELD BETWEEN THE MARket and the church is packed an hour after the morning market shuts down. People arrive with folding chairs, or spread out blankets with coolers and baskets of food. Some have colorful parasols to guard against the sun, which will be high and hot in a few hours.

Lillian sits at the end of a long wooden table, alongside eight other *Inyangamugayo*: local judges who are teachers, bankers, farmers, and business owners during the week. She had to become a Rwandan citizen for her name to be put on the electoral ballot three years ago, but after living here for three decades she didn't think twice about it. There are no Hutus or Tutsis. The identity cards issued by the past Hutu governments are meaningless; they are all simply Rwandans.

What would Reverend King think of this grassroots justice? It's not perfect by any means, slow-moving and reliant on circumstantial evidence. But the reverend would appreciate the sentiment: reconciliation and forgiveness. When it works, it is truly miraculous. Healing.

She has seen it work more times than not over the past year, with both the victims and the accused telling stories they have secreted away for nearly a decade. There's restitution more often than jail sentences. Hutus and Tutsis work together to rebuild homes. The bodies of loved ones are recovered and buried properly. Apologies are offered and received. It is not enough; there can be no real restitution or redemption. The horror of what happened is too large. All the victims and the accused really have are their stories.

People are settling in and the judges are all here; it's time to call the first witness. Lillian smoothes back her hair, now long and mostly gray, braided in a loose coil around her head. She tidies the stack of files in front of her, moves a wooden vase of red dahlias plucked from Nadine's garden, now blessedly overgrown, a bit closer. She's been waiting a long time for this day. It's her daughter's turn to finally tell her story.

Time seems to slow down as Nadine walks toward the table of judges. Lillian's vision isn't what it used to be, but each face is clear as she gathers her family in her heart. There is Nadine's fiancé, Lawrence, beaming at her as she stands to speak. There are Tucker and Rosie, who is a beautiful young woman now. Living in London is doing her good. There is Rachel, beside Tucker, the cherub-faced baby girl they adopted last year asleep in her arms. Christian sits with his family; he doesn't have to be here but he came of his own accord from Uganda to testify and support Nadine.

Nadine stands tall as she speaks. "The mission of the *gacaca* is truth, justice, and reconciliation," she says. "Perhaps none of these things are possible. Today, I come here hoping to find *amahoro*." Lillian notices that Nadine's hand is shaking a bit as she picks up the envelope of photos that was buried under the mopani tree. She holds up the photos, one by one, and lays them out on the table.

"I was told that I must stay alive, at least for a while, to be a witness," Nadine continues, looking to Lillian for strength. "That was part of my punishment for being born Tutsi. These images have haunted me, kept me prisoner in the shed behind the church where I hid… I have been afraid for ten years. These images will never leave me, but today I am letting go of the fear. Today, I will tell you everything that happened at the church where my friends and family were murdered. Where I was tortured. Raped."

As Nadine begins to tell how she and her family were kept prisoners in their own home, her new family members step forward and gather around her. In Lillian's mind she sees snapshots, not of the past but the future: a wedding, a birth and a funeral. Nadine and Lawrence exchanging vows on the back porch of Kwizera, which will become their home. Tucker and Rachel standing over a bassinet with blue ribbons tied on it. The baby has Henry's dark, sparkling eyes. She sees Ebenezer Baptist Church in Atlanta for the very last time. Kaleidoscopic light—red, green, purple, gold—shines through the window, warming her. She is at peace.

She nods at her daughter. *Amahoro.*

ACKNOWLEDGEMENTS

I need to start by thanking my wonderful agent, Valerie Borchardt. I will always have immense gratitude and respect for Valerie, who thoughtfully and diligently worked to find the right publisher for my novel—and me.

I could not have conjured up a more passionate and just plain smart publisher than Michelle Halket. She has been an advisor, a mentor and a friend during this rollercoaster ride of launching a novel into the world. I have endless appreciation for the sales team at IPG for their hard work getting this novel into bookstores, and the independent booksellers who were early supporters.

I spent eleven years imagining and revising this story. I am grateful beyond words for the support I have received along the way. Adrienne Brodeur, you are my Fiction Angel. To Wally Lamb, Brenda Peterson, Priscilla Long, Dani Shapiro, Claire Dederer, Dawn Tripp, Caroline Leavitt, Susan Henderson, Jenna Blum, Christina Baker Kline, Jessica Keener, Steve Yarbrough, Jill McCorkle, Ann Garvin, Jennie Shortridge, the list goes on and on (forgive me for cutting it short): You all showed me throughout the years that a satisfying writing life is not just about the work but also about being kind and generous to other writers and readers. You have all been incredibly kind and generous with me.

I am honored to have had the support of writing communities including Aspen Summer Words, Hedgebrook, Hugo House, Mineral School, Sewanee, Squaw Valley, and Tin House. I won't even attempt to thank everyone in Seattle's strong community of writers and independent booksellers. I am proud to live in this City of Literature. Special thanks to Elizabeth Dimarco, Sonja Brisson, Ingrid Ricks, and my sister Essayistas!

I could not have persevered for over a decade without the love and support of my family: Eric, Drew, Justin and Kodi. You are all pieces of my heart. You give me moments of joy, even during the roughest days. Ellen, you are not only my sister but also my best friend, always there for me. I thank my parents, Richard and Nina Rieselbach, for their encouragement and support.

Lastly, but certainly not least, I will forever be indebted to the people of Rwanda who welcomed me, watched out for me, and shared their stories with me. I am honored to be a conduit to share these stories of finding *amahoro* with the world.

A CONVERSATION WITH JENNIFER HAUPT

Q: Why did you go to Rwanda in 2007?

JH: The short answer is that I was a reporter exploring the connection between grief and forgiveness. I went there to interview genocide survivors. I also went to interview humanitarian aid workers about why they were drawn to this tiny, grieving country a decade after the 1994 genocide.

I had a handful of assignments for magazines, writing about humanitarian efforts in the capital city of Kigali. Within the first week they all fell through for one reason or another. That's when I decided to hire a driver and go into the ten thousand hills to visit the small churches and schools with bloodstains on the walls and skulls of anonymous victims stacked on shelves. I wanted to trace the steps of the genocide and talk with the survivors, mostly women, who were guides at these rarely-visited memorials.

Q: What did you find in Rwanda that was surprising?

JH: I didn't even realize until I was in Rwanda that I needed to address my own grief for my sister who died when I was age two. There was an unspoken rule in my household growing up: It was forbidden to speak of Susie. That's how my parents dealt with their grief and I respect that. In Rwanda, it felt safe to grieve for the first time. My grief was miniscule compared with the genocide survivors. And yet, we shared a powerful mixture of emotions — compassion, sorrow, longing — that crossed the boundaries of race and culture.

What struck me was that many of the aid workers I interviewed were also grieving over the loss of loved ones. They came to Rwanda as a way of reaching out to help others, and also to heal their own souls. Most of the people I spoke with, no matter if they were Rwandan, American, European, were, in some way, grieving. I had always thought the universal commonality that connected all of us was love, but I learned in Rwanda that grief is an equally strong bond. Grief and love form the bridge that connects us all.

Q: How did your Jewish background affect you?

JH: Fifteen years before I went to Rwanda, I visited the Dachau Concentration Camp Memorial site in Germany. The site is an impressive museum with photo exhibits and artifacts. The former prison barracks and crematorium where some of my relatives may have been imprisoned and murdered were now scrubbed clean. I went to Dachau expecting to feel sorrow, maybe anger, but instead I felt a disturbing emptiness. Nothing.

During the two weeks I spent traveling in the ten thousand hills of Rwanda, I couldn't help but think of my visit to Dachau. Thousands of people visit Dachau each year; we Jews vow to remember the atrocities that happened there. *Never again.* It struck me that I was nearly always the only visitor at the dozens of tiny bloodstained memorials

I visited. There was always a guide, usually a woman, a lone Tutsi survivor whose family members were murdered at the church or school.

I remember at one church, I was met by a woman named Julia who was in her mid-forties, around my age at the time. She had survived by laying on the floor among the dead bodies. Now, she gave tours so that no one would forget. I talked with Julia about her family members and friends who had been murdered here. We cried together; my tears were, in part, for my relatives and members of my tribe who had been murdered during the holocaust. I experienced a powerful connection with this stranger who lived halfway around the world from me, in a culture so different than mine, through both love and grief. I wanted to share that experience with others through the characters in my novel.

Q: Why did you write this novel, instead of a memoir about your time in Rwanda?

JH: *Amahoro* is a Kinyarwanda greeting that translates literally to peace, but means so much more when exchanged between Hutus and Tutsis since the genocide. It's a shared desire for grace when there can be no forgiveness. It's an acknowledgement of shared pain, an apology, a quest for reconciliation. I wanted to be the conduit for telling the stories of *amahoro* that I had heard in Rwanda, from Tutsis and Hutus. I wanted to explore more deeply the meaning of *amahoro*, from many different world views. I wanted to excavate my own grief more fully and, perhaps, find my own vision of *amahoro*. I could only do all of that, I felt, as a novelist.

Q: Why did you choose to tell this story through the eyes of three women of different ages and cultural backgrounds?

JH: I wanted to offer Westerners a window into a very different world, and to do that I started with an American protagonist leaving everything she knows to try and find *amahoro*. Rachel Shepherd is searching for her father, Henry, in Rwanda. She is also searching for the piece of her heart that he took when he left her twenty years earlier. The piece that knows how to love: like a child, like a wife, like a mother.

I also wanted to connect the African-American civil rights struggle with the struggle for civil rights of the Tutsis in Rwanda. That's where Lillian comes from. Once I decided that she and Henry Shepherd had an ill-fated interracial love affair during the late 1960s in Atlanta, their story took on a life of its own. Lillian is on equal footing with Rachel as a central character in this novel.

Originally, this was just Rachel and Lillian's journey: The intertwining stories of two women searching for the man they both love. Two women trying to piece together a family. I didn't add Nadine's story until eight years after I started writing this novel. She's based on a 19-year-old woman I met in Rwanda who had left after the genocide and was returning for the trial of a Hutu man, a former neighbor, who she had seen shoot her mother and sister.

Nadine is a fusion of this woman's story as well as other stories I heard in Rwanda — and then, of course, my imagination. She's the lynch pin that holds together the stories of Lillian, Henry, Rachel, and Rachel's love interest in Rwanda, an American doctor running from his past who has become like an older brother to Nadine.

Q: Is this a political story about the genocide?

JH: No. This is a story that is set against the backdrop of pre-genocide, the genocide, and then after the genocide. I conducted a lot of research about Rwandan history but I don't claim to be an expert on the country's politics or tumultuous past. I do present some background about the genocide, which is factual, but this is historical fiction. The story is about the experiences of the characters during this time in history.

Jennifer Haupt went to Rwanda as a journalist in 2006, twelve years after the genocide that wiped out over a million people, to explore the connections between forgiveness and grief. She spent a month traveling in the 10,000 hills, interviewing genocide survivors and humanitarian aid workers, and came home to Seattle with something unexpected: the bones of a novel. Haupt's essays and articles have been published in *O, The Oprah Magazine*, *The Rumpus*, *Psychology Today*, *Travel & Leisure*, *The Seattle Times*, *Spirituality & Health*, *The Sun* and many other publications.

In the Shadow of 10,000 Hills is her first novel.

jenniferhaupt.com